APPENDIX A

Also by Hayden Carruth

The Crow and the Heart

HAYDEN CARRUTH

APPENDIX A

THE MACMILLAN COMPANY, NEW YORK
COLLIER-MACMILLAN LIMITED, LONDON

First Printing

Printed in the United States of America

The Macmillan Company, New York
Collier-Macmillan Canada, Ltd., Toronto, Ontario

Library of Congress catalog card number: 63-17512

DESIGN BY R. A. KASELER

With thanks to Peter Laderman.

PUBLISHER'S NOTE

Although this document was written in fulfillment of a prior contractual obligation, it would not have come to the attention of the publishers if it had not been through the agency of persons acting in what may best be described as a semiofficial capacity. It is now, in fact, part of a subdepartmental dossier in the files of a state bureau of public health. No illegality, or any improbity whatever, is attached to its publication, but considerations of private sensibility nevertheless dictate that no further identification be made. The reasons for publishing it in this uncorrected state will be, we hope, evident to those who read it. Publication has been arranged with the author's knowledge, and by the kind permission of Mr. Geoffrey Whicher Carruth, Crossington, Ohio.

PART I

CHAPTER 1

Forgive me for being so late. I always have the devil's own time getting started, if you want to know the truth. You're aware of the type? Continually putting things off? I think of people like Agassiz or Fangio or Goethe, the big doers, guys with a list of accomplishments five yards long, and it's not their genius that depresses me so much, though God knows I feel the lack of it—usually anyway; then sometimes I get hopped up on an idea for a poem and I wonder what genius is anyway, who's got it, whether anybody's got it, etc.—but as I say, it's not the ability of great men that depresses me so much as their goddamned readiness to begin. Don't they ever stop to think of the complications that are going to come up? Or how bored and fed up they are going to be before it's over? Believe me, that's what I think about. Only you can't really call it thinking, just brooding.

Take Casanova. Must have been innocent as a child. How else could he manage all those beginnings?—that first inquisitive look, a soft word, and then: *Allow me to bring you another cup of that splendid Málaga,* and *Wouldn't it perhaps be somewhat refreshing to stroll in the rose garden*—whammo! he's in again, and God knows what catastrophes will ensue; as like as not a stiletto in the small of his industrious back. Did he never falter?

Me, I falter. I'm the greatest goddamned falterer of all time. Seduction is a fine and wholesome thing, a pursuit to be cultivated with close attention; but the beginning, a new one each time, is tough. I mean that point where the first look is just giving way to the soft word; the point, I imagine, at which the redoubtable Don

3

swung closed the casements of his mind, shutting out the light of good sense—presuming he had any. Which is not a very nice way to talk about the first Spanish antifascist, especially since I claim no particular good sense myself. Nevertheless, that point—when the look is leading to the word—is precisely the point at which I light another cigarette and begin thinking about getting the hell out of there. Not from nerves; not any more; I've reached the somewhat less nervy time of life; and besides, seducing the women I'm likely to come up against in my line of work is more or less like feeding herrings to the sea lions: once they get the idea there's not much holding back. Damned little gratitude you get, too, when the herring's all gone.

Here I am, talking about sex already, and I've only just introduced myself. Not much of a way to make a good impression, is it? Not much of an introduction, for that matter. But I haven't time for anything further about myself at this point—I'll get to it later. The main thing is, I wanted to establish friendly relations right here at the beginning of this novel or autobiography or dissertation or whatever the hell it is—I haven't really decided yet. I'm going to be relying on you a good deal from now on, you see: for patience and understanding and all that; and so I thought I'd best start right out by addressing you directly, though of course I realize it's an unusual way to begin a book. But it isn't quite the same as sticking my foot in your door, is it? I hope not; I've no desire to be unmannerly or overbearing—not like some of the young guys writing nowadays. You can always shut me out any time you want to, just by closing the book.

I had intended to make this introduction some time ago. On June 1, as a matter of fact. That's when I came up here, after having been in another part of the country for a long time. "Up here," of course, is the Berkshire hills in northwestern Connecticut; and I don't know why I say "of course" except that it's now July 24 and I have been here for nearly two months and the place seems so familiar and real to me I can hardly imagine you don't feel it too. But naturally you can't. A nice little cottage, white clapboards and black shutters and a stout chimney, all the usual refinements, shut away at one end of a small valley where the pines and hemlocks stand around like old men diddling themselves. A friend loaned it

4

to me; otherwise—hell, I'd still be back where I came from. A fine place to write, my friend said, and I thought so too; at first anyway. But that was two months ago, as I say, and it has taken me all this time to get started.

Scared? Scared stiff—that's the simple truth. Scared of sitting down and starting a *book*. Sure, I've written plenty of things before —poems mainly, and a lot of reviews, essays, sketches, reports, and so on—but never a whole book at one shot. Jaysus, I said to myself, that'll keep going for months, maybe years; and I'd never written anything I couldn't pretty well polish off in a couple of afternoons. Scared stiff—so I was, and so I still am. Scared I won't have the courage or the intelligence or the simple strength to get through everything I've got to say. Scared it will be awful, rotten, unread-able. . . . You know, though, these hills are full of writers, so I've discovered, and maybe this will turn out to be a good place after all for what I have to do, now that I'm started. You can hardly turn around up here without knocking into a writer—a poet or a critic or a novelist. Rich, fat, healthy guys, most of them, with puffy backs and freckles on their bald scalps, hanging around the post office at ten o'clock in the morning, like the old men and the boy with the twisted leg. Plenty of money in their pockets. Most of them haven't stirred from here for years (except to go down to New York every off month to get plastered), but they always look at you as if they'd just come back from Mount Kilimanjaro or somewhere. Tell the truth, I felt a little that way myself when I first came up here. I had some money in my pockets too; but the main thing is I had a contract. I mean this Mr. Meredith at the Macmillan Company, he likes my poems—which is okay, because I'm a pretty fair hand at poetry—and he said he'd advance me some money against "expected future royalties" and give me a contract to go with it. Fact. I've got the damned thing in my desk drawer right now, signed, sealed, and done up in a blue paper binder.

Of course there's nothing in the contract says Macmillan has got to publish this book if Meredith doesn't like it after I've finished it and sent it on to him. Nothing at all. In a way I can shove off some of the responsibility for what follows onto him. If you've gotten this far, then you know Meredith has liked what I wrote and has agreed to offer it to you (for a price), which means that

5

whenever you don't approve of what you read in this book—some of which is going to be undeniably raw, I warn you, and some unavoidably abstract—you can blame him as much as me. But I don't know if he'll give you your money back.

A further point; or rather two. Meredith and the Macmillan Company aside, I'm writing this book because it must be written. *Must*. You'll see. If the things I am going to say can't be put down here at last in some kind of decent order, then it will mean the damnation of us all.

Anyway I need your help. Your forbearance, your good will, your trust. If I possessed the genius of a Joyce or a Proust—or their blindness, insensibility, pigheadedness, whatever it was that enabled them to scrawl out on paper, year after year, all their own purgations and self-betrayals—I still could not say clearly what must be said in this book. Not clearly enough, that is. It could never be clear enough. We must muddle along and hope for the end, recognizing that none of us may get out of this with his skin. I shall be calling on you often—and quite directly, though I know this runs counter to all the rules of fashionable writing—for your help.

Bonne chance!

CHAPTER 2

The tone of that first chapter is uncertain, I know; timorous, hesitant, stumbling, a touch forlorn—in the conventional manner of ingratiation. Never mind; I'll go back to it and fix it later. The important thing now is to get on with the business at hand while the starting momentum is still with me.

First, I find I'm obliged to say something about the city of Chicago, Illinois. Much has been said already about the city of Chicago, Illinois, of course, by writers of many persuasions and in many times and places; and 90 percent of what they have said has been defamatory, as we know. But true. That's the hell of it. Chicago *is* cruel, corrupt, filthy, stupid, libidinous, etc., etc.—all the things that anyone has ever said about it. I've lived there and I know. Anyone else who has ever lived there will tell you the same thing; and quite cheerfully, too; Chicagoans are, above all, realists. Since I also am a Chicagoan (now in spirit if not in fact) and hence a realist, much of what I shall say in this book about Chicago, which is where the events I want to explain to you took their course, will be defamatory and—in my memory at least—true. But before I get into that, I'd like to point out one or two things on the other side of the account.

People talk about Chicago. Perhaps they do so because they despise Chicago, because they fear and revile the city of Colonel McCormick, Potter Palmer, the Capone brothers, and the Century of Progress; but people do at least talk about it. They do not talk about Omaha, for instance. Or Minneapolis. Characterless cities. When was the last time you heard of anything happening in

7

Omaha? If the truth were told, all I know about Omaha was the occasion—Independence Day, 1919, I believe—when the mayor's daughter, who was a member of the company on the speakers' dais at a Populist rally, bent over to retrieve her glove and was accidentally goosed by the cane of William Jennings Bryan. "Jesus Christ," she said, "watch where you put that thing!" I don't say it's true. I don't say anything's true.

As I remarked, this levon, which is what I've decided to call this book—a feeble invention, but let it pass; I'll explain when I get a chance—will contain a certain amount of unpleasantness anent Chicago. Inevitably so. But now it is a question for me of two places and two times: the present here in Connecticut, these hills with their gracile birches and lugubrious hemlocks; and that other time ten years ago, my memories of Chicago's frayed concrete and eaten chrome. A polarity—the fashionable mental stance. Yet of the two, my affection attaches itself, whether I will or no, to the city, to the place of corruption and decay; I am pulled there by sights and sounds so deeply a part of me, even after a decade, that I feel almost like—well, it seems absurd to say so, but I do feel *pulled*, stretched like taffy, wrenched and racked away from these hills and toward the city. Absurd. From every standpoint. Not the least of them being this tranquillity, which I've never known before.

Chicago has the best waterfront in the world, bar none. This is extremely important, because Chicago, a far from characterless city, as I have said, takes much of its character from Lake Michigan. "Waterfront" is technically the correct term, but isn't precisely what I mean, since it conveys an impression of wharves, warehouses, bristling cranes, ships, etc. Chicago has a waterfront in this sense too, down to the south in the region of Calumet where the ore boats, upon whose drudgery the city's prosperity relatively depends, put in to discharge their cargos. This is a fine arrangement, because it leaves most of the rest of the city's long lovely margin free for other uses. Incidentally, Chicagoans do not call it the waterfront; they use the term "Lakeshore," and the huge *autobahn* which runs its length and furnishes the quickest means of transit from the North Side to the South Side is called Lakeshore Drive. The Lakeshore itself falls southeasterly in a scraggly line, down from Evanston and Milwaukee and beyond, to the coastal sweep of

8

Indiana; an ancient lacework of whitecaps fringing the threadbare carpet of the city and the prairie; twenty or twenty-five miles in length, I imagine, with beaches here and there, parks and lagoons, several marinas for private watercraft, and a great drawbridge which divides and rises above the Chicago River like two stubby thumbs; and at the low places along the edge of the lake there are parapets of stepped stone to hold back the waves during storms. One remembers, when walking along the Lakeshore, that "Chicago" comes from an Indian word meaning "swamp," according to one derivation, and that many points in the city are below the level of Lake Michigan; in fact, a good deal of the Lakeshore as it appears today, including some of the parks and the flossiest residential quarters, has been created artificially by means of dumping enormous quantities of rubble into the swampland and even into Lake Michigan itself. I'd be the last to disapprove. Once you grant that that part of the earth may as well be occupied by people as by ducks and herons—not to speak of mosquitos—then the new Lakeshore is certainly more charming and salubrious than the former quagmire must have been.

Chicagoans are seldom aware of living in a port. Some people may consider this a misfortune, people whose images of waterfronts derive, for instance, from old lithographs of Thameside—a jungle of masts with lianas of rigging, bowsprits mounting the wharves like unicorns, odors of hemp and spice and pitch, a cosy grogshop across the street. You won't find anything like that in Calumet today, nor in London probably. Only rusty monsters, spritless and scant-masted, leaking at dockside like flensed whales. Cargos boxed tight or cosmolined, ladled into the holds by mechanical hoists, like evil-smelling offerings to Moloch himself. Anyway, you can't get in. The docks are shut fast behind board fences, and the gates are manned by stooges demanding to see your union badge; the grogshop across the street is Harry's Blue Anchor Bar & Grill where the beer hasn't been washed off the floor since the Pullman strike; even the longshoremen wouldn't go there if they could figure out a way to keep beer from going flat in a thermos bottle.

Lake Michigan is the largest lake in the world, but still a lake. There are other fine bodies of water beside which to raise one's habitation, I'm sure. You always hear about the Bay of Naples. I was billeted in Naples once, waiting for a ship to take me home after the war, and it's a splendid sight, no doubt—the extraordinary blue catching spangles of sunlight, and at night the velvety darkness wearing the lamps of the Esplanade like a tiara. Yes, a fine body of water. But is it a body, after all—in any meaningful sense? If so, then a horrible one, gross, spreading illimitably beyond the horizon, a vast vague dispersion of flesh. People speak of the mystery of the sea, and of the benefits bestowed upon those who live by it and atune their thoughts to it. Maybe so, I don't deny it, given a certain temperament. But how does a mystery reveal itself? In extravagant and sentimental intimations, I believe: thick pasty blues, sunsets like gore, always a heavy emphasis and insistence. A lake is another matter. When you stand by the Lakeshore you can't see the other side, but you know it's there: the lake is a real body, enclosed, firm, palpable, beautiful, revealing herself continually in new subtleties; lights and shadows, pastels, running wavelets, storms, smiles and despairs; sometimes all these together at once; changeable, various; manifold. Chicago is ugly and often mean, like all lovers, but this mistress has the real womanly greatness which accepts and dispels everything. It's a greatness which resists all efforts of simplification. Think of that. If the men of the Mediterranean had lived beside lakes rather than by the sea, they would not have left us all this useless wreckage of oversimplifications to regulate the world.

Fresh water, not salt. Neither the gray salt of the granitic rollers, nor green salt of algid wastes, nor blue salt of oily equatorial pullulations. Fresh water contains a thousand smaller lights, every tone and demitint. Would you wash your eyes with brine?

Appearances:
A. April; morning; ten o'clock. Housecleaning time. From the parapet Alex and I watch the cleansing wind, the clouds torn and whisked away. A motley sky; ragged; patched with gold, white, gray, black, threads of green and purple; the blue flesh, elbows and knees, poking through. Alex is watching the water. "Look, the lake has even more color than the sky."

"Perhaps because of the waves."

10

"Yes, so many surfaces; each second differently tilted, like little mirrors strung on a fishnet."

"Not only reflections, however. Refractions to break and scatter the lights."

Above each gem-cut wavelet is a whitecap, small and sharply white, dispersed; not ocean's stately combers, but runaway daisies fluttering pell-mell to Michigan; and the wind from the prairies and the great mountains a thousand miles away carries with it the freshness of newly turned loam. A multiety of color, not heavy, not drenching—no canvas smudged with oily hues; but clean, washed, translucent, quickly sketched. Alex points high over the lake's horizon. A straggle-tailed V of wild geese is moving northward. They have a long journey to go before they find the reedy bays where they may alight safely. Alex says nothing.

B. In January the bitter night glides down from Manitoba and Hudson's Bay, silent, barbarous. The lakewater is almost still, rather stealthy and tentative . . . dark occasional whispers speaking to the ice-locked shore. The sun rises, long after the first eastern glow. Ribbons and patches of mist drift on the lake, lighting to rose and saffron and mallow in the dawn. Ice on the lower steps of the parapet burns briefly with running fire, and on the higher steps, rising nude from the ice-skirt, rime glistens. Aslant, an old piling has acquired fantastic shape from the drenchings in frozen spume; it is bulbous, fleshed in ripe swellings of icy tissue, a dead, brilliant, vulgar fungus blushing hugely in the sunrise. The shame of even simulated life in this interstellar emptiness, or so it seems. An inch above the horizon, the sun pales, the lake turns to bleached slate, and the cold breeze, miserable and dusty and very ancient, gnaws your neck with its rats' teeth. You snuffle and turn toward home. Little pains explode like Chinese crackers in the muscles of your calves when you stumble and hurry. A touch of chilblain, no doubt. Was it worth it, ten minutes of technicolor in exchange for all these frost-riven cells given to death?

C. In November the black storms come to Lake Michigan. Shadowy snow and freezing sleet are hurled into the water like buckshot, striking in bursts of pellets, a fierce swish-swish. In the

11

hollows of the waves the water is purple, gleaming dully like slag from old iron-smelting furnaces. Above, the wave tops are ripped away, flung to the parapet, or even higher; sometimes whole waves leap up and over like terrified horses. They crash down on Lake-shore Drive, bodily. Policemen in clumsy rubber coats motion traffic toward the one lane still open. The police scuff their boots and hunch their shoulders against the shot-laden wind. Overhead, clouds crunch, scream, jostle, stumble, press—a southward-stream-ing herd: suddenly broken, and for three seconds a blinding sun-shaft cants through the smirch. Thor's javelin; the policemen shrivel in their Gothic hearts. This is the year's swift fall, a crash-ing end before winter drives the life of the city into its million lairs. November. Much is dead already, as a matter of fact. Lake-wrack tumbles lifelessly on the stone parapet: black sticks from the forests of Michigan, ship refuse, garbage, a dank-feathered gull, fish oozing their thin fish-blood, the curious straw and chaff that always appear on the edge of storm-driven water, a choked eel; everywhere the scum and froth of death; decay hastened in the splintering water; filth; the hard sleet and snow, rice of death, flung in a monstrous nuptial.

Alex is impatient. "What in God's name do you want to look at this for? Come on, let's get some coffee."

D. If you look at a topographical chart of North America, as I am at this moment, you see that the color green, signifying a low elevation, extends outward from Lake Michigan in all directions: easterly to the Catskills and Poconos; southerly to the delta; north-erly to the Canadian wastes, Hudson's Bay, and the islands of the ice-jammed Arctic; westerly to Cheyenne, Denver, the Black Hills and the peaks of Laramie and Big Horn. Chicago is a house whose front yard is the lake, clean and bright, the portal and the focus of family life; but the backyard and the side yards are the plains, un-protected, sweeping out to . . . to what? Chicagoans are as well schooled as most people and have studied their geography lessons in childhood, yet in their hearts they don't know what lies beyond: space, distance, the incredible vectors and tangents of the nebulae themselves. The places where the weather comes from. The winds pour in relentlessly, and their source, wherever it is, whatever it is,

12

is never depleted. Sometimes the winds blow hot, sometimes they blow cold, and sometimes—quite often in fact—they blow both together, especially during the evenings which succeed the warm afternoons of May. Which is, annually, perenially, a considerable inconvenience to the city's fishermen.

No, not to those whom the old man—*pace*, Papa—would have recognized by that name: stalwarts, numb to the armpits, who fling themselves up icy headwaters for the sake of depositing in a particular dark pool a particular bright fly. The fishermen of Chicago are another breed. They fish at night from the steps of the parapet, and their manner of fishing is this: strong cord, not too thick, is weighted with iron pipe at both ends, one end being placed on the parapet, the other flung into the lake; a forked stick is then erected on the parapet and the cord is strung through the fork, so that the cord runs on a taut incline from the fork to the iron pipe on the lake bottom; then the main fishing-line, by means of small brass rings, is threaded along the inclined cord, while from this main line hang four or five shorter lines, hooked and baited with minnows; finally, at the landward end of the main fishing line is attached a small brass bell which will tinkle when a fish is hooked, telling the fisherman he must draw in his line, remove the fish, rebait the hook, and permit the line to slide downward again into the black water.

But, as I say, the weather is changeable. An evening which begins in warmth may decline quickly into chill. The fisherman, in order to keep himself warm, brings a blanket to spread across his knees while he sits on the stone step and waits for his bell to tinkle, and he builds a little fire at his feet out of drift-sticks and fragments of orange crate; then, in order to keep himself cool, he also brings a bucket of ice containing cans of beer. There he sits; wrapped in his blanket, his pipe smoldering, his fire wavering in the night air, his beer can resting handily on the stone beside him; and as often as not his wife beside him too, sharing his blanket, his beer, and sometimes his pipe; old couples, stumpy-handed, ravaged of countenance, patient and serious; seldom loquacious, content with a gutteral phrase of the comfortable Plattdeutsch or Lettish or Croatian, or whatever it may be—Gaelic was common not so long ago—to tell their thoughts. Hundreds of couples, perhaps thousands

13

on a Friday night, are sitting a few yards apart along the parapet, their fires extending like lanterns for miles down the Lakeshore; and the tinkling of the fishing bells makes a delicate treble against the mumble of the small tide nudging the stone. But perhaps the tinkling of a bell only means that a fisherman has pulled in his line to see if the bait is still there.

They catch perch and white bass mostly, I guess, usually quite small. Sometimes a lucky fisherman hooks a whitefish, a fat two-footer, and then everyone comes to look at it, standing to admire and gossip awhile before drifting back to their own firelit posts.

At ten o'clock, or ten-thirty if the night is fine, there is a general tinkling of bells and stirring about as the fishlines are dismantled. The couples trudge home, carrying their tackle and their beer buckets (now turned into aquaria for the still living victims of the evening's sport), back across the passenger bridge over the Drive, into the city, dispersing like autumn leaves in a forest; each to his incogitable street and number. And I have no doubt all those fish are scraped, gutted, cooked, eaten, digested; thus becoming, *in transitu*, cells of human flesh, particles in the mass. Cats get the heads.

E. Alex: "What'll you have?"

"Salt," I say.

"Here. Don't spill it."

I open the matchbox which holds the salt, and sprinkle a pinch on a slice of roast beef, coral pink, as thin and limp as kidskin. Should have told the delicatessen man to slice it thicker. I put on another piece of beef, then the top slice of bread to make my sandwich.

Alex: "Hell of a fine day for a picnic."

"Ummmm."

"Won't be many more. End of September already. And the sky looks like October, really. You know? Not a cloud. And so deep and blue—cerulean."

"Don't use that word."

"Why not?"

"If you saw a whole sky of cerulean you'd be scared out of your wits. Too brilliant."

14

"What should I say then?"

"Dresden maybe. Just say blue."

"All right, it's blue. But the way it arches at this time of year, higher and deeper—I never remember from one year to the next, it's always a surprise. You can almost look through the sky, like looking through a sapphire. Or maybe it's the opposite—the color comes down somewhat, inside of you."

"Ummmmm."

"And the lake catches it, and the whole thing goes round. Sky and water, all blue, a perfect globe. And you're on the inside—like the little man in the glass ball."

"Where's the beer-can opener?"

"In that bag with the potato salad, I think. Why don't we go sailing sometime? I've never been out. See that one, a little off there—no, to the left—a little triangle on the horizon?"

"Scalene."

"What?"

"Scalene triangle."

"— to you." With gestures.

F. In Indiana are the Dunes. Students of geology come from great distances to look at them. I wouldn't go that far myself, but let each rejoice in his own folly, I say. For a very long time, you see, the prevailing winds have been northwest to southeast, driving the waters of Lake Michigan down toward the Indiana-Michigan shore, and in consequence that part of the shore is the only part which is naturally sandy. The Dunes, large hillocks of this sand, reach inland, at some places, as far as five miles, and must originally have resembled a desert; but tough weeds and hardy grasses have taken hold there now, along with homely scrub pines and cedars, so that the primeval and austere beauty of the Dunes is covered. The process was speeded somewhat, as a matter of fact, by people who came in the last century to build summer homes there and planted desert grass on the sand to keep it from shifting. Some of the dunes are a hundred feet high, the highest elevations in that level country, and if you stand on the top of one of them and look across the lake you can see a good distance, even to Chicago fifty miles away. When was the last time you heard of anything happening in

15

horizon like golden jackstraws. Or like a filigree of enchanted castles. It's the city all right, you know that—bleeding chrome and glass and stone, filth and rancor and pollution.

Sometimes on hot August afternoons thunderstorms blow down from Wisconsin, driving fast under tall thunderheads. You are standing on a dune, looking toward Chicago. You see the storm coming, a high cloud, black beneath but swirling like cotton above, bubbling and mushrooming. All the rest of the sky in every direction is hot and blue and still, like a Venetian sky in a painting by Tiepolo. When the storm is directly over the city, you see the drama distinctly, as if through the wrong end of a pair of binoculars: the miniscule cloud writhing, the darkness beneath, the tiny sparks leaping to the matchstick buildings. It is fury reduced to the scale of the ants and weevils. You say to yourself: *Aha, you bastards, you're getting it now, aren't you, and I hope you get it good and hard, I hope you're all blown to hell, you scummy bums, and wouldn't that be fine?* Twenty minutes later the storm has reached Indiana, and you are crouched indoors, if you have a house to go into, with your own heart hammering in your ears.

G. *Solstice* is a lovely word, full of mankind's slowly gathered feelings and speculations. It means the time when the sun, *sol*, stands still, *sistere*. This is no jargon of meteorology, with its balloons and rockets and hairspring contraptions, but a word from the time when each man was his own weatherman and knew from his own observations at dawn and dusk the precise times of the year when the sun rose and set at the same places on his little horizon. I think that although *sistere* comes from the root which means standing still, actually it meant more than this as it grew over the centuries in countrymen's minds: it meant peace, quiet, contentment. As in *armistice*, the time when the weapons stand still.

The summer solstice, when the sun is with us and earth pays us homage in greenery and blossom—this at least is a time of contentment. Don't we pray for it? The lake is blue, no pasty Caribbean cobalt but the blue of a Swedish girl's eyes, lucid and immaculate. Puffs of cumulo-stratus, the snail cloud, proceed unhurriedly and in irregular groups down the horizon, like families going to church.

16

The beach is dense with bathers, more are coming over the foot-bridge that crosses the Drive. Traffic whines on the Drive, two or three airplanes drone overhead. Naturally one looks at the young girls, bodies flushed with sex, brimming from tight suits at breast and buttock. Just as naturally, one looks at the old ladies, their squalor and desuetude—is it animate, that heap of toneless flesh, does blood flow in all those mounds and subsidences, or is it refuse the owner has forgotten to discard? A tumulus; a barrow. Watch where you step: it is easy to put your bare foot down on a beer-can opener or a burning cigarette. . . .

One lifts one's eyes. On the thin line of the horizon move the boats, a long way out, in slow procession; each with a plume raised from its single funnel, set far aft. In the mid-distance are sailboats —catboats mostly, sometimes a ketch or a larger vessel—and the motor launches of the wealthy. Near shore buzz the speedboats, cutting as close to the bathers as the pilots dare; and the beach-squatters hem and harrumph. . . .

What contentment, then, amid such activity? I don't know. Babies squawl, adolescents race and wrestle, old women babble. Afterward you wonder. But on the beach a matrix of sun and water envelops the afternoon in serenity. Yes, even your own easily unbalanced moodiness.

Eventually it is time for supper. Many people go home. Many others come, bringing hampers and thermos jugs. The footbridge over the Drive becomes a seat of contest, since its designer did not foresee such a traffic of Horatios battling in both directions, bur-dened with blankets, bundles, baskets, babies; while the cars whine underneath.

Toward ten o'clock the moon rises, close above the horizon. Color of Smyrna tile. The moonlight skips on the crests of wave-lets, coming toward the shore on a broadening track of orange tracery. This is the lake's only lapse into sentimentality, as I point out to Alex. "You are not old enough," I say, "to remember the third-rate dance bands of 1927. They always had a scene painted on the face of the bass drum, and nine times out of ten it was a lake with a track of moonlight running across it, and of course a young couple in a canoe." "You aren't old enough to remember yourself," Alex says. "Just barely," I answer. From the parapet on

17

the Promontory at 55th Street, one looks across the water toward the Loop, and the lights from the tall buildings glimmer in the lake. A crisper light than the moonlight. It is good to let one's feet hang over the edge of the bottom step, just touching the surface of the water as it rises and falls. It is also good to drink beer or, if one has had foresight, chilled hock.

Much later—long after midnight—the voices are gone, the moon is pale in the west, the remaining light is dim starshine. The ripples accost the stone like the greetings of old maids, and recede shyly. In the gray light the rats come out on the parapet and play. When you are standing at the front window of your third-floor apartment on a late afternoon in winter, and you see a gray rat slink down the gutter of the street and turn into the areaway of your apartment house, as if he were any other tenant coming home from a day's work, your attitude toward rats—gray city rats—is cold and friendless, and the words "bubonic plague" switch on like a neon sign in your brain. But on a warm summer night in starshine the playing rats, scarcely distinguishable, seem not unamiable sharers of the stone. Perhaps they aren't playing. In fact, I expect that rats, being irredeemably rats, don't play and don't know how to play, they are just scurrying around on the stone to scrounge a few fishheads or picnic remnants. Sometimes they squeak, like dolls. But everything else is quiet: rats' feet scurrying, ripples rippling, occasional late cars whining on the Drive. The city seems almost undone, as if an angry goddess had put all but a few chosen acolytes into a dreamless sleep; while the rats and the water do their work. One such night, in the darkness under a branching spirea bush, Alex and I made love on the grass, rats and all.

CHAPTER 3

You should see yourselves. Lips blanched like a halibut's, eyes bruised and frosty as scuppernongs left too long on the vine. Well, I'm sorry. I didn't realize what a blast that sentence might be until I'd already written it, and then I decided to let it stand. You see, Alex is short for Alethea, and there's nothing to fear. To me, Alex signifies something so essentially, hotly, completely female that for a moment it simply didn't occur to me you might take it to mean anything else.

Still, I might have intended it—that dirty trick, I mean. It is a legitimate device, and has been used often enough by other writers. Anything is legitimate, isn't it?—that's the art of writing: the dirty trick played on the reader, the practical joke, the illusion of reality. Or the illusion of unreality. And the secret of all esthetic theory, it seems to me, is precisely that you, my friends, like it; you adore the dirty trick, you come back to it again and again. Why? It's so plain that one wonders how it can have been the object of learned confusion for three thousand years. You like the practical joke of art because it gives you pleasure, while the practical joke of life gives you . . . well, boredom most of the time, I suppose, but now and then a pretty effectual kidney punch for most of us. Hence the continuous effort to escape from life into art; but it can't be done —can't be done because life and art are the same thing. Just as pain and pleasure are the same thing. How can pleasure and pain be the same, you ask, when they are opposite extremes? Because each contains the other in principle, like a pair of old-fashioned pince-nez that fold together: each always folds into the other.

19

Moreover, no one knows for certain which is which; and although you may find several people who agree that a pain is a pain, you can certainly always find several more who will say that it is a pleasure. Just so with life and art: extremes, each containing the other, controvertible. Perhaps it is best to abandon the pain-pleasure-life-art principle entirely, the search will only lead you into a shifting, unreliable countryside where no landmark can be found again. Instead we must look for something else. What shall it be? What shall we agree on? Not Truth, certainly—a grandiose idea, okay for the old-timers, but we are more realistic. Maybe, even so, we can find one or two true things upon which to peg our feelings.

Is it possible? For that matter, is it necessary? What's the good of it? Why should we trouble ourselves? . . . Out of a sense of duty? Odious concept! Duty to God, duty to society, duty to family, *duty to oneself*—how they have rung the changes on that old piece of wormwood.

But I might do it for love.

At any rate, I won't put down anything on these pages that isn't true. I couldn't, in fact—because I haven't the faintest idea how to invent a fiction.

CHAPTER 4

Without doubt a proper author would have begun with Alex on the first page. Perhaps in some such terms as these: the first time I made love to Alex was more or less like this, etc., etc. But do you see?—already these few words are meaningless, turning themselves into abstractions. You had to know something about me before the words could even be spoken, and now you must know something about Alex before they can be intelligible; if I reversed the order it would be simply that—a reversal, an evasion, a trick, and an untruth.

I shall say something about the woman herself. The word is important: woman, not girl or lady. Nor broad, pig, tomato, etc., though she was all these things too. I think she was born a woman perhaps, her first cry, as she pushed her way from the womb's darkness, already a proclamation of her sex and of sex in general. Shortly afterward, at any rate, she was named Alethea, her mother's name before her, chosen by her grandmother from one of Pushkin's stories. Once when I asked Alex if she had read the story in question, she replied that she had never looked for it and didn't know its title. All she knew was that it was a horrible name, even her parents found it *gauche*, and soon everyone took to calling her what she herself, as soon as she could talk, declared her name to be—Alex. It stuck. Later, when she was in high school and became embarrassed at having a boy's name, she changed the spelling to Alix, even for a while to Alics; but the embarrassment passed; and eventually, when she learned that her name had become, like her body, an indelible aspect of her personality, hers alone, she was

21

quite pleased with it. Alex was never known not to be pleased with anything she was or did—after she was about seventeen.

She was Jewish; that is to say, half Jewish, her father, Herman Silverstine, having married a Polish girl in Prague in 1904; but a half is as good as a whole in Atlanta, Georgia, where Alex was born. She was the only child of parents who had given up hope of offspring, and made her entrance in 1926 on a surprising day in July. Surprising for Mr. Silverstine. First, he had not yet entirely acquitted himself of the disgruntlement which had grown, like the habit of chewing his mustache, during the twenty-one years of his doe-eyed, dun-haired, gaunt-sided wife's infertility. During her pregnancy, he had seen her belly grotesquely hunch and tighten in the horned scales of her pelvis; it looked as if she were carrying an apronful of stones, not a child. (I am imagining some of this, of course, though it is close to what Alex told me. She also said that her father loved her mother dearly, that her mother did indeed look like a starveling, and that he made love to her passionately "practically all the time.") When Mr. Silverstine saw that his wife's body had indeed produced a life, not a thud of falling stones, when he saw the infant's bland face ("My mother always told me I was born with a smooth skin, not all wrinkled up like most babies") and heard the indubitable protestations, his long-accumulated but scarcely recognized resentment of his wife's supposed barrenness exploded with, I imagine, a kind of soft internal shock; he was, in spite of himself, surprised. Secondly, he had thought it was going to be a boy. Nevertheless, he rejoiced and he continued rejoicing. His business, a hardware store, prospered; he acquired a large bank account, at least in terms of his station in life; he opened two branch stores, he joined a club, he bought a house in a carefully landscaped colony north of the city, and he was just on the point of expanding his business by becoming a wholesaler when, six years after his daughter's birth, his fortunes were demolished in the middle of Peachtree Street by a taxicab with failing brakes. His face was removed by forty feet of abrasive concrete, and he entered the kingdom of heaven, two hours later, in a state of excruciating anonymity.

His wife is living yet.

Alex seldom spoke of her childhood or her family; what I have put down here about her father is all that I know of him; and I know even less of her mother. When, after three years at the University of Georgia, Alex decided she was not leading the life she wanted and in consequence set off on her own, she apparently broke with her mother. But no; I imagine that is putting it too strongly; there wasn't a break between them, so much as a mutual relinquishment, a letting go: very reasonable and fortunate in the circumstances. When I knew her, Alex wrote to her mother five or six times a year, and I have no doubt her letters were warm and affectionate, but also, I suspect, vague, insubstantial, and devoid of real news. The mother, so far as I know, wasn't the least distressed, I never heard of any protests and I don't think that letters were any more frequent in one direction than in the other. You may ask how much was Alex's half-Jewishness responsible for this withdrawal from her family? I don't know. Her early years had of course been spent in a Jewish context; her father's club was a Jewish club, naturally; he couldn't have been admitted to any other; and the community in which he had bought his house was specifically a Jewish community. But he wasn't a religious man, I gather, nor was his wife a religious woman—in order to marry at all they couldn't have been. Their miscegenation brought them a certain degree of aspersion from the strict elements of the Jewish colony in Atlanta, but these strict elements were not strong. In the South, confronted with the continual spectacle of abomination heaped not upon them but upon others, the Jews forsake their own sectarian austerities, and live, like their Aryan and Negro fellows, in an atmosphere of careful easygoingness: I say careful because the limits are there, strict limits, though everyone keeps quiet about them most of the time. But it is well known that the transgressor, even the inadvertent transgressor, will be peremptorily and perhaps brutally reminded of them.

After Mr. Silverstine died, Alex's mother continued to live in the house he had bought, and for a while kept her membership in his club, primarily for the sake of the playground and pony rides for members' children. Alex was a little Jew girl. Everyone believed this, and in time Alex grew up enough to believe it herself. In school her friends were both Jewish and Aryan, but mostly Jewish. There was never any trouble, not even inconvenience; yet she knew,

23

as she progressed through grade school and entered high school, that there were houses where she would not be admitted, hotels that would not serve her, beaches and playgrounds closed unequivocally if irrationally to her emerging charms. When she reached the university and found that she was, by virtue of her surname and an inconspicuous initial entered in a square on her matriculation card, deprived of admittance to any but a Jewish sorority, her mind absorbed this indignity without any apparent disturbance: she signed up with the proper sorority and went through the rituals as if she had never desired anything else. I very much doubt that she ever *had* desired anything else, at least not in the active sense usually meant by the word. Alex's desires were powerful but personal; matters of blood and nerve, seldom matters of conscience. Nevertheless, in November of her senior year she celebrated her twenty-first birthday, and the next morning packed her bags and departed without saying so much as good-by to anyone at all. She went home, stayed two days—long enough to repack her luggage with a better feminine regard for method—and took the Pullman to Chicago with a new, blue-leatherette checkbook in her purse, by means of which she intended to draw against the moderate but adequate inheritance left by her father; it was hers to use as she liked, now that she was twenty-one. Her reason for choosing Chicago instead of New York, where otherwise she would have preferred to go, was that she knew no one at all in Chicago, while New York, always a virtual Field of Mars for Atlanta, was full of people who would seek her out, give her advice, help her to find living quarters, and introduce her to other people—mostly other Atlantans. She wanted none of this.

What was in her mind, that outrageous, outraging, but never outraged faculty? The question has been asked often enough; not, to be sure, about her reasons for leaving Georgia, but about later aspects of her behavior. Her reasons for leaving Georgia are probably not worth much inquiry. Most intelligent Georgians leave at one time or another, or at any rate hope to. Not that Alex was intelligent; sometimes I wondered if she had a mind at all, at least in the ordinary sense; but that was absurd, because I couldn't really say she was unintelligent either; for months during the period when I knew her I simply couldn't see whether she was

24

intelligent or not, and it wasn't for lack of trying. Sometimes she could astonish us all, at a party or when we were sitting around in somebody's apartment. She would say: "It's always better to get your philosophy at second hand, that's why Thaïs was a better Aristotelian than Alexander." Or: "I knew a prodigal son who went to the psychoanalyst to be cured, but at the end of two years his father quit paying the fee." As a matter of fact, Alex could manage well enough at the South Side cocktail parties where the bright young men held forth. She didn't contribute anything, of course, except her disquieting substance; but she had the knack of introducing remarks so pointedly enigmatic, so mockingly condescending, that the bright young men must have all gone home feeling that she despised them utterly; which she did.

It was a knack only, nothing more. No doubt Alex left home for the usual reasons—boredom, hostility, spirit of adventure—plus in her case a desire to escape her half-Jewishness; but the important point is that all these motives were totally unrealized within her. Alex moved as an animal moves, in response to whatever winds touched her skin, whatever fragrances touched her nostrils; drawn always by the unrecognized stimulus; drawn, I might add, in a movement whose languidness was equaled only by its determination. If her Jewishness troubled her, she never showed it to me. In fact, I wonder why I have been making such a point of it here. When I knew her and was with her, I never thought of it. But in looking back I think I can see that when she arrived in Chicago she advanced instinctually upon that part of the city and that element of the population in which her Jewishness, or anyone's, would be of no meaning whatever; I mean the half-arty, half-academic, wholly unconstrained neighborhood of the university on the South Side; and beyond that she simply avoided, effortlessly, the places where her race could cause her the slightest inconvenience. But she did nothing dramatic—she might have changed her name, for instance, but she didn't. Alex Silverstine never did anything dramatic; or rather she constantly did dramatic things in a way which made them seem uncalculated and commonplace.

In her Pullman room, Alex slept. The train grumbled up the mountain, clacked down the other side, burst with Vulcanian splendor across the river, forged at last in sedulous concentration

25

across the colloidal damps of Indiana. Alex slept, I imagine, as she always slept; deeply, strongly, aggressively; drinking her sleep, eating it, battening on it, serving it as if it were a lust continually satisfying and renewing itself; she engaged sleep as a naiad engages the stream into which she leaps. Consequently, it isn't surprising that she snored.

CHAPTER 5

Hemlocks define this valley like a Greek *choros*, men on one side, women on the other; silent now, bowed, arms folded, dark. At the back the sun is going down, incarnadine—an amateurishly painted backdrop. In the center an apple tree appears, subsiding from the day's agony; her intricate shadow lengthens, her boughs are already heavy with leafage and the young fruit. It is quiet everywhere. The drama is ending; but the final moment is in some respects the most moving, as in all dramas of gender.

Gender is a better word than *sex*; more restful, more expressive, and ultimately more meaningful. A famous man once remarked that there is between a man and a woman the difference of plumbing—so great and so little. *Gender* gives us this meaning almost perfectly, being related to both *genital* and *engine*; whereas *sex*, coming from the word which means to divide or cut, is an ugly, brutal, destructive term. *Gender* is related to other fine words too, such as *ingenuity, gentle, genial, genius, generous, genuine*— some of our most beautiful words—and of course also *genesis* and *generation*. Notice how the words fall into two groups, those having to do with generation and those having to do with thought, the indispensable reciprocity of skull and pelvis upon which all our art and philosophy and understanding rest. Perhaps the real tragedy of our civilization arose in the contest of meanings when *gender* was displaced by *sex*.

CHAPTER 6

Later; a good deal later; middle of August. I've been put off by one thing and another, and my progress is shamefully slow. One distraction was the damage done to the garage when lightning struck last week. The storm had risen in the Adirondacks, and came blasting across to us with wind, rain, hail, lightning; it dived on us like a locust swarm. The bolt struck the cupola, which was a fake cupola anyway, flimsily put together long ago to suit the unknown builder's fancy; I found some splintered parts of it a hundred feet away in the meadow, where they had been hurled by the lightning's force. The roof was damaged too, a couple of rafters split and the shingles torn up. The unknown builder had made a pigeon cote up there in the space under the roof, complete with little arched portals at either end for the pigeons to use in their coming and going; but since I've never seen a pigeon in this region, I thought the pigeon cote was another piece of fakery. I opened the hatch in the garage ceiling and climbed up to inspect the damage. I found that my supposition was wrong, the pigeon cote had actually been used, though it must have been years ago. The dust was an inch thick or more. Pigeon droppings were thick too, shiny and smooth like old paint. The dust was gray, that mysterious silt which drifts and settles in closed recesses, and at first I didn't notice the skeletons; but when I saw them they were unmistakable —fragile and intent like Chinese calligraphy in the dust. The snake's vertebrae formed the most delicately carved necklace you can imagine, with tiny ribs like filaments of Venetian glass. The pigeon skeletons, ten or twelve, mostly adult but a few smaller, lay

28

in scattered attitudes, breasts broken and wings turned under, their little skulls as thin as old silver thimbles. How the snake had managed to climb into the cote I have no idea, but clearly he had encountered more than he expected. The pigeons, more accurately called doves, had finished him off, though they lost some of their own number in the fray. It was no doubt a furious battle, but perhaps strangely silent; no need to sound an alarm at that point; feathers whirled in the dim light, a violence of wings flogged the hot air, the serpent coiled and spun; a cataclysm in a hot world, up under the rafters. Did the owner climb up to see what had happened and then, finding the havoc, shut up the cote forever, the owner who had brought the pigeons there in the first place and in consequence the snake as well? Or had he perhaps moved away some time before?

At any rate, it took me most of a week to see that the damage done by the lightning's revealing stroke was repaired and the cote sealed up once more.

CHAPTER 7

The day in question, the day I set out to record some pages back, was one which some authors of the older and more radical generation would have arrayed in sonorous monumentality or, by opposition, in ironic triviality; and I can myself easily imagine the events of that day falling into either pattern, given an author with the imaginative force to exert such a degree of control over his materials. I lack it, at least in respect to this particular day. It remains in my memory with a clarity and individuality which renders it virtually autonomous, exempt from my creative authority. Simple veracity is all I can hope for. Which is perhaps enough: this day, like all days, was autonomous, unique, and what could be more interesting than its simple history? It's a point I wish to hold to, the uniqueness of days within their multiplicity.

Hence the universe was, on that particular day, in a condition never known before and never to be duplicated again. Do I understand the universe rightly? It's exploding, isn't it?—that's the current belief?—stars and nebulae flying apart at a rate of thousands of miles per hour? A frightening thought; yet no more frightening, perhaps, than the bygone accounts of astrologers, now fallen into ill repute. Here also I am ignorant. I have no idea what scandalous conjunctions and domiciliations may have been occurring among the celestial folk in midsummer 1951, but something must have been afoot. . . . One decade ago, no more than that, and perhaps to the very day. This is a frightening possibility too, though I don't see precisely why. Here in my hemlock-lined valley on a mid-August day in 1961 I am safely removed, you might think, from the time and place of that other August day ten years ago at Lake Jones.

A well-named lake, believe me. At least if you grant that Jones, while respectable enough, is undistinguished. Inigo, John Paul, Bobby, Philly Joe—that's about it as far as the Jonses are concerned. Well, there was an emperor too, wasn't there?—so perhaps I shouldn't be hasty. At any rate, Lake Jones lies twenty miles, more or less, over the Michigan line when you drive eastward from Chicago around the bottom of Lake Michigan. It is one of the many small lakes that lie close around the Great Lakes like boulders fallen from a cliff. Their main attraction is that so many people vacation on the shore of the big lake that few have discovered the little ones. Lake Michigan occupies 22,400 square miles of the earth's surface; Lake Jones occupies about four acres. A modest lake. Longer than it is wide, extending north-south in a kidney shape, the farther convex shoreline giving way to reedy marshes and meadowland while the nearer concave shoreline rises among large pines whose roots twist along the surface of the bare ground; bare, that is, except for a covering of thick, slimpsy pine needles. What with the pine needles and the exposed pine roots, it's worth your life to walk up that slope after dark—on your way to the outhouse—and the chances are you will stumble and skid and fall and spend half an hour hunting for your flashlight—which always goes out when it drops—while the blood worms viscously down your shin like primeval ooze and coagulates in your sneaker. Above the slope the trees thicken into a wood that extends about two miles and conceals Lake Jones from the main highway; the pines give way to beeches, ash, thickets of hawthorn, a good deal of underbrush, cut by paths and opened here and there by small grassy clearings. Through the wood runs a road—two ruts with grass between—from the main highway to the north end of the lake, and along the slope, under the pines, is a scattering of "cottages," really no more than shacks: four-room, weathered matchboard houses on stilts, with porches and steps in front, and of course outhouses in the rear. Matchboard lichened and warped; windows lopsided; screening rusty, broken; one naked electric bulb hanging from the ceiling in each room; rusty rectangular iron sink in the kitchen; water from a hand pump at one end of the sink;

31

kerosene stove for cooking, with wicks burned down unevenly. What can one expect for $200 the "season"? Even so, three or four of these cottages were occupied all summer by retired couples who cleaned them, mended them, painted them, and in fact made them almost presentable. Ours, used only on eight or ten weekends, remained in its pristine degradation. The swimming was good (except for the leeches) and a workable rowboat went with the cottage, so it wasn't bad for people who simply wanted to loaf and wear dirty clothes and drink beer and read; who wanted, in other words, to escape Chicago's unbearable summer heat by going completely to pieces for a few days. Which is what we did.

No, I'm wrong, Alex didn't wear dirty clothes; she was usually rather spiffy, in fact; and damned well ought to have been, since you could have laundered her entire weekend wardrobe in a teapot without any difficulty at all.

And now I remember why I began my previous remarks about Alex by saying that she was half-Jewish. It has to do with her looks. Curious I should have forgotten to go ahead and say something about her appearance then. I suppose her physical presence is so much a part of my memory that I thought I was conveying an impression of her great magnificence to you merely by mentioning her name; whereas actually the name itself—four black marks on the page—still means almost nothing to you. . . . One doesn't need to be an anthroposomatologist to know that the most beautiful women are products of miscegenation. This is a universal belief and perfectly justified. Eurasian girls are exquisite. So are certain Latin-American mulatto types. In our own culture many of the national female sex personifications have been of mixed Jewish and Aryan strains: I think particularly of those who have retained undertones of Levantine softness and shadowing with a northern overlay of brightness, blondeness, and angularity. Alex belonged to the suborder Fair, but was in no sense Nordic; she throve in summer—none of the flaking and bleaching and blotching which calls attention to the delaminated Anglo-Saxon in July. She was a good tennis player, when she wanted to be. Her skin gave the effect of deep light, as from the bottom of a glass of Rhenish wine. It gave off many lights, many colors; but not harshly—deeply and warmly like gold darkened with age. You could find a spectrum in

32

her presence: the purple shadow under her anklebone, the tender white, like fish meat, at the back of her knee, the claret flush, very faint, of her cheek, the deeper pink, though lucent, of her lips and nipples, the papyrus of her soles, the lavender vein in her groin running into pubic hair the color of beach sand that was wet and is now beginning to dry, the russet of eyebrows, the cream of abdomen, the tanbark of sunburned shoulders fading to honey-colored arms and hands. Her hair was the shade of tufa stone or pine wood, yellow with lighter and darker strains, and it was ringleted like a Bedlington's coat; she wore it short, cut close to the skull. Her eyes were light gray and the pupils were too small; her eyes could scare you half out of your wits if you looked into them too long, they were so blank.

Coloration appeals to taste. Blondes are preferred only by some gentlemen, as a matter of fact. But the torso is a subject for general agreement, and moreover, as the Orissan sculptors knew well, is the chief feminine ornament. Here is Alex from collarbone to kneecap. Full breasts, rounded, firm, not pointed, sloping smoothly over the glands of the upper chest, rounding snugly into the midriff; slight suggestion of ribs; blonde down, unseen except in slanted light, curving toward the deep navel; pelvis somewhat small; abdomen nearly flat; buttocks with a modest flare; long thighs with a soft inner part that flexed marvelously as she walked toward you. She was young, strong, slender but not thin; not hungry-looking like the women in fashion advertisements.

What the hell?—the ordinary Hollywood type, the sexpot. Granted, but don't make the mistake of thinking Hollywood invented the type, or has given it more prominence than it might have or ought to have. Look at the Konarak temple statuary, or the traditional Tarot pack, or for that matter Aphrodite of the classic period, though the Greeks (or their Roman copiers) took the life out of the stone. The type of perfection in the female principle, no more, no less; and deviations from it have been either decadent (stereotypes) or sentimental (spiritualizations). Whatever Hollywood has done wrong—plenty, God knows—it has at least preserved the genuine, natural image, which no degree of paint and technicolor can disguise, and in an age which has few other images either genuine or natural this is something to be thankful for.

33

The flesh of Alex—her impressionable part, so to speak—was Jewish, an olive-golden, eastern mode of being; but in her skeleton she was pure Slav: a thin nose with a precisely modeled bridge, eye sockets deep and large and wide, prominent cheekbones with hollows beneath, a strong jaw line and small teeth, though her mouth was rather large and her lips were full.

There are, praise the gods, enough such women in the world to permit every man to see one from time to time. On an unknown street in an unknown town—or better yet, on a known street in your own city—you look up and one is coming toward you. It's frightening and at the same time painfully exciting, frightening *because* it's exciting: like watching one of the big cars come off the straight a tenth of a mile per hour too fast. You can imagine how the ancients felt in the presence of the goddess, you can imagine why Actæon had no choice but to look at Diana in her bath. As for me, not only have I seen such a creature, I have known her.

Saturday afternoon, then. About two o'clock, the long hot hour after lunch—and that weekend the dog days were being as doggish as I've ever known. Damp, suffocating air clung to everything, even to the gray surface of Lake Jones, where the atmosphere lay in tangles like a broken cobweb. I was on the cottage porch, tilted back in an old, half-broken, cane-bottomed chair, my feet on the railing; I was reading a book by John Dickson Carr. The sweat drained down my spine where my T-shirt was pulled out of my pants by the way I had slid forward in the chair. Alex was sitting on an overturned beer case that we used for a hassock in front of the sofa which slumped, wounded and petulant, against the rear wall of the porch. We were alone. The beer case was low, she sat with her knees sharply raised, her elbows resting on them, her chin thrust despondently into her palms. She held a cigarette in her right hand, and the smoke rose above her head, coiling greasily in the heat. From time to time she tapped off the ashes with her forefinger in a gesture of controlled asperity. She wore tennis shoes, newly white, very short green shorts that creased the top of her brown thighs, and a white halter tied behind her neck. The sweat on my forehead coagulated in my (somewhat ample) eyebrows and fogged my glasses; I took them off, and then, after a moment, reached back and placed the book and the glasses on the sofa. Alex

34

very carefully dropped the butt of her cigarette through the neck of an empty beer bottle, and it hissed in the dregs. Out of sight, at the other end of the lake, children shouted and oarlocks creaked. No other sound; not a stirring anywhere. I tipped my chair forward, letting it thud to the floor, and got up, and then went and stood behind Alex—I don't know why, I guess I had it in mind to say something; but there was nothing to say. I looked down at the top of her head, noticing how the hair curled loosely away from the part. When I said nothing, she tilted her head back and looked up at me, upside-down. I could see past her face into the opening of her halter, the softness there deepening into shadow, and I could see the distention of her nipples against the white cloth. (It is all perfectly vivid in my mind.) I leaned forward, lowering my hands over her shoulders, crossing them beneath her throat, cupping her breasts in my palms; I pulled her gently back against my belly.

Alex lowered her head, placed her hands over mine, and hugged. N.B.: a curious embrace; she was hugging herself, yet I was closely caught into it.

I felt myself losing my balance, however, and straightened suddenly, steadying myself for an instant with my hand on her shoulder, wondering at the same time what I should do next; but I had no chance to be apprehensive. She turned and put her arms around my thigh, laying her cheek against my side, and with her hand she began to stroke me. It was damned near more than I could stand. . . . I shivered. Alex held me tighter, and the tremor passed. My hand was still resting on her shoulder, sticky with sweat, hers and mine. Half unconsciously—99 percent of my being was caught in her blazing touch—it (my hand) moved toward the cloth tied at the back of her neck; but she reached over her shoulder and intercepted the movement.

"No," she said. The first word either of us had spoken.

Again a flicker of nerves made my hand tremble. And again Alex moved quickly. She stood up and walked down the steps and around the corner of the cottage. Not hurriedly: decisively. She could have been going away from me in order to be by herself— for that matter, she could have been heading for the outhouse—but I know these thoughts didn't occur to me then. I walked down the

35

steps too, somewhat gingerly, and turned, going around the opposite side of the cottage.

The children's shouts and the squeak of oarlocks oozed through the heat that lay like a bandage over the lake.

I met her in back, near the outhouse. She hadn't stopped walking, but was going on ahead of me up the slope, stepping on the pine roots. I followed. She went into the woods, entering by a path between pine saplings where the branches were tangled in bindweed. She walked as if she knew exactly the place she wanted, and I wondered where it was. This was the beginning of my return to some semblance of higher consciousness, though still disconnected; but now I felt the emergence, steadily stronger, of an objective self. I became capable of looking with detachment at my own actions. I was doing what I was doing, and at the same time I was observing what I was doing—two people, the wholly sensate, compelled creature of sexuality, and the detached mind, observant, even faintly amused, but without any capacity to interfere. A long rough-edged blade from some tall weed cut my forehead. I believe this schizoid effect, the distinct separation of the feeling and thinking centers, is characteristic of men's response to extremely unusual situations. In modern warfare, where instantaneous and unseen annihilation surrounds the body, the mind detaches itself, departs elsewhere, sits and observes, watches the foolish body crawling through mud and bullet-riddled air; observes dispassionately, casually, remotely, in complete abrogation of its responsibilities to the body, which continues to crawl forward through filth and peril. A horsefly began circling my head, then lit on my sweat-soaked shoulder and bit me through the T-shirt. The bastard. I rubbed away the sting. My distant observer chuckled.

That damned oarlock still rasped like a fly too, a peevish fly, through the dense afternoon.

The place Alex had in mind turned out to be a small clearing under a half-grown oak, screened around the edges by saplings, scrub pines, and weeds. The ground, which sloped upward toward the oak trunk, was bare between clumps of brown grass. Alex walked into the clearing, unbuckled her shorts, dropped them, kicked them aside almost viciously. The white skin, where her sunburn had not reached, gleamed against the background of tree-bark

36

and dark foliage. When I came up to her, she reached her arms around my neck and shoulders and embraced me with surprising strength; she pushed her thigh between mine; she kissed me: long, hot, hungry, wet, ferocious, mobile, sweaty, abandoned. The combination of sweat and saliva was like blood. My hands pressed her into my body. She went down then, to the ground—not sinking, not sprawling, but lowering herself in slow balance, like a powerful dancer—and drew me after her.

My talent for lyricism is weak and uncertain; but judging by what I've read I doubt that anyone's is great enough to make a useful representation in written language of the subjective aspects of sexual experience. Let the watcher in the treetops, or wherever he was, take over.

We lay at full length on the ground, crushing the grass clumps under us; some of the blades tickled us through our sweat. There was a smell of dust. We kissed again, and a third time, I kissed her throat and breast and the hollow of her collarbone, where the perspiration had collected. Sensations of haste then: urgency, awkwardness; foolish clothes; the momentary shame men feel upon seeing their own nakedness exposed before the elegance and subtlety of a woman. We began. A bird rustled in nearby branches. . . . I hoped it was a bird. We were sweating rivulets now; torrents, cascades, niagaras. Our bodies slipped and smacked as if they were greased. The ground moved under my knees, crumbled . . . so it seemed . . . and in fact our movements had carried us forward, Alex's head was pushed to one side by an oak root that thrust along the ground at the base of the tree; but she continued rocking her head from side to side. I lifted my chin, moved leftward, came down again on her other shoulder. On the end of a drooping blade of grass, not two inches from my nose, a green inchworm humped and flattened, humped and flattened, on his fatuous journey to nowhere. I closed my eyes. With her right hand Alex was beating my shoulder, palm open; soft blows at first, then harder; her left hand pushed upward against my chest. I raised myself on straight arms, opened my eyes and looked at her, then lowered myself and kept going. Alex arched her back, threw up her chin, striking me on the forehead. I opened my mouth against her soaked flesh. Fury now; mounting; going up very fast. Pulsations quickening. And at last,

37

with every ounce of strength, the final surge. And—inevitably—the collapse.

"God, it's over," Alex said.

She was gasping, so was I, we were making movements of subsidence; the bird—if it was a bird—still rustled in the leaves, and we regained our breath gradually. Finally Alex sat up, cross-legged like an Indian, and looked down at me. She smiled, sweetly, and leaned down to kiss the back of my hand. She stretched, doubling her fists behind her ears, pushing her breasts tightly into the soaked and rumpled halter she still had on. Then she got up, brushed off her fanny, walked to her shorts and picked them up; she put them on with a certain effort of concentration, lifting her knees alternately to place her feet through the leg holes.

"Lord, the heat!" I said, and thought to myself what an asinine thing to say.

I got up too, and put on my clothes. We turned toward the edge of the clearing where the bent weeds showed our entrance, and as we were stepping through them we heard the Ford shift and turn off the highway into the back road toward the lake; it passed through the woods, fifty yards to our left. Impulsively we both ran a few steps; but then Alex stopped, turned to face me, and kissed me again, lightly, on the cheek. We walked slowly back through the woods, down the slope under the pines, around the cottage (which had no back door), and up the steps. Inside, Charley was hefting a new twenty-pound cake of ice into the old icebox, and eight dewy beer bottles and a head of lettuce lay on the floor at his feet. (The icebox was in the "living-room," I don't remember why.) There was a bag of groceries on the table, and a carton of warm beer. The ice fell into position with a thud, and Charley sat back, squatting on his heels.

"Hi," he said, looking up.

"Hello," Alex said. She rumpled his hair. "We took a walk."

"So I see. Looks as if you've been mountain climbing."

"We were running," I said. "We heard the car." I guess it sounded all right, though it wasn't much of an explanation.

"We're bushed." Alex blew a drop of perspiration from the end of her nose. "Let's have a beer."

"Damn right," Charley said. "Going to get into my trunks first though. You open the beer."

"Okay," Alex said, half under her breath. She could imitate perfectly the way people say inconsequential things when they're thinking of something else. (Or perhaps she really wasn't trying for an effect?) She reached for the bottle opener hanging on a nail I had driven into the side of the icebox, where it would be handy.

Charley stood up and went through the kitchen to the bedroom. As you know, he was Alex's husband.

CHAPTER 8

That's that. It wasn't easy, and I still make slow progress, far slower than I had expected. May I remind you—if you are out there at all, if you haven't been incinerated long since—that this is the summer of 1961? Troops are being mobilized; reinforcements have been dispatched to the Berlin garrisons. The Wall has been closed. And the lunatic element, the paramilitarists that we Americans never can get rid of entirely, are making louder and more vicious noises than I have heard before; even on the radio, which ought to be an instrument of the public trust, but obviously isn't. They cry for the bomb, they plead for the bomb—their voices, like those of all addicts, rasp with hysteria. It's not easy, I say, to write a novel . . . levon, that is . . . it's not easy to write anything when you are aware that before you have finished, long before your reader has looked at the product of your labor, you and the reader and the manuscript may be no more than a handful of cosmic dust. It's damnably hard, in fact, and all the more when you are writing about Alex. Let me say this: the episode just recounted was, whatever its consequences and concomitances, its awkwardnesses and banalities, in itself good; the act was good; it was an act of love, literally, and I cannot regret it. Not in these times. If the bomb has not yet fallen, it may be because the event has been forestalled by just that little extra ounce of love and sanity buried in the world's history. *Love.* . . . There's no lust, I think; not among human beings, unless you count the unhappy ones we call defective. But those who can speak to one another—no, they have no lust, although in the vigor of their good years they may make love power-

40

fully. Because language is love; touch is love; being is love; everything and every thought is love; the whole ocean of existence in which the individual person swims onward from the moment of his conception, this is love. Oh, I'm not fool enough to deny that it is often enough corrupt and dirty, fouled beyond recognition by distortion and insanity; but have you noticed?—love is the one thing in the world which even those who have never known it themselves can always understand. It is our substance. The other feelings, those which are not love, have no meaning—no form or articulation—to the individual person; they come into being, like all epidemics, only in circumstances of overcrowding—then love falls out with itself, having too many referents. . . . Now, when the air itself drips with hatred, to write about love seems difficult and presumptuous; a labor too painful to be borne, and doomed, in any event, to futility; yet never have I been more aware of the need for it. Never have I been more aware of the need to make myself one person, one man, apart from destiny.

CHAPTER 9

Those who wish to know who I am may look at the title page. I had considered the advisability of a pseudonym, but decided against it. For one thing, you have to go to such lengths of circuitousness to make the thing stick that it scarcely seems worth the trouble; besides, the truth generally leaks out sooner or later anyway, mostly sooner. People who use pseudonyms aren't interested in being genuinely pseudononymous: they simply think a *nom de plume* will give them added distinction. Sometimes it works. As in the case of Le Comte de Lautréamont, whose real name was Isidore Ducasse; nobody ever mentions him without pointing out that he tried to disguise his origin with a phony title. Which is a kind of distinction, I dare say, though he was a good enough writer not to need it. If my name were Isidore I might hide it too. As it is, I'm well pleased with my name, a good Caledonian name. I like to think it goes back to the Pictish, that virtually unknown tongue in which God knows what fierce epics may have been composed; by all accounts they were, those people, a fine and fierce nation. But naturally I have no way of knowing.

Appearance may mean something, however. At least my chromosomes didn't come in with the Saxons or the Danes. Pure black Caledonian, such is my color: black hair, black beard, black brows, hooked nose, a body like a barrel. I've a pot now, but ten years ago I was flat-bellied: height 5' 10", weight 180. My lower eyelids are drawn down in such a way that the whites of my eyes are exposed all around the bottom, which lends a fierce and piratical appearance. Ugly as sin itself, of course; but I like it, probably because it so clearly belies my nature. I am hopelessly mild-mannered. The only time in my life I got into a fistfight was in Rome during the war, when I was well crocked and took an awful beating from a paratrooper. I didn't know what to do with my hands, which seems odd—perhaps revealing—when you consider that I've spent a good deal of time punching the bag: that's what I like, whacking away at inanimate objects, punching the heavy bag or chopping wood. I'd be a great rock breaker on a chain gang. My looks have always been a source of comfort to me, and in the subway or on a bus all I need to do is look unsmilingly at somebody to see him (or her) turn pale. At one time I wore a long thin black mustache, but it was a nuisance and I shaved it off.

I was and am—as I said at the beginning—a poet. Not much of a poet measured in the scale of eternity, which is how poets un-happily measure themselves, but good enough; hard work has made up in some degree for a lack of native talent. I began writing verse early—when I was eight or nine years old, I guess—and I've been at it ever since. Not pretty poems probably not powerful poems either, but honest ones, most of them, genuinely felt and experienced; and that is as much as I can, or care to, produce. But don't think I am a trifler. On the contrary, I make no apology for being a poet and I am deadly earnest about my poems; I love poetry and have worked hard to learn something about it. Poetry is, of course, only one means of coming to terms with life, not the most successful; but not the least successful either. In 1951 I was editor of a magazine called *Pegasus: A Monthly Exhibition of New Verse*, which had been established in Chicago in 1897 and which had, since about 1910 or so, been closely associated with the modern movement in American literature: a distinguished magazine, whose contributors included most of the distinguished American (and British) poets of this century, although it had been permitted to lapse into dull-ness and mediocrity at more than one point in its history. Still, I enjoyed a good real of respect, as the editor of *Pegasus*, among most professional writers and critics, except in some of the fruitier quar-ters. More about this later.

Speaking of the fruitier quarters, however, I should perhaps make it clear that my literary life has been solely professional: my friends, generally speaking, have not been poets. You see, I know perfectly well the disesteem in which some of you hold poets, and I don't blame you. The fact is that many poets are splendid people, including most of the great poets of our time, but these are just the ones you are least likely to meet in the centers of so-called literary life; instead, they are often virtually inaccessible. Perhaps the greatest disappointment of my young manhood was learning that the literary life, which is described so attractively in the books that are written by the sort of people who write books about the literary life, is in fact a hideous compound of vanity, backbiting, ambition, greed, politics, neurosis, and perversion; and I discovered, somewhat ruefully, that I had best stay away from it. I ought to add that, among the perversions, the sexual categories, though obnoxious, are by no means the most dangerous.

I was born in the city of Fort Wayne, Indiana, on 3rd August, *anno Domini* 1921. Married 1941; divorced 1947. No children.

That's as much as need be said at this point about the author.

CHAPTER 10

The rest of that weekend at Lake Jones was awkward. For me, at any rate—Alex didn't appear to mind it. Not once could I catch her aside, or provoke so much as a secret smile from her, a touch in passing, a meaning glance; not one comforting acknowledgment of complicity; the episode in the oak clearing might as well have been a dream, since there was nothing to show that it had happened—no change in Alex, no new element, however slight, in her behavior toward Charley or me. I had only my indubitable sexual itch to remind me, by raising hopes for the future, of what had occurred so recently in the past.

One aspect of this category of experience which everyone remarks about is its suddenness. Perfectly true, Lord knows, in this case. I had known Alex for some time; along with half the other inhabitants of the South Side I had regarded her as a notable sexpot, but wholly outside the range of my own possible interest. As nearly as I can remember, she hadn't even entered my sexual fantasies—certainly not seriously. She was Charley's wife, Charley was my good friend; but that was only part of it: beyond this was the extreme difference, so it appeared, between us, the widest imaginable gulf separating our personalities, predilections, backgrounds, etc. It seemed until that Saturday afternoon as if we scarcely spoke the same language. Neither of us had ever listened seriously to anything the other had said, I'm sure. The idea that either of us ever could be desperately interested in what the other said had never, I believe, entered our heads.

Yet there on the cottage porch that afternoon, as the three of us

45

drank our beers—Alex and I still wet with the serums and ichors of our exertions in the sun—I knew myself to be sinking like a leaky scow into the sea, the enveloping ocean of tenderness, longing, warmth, (if you will) sentimentality; I was inextricably in love; my look rested upon her as softly and possessively as morning mist in a valley, and returned to her as ineluctably. Scarcely an hour earlier I had been looking at her with perfect composure and detachment. In old romances the hero at such moments was said to have been *transported*, and this was the case with me exactly: still at the cottage, still at Lake Jones, still dressed in my tawdry skin and wearing my piratical face, I nevertheless had been moved to an entirely new country where nothing, not even the most familiar object, presented the appearance by which it could be recognized.

Romance: a terribly mistreated notion. Permitted any dignity at all only in myth and fantasy. Yet no less a part of our steely, stony, actual days. I have read critics and historians who attribute the origin of rottenness in our civilization to the ascendancy of romance—no doubt you know the ones I mean. But I say romance is all that makes the rottenness bearable.

Alex was, as I said, très cool that weekend. I didn't know what she was thinking, and for that matter I never found out, except by inference. We had hamburgers and salad and a bottle of Chilean Chablis (so-called) for supper that Saturday, then about sundown went out in the boat, rowing quietly—Alex at the oars—and drifting toward the eastern shore, where the last rays of sunlight slanted orangely on a convocation of stout-trunked, misshapen willows. At water's edge grew short grass, sparse in a bed of sand; a few feet offshore floated a nearly waterlogged willow branch caught in some dark species of water growth. This log was a favored sunning spot for turtles and water snakes during hot afternoons, but at sunset, or a little before, it was appropriated by the songbirds that came from neighboring woods and fields to drink and bathe before the night. It was a sight worth beholding. We weren't bird watchers, Charley and Alex and I, not by any means, but we never failed to go and see the birds on sunny evenings. Bluebirds, goldfinches, purple buntings, tanagers, catbirds, robins, yellow- and orange-colored warblers that we were too ignorant to identify, jays, thrushes, waxwings, vireos—all came, fluttering, chirping, dipping

46

their beaks down in formal bows to drink. Frequently, too, we even distinguished minute hummingbirds perched apprehensively on one end of the log, away from the others. Overhead swifts and night-hawks cavorted, bats zoomed and veered. We drifted, that Saturday evening, to a point about thirty feet offshore, where we could see the birds well, keeping quiet so as not to frighten them. Alex let the oars trail from the tholepins, and pushed herself back off the seat so that she was sitting on the bottom of the boat, her back resting against Charley's knees and her feet cocked against the rower's seat. Charley's hand rested on her shoulder, beside her throat. I was facing them from the forward seat. "Look, Charley," she whispered, "aren't they beautiful?" He said nothing, but I saw his hand close gently on her shoulder. The sun slanted lower and the light deepened, combining with the heat haze in such a way that the grove of willows and the little scene below intensified against the darkened water which reached back of us on either side; it was like a stage, strongly lighted in the darkness of the rest of the theater, where the actors in their bright costumes—the song-birds—were diminutive and distant, as if seen from a seat in the gallery; and the sound of them speaking their lines—chirping and scolding—came as if from a remote and separate place across the surface of the water. Everything else was still; even the children at the other end of the lake had gone in to bed. But just before the sunrays lifted from the scene and over the end of the lake, leaving the stage dark, Alex threw up both arms and both legs and shouted, "Aaaahhhhhheeeeeeeeeeeeeeeeee!"—an enormous noise after the quiet. "Fly away, fly away home, you little bastards!" she yelled. And of course that is what they did, with consternation and confusion. We had known Alex was going to do this; she always did; every time without fail; we had been waiting for it. But we never knew the exact moment when the spirit would move her; and so we were startled anyway, and both jumped, Charley and I, half out of our skins. "Alex!" Charley said in good-natured exaspera-tion, "you'll give us failure of the heart." Alex snickered. At that moment the mosquitoes found us, as they always did sooner or later. Alex sprang into the rower's seat, seized the oars, and began rowing maniacally, while Charley and I rowed with our hands, and the boat slithered and lurched over the water to our sector of lakefront, where we scrambled out, hauled the boat up the bank, flung the chain around the post, ran to the cottage, shut all the doors and windows, and turned on the lights. "Beer, for God's sake," gasped Alex. "Beer for the troops." Charley opened the door of the ice compartment and reached behind the ice cake; he turned toward us, holding out a bottle of American champagne.

"Charley," Alex intoned gravely. "For me?"

"Pig," Charley said. "Be thankful if you get any . . ."

"Very extravagant, Charles," I said. "You better let me chip in something toward the expense."

"No," Charley said. He had taken off the foil, and was working circumspectly at the cork. "What the hell, in France one believes in champagne now and then—to keep up the spirits. No? Very good for the liver too. Only trouble is," he remarked seriously as he drew out the cork and set the bottle down softly on the table, "over there we got better wine for less money."

Alex had brought three paper cups, decorated with cerise polka dots, and Charley poured out the wine. "We need a toast," he said to me. "You're the poet, that's your department."

"But it's your wine," I protested.

"I never can think of what to say."

"Well, for sweet Pete's sake, hurry up," Alex said. She clenched her teeth in a grimace.

"Okay, okay," I said. I elevated my cup with mock elegance. "To Lake Jones, by whose pacific waters may good fellowship forever dwell."

"Damn right," Charley said. He had taken me seriously.

We all drank then, swallowing deeply. The wine was cold and —in that time and place—delicious.

Then we sat down at the scarred deal table, sweaty and contented—even I grew calm at that moment, under the sedative influence of the wine and the warm night. My guilt and longing fell away from me, and I felt as I had always felt with these two friends, as if the transaction in the oak clearing had been somehow canceled. We lit cigarettes, and talked, leaning our elbows on the table, looking at the deep shadows cast in each other's eyes by the dangling light bulb overhead. We spoke of our memories of childhood, fondly, smilingly, basking in one another's remembered

48

gladnesses; we sipped the wine; and when it was gone we continued smoking and talking until after midnight, and then we went to bed. As I undressed, I heard an owl barking—*whuff, whuff, whu-whuff* —in the woods. Once I was alone in bed, naked as the light bulb and just as hot, dripping on the damp sheet, then the night turned vicious, of course, and the guilt and desire returned. Alex and Charley slept in the room off the kitchen, I in the room off the living room, and our bedrooms were separated by a single wall, a thin partition of smirched fiberboard. The beds were iron bedsteads with cotton mattresses and noisy springs. I heard the creaking of the bed in the next room; shaking with jealousy, I reached to turn out the light—and burned my fingers on the hot bulb. Perspiration jumped out all over my skin. I wondered, furiously and dismally, if he was giving her as good a time as I had. But the creaking stopped, and I decided they had simply been moving around before settling into sleep. . . . As a matter of fact, this had happened every night we had spent in the cottage together, though previously I had been only curious, not insane: the bed in the next room had always creaked, I had always wondered if they were actually doing what my mind depicted them as doing, the creaking had always stopped, I had always decided they were simply going to sleep; I had always decided, in plain truth, that Charley's ingenerate sense of delicacy in such matters, in *all* matters, joined with his knowledge that the beds could clearly be heard through the partition—for certainly they could hear my bed squeaking too, especially when I tumbled about in a fit of insomnia, as I often did—all these considerations would prohibit any active conjugating between them as long as a third person was in the cottage. In the past, though, I had smiled, half fondly, at Charley's sense of decorum, and had wondered idly if his reserve was shared by Alex. This night I did not smile, or wonder.

My fit subsided, somewhat. But was replaced immediately by the jitters. In the night my worries exploded into a mass of half-formed fears. Alex and I had committed our joyous transgression in the oak clearing without taking the ordinary precautions recommended in a technological era, and I desperately wanted to get her aside and ask her what time of the month it was. What agonies a man lets himself in for! Women too, of course, with all manner of

49

ensuing psychogenic disturbances, as one very well knows; and Alex's calmness should have reassured me. But I suspected that she would be calm in the face of anything—for example, a Tartar rape —and besides, at that point I was beyond reassurance; I was as high as a kite, drunk with wine, heat, fatigue, nerves, and prurience. Not that I wasn't perfectly willing to sire veritable hordes upon that luxurious body; but not now, not so soon. Let it be done properly, decently. I didn't have the faintest idea what—in those circumstances—could possibly constitute propriety or decency, but I thought, hoped, wondered, believed, feared, demanded that some accommodation could be arranged. I was gone, flipped, out of my mind.

Sleep was impossible. I tossed and struggled in my bed, though as gingerly as possible so as not to disturb the sleepers—if they were asleep—in the next room. Eventually I got up, stepping softly, put on my pants and sneakers, went to my suitcase and fumbled in the pocket for the bottle of Seconal capsules, went to the icebox and got out a bottle of beer, and then retired to the sofa on the porch. Naturally I had forgotten the opener. I went back and got it, and the floor creaked like a windlass. I swallowed a capsule with a gulp of beer, lit a cigarette, and leaned back against the musty fabric of the sofa, staring into the darkness. The sky was black, filled, it seemed, with black smoke—no moon or stars. The night dripped. I agonized as before, without much purpose. By the time the second cigarette was finished, I had collapsed at last, leaden-skulled and numb-bodied, with just enough strength remaining to set the beer bottle, still with an inch of beer in it, shakily on the floor and creep into the crotch of the sofa. I woke again at four o'clock when someone split my head with an axe. It was only a crow cawing, but the wound remained—all day. I was stiff and cold.

I remember, though, my first waking thought: idiot (to myself), why didn't you think of it before?—there's nothing whatever to worry about, a woman like Alex would have had herself spayed. The bitch!—what a horrible thing to do. . . . It wasn't true, as a matter of fact; yet my intuition of her character, even at that ghastly hour, perhaps because of that ghastly hour, was accurate enough. It almost could have been true. In another time and place I'm certain she would have done it without a moment's hesitation.

50

But do you see how soon love mocks and doubts itself?—how soon the objective mind begins recording its reservations? This was the horrible part: I knew I was in love with a soulless woman and I knew I would go on loving her just the same.

CHAPTER 11

The following day—Sunday—was ugly and brutal, a killer.

After I had awakened at four o'clock, I returned to my bedroom, but lay sleepless a long time while the early summer morning brightened, my head aching and my stomach uneasy. There wasn't any booze; we usually didn't bring anything hard with us on these weekends at Lake Jones. I thought about getting another bottle of beer, but my gut quavered at the notion. I dozed finally, and found myself among macabre dreams—I don't remember what, but I do remember waking in a fright, ill and worn out. Alex was messing around in the kitchen. It was about eight-thirty.

Of course, the first thing I thought was that maybe Charley was still asleep, in which case I might have a few minutes alone with Alex; and I got out of bed quickly, tipping the contents of my skull like pebbles in a bucket, and dressed hastily; but Charley was just coming out of his and Alex's bedroom as I entered the kitchen. "Hi," he said. "You look awful."

"No doubt, no doubt," I grumbled. I went to look at myself in the cracked mirror with the tarnished, curlicued brass frame that hung over the iron sink. I've seen better looking squashed frogs. It's bad enough to be able to see practically the whole lower half of a man's eyeballs, but when they're bloodshot to boot, you have a pretty god-awful image confronting you. I snorted, half expecting flame to spurt from my nostrils. But it didn't. I raised the pump handle and leaned on it, and stuck my head under the spout. There's one thing about pump water, or rather two things: you have to work for it, but when it comes it is cold and delicious. I

52

soaked my head and drank from cupped hands. Charley appeared, with two aspirins in his outstretched palm, and I took them and swallowed them. "Thanks," I said. "That's more like it."

"Bad night?"

Before I could answer, Alex held out a mug of coffee to me, holding it by the handle so that I had to grip the bottom. I burned my fingers again. "Thanks," I said, putting the cup down in the sink.

"Well, drink it," Alex commanded. "It'll do you good."

As a matter of fact, it did. It was good coffee. Alex was a marvel. Maybe other people could get good coffee out of a rusty percolator and a kerosene stove that smoked like the town dump, but I doubt it. I leaned back against the far end of the sink while Charley doused his head; I sipped the coffee. When he looked up, I wagged my head sympathetically at him. His blond hair hung darkly and limply over his forehead, and he took the towel and rubbed his head vigorously. "That's better," he said. "Well, did you or didn't you?"

"A rotten night," I answered. "Slept on the porch part of the time."

"Humpt," he said.

I put down my coffee again, took the comb that lay next to the cylindroid box of salt on the shelf, went to the mirror and combed my hair. Then I picked up the coffee, got my cigarettes from the bedroom, and sat down at the deal table in the living room. I lit a cigarette and drank some more coffee. I had felt uncomfortable in the kitchen, and I was glad to get away.

Alex had been standing over the stove—in front of the stove, before the stove—tending bacon and eggs. She was wearing pale green pajamas that obviously hadn't been slept in, made of some soft, lustrous fabric. (Don't ask me what it was; I know nothing of such things.) The effect produced by the soft cloth falling smoothly over her body was an impression of absolute deliciousness, nothing else—softness and firmness conjoined, pliancy (compliancy?) and strength, youthfulness and ripeness; and the color, which by itself, I imagine, would have been enough to make one retch, especially at that hour of the day, was the perfectly matching complement to her brown skin and dark golden hair. But then, so

53

were all colors. . . . It was femininity heightened. But the word is wrong, suggesting as it does the etherealized sentimentality of lace and frills and pallor. The concept is better (though more awkwardly) expressed in the word *femaleness*, the gender embodied (put in a body) and functioning. I felt my hands going out to touch her, like the will-less hands of a starving man going out to food; her soft-clothed flesh demanded to be touched. But of course Charley had been there too, the husband, the friend; like the glass that separates the starving man from the goods displayed in the bakery window. Believe me, adultery is no game, no lighthearted adventure, as the authors of comedies and romances would have you think; it's a serious business, atrociously serious. Consider the emotions I felt then, leaning against the sink and sipping my coffee and looking at Alex and Charley. Engulfing, staggering, starving devotion to Alex, mixed with blank astonishment that this should be so; and for Charley . . . ? Guilt, of course. Guilt first and paramount, a nerve-twisting sense of culpability. His presence in the same room was a shouting, strident accusation of duplicity, evil, against which I was defenseless. And then affection too, almost a fraternal affection, a desire to protect and help, for I was never unaware of the tragedies of Charley's life. And also respect for him, for his modesty and goodness. But again, again, again, and ever again: jealousy, anger, hatred, fury lashing at the one who stood in my way. . . . And finally, for myself, Fear.

These feelings went to work on my mind and body like a wrecking crew, attacking every cornice and buttress. I tottered, the brick and timber and plaster cried out and fell; so it seemed at least, though if I shook outwardly, Charley must have put it down simply to my insomnia.

Sitting in the other room with my coffee and cigarette, I experienced the old sensations of lost selfhood: disorientation. My center of consciousness had been struck like a globule of mercury with a hammer, and the bits and pieces had fled in all directions. I looked up and searched for the outside world through the smeared window, half expecting the objects out there—trees, lake, stones—to be showing evidence of independent existence, to be moving or conversing under their own power, as if they had expropriated my

54

identity and were sharing it out among themselves. But nothing moved—even when I looked back again quickly.

Alex came in with a plate of bacon and eggs in one hand and a baker's carton, containing a coffee ring, in the other; and Charley followed with two more servings of bacon and eggs. They both made a second trip for the coffeepot, silverware, margarine, etc. Then we ate. We sat around the table as usual, but this time in silence. No one said anything. This had happened before, of course, and I had taken minor satisfaction in the knowledge that we three could sit comfortably together without talking, as good friends should. But not this morning. My apprehension was nearing the point at which it would be more than I could bear—the pressure mounting up— and then suddenly, catastrophically, the idea came into my mind for the first time that Charley already knew. Alex had told him. The bitch! And Charley was keeping silent because he was trying to think of a way to begin. In a minute the whole ugly, hot, shameful secret would be out, lying on the table before us like a bloody cloth. My mind, shattered, began running like a cageful of mice, searching for a word, a gesture, anything to divert the impending blow and restore an element of rationality, or at least decorum, to the collapsing reality of the scene. I found nothing. It was a case of demoralization, complete and dangerous.

What saved me, of course, was the mind's (already noted) detachability. I became an objective register of the scene, escaping into remoteness, seeing the room, the breakfast, Alex and Charley and myself, from a distance, seeing that the tension was all in myself, as I should have known from the outset. There was none in Charley; he could not have disguised it; he was eating his breakfast with his ordinary calm, musing unhurriedly about something. Soon, I knew, he would speak. And he did: "Damn good eggs," he said. And then Alex, "Have some more coffee ring." I felt better immediately, and in fact felt so much better—a sudden onrush of cordiality—that the danger now swung to the opposite vector, and I could have spoiled everything through simple exultation. I was going to get through the breakfast after all! It was a triumph of luck and I was ready to shout. I controlled myself, however, and said, "Yes, thanks," and took another wedge of coffee ring. By the end of the meal, I was more or less fully restored.

Charley was right—it's food that does it. They *were* good eggs. It's marvelous, really. Normally I'm not enough interested to go to any trouble for the sake of my stomach, but I wonder if this isn't a mistake: I've noticed that people who think about food a lot seem to be the most pleased with life. At any rate, getting some chow into the belly does wonders for the nerves. If I had spoken these thoughts aloud, Alex would have remarked, "Oral satisfaction," while stuffing an extra large piece of margarine-coated coffee ring into her mouth. Maybe so. But I'm inclined to think there's more to it than that. I can imagine that a mouthful of nipple and a bellyful of mother's milk—98.6° of warmth; ugh!—might teach the infant to value comfort and digestive lethargy; but I don't see how this alone can also inspire him to undertake foolhardy and strenuous enterprises. Whereas it is well known that knights of old, to say nothing of today, did not sally forth to rescue maidens with much gusto unless they had some proteins, preferably wine-sodden, floating in their vitals.

After breakfast we sat for an hour, drinking coffee and smoking, then Charley and I cleaned up the dishes while Alex dressed. Charley said he would go for the paper; and I immediately tightened up, of course. Alex—her perversity by this time was destroying me—said, "Oh, let's all go," so we all went; cruising into Niles, Michigan, the nearest town—some president was born there, I forget which, one of the ones you never can put a face—or a time—to. We went to the drugstore and bought a South Bend paper for me and the Chicago *Tribune* for Alex. So far as I know, there isn't a newspaper worth reading between Philadelphia and Denver, so I always buy whatever comes easiest to hand so long as it isn't the *Tribune*; but Alex used to read the Sunday *Tribune* practically word by word, sitting on the floor with the different sections strewn around her. We bought ice cream cones too, but had to wolf them down quickly because they melted so fast. As usual, I got a toothache. The heat was coming on fierce, worse than yesterday. We drove back to the cottage, read the papers, had lunch, loafed, went swimming, drank beer, etc., etc., but there was no doubt about it, Sunday afternoon was a hideous drag, the sun spattering down like volcanic rain through the steaming atmosphere, all of us sweat-sodden, bored, and pooped. No one was sorry when, about

56

five o'clock, Alex said, "Oh, the hell with it, let's go back to town and have dinner there."

"It'll be awful hot, driving," Charley said.

"Who cares? All the more reason to get it over. I can't be any hotter than I already am anyway."

"Yes, she is right. No?" Charley looked at me. His ordinary speech was very nearly standard American, but occasionally he injected, possibly with conscious intent, a touch of accent and a suggestion of European syntax, as he had here.

I agreed. I knew I wouldn't find any way to resolve my various enigmas as long as we remained together in the cottage, and besides, by this time I was tired out, and I thought I'd be glad to get away from both Alex and Charley for a while. It would be a hellish drive back to town, no doubt of that. We usually waited until late at night, or even Monday morning. "Okay, let's go," I said. Twenty minutes later we were on our way, having shoved our belongings into suitcases and locked up the cottage. At the last minute, when we had already turned into the lane heading toward the highway, Charley remembered the icebox, and we went back. Charley and I, grumbling at our absentmindedness, went into the cottage, and I emptied the pan underneath while he put what was left of the ice cake in the sink. We left the beer in the empty ice compartment, and I threw part of a head of lettuce and two eggs down the hole in the outhouse, which I don't suppose added anything, come Tuesday morning, to the general aroma of sanctity at Lake Jones.

We never knew. As we churned with intentional arrogance through the sweltering gentility of Niles—whose houses, with walls of ulcerating gingerbread, pillars of tallow, lawns of yeast, eyed us through watery, lidless windows—and then turned westward across Michigan's still lovely farmland, going toward St. Joseph where we would pick up the main speedway to Chicago, our conversation was more or less like this:

Alex: Why in God's name do we keep doing it? We must be idiots?

Ego: Granted.

Charley (lighting a cigarette with the dashboard lighter): Doing what?

57

A: Coming out to this g.d. Lake Jones every weekend, what else?

C: Well, it's better than—

A: Oh, Charley. When it takes three hours to drive out and three hours to drive back, with all the traffic and the stink and the rotten heat? And what do we get for it?

E: I think we've been through this before.

A: I know. But just look at us. Bored and bushed and stinky. And we haven't even *done* anything.

E (wincing): Well . . .

C: You wait. Next Friday afternoon you'll be saying you can't wait to get away from the city. You'll be even hotter and more pooped—isn't that so? (He glanced toward me.) And all you'll be thinking about is sitting on the porch and drinking cold beer and going swimming and—all that. By six o'clock Friday afternoon we'll be on our way again, heading for Lake Jones as fast as we can go, you wait and see.

E: He's right, you know.

A: Nope. Not me. I've had it. I'm fed up to here. I don't know why we ever thought it would be any good in the first place. Seriously (she leaned forward and wiggled her fanny on the seat) look at that cottage. Cottage, my toenail! It's nothing but a shack and you know it.

C: But we can't afford—

A: All right, if you can't afford to go to a decent place in the summer, then I say you should stay at home.

E: It's pretty shabby, all right.

A: Shabby! It's a—a goddamn pigsty.

C: I know. We all wish we could do better.

A: It's not that, Charley. And you know it. Nobody's saying you ought to be rich. It's just that we . . . well, if you haven't got much money, that's when you should be careful how you spend it, isn't it? That's when you should get the most for what you've got, isn't it? (Looking at me, she said it again.) Isn't it?

E: I guess so. But . . .

A: Of course. Listen. How much did we pay for that shack— two hundred for the season? All right, suppose we took that two hundred dollars at the beginning of the summer, plus all we spend for gas and oil and provisions and all that, and put it aside. And suppose we divided it up, a part for each weekend in the summer. How many would that be—twelve weekends? Okay, then we could spend the money on some good meals in air-conditioned restaurants. And we could go to some good air-conditioned movies. That's the way to beat the heat. And if you want to go swimming, hell, you got the biggest lake in the world no more than three blocks from your front door. As for me, I can do just as well in the bathtub.

C: But isn't it nice to get out in the country?

A: Balls with the country! . . . Oh, well, all right, yes, once or twice or maybe three times in the summer, of course—but then you can go to different places, not to this same god-awful Lake Jones all the time, you can drive up to someplace in Wisconsin or to that lake in Indiana, whatever it's called—

E: Shafer Lake.

A: Yes, and to . . . to . . . hell, I don't know, you can go *any-where*. But you can do it properly—get a decent cottage for a night or two, or stay in a hotel; you can be clean and comfortable.

C: We'd never have enough money for much of that sort of thing.

A: I don't care. I'd rather have a decent weekend *once* in the whole summer, if that's all we can afford, than go out to that grubby whatever-it-is, that *pigsty*, every bloody weekend from June to September.

E (conciliatory): We've said it all before, you know—every time on the way back. It doesn't have to be settled now, does it? Let it ride, we'll see how we feel later.

A: Well, I know how I'm going to feel. No more Lake Jones. I've had it.

C: But it *is* nice to get out to the country. No?

A: Ah . . .

She didn't complete what she had intended to say, however. Instead, she fell back against the seat, brushing a wisp of damp hair from her temple. "Give me a cigarette, will you?" I gave her one, and held a match for her, cupped in my hands against the airflow from the window. Alex subsided, smoked. She didn't say much for the rest of the drive. But as a matter of fact her feeling turned out to be right; we never went back to Lake Jones, the

59

enthusiasm we had had at the beginning of the summer, when we rented the cottage until Labor Day, thinking that any respite, no matter how inelegant, from the oppressiveness of the city would be a benefaction to ourselves, having utterly evaporated, even, I believe, in Charley. He was a little tight, in plain truth, like many Europeans; and his main argument, if he had felt he wanted to expose it, for continuing to use the cottage would have been that we had paid for the place in advance for a whole season and ought to get our money's worth. But we never returned, and about a month later I mailed the key back to the owner.

We were coming into St. Joseph now, a couple of miles of drive-ins, gas stations, tackle and bait stores, marine supply depots, secondhand car lots, novelty shops, etc., stationed along the Lake-shore and flanking a broad, fuming concrete strip. The sunrays burned in from the west, directly in our faces. Charley's '47 Ford coupe was as hot as the inside of a chicken pie, and about as glutinous. Charley was driving, leaning forward, his left elbow cocked on the door. He loved to drive. So did I, of course, but it was his car and he drove. I sat on the other side, and Alex was between us. Cramped quarters, especially in such heat; and for a while I rested my left arm along the back of the seat in order to make additional space, feeling the back of Alex's head against my forearm; but then my arm went to sleep and my shoulder stiffened. I changed position, and Alex and I sat shoulder to shoulder, our perspiration gluing us together like mucilage. We stopped for a red light and Charley jazzed the motor to keep it from overheating. Charley's car was upholstered in the standard automotive plush of those days, the most unlikely fabric in the world. Plush, for God's sake! It must be the best clue we have to the American mentality of the 1890's, the days of the Oil Barons and Railroad Magnates, people who could tolerate such upholstering in their carriages and railway cars simply for the sake of its expensiveness; until the word itself came to signify wealth and luxury. Remember Lord Plush-bottom? Must have been a damned stuffy lot. But maybe it's a clue to our own mentalities too, I mean the fact that automobile manufacturers continued to use it for upholstering cheap cars long after it had passed out of high fashion, until nearly the middle of the century, in fact, simply because poor people (meaning middle-

60

class) continued to accept it as a snob symbol. That's over, anyway. Something to be thankful for in the general despondency. The point is that that plush used to be torture in the summertime; the pile or nap or whatever you call it would stick through thin, sweat-sodden clothing like pins, irritating your skin, making it burn and itch.

Traffic thickened as we left St. Joseph, and would continue to thicken all the way to Chicago as more and more people heading home from points along the Indiana shore joined the stream. The concrete highway was a steady rolling formation of cars, like a railroad train a hundred miles long. At first the pace was quick, but then it slowed, cars jammed up, sometimes there would be a crescendo of aphonic squeals as drivers, one after another, jumped on their brakes; for a mile ahead in the late afternoon light you could see red glowing taillights, and the air would turn blue and acrid with exhaust fumes from idling motors. My headache returned, and with it my tension and jitteriness—Alex and Charley's little disagreement hadn't helped my nerves either. When the jam-ups occurred, I could feel a suppressed scream against my pharynx, and the muscles of my arms and legs tightened in an impulse to throw open the door of the car, leap out, and run for safety in the woods. Charley only mumbled under his breath— "Schirzzzulschiffivitchesserz!"—when we got hemmed in. Aside from that, no one spoke for a long time.

By the time we passed through and out of Gary, it must have been nearly eight o'clock; the sun was setting; thunderclouds heaped up around the horizon rather spectacularly, lighted like endless celestial chambers. Sharp gleams of lightning played intricately among the clouds. We all looked, but no one said anything. The sky darkened quickly as we drove on, one car among thousands, through the industrial sections south of Chicago; and as we passed a petroleum refinery, which was located next to a field filled with huge storage tanks—glistening silvery globes in rows, like a formation of military balloons—the storm broke over us; pelting, smashing rain, with thunderclaps exploding like howitzers all around us.

61

CHAPTER 12

At an early point in the storm, the low clouds, roiling swiftly over us, parted for an instant, and the last upward rays of the sun, which must have been setting somewhere to the west, near Davenport perhaps, were caught briefly against the white upper clouds, a fiery spectacle. It looked like a great animal hide nailed up to dry, bloody side out. . . . A sign from heaven? It could be a cross too, I saw at once, a cross leading us onward, as the children had once been led onward into their devout terrors during that inconceivable crusade. A sense of religious presence stirred in me. It was a cross certainly, painted in the royal hue, compelling and awesome. A Cross of Lorraine, the central rod and the upper and lower transverse bars, standing majestically in the sky. I thought of Domremy and the girl there, La Pucelle. (All this occupying no more than a second, or a small part of a second, in my mind.) I thought of Rouen and the woman there. And I looked, sidelong and furtive, at the person beside me.

I had been doing this, in fact, during most of the drive from Lake Jones. The temptation was too great to be resisted. Brown temple, hair of darkening lights (like candlelights), cheekbone and jaw rounding and dipping and curving, full-petaled mouth, beadwork of exquisite moisture. I was drawn, pulled, turned, torn, commanded, subjugated, unwilled. . . . As powerful fish striving upstream in floodtime are nevertheless carried slowly backward by the force of the current, so my eyes turned slowly toward Alex, catching each time a blurred vision of her through the edge of my lashes and across the bridge of my nose. . . . I don't know whether

62

or not she was aware of this; but when I turned now to look at her, with the thought of Joan in my mind, I suppose I had a look of exceptional tenderness in my eyes—if such a thing is possible with eyes like mine. At any rate, she gave me a nudge with her elbow, no more than a suggestion against my arm. But it was the first intimate sign I had had from her since the day preceding, and I went immediately into a state—I confess, I bemoan—scarcely short of certifiable dementia.

Ahead, the break in the clouds had closed again. The rain was driving hard, the wind was strong, and we were passing an open field of floccose daisies, bubbling with commotion. But I saw that Charley was only now rolling up the window on his side, and as I cranked the handle on my side too, I realized that the whole episode of the cross had required no more than an instant as the rain began to fall.

CHAPTER 13

C: Hell of a thing to have to roll up the windows just when the air might be getting a little cooler.

A: Leave them open then.

C: We'd get soaked.

A: I'm soaked anyway.

C: Okay.

Charley dutifully rolled his window down again, partway. I rolled mine down too. I thought: *Charley and I will be the ones to get the rain, not Alex—she's in the middle.*

E: That's the trouble with thunderstorms, you always have to close the windows just when the cool wind might do you some good.

A: Why? What's the difference if things get a little wet?

E: Not on account of the wetness. It's suppose to be safer.

A: Why? You mean lightning might strike or something? That's an old wives' tale.

E: I don't think so. Lightning is supposed to follow air currents. If you open your windows you let out the warm air inside, it might make a current of warm rising air that the lightning could follow right into your house.

A: Piffle.

C: No, I've read that too. Just the other day, in fact. Man, wouldn't it be nine kinds of hell if lightning struck those gas storage tanks back there?

A: Let's get going then. Let's get out of here.

E: No danger. They probably got lightning rods all over them.

64

C: That's right. That'd keep the lightning away from them.

E: Where did you get that idea?

C: What idea?

E: That lightning rods keep the lightning away.

C: Why, what else are they for? . . . I read it in the paper a couple of days ago.

E: That's the *Tribune* for you, full of misinformation.

C: What do you mean misinformation? Hell, everybody knows that. I've read it other places too.

E: For Christ's sake. Look, Charley, the lightning rod is put there to *attract* the lightning—in a sense anyway. If the lightning gets close enough to strike, then it will hit the lightning rod, because the lightning rod is made out of iron and has a sharp copper point—it makes the best conductor, see? So then it's grounded somewhere so it can carry away the charge without letting it do any damage.

C: Maybe. That's not what I read.

E: Be sensible, for God's sake. How in hell could a lightning rod—a stick of metal—*repel* the lightning?

C: I don't know, I mean I don't remember the details. Has something to do with gasses or something.

E: Gasses, my foot. Gasses?

C: That's what I said.

E: Balls of fire. Charley, where in hell are any gasses going to come from?

C: I don't know. I told you I don't remember the details.

E: I reckon not. Gasses, for Christ's sake! It's that paper you read, gassiest rag in Christendom.

C: It's a damn good newspaper. Got more news than those radical papers you read. How come you know so much about it anyway?

E: Hell, anybody studied a little high school physics knows lightning rods don't keep lightning *away*.

C: Well, maybe I didn't study physics in school, but I damn well know what I read.

E: Okay.

C: Goddamn it, maybe I don't remember all the details, maybe

I don't even understand them, but at least I remember the main point.

E: Okay.

C: What do you think I am, some kind of a moron or something?

E: Well, don't be so gullible then. You don't have to believe all the crap you read, do you?

C: Listen. It isn't crap. You hear? And I'll believe what I damn well want to believe, and I don't need any two-bit wise-guy poet like you to tell me either.

I shut up. Two-bit wise guy, eh? The hell with him.

I sat in silence.

As I discovered some years later, Charley was right; or rather we were both right, or possibly—probably—both wrong. The fact is, neither of us knew what we were talking about. I hope I've made that obvious.

Keraunology is a branch of meteorology that even the meteorologists—so I'm given to understand—don't know much about.

We were out of the storm now. It had been brief and hadn't done any real good. The air was still thick and hot and steamy, the pavement was half obscured in little feathers of mist. We were in Chicago, nearly home, heading north on Lakeshore Drive with the lake on our right. It was dark now, but lights shone on the beaches, and other lights flickered out of the darkness of the lake —riding lights on boats, lights on the pumping stations of the Chicago water system. Irrelevantly—or perhaps not irrelevantly —I noticed the absence of fireflies—don't we call them lightning bugs?—and I remember thinking that we always notice when the fireflies come, on the first warm night in June when they appear in the gray shadows under the trees at twilight, but we never notice when they go. Alex broke the silence.

A: Why don't you two go soak your heads?

C: At ease in the ranks.

A: I will not. Asses, both of you—two ignorant fools that don't know what you're talking about. You know it.

C: It's nothing. Just a little friendly disagreement.

A: By God, you men are all alike, you really are. Friendly disagreement? When you're ready to jump at each other's throats right this minute?

66

C: Don't be silly, Alex.

A: Think I don't feel it? Murderous, both of you. You'd kill if you could.

E: Alex, don't be extravagant. You know us better than that.

C: Of course. Just a little friendly disagreement, isn't that right?

E: Sure.

C: I'd never kill anybody.

A: Sure.

C: No, I mean it. I'd never kill anybody—I know that, just as sure as I know . . . oh, what my name is, or anything else you like.

A: How can you be so certain? People do kill other people. It happens all the time.

C: Oh, well . . .

A: No, I'm serious. I know what you're going to say, that it's just in the papers—crazy people killing each other, nobody we know. But how can you tell they're crazy? I bet a lot of them are exactly like us. It stands to reason they can't all be crazy.

C: Not insane maybe. But you can't call them normal. Not if they kill somebody.

A: I don't know. I'd call them normal. In certain circumstances killing somebody might be the perfectly normal thing to do.

C: Self-defense—

A: No, I don't mean that either. You say you wouldn't kill anybody because right now you don't have to. The situation you are in doesn't require it, you are so far away from it you can't even imagine yourself in such a situation. But it could happen. It must happen to some people. Terrible things happen all the time. How can you predict for certain that someday you won't find yourself in a . . .

She shrugged and let her voice drop into silence.

C: That's not the way to look at it. Everybody isn't the same. I think there are people who would never kill anybody no matter what situation they got into. Why, there are some people who wouldn't even do it in self-defense, they'd let themselves be killed first.

A: Maybe. They're not the ones I'd call normal.

C: Everybody doesn't have to be like an animal. That's not what normal means. I know what you're saying. You're saying it's *in* everyone, no matter what. And maybe it is in a lot of people,

67

maybe even most people. But I still say there are some who can always . . . What I mean is I think there are some people in the world who hate killing so much that they would always remember how much they hate it no matter what happens to them. And if it's in them, they wouldn't let it out. Well, I'm one of those people—I know I am.

A: Then what do you keep a gun for?

E: Charley keeps a gun?

C: It's nothing, nothing. Damn it, why did you have to mention that?

A: It's true. Are you ashamed of it?

C: No—yes—I don't know.

A: Well, don't worry about it. It's no cause to be embarrassed.

C: I'm not embarrassed.

E: But Charley, after all you were just saying—

C: I know, it must sound screwy. I just bought the damn thing one day. No particular reason.

E: I must say I'm surprised. A good deal surprised. It doesn't seem like you in the least.

C: Well . . . it's a pretty neat little machine, you know. Damn well made.

A: Oh, Charley, come off it! You don't keep a pistol around because it's a neat little machine. Besides, what good is a machine if you don't use it? How can it be neat if you never make it work?

C: I've never used it.

A: But I'll bet every time you look at it you have the idea in your mind of how it works. I'll bet you can just see it firing and the bullet coming out.

C: Maybe. That's natural, isn't it?

A: Of course. That's my whole point. What could be more natural than keeping a gun? You're not dead, you're not some kind of a . . . a. . . . What I mean is you're alive, you're a man, you're all there. You're not some kind of a saint or something, you're not Mahatma Gandhi. Is there anything the matter with that? . . . Having a gun just proves what I was saying, that's all.

No one spoke for a minute. When Charley broke the silence, it was clear he was worried and deadly earnest.

C: I never looked at it that way. I still don't know. I still think

68

there are people in the world who would never kill anybody, perfectly normal people. I think I could find examples of them in the history books—famous men, and women too. But me? . . . I guess no one can ever tell what he's going to do in the future. Not until he's dying anyway, maybe not even then. It's hard for me to think of anything that would make me want to kill somebody. But maybe I would. It would have to be an awfully tough situation, I know that. I wouldn't just do it for money or anything like that, that would be silly. I don't think I'd do it to save myself even, at least not if I had a minute to stop and think. And I wouldn't do it for a friend either—that would be like doing it for yourself. Then what? . . . For you. Maybe for you. You are what counts most. Yes, that would be it, I guess—if somebody was hurting you, or trying to horn in. . . .

He was talking now as if I weren't there.

I hope it's plain that this was the damndest conversation I ever sat through in my life. I've got it verbatim here, I think, or very nearly; the words still reverberate in my head. At this point I was having a new attack of nerves, of course, the worst I'd had all day. I was as tight now as an animal that's been shot in the stomach, rigid with shock and fright. Me!—yes, me; obviously Charley was going to kill me. He was going to come after me with that surprising gun of his, that unbelievable gun. Soon, very soon: the secret couldn't last long. And this meant only one thing. I would have to kill him first.

By the time I took notice of where we were, we had turned off the Drive and were making our way slowly up 47th Street, two blocks from home.

CHAPTER 14

At home, I begged off dinner with Alex and Charley, and went straight to my own flat, where I sat for hours in my leather chair, with quinine water and gin to defend me against the heat. The night was oppressive and ominous. I tried to think, but wasn't capable of anything resembling consecutive deliberation. Instead I worried the weekend as a dog worries a rat—shaking it, tossing it, chasing it into corners, pouncing on it. Like a rat, the weekend died, and was found to be worthless—not even edible. I went to bed at last, but slept fitfully, half aware of a new thunderstorm breaking over the city. I dreamed that the apartment house was falling down: slowly: wall by wall: each segment peeling away and subsiding in an indolent crash. One by one the sleepers were tumbled to their deaths in the rubble. When my time came, I fell sickeningly, and my body was broken and mutilated on the jagged brick and splintered wood. It lay grotesquely, its open eyes showing nothing but white. Along with the other spectators, I walked over from the street to inspect it with interest.

PART II

CHAPTER 15

Yes, Part II. I hadn't anticipated, when I began this work, that it would fall into "parts," but now I see it must. Something concerning Charley's prior life and circumstances is required, something about the events which led up to the weekend memorialized in the preceding pages. This is unfortunate and I don't approve at all. It's okay, I suppose, for the bright, buttoned-down lads who write books shining with technique; but for my taste such books have always seemed to convey a false or merely external impression of formal structure, like cowflops on which a crust has begun to harden. I had thought I could stick to a straight narrative order —beginning, middle, and end. Probably you are asking why I couldn't foresee the breakdown of such a scheme; it looks obvious enough, after all. But believe me, I did begin at the beginning. At any rate, I began at the only place where a "beginning" could be made. Begging the question? The difficulty lies in the defective chronology of the very material with which I am dealing. The "story," as I see it, can only be the events which I experienced; the rest—the "background"—is the knowledge which came to me after the "story" began. (I put "story" and "background" in quotes because of the very real possibility that they ought to be reversed, or that they are at least freely interchangeable and hence meaningless.) The point is that in order to carry on this analysis with even a modest degree of comprehension—yours or mine—we must "proceed" (sorry, more quotes) from the "beginning" to the "end" by means of "retrogression."

Which leads me to say, before I continue, a word or two about

73

this levon itself, about what I mean by a levon. First, obviously *levon* is *novel* spelled backward. Very good; as I've pointed out, the necessity of going backward is something we must bear constantly in mind. Secondly, *levon* is associated—in my thoughts at least—with the prefix *levo-*, meaning lefthanded. Better and better; backward and lefthanded. Thirdly, *levon* is pronounced very much like *leaven*; which makes a pun, a bad one, but for our purposes a possibly significant one. Here you have it, at any rate: a backward lefthanded leaven. Why? I hope I have made it clear in what I have written so far that a desperate need underlies my words. Make no mistake, this book is propaganda; but to be effective it must, like all propaganda, be indirect, and you, the reader, must not only recognize its indirectness but accept it, acquiesce in it, gladly, as such.

The experiences considered here are important for three reasons, of which the first two—(a) because they are interesting to me, and (b) because they are interesting to you—are less demanding than the third—(c) because they are interesting to the Devil. As many of us as possible must align ourselves on the right side, for the Devil is sure to take the wrong. He is sure to insist, *par example*, that these experiences are true. Join me, my friends, in resisting this imputation; join me in affirming, over the Devil's insolence, the eternal, incorruptible, final mendacity of everything we write.

Item: the identity of the person on the title page. Obviously a fake: Mr. X, Old Pseudononymous, W. W. Noman. Then what about the rest of the people whose likenesses appear (or do not appear) in these pages? I have known them all; except for Charley they are alive today, living in this country. They are real, aren't they? . . . Charley, of course, is dead. Which means that he is the only one about whom the truth may be told, the only one who really exists here on these pages, *the only one we know*. . . . Still, he is very dead; buried in the ground somewhere, I'm not even sure where; rotten and gone to pieces. . . . Lies, lies, lies, it is all a pack of lies.

Christ, what a mess!

In 1941 the state legislature of North Carolina determined by statute that the official flower of that commonwealth should no longer be the common field daisy, but the flowering dogwood. You see what can be done with words?

CHAPTER 16

Charley was born, 23rd January, 1929, in Gespunsart, a village in the Ardennes, not more than a rifle shot from the Franco-Belgian frontier. On the following 11th February, he was taken against his will to a neighboring sanctuary of the holy spirit and instructed to rejoice in the name of Gaston Louis Marie Silvestre DuPont. His response was an audible dilation of the sphincter. So his sister Angélique told him some years afterward; she had been age five at the time. The priest, she said, coughed inauspiciously.

Nothing of further importance happened to Gaston for nearly ten years. An outrageous statement, obviously; it means that the events of his life during this period, important or unimportant, are unknown to me. Even then, moreover, ten years later, the event was scarcely world-shaking; in October, 1939, he received his first letter, no more than a picture postcard, one of those sepia mezzotints that look as if they had been printed in manure, depicting in this case the cathedral of Dijon and inscribed on the back with a message of poignantly depressing formality from his father. M. DuPont had been called to defend the glory of France some months before, and was doing so in the jaundiced hayfields of the Côte d'Or, as bravely as possible in the circumstances, I'm sure, although the value of bellywalking over rancid hay stubble with a dummy carbine gouging his back must have seemed problematical at the time. Gaston treasured his father's postcard for nine days, reading it once each day before breakfast and twice before going to bed, but then he put it for safekeeping among the pages of a book on Flemish history which belonged to his father, and he never saw it again.

He was a thin child; not frail; somewhat taller than most ten-year-olds; inclined to be stoop-shouldered. His hair, which was blond and cut like a burlesque comedian's wig, hung down in front and partly obscured his deep-set eyes, giving him the expression of an Eskimo emerging from his igloo after a long dark winter. One can't quite tell, from the single early snapshot on which I base my description, whether, in looking at the world, Gaston (as I shall call him now) was astonished to find it still there or disappointed to find it still unchanged.

In the following spring—May, 1940—an event occurred which was considerably more momentous than the postcard, not only for Gaston but for everyone in his part of the world. Of course, it had happened before; many times; but human beings are by nature perennially unprepared. They possess what the other animals have never required—hope. In consequence, when the armies of the Third Reich crossed the border from Belgium there was a good deal of flurry-scurry-worry-hurry among the civilian inhabitants of the northern French provinces. I needn't describe it. We have seen it in the movies, read of it in hundreds of novels and memoirs: panic and despair, recounted in tones of monotonously convincing anguish by people who, unlike me, were actually there. Mme. Du-Pont gathered together her two children and a few belongings, and headed down the road toward Reims in the family's ancient Renault. The highway was crowded with other fugitives, driving was difficult, and in any event the car conked out after a mile or two, owing to a broken fan belt. The three DuPonts got out and walked; they were enlightened a half hour later when their car clanked past them, filled to bursting with ripe-red farm women and driven by a lusty 4F'er—I don't know the French term—who had no doubt got the generator going by substituting his shoelaces or a piece of suspender for the broken belt.

Night on the roadside: cold dew, hard stones. Blisters. A sip of fiery cognac in the stomach. How many kilometres to Reims? *Hunger!*—that is an awful word. And then, inevitably, the motorized German troops overtook them, scattering them like chickens. There was some shooting, I gather, and artillery fire in the distance; and weeping was heard—occasionally screams. Gaston lost his mother and Angélique, and took up with a well dressed, middle-aged woman who was slightly dotty and kept brushing her muddy

76

tweed skirt with a silver-backed comb; she had a large purse full of chocolate bars. Then he lost her too, and wandered by himself for two days among the increasingly tattered, fear-ridden crowds, one of thousands of detached, filthy, and (at that point in history) absolutely useless little boys. He never got to Reims.

Instead he was picked up by a German supply outfit moving east from Karlsruhe to join the main forces in the push toward the coast. Anyone who has ever served in an occupying army knows what happened; Gaston was adopted as the mascot of the enlisted ranks, the errand boy, the jester, sometimes the scapegoat. He was fitted out with a cut-down uniform—soldiers in the services of supply live well and enjoy plenty of graft. He lived by his wit, learning quickly that when he could make his benefactors laugh at him it was usually good for a cigarette and sometimes a gulp of wine. On the whole the Germans treated Gaston well and were, I imagine, genuinely fond of him. He was blond and thin and tough, or soon became so. In later years, when anyone spoke of Nazi brutalities in his presence, Gaston would look uncomfortable; the kindnesses done to him by the German soldiers, his surrogate fathers and brothers, simply didn't match up with what he learned later of Dachau, Buchenwald, and the rest—not that he doubted the facts of Nazi history, or had any sympathy with the doctrines upon which it was based. . . . The supply outfit moved across France by fits and starts, and came to rest in late summer on the outskirts of Honfleur, where it remained until the Allied invasion somewhat less than four years later; it was part of the huge organization assembled, with Teutonic proficiency, to supply the Normandy defense establishments, its sphere of action being the production of bread—large, round, mealy loaves. Gaston throve. Shoes were his main difficulty, but the soldiers chipped in to buy him secondhand boots on the local market. He was clever; learned to speak German quickly; learned the military argot—its filth, its sex-hunger. As I say, anyone who has served in an army overseas knows the type: native boys living virtually as soldiers, begging, stealing, fighting. Gaston worked in the kitchens, measuring out the powdered eggs, tipping hot loaves onto the cooling racks. He spoke quietly, I think, but sharply when necessary; he was serious and somewhat melancholy, and perhaps was the special friend of

77

the middle-aged men in the outfit, those with sons of their own at home. By the time of the Normandy invasion, he was fifteen years old—tall, stooped, hollow-cheeked; blond hair combed back with water from his wide forehead; dark blue eyes with thin, sleepy lids and a slight tic that came on in the right eye during periods of anxiety or fatigue.

How we are betrayed by our suffering! Gaston knew it. He was ashamed of that tic for the rest of his life; a relic of a boy's longings. I believe he actually came to think that the tic in a sense was not a true part of himself. Perhaps it wasn't. Nevertheless, we can imagine the biography of that tic.

When Allied troops landed in Normandy, Gaston's friends soon knew that they would be on the move again, and they knew that Gaston had no place in the disorganized ranks of a retreating army —like all enlisted men, they could smell defeat before the generals could plot it on their charts. At the same time, the Germans were well acquainted with the plight of neutrals caught between opposing armies; they couldn't leave Gaston behind, couldn't merely let go of him, like a lizard letting go of a useless tail caught in the mouth of an adversary. Gaston was piled aboard a supply truck bound for the rear, his tiny bundle of belongings hanging from his hand, and dropped at an orphanage near Rouen, where the good sisters were charged on pain of imminent debauch with his welfare and tutelage. (Why does the German imagination fail at the crucial moment?) Life in the orphanage, where most of the inmates were younger than he, was dull, prim, unattractive—a continual exacerbation after the rude amiability of the bakery. Gaston was depressed. Once more he felt completely unattached. The good sisters—perhaps they rejected his German auspices, perhaps they were simply too busy with their other charges—made no effort to capture his affection or even his approval. Hardbitten souls they were, like all God's functionaries. Gaston stood it for eight days. Then he departed, choosing the same means that others had chosen before him: he began running, over the fence and through the fields and woods, and he kept on running until he dropped; whereupon he looked around and discovered that there were no pursuers. They hadn't bothered. It was a flight of despair, of course, an escape less from the orphanage than from . . . war,

78

homelessness, fear, the whole unbelievable chaos of his life. After three days of wandering, he found himself at dusk behind the American lines, coming out of a wood on the road from Caudebec, though he had no idea where he was at the time: soaked, starved, without hope. The road was crowded with military vehicles of all descriptions, convoy after convoy grinding over the mired pavement toward the lines. Rain fell continuously but, it seemed, slowly —like the confetti Gaston had once seen in the square at Charleville on a July 14th: a gelid, numbing confetti that for some reason smelled like camphor. Gaston turned in his sodden shoes; headed down the roadside in the direction from which the trucks were moving; shuffled through the dank weeds and black mud. He walked for a long, long time. He knew he was going to die. At intervals he became exceedingly frightened, and his heart jumped like a fish. Betweentimes, he examined his fear and decided it was nothing: he would get through this dying somehow. Eventually he came to an intersection.

The trucks like great beasts of labor plodded toward the crossroad from two directions, rain streaming from their gray tarpaulined flanks; they converged, exchanged lowering nods of recognition, and lumbered off again in the two remaining directions, lurching and sighing. The pavement cracked under their weight; cakes of ancient asphalt skittered away, escaping the pressure of a monstrous tread. Mud oozed from the holes. A human figure stood in the middle, faceless, clad entirely in rubber, wordless, communicating solely by means of a red flashlight, directing the beasts to their proper destinations. Any one of them could have trampled him squashily into the mire in an instant; but they obeyed him unresistingly, like brokenhearted elephants, and their despair was imparted to the scene at large—the teary roadway, the listless sea-creature in the center with one bloodshot eye swaying at the end of an anguished peduncle, the black untrimmed privet thrusting choric hands toward the sky at the edge of the lighted area.

The minds of soldiers are blunted—at some cost—to such sentiments, however, and the group at the side of the road was cheerful enough. Three more fish: gleaming in rubber capes and hats with long downswept brims. One was asleep in the back of a jeep parked halfway in the privet hedge, and the other two, a sergeant and a

79

pfc., squatted on either side of a number eight can of burning diesel oil; the smoke coiled upward blackly, greasily. Gaston approached. He stopped ten yards away and stood. "Hey, you Frenchy." The sergeant's grunt could have been a question, an exclamation, or possibly a command.

Gaston said nothing.

"You français?" the sergeant said, a question this time, elaborately and incorrectly pronounced.

Gaston raised and lowered his head once. His hair clung in gluey fingers over his eyes.

The sergeant took a Hershey bar out of the interior of his cape and held it out toward Gaston. When Gaston didn't move, the sergeant made a tossing movement with his hand. "Here," he said, "take it."

Gaston came forward, took the chocolate bar, retired a step or two away, and squatted. With an exaggerated gesture, the sergeant waved him closer to the fire. Gaston came forward, squatted again, and began to take the paper off the chocolate. "Danke schön," he said.

The sergeant looked up quickly, moving only his eyes—like someone in a movie. "Hey, you hear that?" he said to the private. "I t'ought he said he was a wog. Huh? That's kraut talk."

"Yeah," the private said.

"A spy or somethin' maybe, huh?"

"Ain't old enough."

"Yeah."

"Anyways he wouldn't be walkin' around like a busted duck, would he?"

"Yeah."

The private lit a cigarette, drew on it as if he were going to eat the smoke, then held it cupped under his palm against the rain. Some seconds later he exhaled noisily; practically no smoke came out; perhaps he did eat it. The sergeant rubbed his nose with the knuckles of his hand. "I don't like it," he said. "I'm gonna call in."

"Yeah," the private said.

The sergeant went to the jeep, sat in the front seat, took off his hat, picked up a walkie-talkie from a case under the dash; eventually he said, "Yeah, it's me. Lemme talk to the lieutenant . . .

80

Yeah, it's me . . . Yeah, they're rolling now okay. Had a six-by with a busted axle; nothin' special . . . Yeah, look, I got a kid here, you know, says he's a frogeater, but I dunno, he talks kraut, you know?—somethin' screwy, Lieutenant, yeah, that's right, he talks kraut, like I told you . . . You want I should hang onto him, huh? . . . Yessir . . . Yessir, okay, yessir, I can handle him . . . Naw, just a punk kid, that's all, says he's a frogeater, but I dunno . . . Yessir."

When the sergeant came back to the fire, he said, "Talked to Sinky. He's coming down. Says to keep a lid on this motherfucker. You know?"

"Yeah."

"That's all, just keep a lid on him, you know?"

"Yeah."

"That's all."

"Yeah. . . . Say, if the frogeater's a spy or somethin', he can probly talk American too. You think so?"

"Yeah. . . ."

The sergeant edged three inches backward, rocking on his hams. "Yeah," he said.

CHAPTER 17

First Lieutenant Stanislas Pawel Cienkiewycz was called Pawel by his mother, Stanko by his father, Espy by Frank Lloyd Wright (under whom he had studied at Taliesin), Stan by his friends, and Sinky or Stinko or Stinkopisser by the men of his command; since these last were terms of affection, they were never in any circumstances used for direct address. Nevertheless, Cienkiewycz knew about them, and was justifiably proud of them. Both he and the men who served under him were secretly but gravely embarrassed at having been assigned to the Military Police in the first instance, but Cienkiewycz, a man of sense as well as sensibility, had managed in the course of a year and a half to soothe the feelings of injury among the ranks. He had brought his company to a state of functional well-being which pleased both his architectural and his military temperaments. He was well liked. At the same time, he was an advocate of good discipline, which he defined as an amiable but rational differentiation of authority. He had learned very early the first rule for being a good company commander: to make known to one's men the low regard in which one holds the foolish commands which come down from above, but to do so in such a manner as not to forfeit the authoritativeness of one's own foolish commands. He was tall, square-jawed, blue-eyed, and thirty-five years old; his hair was dead white and cut close to his skull. He had been born and raised in Gary, Indiana, and had been a junior partner in a firm of architects in Chicago before he had entered military service.

Who ever heard of a square-jawed Pollack? A just and inevitable

82

reproach. The lieutenant, however, had inherited his jaw from his mother, tenderhearted Mme. Cienkiewycz, whose maiden name was Gauss and who was a native of the easterly village of Parchwitz. Thus Pawel, through his mother, bestowed supplemental honor upon the village otherwise esteemed as the birthplace of Field Marshall Hermann von Kesten-Kesten Schlie, hero of Martz-Lestray, and Fräulein Rose Marie Dorn, the Silesian Sleeping Beauty.

CHAPTER 18

The lieutenant's jeep bumped down the edge of the roadway, past the column of trucks. Cienkiewycz was driving. He was a good driver, and he hunched forward over the wheel, peering through the clear fanlight left by the windshield wiper on the muddy glass. The other wiper wasn't working; the blade was gone and the nub of the bare wiper arm squeaked back and forth over the glass, leaving a thin arc traced in the mud: the private who sat in the passenger's seat couldn't see anything ahead, hadn't been able to see anything ahead for weeks, possibly months, and in consequence sat like the Detroit-bred quietist he was, his hands in the pockets of his field jacket, his eyelids lowered, his head flouncing with the jeep's saltatory progress, his expression denoting utter composure and faith in whatever dispositions of wayfarer's luck Providence had arranged for the highway ahead of him—all this with a dead cigar stub set squarely between his teeth. He said nothing; he seldom did: his miltary career consisted entirely in listening to the lieutenant. He cherished the hope that if he listened well enough he would eventually become a corporal.

Cienkiewycz said: "Nothing to it, nothing to it, what would a German agent be doing wandering around in—*blast and digitalis!*" He rammed the jeep into second and climbed out of a pothole. "It's all foolishness . . . like everything else in this—*move over, you crystalline crump-head, you—*" Etc., etc.—mumble, mumble, mumble. He punched the horn button savagely; nothing happened. "Wozzeck, why in hell don't you fix this three-cornered horn, why in hell don't you fix that croxy windshield wiper, why in hell don't you get up off your pneumatic duff once in a while?" The private,

84

whose name was Woodside, said nothing. The windshield wiper said squeak, squeak, squeak, squeak. A drop of rainwater fell from the jeep's soaked top and ran down Cienkiewycz's nose.

One of the points of military life which disturbed Cienkiewycz especially was the unimaginativeness of the swearing. He made up his own as he went along.

Headlights: saffron tusks drooping toward earth. Taillights: a line of creeping ladybugs. The pavement: gray as a whaleback. The rain: ten thousand tiny *entrechats* on the roadway. As in certain surrealist paintings, the alien images were unified in the prevailing *tendresse*.

The jeep lurched finally into the roadside clearing where Gaston was being kept, unknowingly, under a lid. Cienkicwycz said blessings-on-thee-little-jeep under his breath, reached into the back for his rain hat, clambered out, looked ruefully at the pot of smoking oil, thought instantaneously of his wife's lobster casserole, and squatted in true soldierly fashion—*vide* Xenophon—beside the sergeant. He picked up a wet pebble and threw it into the can of burning oil. "Keeps it from boiling over," he said, wondering if it did. The stone hissed, the pot emitted a gasp of steam. "Now what the hell is this parboiled crap about a German spy?"

"It's like I said, lieutenant, this here frogeater, when I ast him somethin', ya know what I mean?—he answers Dutchy like, he don't talk frog, I mean he just comes out with this here kraut talk without thinkin' like, ya know what I mean?—so I figures he's a kraut maybe, just off his guard a minute maybe, or somethin'."

"Him?" Cienkiewycz pointed his thumb at Gaston.

"Yeah, lieutenant, that's him. Like I said, he just come up like from down the road there, ya know what I mean?—just come up out of nowhere. And he looks kinda punchy so I gives him a Hershey bar, ya know what I mean?—and then he says . . . aw, you know, kraut talk, I kin tell it was kraut right away, ya know—"

"What'd he say?"

"Aw, lieutenant, how do I know, huh? Kraut talk, that's all. Donkey shayne—somethin' like that, how do I know, huh?"

"Take a look at him, sergeant."

"Who, him?"

"Yeah, the kid."

The sergeant looked at Gaston across the smoking pot, and Gaston looked back. The sergeant blinked, but Gaston did not. Gaston peered from hollow eyes between the streaming twists of his hair, pale and thin. His expression seemed at the same time much older and much younger than his fifteen years.

Then the sergeant blinked a couple of times at Cienkiewycz too. "Aw, ya know, I wasn't sure, ya know what I mean?—I was jest trying not to make no goofs, like you said, lieutenant, ya know what I mean?—in case some of them frogeaters turn out to be—"

"Okay." Cienkiewycz turned toward Gaston. "Na du."

" 'N'Abend." Gaston spoke in a low voice.

"Bist du ein Deutscher?"

"Nein."

"Was bist du denn?"

"Ich bin ein Francose."

"Porquoi parley-vouz en l'Allemagne?" The lieutenant's French wasn't up to his—or his mother's—German.

"Ah, monsieur le capitan," Gaston began. But he stopped; the effort was too great, he was too tired, what could it matter anyway? And his French came back to him in formal phrases, hard to search for.

"Ich bin ein Leutnant," Cienkiewycz said, reverting to German. "Wie heisst du denn, Junge?" His tone softened and he smiled.

Gaston murmured: "Je suis appellé Gaston, monsieur le lieutenant."

"Okay. Komm mit mir, Gaston."

Cienkiewycz stood up, and with a small friendly gesture waved Gaston toward the jeep. Gaston climbed in the back. "Wozzeck, give the kid your jacket." At first Gaston refused it—"Non, monsieur"—but put it on when Cienkiewycz said, "Nimm's schon." Cienkiewycz took off his rain hat, lit a cigarette, started the motor, then turned and shouted to the sergeant: "It's all right, it's okay. Carry on. When's your relief due?" But he revved the motor and drowned the sergeant's answer. "Don't shoot till you see the whites," he muttered, and drove off with a wave of his hand, headed back in the direction from which he had come.

The sergeant looked at the private. "You hear that, huh? You hear the lieutenant talkin' Dutchy with that there kid? What you think, huh—Sinky's a goddamn kraut too!"

86

CHAPTER 19

November 30, 1961. I write down the date—thus unapologeti-
cally—at the top of the page. By way of apology, however. Indirect
apology and, of course, confession—a confession that time has
flown and I have been lazy. Pages have been written, read, rewrit-
ten, and torn up, all to no end but worry. . . . But really, there's no
point in going into all that.

The summer went quickly, far more quickly than I have been
used to, and now autumn has ended too. A late autumn this year,
here in the hills; the brilliant colors lasted until nearly Thanksgiv-
ing, and there were many warm days when hazy sunlight filled the
meadow and it would have been foolish not to go out and savor the
smoky air under the hemlocks, not to go out and watch the apple
tree twisting and flaunting its brilliant skirts in the sunlight. You
would have too. One day there was a girl who came wandering in
the dimness behind the hemlocks, toward the woods; a thin, pale
wisp of a girl; and she didn't see me at first, as she stepped here
and there in the duskiness, touching the branches with her finger-
tips—a girl white and pallid moving behind the line of trees, as if
she were an understudy waiting in the wings, dancing alone, hidden
from the audience, while the red apple tree danced in the sun. But
I was there.

She and I spent many afternoons together under the hemlocks,
where the Indian pipe and false beech drops gathered shyly, according their lovely pallid grace to the needle-strewn earth. Wonderful
afternoons. I almost forgot Charley. . . . No, that isn't true. I was
driven as always; driven each morning to these pages, laboring

87

among the words, sending out my sentences like little desperate sallies into the no-man's-land of memory, patrols ordered into action by an insane general. Not much was accomplished. The terrain had been familiar but seems strangely altered now, and remembered impressions aren't verified by our reports. There is a good deal of confusion. I'm told that this is the sort of indeterminate stage which occurs sooner or later in every campaign. I would have been quite lost without Linda's help.

Not that she could give actual assistance in these difficult matters. Even if she knew anything concerning them, which would be impossible, what could she do?—poor Linda, deaf and dumb, as silent as the trees, as unlettered as the earth. Nevertheless, as you can imagine, she helped. The help she gave required no speech between us; and although I would not have thought this possible before, it really is better—more lucid, more *intelligent*—for having no intrusion of words.

Her name, as you see, is Linda. And she is deaf and dumb. Those are the indispensable data.

Now the cold weather has come, a sudden descent from the north, cracking the air, making the cottage creak and groan. Snow fell all night. The valley is thickly white, the apple tree black and contorted. The chorus of hemlocks stands bowed on either side beneath the heavy mantles of snow. Linda is staying here now. A day or two after she came, her father, who is a farmer this side of Goshen, arrived at the cottage in a quarter-ton truck, bringing a smell of manure. He wore overalls, rimless spectacles, and a long-billed cap pulled down close to his eyes. I was scared stiff; but he said: "It ain't proper, mister, but I'm obliged to you. Keep her as long as you like." He handed down to me a cardboard box of Linda's "things"—a red plastic hairbrush, two dough-colored dresses and some other garments, a china dog, a mirror, a bundle of picture postcards done up with elastic, a calendar for 1957, a Copenhagen snuff tin filled with pebbles, a tennis ball, and her bells. Bells are Linda's obsession, which is natural enough if you consider that the only sound she has ever "heard" were the bells at Kent School years ago: by accident she and her family—their old Model A having come to an inglorious halt on Route 7—were present when the change ringers were at practice. Her collection

88

includes dinner bells, cowbells, the fake Hindu bells that hang on a colored ribbon, Chinese gongs, a locomotive bell, little brass bells, a child's glockenspiel, a cracked wooden bell, a bicycle bell, some broken wind chimes, several glass bells, even a pastel print of Canterbury bells in bloom. None of these produces enough resonance—except possibly the last—to penetrate her deafness, of course, yet she can at least imagine their sound. No other sound is conceivable in her mind. Her favorite bell is in the form of a doll: a head and body of stuffed cloth with a cloth skirt which covers a bell of crudely cast bronze. When she turns from me to fall asleep, this doll-bell is clutched to her breast, though now somewhat heedlessly; and later in the night it sometimes falls to the floor, making a sound like a dull thud, which awakens me. The first time I woke with this sound in my ears I thought of a skull falling, and I have never been able to keep from thinking the same thing each time since. But Linda never stirs.

CHAPTER 20

The static hysteria—I pick up my thread as well as I can—of the confrontation across the pot of fuming oil had stiffened Gaston's tic to a point of feldspathic rigidity: he had been damn near fossilized. In the jeep, however, his rigor melted and his tic came to life, like a minnow emerging from the mud. He hunched himself forward on the seat so that he could rest his head on his hand, his elbow on his knee—immemorial stance of *le penseur*, decidedly uncomfortable in a lurching jeep; but what else was there to do? So he reasoned; he must cover the tic. Immediately his fantasy took up the whiplash of his fear. "Whatsa matter?" the lieutenant would say. "You sick?" And Gaston would murmur: "Non, monsieur." They would be watching him covertly; he would faint; they would stop the jeep; they would throw him into the—no, no, no, they wouldn't do that, they would take him to the hospital, yes, and the doctors would assemble over him, talking, talking, talking, and there would be bright lights, a bad smell, and then questions, questions. . . .

His lower eyelid jumped and jumped but could not get free, a silvery fish in a net.

Shame, shame. And bitterness, the fruit of shame. They determined the form of Gaston's life, of course. As they determine the form of nearly all our lives.

In point of fact, however, the lieutenant and the private up front paid no attention at all to Gaston, nor to each other apparently, and the jeep pitched and slued through the wet night, slithering down the highway like a pine chip in a rapids. Traffic was heavy, mostly moving against them—the convoys of elephantine trucks—but some were going in their direction too, and several times the jeep squirted past a slower vehicle with a veering and swooping motion, grazing hedges, leaping ditches with a club-footed pounce; and Gaston's head would bob, his chin would crunch into his palm, his elbow would slip from his knee. Fantasy: his head came off and rolled on the floor of the jeep and came to rest face up, the tic twitching feebly like a stranded minnow in the ebbing wave of a truck's headlight. . . . Once or twice the jeep stopped and the lieutenant got out to conduct his unknown business; Gaston did not look up. He did not look up when at last the jeep squished through the mud of a farmyard and halted by a whitewashed door: the motor died, coughing, and the headlights decayed swiftly in the darkness of mud and of black, gnarled apple boughs. They were in a small courtyard. The lieutenant and the private climbed out—skillfully; swinging their feet clear and alighting with one experienced leap—and Gaston clambered after them, and cracked his dome against the plexiglass side screen. "Scheiss-dreck," he said.

The lieutenant hesitated an instant in his gait, then shambled on toward the whitewashed door. "Alas," he said softly and sadly, "goddamn and alas."

The farm had been commandeered by Cienkiewycz for his temporary headquarters, and he stepped into the kitchen without knocking. A frightened French farmer and his indignant wife sat side by side on a bench in one corner, while a private in a muddy field jacket typed on a portable typewriter at the white enamel-top table in the center of the room. A stove at one side gave off warmth. Gaston spent the night in the farmhouse. With scarcely a word the American soldiers befriended him—an alien kindness he could not understand after his recent experiences, though it brought him within a few minutes a change to dry clothing, a box of K-rations, a blanket, and a bed on a horsehair sofa in another room. Gaston was close to dangerous exhaustion. Before he went to bed, however, he ate the K-rations, slowly, methodically, and completely—canned egg-and-bacon, hardtack, salt, everything; and he smoked the two cigarettes, and he chewed the chewing gum, and he looked thoughtfully and perhaps sorrowfully at the toilet paper before putting it away in his shirt pocket. Then he went to bed. The rough fabric of the sofa's ancient upholstery briefly burned his cheek, and he sighed and slept the sleep of the just, the poor, and the ignorant everywhere.

By what warrant, you may be asking, do I declare Gaston at this time—years before I knew him—either just or poor or ignorant? How can I presume, for that matter, to reconstruct events, thoughts, and utterances so far removed from myself, never heard, never seen, never felt by me? It is a question of some importance; not to be answered by mere recourse to "the artist's prerogative," or other such metaphysical nugacities. Believe, if you like, that I am drawing reasonable inferences from skeletal data furnished to me by Gaston himself in later years. Me, I'm not so sure. I may have been present at these events after all. Very likely I was. Perhaps I was even Gaston himself. . . . Whatever the case may be, names are untrustworthy. Consider Linda. Her "real" name is Lucinda-Mae: Cindy to the farmfolk and villagers, Crazy Cindy, wanderer of the weedy fields. I call her Linda. But what does she call herself? Remember, she has never heard any name that has ever been addressed to her by anybody. Who is she then? The brutal kids from the farms call her Crazy Cindy to her face, her poor, mute, quiescent face, but she has no ears to hear. Once I wrote "Linda" in big letters on a piece of wrapping paper, and pointed first to the name and then to her, pressing my finger against her breast. It was evident that no connection formed in her mind. *Horror of horrors, she does not know what a name is!* . . . It has been said sometimes that without a name a thing cannot exist. . . . I wonder if, in putting my finger against her breast, I touched the right part? The conventional part, certainly. But she knows no convention. Where does her being lie? Should I have touched her belly, her forehead, her crotch, her hands—her hands upon whose senses she relies for so much? Perhaps I should have touched the bell-doll. I have been with her now for several weeks, and in fact I think there is real doubt that she knows who she is. How often she must question, too, how and why she is!—if she can ask questions at all. But although she may not know these things, I think she does have a strong sense of her external consciousness, and it lies in the bell, of course. In an esthetic sense only, if you like; but nevertheless far

92

more decisively, I should say, than a painter's self ever lies in his paintings, or a poet's in his poems. Perhaps on this account—her confidence in the bell—Linda is to be envied after all. . . .

Let me get on, however. I can make short work of Gaston's life among the American soldiers. Really, there'd be no point in spinning it out; it is a familiar tale. He remained with the MP outfit until Christmas, 1945. I don't mean to suggest that the experience was uneventful, or that it was unimportant in the formation of Gaston's character; but what the hell?—I must get on to other things if I'm to make anything out of this levon at all. I shall say merely a word or two about the remaining eighteen months of Gaston's military service.

Do not be taken unawares by the term. Military service was exactly what Gaston's life from age eleven to age seventeen was, and if he never fired a shot, neither did most other soldiers in that highly technological prelude to the push-button war which is coming up next. I myself sat at a desk in Casablanca for two years, ciphering and deciphering the pig-English in which generals strive to communicate with one another.

The twisted routes of rear-line traffic which raddled Normandy and Brittany, like yarn tangled by a kitten, during the first weeks of the liberation of France were ultimately "stabilized"—the proper military procedure, viz. a ceaseless formalization of pandemonium. Lieutenant Cienkiewycz and his company were reassigned to duty in Cherbourg; the event was signalized by the commander's promotion to a captaincy. Police duty in the port city could be rigorous, since it consisted primarily in shepherding drunken soldiers to the pokey, where they did not want to go. Gaston wasn't involved in this, of course, but was assigned to work in the company compound—in the kitchen, in the motor pool, in the enlisted men's barracks, wherever he could be useful. Until his sixteenth birthday, he was retained on the same basis he had enjoyed among the Germans, i.e., company mascot, but when he became sixteen Cienkiewycz put him on the payroll as a civilian employee and found him a room with a nearby French family. Gaston learned English as quickly as he had learned German four years earlier, and he found that his old tricks served as well with the Americans as they had with his former benefactors: his grimaces, his jokes

93

against himself, his sly sarcasms at the expense of the officers or especially at the degradation of his own nationality, etc.—these brought him coins, cigarettes, gifts of candy. Never wine, though. Gaston was puzzled at first, just as he was puzzled when some of the MP's took him aside and admonished him not to use certain English terms which he heard commonly every day. He was a tough kid, and he knew it: a camp rat, a European rat, one of the swarming horde of rats that was scrounging, kicking, biting, scavenging, from one end of the continent to the other, in every city, around every military installation; in his circumstances illusions were impossible and he knew quite well what he was. He would have known it even if his former benefactors, the Germans (Europeans themselves), hadn't told him continually. But the Americans? A deluded race—thinking a sixteen-year-old European rat fighting for every crumb he got should speak like a . . . well, like some sort of an American pussycat, scrubbed and brushed and tied with a ribbon; he had seen a photograph of such a cat in the *Stars & Stripes*. As for wine, their attitude was absurd, of course. The Americans only drank it to get drunk, he soon learned, and he longed to get drunk himself, but the older men in the outfit sought to prevent it. It took him somewhat longer to learn that this was because they were fathers and had sons in the States (as they called their home) whom they loved with a fury that was entirely beyond Gaston's comprehension. Still, he was more or less content, without wine and without the independence of will which he was, nevertheless, beginning to covet secretly.

It was the Americans, of course, who changed Gaston's name. "How come you call yourself that chicken name?" they said. Thenceforth he was Charley, short and simple—Charley Dupont. (The "p" got made a small letter at the same time.) And since that is the name by which I knew him later on, I'll revert to it now.

Charley throve. A rat couldn't ask for better foraging. The deluded Americans even made him an assistant in the distribution of PX supplies, until his thefts of candy and cigarettes and chewing gum became so embarrassing to everyone that only his summary reassignment to other duties could restore good form to the compound. It was done; but not before Charley had peddled his candy, cigarettes, and chewing gum to the underground merchants of

Cherbourg, certain tight-belt-and-fedora types who inhabited the purlieus adjacent to the waterfront. Alas, they cheated Charley, gave him short prices and short change. He had the heart for thievery, but not the head—at least that is what the men of the company believed. But Charley himself knew that his defeat at the hands of the sharpsters was also a failure of nerve, since their evil faces and abusive tongues invariably set loose his tic. That unnerving twitch—like a worm of conscience dwelling in his eye—reduced him immediately to confusion and unfitness before the sharpsters. He also knew that the act of theft itself, stuffing the carton of Camels under his jacket, was no sign of bravery, but only a dream of greed, a fantasy of possessiveness, in which he, the actual possessor of nothing at all, moved like an automaton toward objects that he could—might, would, should—identify as his own. Here he touched the heart of his attraction to the Americans, who had for him a quality far different from anything he had seen among the Germans or among his own people, that overrode their delusions, their foolishness, their sentimentality. Americans were possessors, whatever else they were. Such a treasure of goods. (Goodies, I almost wrote, because objects of possession always take on the aspect of candy in the minds of children, especially in the minds of the child-rats of Europe in 1944.) Here it becomes essential to make the distinction, usually overlooked by enthusiasts of the left, between mere materialism in its various forms (greed, gluttony, venality, miserliness, the profit motive, the power drive, etc.) and possessorship as a means of self-identification—the search for an image of one's own being among the reflections (more properly, refractions) which are given off by the objects that *belong* to one. It's a two-way proposition: the objects which belong to us soon become the objects to which we belong. An adolescent proposition, too—granted. In his adolescent way, Charley could no more make the distinction between greed and knowledge than can the materialists. Yet I think he probably recognized it, instinctively and inarticulately. He saw plenty of examples of the former among his American friends, I imagine, and heard plenty of talk about money, land, jobs—the usual GI gab; everyone is sure to make a million when the war is over. But he also heard some soldiers speak of their cars, for instance, in terms which indicated a personal identifica-

95

tion. The point is that Charley was precisely the same as every other European rat attached to an American outfit during the war: he thought the Americans were absurd in many respects, he resented their naïveté and their excruciating tolerance; but he admired, he passionately venerated and furiously hungered for, the qualities in American life which represented (to him) liberality, social confidence, independence, self-reliance, freedom (not abstractly, but the simple certainty of being able to arise and go), etc., etc., etc.

Cienkiewycz was, and is, a case in point. Charley was devoted to him, and couldn't hear enough of the captain's stories of life at home. Not that Cienkiewycz was boastful; it wasn't his nature, and besides, the truth (to the extent it could be seized and communicated, viz. so far as the European mind was concerned, only in terms of lies) was enough to satisfy Charley. The captain had entered this life in the Polish quarter of the proletarian section of Gary, Indiana; a town whose proletarian section occupies virtually everything within the city limits. There he observed a number of seriocomic episodes, beginning with November 11, 1919, and continuing through the White Sox scandal, *Seventh Heaven*, Teapot Dome, Coué, Dempsey-Firpo, "Keep Cool with Coolidge," Miss Ederle, the Spirit of St. Louis, Sacco-Vanzetti, Kellogg-Briand, St. Valentine's Day, the Sweeps, Max Schmeling, the Bonus March, Technocracy, a Century of Progress, etc.; some of these impressed him, but none so deeply as his reading, in 1923, Sir Henry M. Stanley's *In Darkest Africa*, upon which he resolved (1) to stay at home and (2) to eschew any form of corporate enterprise. (This is an exaggerated statement, naturally; yet these elements of the captain's personality were the most conspicuous, at least in Charley's eyes, and accounted for the appeal which the captain exerted on Charley's imagination: perhaps it is permissible to explain them in terms of the successive simplifications of the captain's explanation to Charley and Charley's later explanation to me.) Late one wintry afternoon, while his mother was stirring the *Kartoffelsuppe* which steamed greasily in its black pot, he asked her what she thought was the best work a man might do, and she said: "Building houses—ja, Pawel, dos ist eine gute Arbeit, natürlich"— an answer which met well with his own predilections, as she knew.

96

No need to chronicle the steps by which young Cienkiewycz rose from a flaking company house in Gary to a splendid home of his own design in Palos Park. It is the American story par excellence. Charley was fascinated by it, however, and heard it, in bits and snatches, many times during his conversations with the captain; he was at the same time deeply moved and involuntarily skeptical; the notion that the education of a professional man could be obtained by a poor boy—this was what took hold of him, lifted him up like a pair of tongs, and deposited him in America; all in his daydreams of course—and in nightdreams too—long before the possibility of an actual emigration was even remotely considered. He memorized the names of the Illinois Institute of Technology, the Art Institute, and Taliesen.

Cienkiewycz's protective attitude toward Charley wasn't apparent to the boy. Often he didn't see the captain for days; like any good soldier he stayed away from the orderly room as much as possible. But then would come a day when the captain intercepted Charley on a walk across the compound or found him in the motor pool when he dropped off his jeep, and the two would talk for a while —ten minutes, twenty minutes—exploring their common mystery. For Cienkiewycz asked as many questions as he answered: about Charley's parents, about the Germans, about the boy's plans, etc. A casual relationship; nothing forced or awkward, nothing that on the face of it looked like concern or sentiment. The captain was adept at establishing, with no more than a word or gesture, a sense of private understanding; it was part of his skill as a military commander—and as an architect. The men of the company were perceptive, and maybe a bit jealous, though the word would have alarmed them. Moments of cruelty occurred. Their nicknames for Charley weren't always friendly. Frenchy and Frogeater were the least objectionable from his point of view; but he didn't like Winky, especially when it was joined meaningfully with Sinky, and for a while he even took pains to avoid the captain. The men found other means of touching his sensitivity too: they sent him with messages to Mimette, the whore whom they particularly favored, and then when he returned gave him the invariable greeting, "Hey, Winky, get yours yet?"—accompanied by a leer and, if possible, a goose. Charley, who had the translucency of all Lorrainaise, blushed uncontrollably, and his eye twitched. Finally, ashamed and afraid, he paid Mimette the necessary two hundred francs and did what had to be done, with all the horrid clumsiness of the initiatory ordeal. Mimette was decent enough, then, to give the word to let up. "Sonna my beech," she remarked, "why dohn yuh leefa da kid alone, huh?" Mimette was Italian, and her real name was Gelinda Nanni: she enjoyed her work immensely, and so did her clients, with the result that her commands, including this one, were usually obeyed.

What the hell?—Charley had no complaint whose gravamen could be more than yours or mine, the rot that sets in when a foetus is exposed to the sugary air. The attitude of cruelty did not prevail among all the men of the company, nor (probably) among any of them all the time. Charley had a lucky deal and he knew it.

The war passed. That is to say, the days, weeks, and months passed while the war remained eternal; and then suddenly and unexpectedly, like the first day of spring in Finland, it ended. On V-E Day, Charley got drunk, again on V-J Day; no one minded, no one tried to prevent it. He was very sick; he had no judgment whatever about how many portions of clobberjuice he could safely put down his gullet (that being the name for canned American beer and 100-proof French neutral spirits mixed two to one). His actual capacity was about half a canteen cup. After the jubilation and the hangovers, life in the MP company returned much to normal; the same duties persisted in peace or war, so long as American troops were in Cherbourg. By autumn, 1945, the rotation of old-timers in the outfit began, new replacements arrived, strangers to Charley and everyone else; strangers also to war and the atmosphere of war. Soon most of the ranks were new. Charley carried on, almost friendless now, serving in the kitchen, the motor pool, wherever he was asked, but simply as another civilian employee earning his pittance, a human anonymity expected to give the proper conditioned response to the slightest administration of such stimuli as "Come on, you!" or "Hey, you Frenchy bastard, quit dragging your ass!" It was humiliating, of course, and Charley, like the others, soon had had enough; but it was difficult to break away—he had no money, no connections. He spent less and less time in the compound, more and more with French friends and acquaintances; but most of these in one way or another were dependent on the Americans too, and suffered the same humiliations and despairs, without any source of relief except what they found, or at any rate sought, in sitting around and bitching. Charley was not the sort who got much help from this.

One sallow November afternoon he was standing nervelessly in a downfall of graupel, squeezing his toes to relish the icy fluid that oozed from his socks, wishing he had a cigarette. The juice in his shoes swished like brine in a barrel; his toes were pickles—numb, warty dills. It was the weather, not of war, but of the peace that comes after a war—hunger, dishevelment, a fuming impatience. The captain sauntered by, slouching inside his glossy pancho. He stood beside Charley and offered him a cigarette. They both smoked, cupping the cigarettes against the wetness, blowing out periodic bolls of smoke. After several inconsequential remarks, Cienkiewycz came to his subject: "I'll be pulling out tomorrow, Charley. My number's up." Charley had known it was coming sooner or later; it was a part of the new order of existence—uncertainty, changeableness. Cienkiewycz laid his left palm gently on the back of Charley's shoulder. "I'll miss seeing you, Charley."

"Yes, yes, I. . . ." Charley stopped, not from embarrassment or emotion but from inexperience.

"What are you going to do, Charley? Going home?"

Charley shrugged, hitching both hands upward in his sleeves—a pointed Gallicism.

"Not much use?" The captain caught himself shrugging too. "Look, Charley," he said, "why not come to the States? It could be fixed up."

"Sure," Charley said.

"No, I mean it. Lots of people will be coming soon, after things shake down a bit. When I'm discharged and get back on the job—" he waved his hand expansively, trailing an arc of cigarette smoke in the granular air "—well, I think I'll be able to guarantee you employment—a job—one way or another. That's the main thing—to have somebody stand up for you. I'll put through the papers when I get home, soon as I find out what they are. Okay?"

"Sure, Captain," Charley said. "Who wouldn't like to go to the States?"

99

"Some people I know."

"You?"

"Maybe." Cienkiewycz GI'd his butt meticulously. "It isn't all black and white, Charley. You think America's great. So do I, but —I've got the right to think so, because I know all the lousy things about it too. But you haven't got that right yet. Anyway it's not going to be what you think, you can count on that. Maybe there would be good reasons to stay here." He waved his hand again, indicating the gray buildings, the wet air growing like lichen on pavement and lamppost.

Charley shrugged.

"Hard to tell," the captain said.

Charley shrugged.

"Everything's a blue-fingered mess now anyway. Isn't it? Who knows what to think?"

"Captain," Charley said, studying his pickled toes, "will you write to me when you get home?"

"Of course, Charley, of course." Cienkiewycz removed his hand from Charley's shoulder, an instinctive gesture of sincerity. "Of bloody damn archepiscopal course!" He saw that most of what he'd said hadn't been taken seriously by Charley. He stamped his squushy boot and turned away, looking back toward the motorpool shack.

Charley wasn't surprised at the outburst.

"Of course, of course," Cienkiewycz said. "And my wife too." He took a pack of cigarettes from his inner pocket and stuffed it into the breast pocket of Charley's tunic. He took out a notebook and wrote in it and tore out the page and handed it to Charley. "Look, Charley, you come to the States, see? To Chicago. Here's my address. Remember, I'll always do what I can for you—understand? I mean it. But you'll have to write first, because I won't know where to reach you. You can't stay here, the outfit'll be gone soon—another month or two probably, no more. And I won't be home for a while either, lot of red tape to get through yet. Will you write?"

"Yes, Captain," Charley said.

"All right. So long." Cienkiewycz saluted informally, and turned and walked away. Charley watched him. At the door of the orderly

100

room Cienkiewycz looked back and waved. Then he disappeared inside. Charley walked away too, down the alley, beside the mildewed hoarding, scuffling his pickled toes, hanging his sodden head. He was thinking that the promise of an American captain about to leave for home was not to be trusted; too much would intervene, too many new joys and worries, and Cherbourg would be a long way in the past. But not for him, he thought, and scuffed his foot viciously on the broken flagstone—he swore when his toe stung from the impact. He looked upward through the wet locks of his hair at the black, rain-driven clouds scudding in from the Atlantic, waltzing like bears across his unknown, unloved, unlamented France—black bears loosed from their masters, reverting to viciousness, trailing their broken chains.

Charley knew he would not write. He knew he would never see the captain again.

CHAPTER 21

Charley made his decision, on St. Nicholas' Day, to leave Cherbourg. In prospect was the bleakest season, to his mind: Noël, the soldier's plague of homesickness; and no doubt it was the bleakest year, the one thousand nine hundred and forty-fifth, of our Lord, the end of Charley's sixteenth. By Christmas Eve he was on the road; cold, tired, wet, and miserable. He slept that night, very late, in a church. He ate nothing. On Christmas Day, however, he stole two frozen potatoes from a rheumy-eyed old man who was pushing a barrow with a little girl in it down a muddy lane: the little girl had a dozen potatoes cradled in her skirt. The old man chased him and yelled at him. Later he picked up a kitten from someone's backyard, with the idea that he would drench the potatoes in its blood, but in the end he let it go; afterward he was sorry, and said to himself that nothing could have tasted worse than the frozen potatoes anyway. On Christmas Night he reached Charleville, where he slept in the railway station, and the next morning he caught a ride to Gespunsart with a Canadian Red Cross officer who was driving to Davos with a pair of skiis; the Canadian gave him a bar of chocolate but no cigarettes.

"Thanks," Charley said when he climbed out of the Red Cross jeep.

"What's the matter, don't you say 'sir'?" the Canadian demanded.

"Thank you, sir," Charley said.

The Dupont house was still standing. Most of the window glass had been patched with cardboard, and many tiles had fallen from the roof. Sooty snow covered the yard and garden. Charley's mother came to the door when he knocked; but she didn't recognize him, and for a while seemed doubtful even after he told her who he was: she stood back, then came forward, then stepped back, and her hands fluttered under her chin. She looked thin and sharp, and had dry, tight, black curls in her hair, such as Charley did not remember. Charley's father came to the door too, stepped in front of his wife, and said of course he recognized Charley and wouldn't he come in. Charley stepped over the doorsill; in the cold, nearly empty room an awkward reunion was performed, alternately tearful and silent. Charley's father showed a bemused expression: he wasn't quite right in his head, obviously. Mme. Dupont, on the other hand, was painfully sane, and for weeks could not decide if Charley was her real son, or only a freeloader; she begrudged the potatoes he ate and said she wished he had not come, but sometimes she would go into the bedroom, where she and her husband slept on a pile of straw, and cry for hours. Charley learned that all the furniture had been stolen by the neighbors who had returned to Gespunsart earlier. But there was no way, then, to prove the ownership of anything.

Charley's father had spent three and a half years as a prisoner of war in Chemnitz, first in a prison compound, then as a member of a farm labor gang, then in a hospital. His mother had made her way eventually, after the flight from Gespunsart, to Marseilles, where she had taken a lover, a crippled customs officer in the Vichy government whose duties were largely imaginary but whose income, supplemented by bribes, was enough to keep their souls and bodies together and pay Mme. Dupont's bill at the hairdresser. The customs officer was seven years her junior.

At first, naturally, Charley resented his mother's inability to recognize him, and thought it strange that a mother should forget her son to such an extent, even after an interval of six years; but in two or three weeks, when he had come to understand that in truth his mother did recognize him but that she was reluctant to admit it and was struggling, in a queer, hopeless, birdlike way, against all the bonds of the family, his resentment changed to a more deeply bitter sorrow. No, it wasn't the few potatoes Charley consumed, for by one means or another he scrounged more for the larder than he took from it, and it wasn't what he was now, a helplessly unhardened, untoughened, unratified rat—these were not this sane woman's curse; nor did she think often of the game-legged customs inspector; these things, Charley saw, were nothing to her, nothing. Her trouble was . . . God knows!—a doctor might have said change of life, a psychiatrist boredom, a philosopher mortality. When she wept it was for the vision of Marseilles harbor, sun and blue waves, the seagulls in an endless ballet by Delibes, warmth flowing like a pulse from Africa. She wanted to die, she desperately needed to die. She lay on her heap of rancid straw in the midst of a rubbled house and a rubbled continent, and she might have been lying in her grave, so close the cold ruins wrapped her. But she had not enough wisdom to recognize her need; and so lived, and became—I anticipate—a doting grandmother in four years, the plumpest beldame of Gespunsart. What folly, when she might have died so easily. . . .

This period entered, for Charley, a state of pastosity. His senses clotted; the village lay under a glut of snow, the guano of February, but he trudged the alleys and backways, searching soft-eyed for lost parsnips, strayed sheaves of kale, a peripatetic morsel of lard. The sky dripped phlegm, and the houses leaked urine—so it seemed. Charley's annoyance centered on a drop of moisture which clung to the end of his nose, a pearl, a jewel, a primitive adornment for some forgotten ceremonial of sex. He squinted down to see it, over his eyes' greasy sill; it lay beyond reach. He waggled his head, and it waggled too but did not fall. He smeared it viciously with the chapped knuckles of his hand, and it re-formed instantly. He went to a black window and studied it in the glass; nacreous, luminescent, charismatic—the orb of his office, Keeper of the Hollow Tooth, Custodian of the Pickled Toe. He turned and trudged on. He could not go home.

He apprenticed himself to a baker and lived at the baker's house. When he met his father on the street, his father said, "Hé, hé, hé, hé, Le Mitron. Oh, bravo! Bravo! . . . Eh, monsieur le mitron, avez-vous une cigarette pour le pauvre soldat?" But work was slow, some days there was no flour at all for the loaves, and you can't make bread entirely of chaff. In April the puddles stood in the lanes. The sun shone hot, the wind blew cold. Charley's father drowned in the Meuse. His burial in the family plot was accom-

104

plished by virtue of the priest's boredom with regulations, and was paid for by the veteran's allowance. Angélique—Charley's sister, remember?—and her new husband, a dentist attached to the staff of an expensive sanatorium at Pointoise, were among the calm cortège, dressed in unimaginably new clothes. They stayed for Easter week, and wore the same outfits every day. Charley, who had cried hard when he saw his father laid out, could summon no tear at the graveside; his weeping, he knew, had been for the indignity, the terrifying indignity of the corpse—symbolized by the expression his father wore, put there by the women's hands, a countenance totally unrelated to the man. Why couldn't they have left him in the river? So much of him had already melted away before he undertook his final fall that the rest would have been gone in no time—deliquesced, solved at last. But no; he was sent to the dark hole, as prim as a judge; and a rat scurried away between the headstones as the funeral procession departed. Charley sneered. When Angélique and her husband returned to Paris, Charley went with them.

"Good-by. Don't worry about me," Mme. Dupont wept. Her hair looked like the sweepings from a barbershop.

Four months later she was married, and considering the times no one thought her hasty. She acquired four new children, eight grandchildren, and a stout bed, giving her house for her *dot*.

CHAPTER 22

The weeks straggle by. Linda is pregnant—curiously, justly, mysteriously enough—and the darkness of early winter nights enters our valley like a foreign incursion. At first the news was appalling. Certainly unexpected—we'd been cautious. One loses so easily the sense of nature. Not that our lovemaking wasn't natural enough, and altogether true, for that matter, to our own, private natures. But nature at large, Mother Nature? Perhaps at the very instant the seed exploded in Linda's belly a star exploded in the remote void; and in neither case was the event attended by the slightest exertion of will, thought, feeling. The mindlessness of it, this is what is so shocking—easy to forget in the agony of searching for a little dignity. Mindless force; the machine with no starter button, no switch to turn it off. . . . When Linda came to tell me, I didn't know what she meant. She held a little silver bell next to her womb, and shook it gently to make it tinkle, but I must have looked more than usually obtuse. She frowned and shook the bell again, more insistently, and pointed with her finger, jabbing herself to show that she meant inside. Of course, her meaning was unmistakable then.

Now I find myself both pleased and displeased; but neither my pleasure nor my displeasure has the quality I would have foreseen if anyone had asked me a month ago. Really, the feeling of smugness is the least excusable—but that doesn't prevent it from forming. My little replica, there in Linda's abdomen, the tiny poet and adulterer, the booby, the victim, as innocent as you please, snug and wealthy—what could be more gratifying? I'm inclined to agree with the Hindus, who hold that the repository of semen is in the skull: if I had anything at all to do with the creation of this small being (as all my instincts assert), then surely he is the offspring of my head. I rest in his perfection, at any rate occasionally.

CHAPTER 23

Charley remained in Paris for two years. During the first year he lived with Angélique and the dentist, sleeping on their living-room sofa with his belongings stowed in a box under the sideboard. The dentist earned a good income at the sanatorium, a large subsidized institution in the suburbs; and considering the housing shortage he owned a good flat, well furnished and clean. Charley wore his cast-off shirts, patterned madras and soft English cloth with bossed shell buttons. There was enough to eat. The trio—Angélique, Charley, the dentist—patronized the cafés, the cinemas, the taxicabs; there was time for strolling, window-shopping, picnicking; Charley discovered the galleries, including one which was exhibiting architectural models and drawings from the Wright workshops. Whether or not any of them were the captain's work was a question which occupied two afternoons' speculations.

Eventually Charley took a job in a factory where radios were assembled, and during his second year in the capital he lived in a dormitory maintained by his union, a huge drafty structure of concrete where old newspapers and cigarette butts soaked on the floor of the latrine. The move had been required by the dentist: Angélique was eight months pregnant, and the husband found he must sleep on the sofa in order to restrain his ardors. Charley was enrolled in night school and carried his books with him everywhere, wore their bindings to threads; but his studies languished. It was hopeless. Mathematics came easily, its language was clear and precise, but the courses in literature and history—they were nothing but dates and names, dates and names; Charley memorized them, stuffing the long lists into his head like hanks of yarn, but in-

108

evitably they knotted and twisted and spilled out in useless tangles: besides, it was too much strain on his French, those pages of Hugo and Voltaire full of obscurity. He had lost French, as one loses a briefcase on a train, when he was ten years old, and had gone traveling off in the opposite direction; and in consequence he still spoke with a child's vocabulary, wrote with a child's scrawl. Angélique did what she could, her forehead hunched close to his under the lamplight on late summer evenings while flies caromed under the ceiling. Charley sniffled, grunted, fidgeted. It was no good.

When one of his dormitory mates lifted the Omega wristwatch he had bought with his savings, Charley spent a melancholy night walking by the river. He leaned on the railing, studying his long fingers in the lamplight that drifted across the bridge like snow; his cigarettes flew away one by one on glowing wings, swooping to the water. He thought of the captain; he thought of the Atlantic, its long gray swells, its black rainclouds. In the morning, on the dentist's portable typewriter, he wrote a letter to Cienkiewycz, gritting his teeth over the unspellable English; and in four and a half months, spent in waiting and pouring over official forms, his emigration was accomplished: he arrived in Chicago in May, 1948. He went to work as an office boy in the small firm of Space Forms, Inc., headed by Cienkiewycz. In time he enrolled in a night school to study draftsmanship. The captain, whose letters to Charley during the period of waiting and negotiation had been perfunctory, even impatient, required only two hours to rediscover his former affection after Charley had arrived.

For two years Charley had thought about his mother, if the truth were known, more than about anything else. But he told me some years later that when he came to Chicago he stopped thinking about her.

"How do you explain her?" I asked.

"I can't explain her to you," he replied, "but I know her, I know her very well. There is so much you don't understand, you Americans. We Europeans aren't what you want us to be. We know that because we aren't what *we* want to be either, we aren't what we are taught to be. It's all fake—the newspapers, the books, the pretty paintings, even the thoughts and longings and dreams. That's all, it's just phoniness—we're fouled up like everyone else."

109

CHAPTER 24

Charley. Bonny Prince Charley. Clap Hands, Here Comes Charley. Charley, My Boy. Do you conceive the qualities of the name? Any of them? This labor has been performed with only that end in view. Charley was born in Europe's misery and came to America in his youth, imbued with the irony of hope—there, it all could have been written in one sentence. But will a man come to you so easily? I dread the errors (crimes) of judgment, having committed more than one person may be allowed. Hence these many memories and images sown like the seed flax on crabbed wolds of language; possibly some of them will sprout.

Because of the identity of names, we associated the song and the man, and would sing *Clap hands, here comes Charley naaoooowwwwww* at birthdays and other ceremonials. But even though Charley always smiled and looked pleased, the song wasn't right. No one would ever have clapped hands when Charley came into a room; any noise, any demonstration, any sportive expression whatever, would have been incompatible with the image of him which each of us carried in his mind; the image of quiet, worried, handsome, modest, inquisitive Charley; dear Charley; lovable Charley. Yes, these quaint terms cannot be avoided, open as they are to misinterpretation. Do not do Charley that disservice, my friends. . . . When Charley came into a room, those who were already there would look at one another quickly and covertly, a glance given and taken in the complicity of affection, in the smugness of self-congratulation, and in the complacency of chosen people: see, the boy has come to us again—isn't he wonderful?—isn't he amusing?—but we must never, never let him know.

110

Charley would find a chair that suited him—a straight chair, without arms or upholstery—and sit with his head hunched forward, his blond hair pushed carelessly away from his eyes, his feet crossed at the ankles, his knees somewhat apart, his hands reposing on his thighs—one hand palm up, the other palm down. I never saw another person take precisely this attitude. This was how I first saw him, though then he was sitting on a wooden bench at one side of the fireplace in the Cienkiewycz house at Palos Park. Remember, he was twenty-two years old now, no longer a boy. But boyish, juvenile, an eternal youth—and the very air of eternality gave him a vestiture of aged serenity that only youth may safely wear. (Forgive me, I'm getting cornier by the minute.) His appearance was *pure*, yet not classical. Preclassical, rather; or pastoral. A structure of bone primarily, abstract, statuesque—if one can use the term, not in its Apollonian sense, but as it might be used by someone who had never seen any sculptures but Noguchi's. A long skull, deep browed, frontal ridges prominent under the forelock, wide cheekbones, a long nose turned up a trifle, a long upper lip, a narrow jaw; the wrists and ankles, always evident, delicately modeled. In his clothes Charley still gave the impression of ribs, vertebrae, collarbones: a paradoxical rigidity of gracefulness. All this supplemented and reinforced by speech. Charley's English was lucid and simple; his accent, almost unnoticeable, hovered between French and German; and if I hadn't known his history I doubt I'd have been able to tell what it was—Hungarian or something like that, I'd probably have guessed. Actually, the accent vanished—from the listener's consciousness—after a hundred words had been spoken. On the other hand, Charley seldom spoke a hundred consecutive words. When he did speak, he studied his hands, and you needed to listen carefully. Like all soft speakers, he enforced—without intending to do so—a submissive audience.

In America Charley learned, through I don't know what combinations of unhappy experience (or perhaps I do), to consider himself not only ignorant but worse: I think he looked on his mind as blighted, depressed, an irretrievable rubble—ruined in the war. It was nonsense, of course. He had a good mind. True, he lacked the tokens of urbane culture at first, the passwords and bywords. He picked them up quickly enough, though. First through the channels opened by architecture, and then through the others

111

which proliferated from his acquaintanceships with the people in Cienkiewycz's shop—mostly university people, artists, writers, etc. He had many friends, Charley did, in every corner of the city, surprising friends from whom he acquired surprising knowledge; and at a party or any gathering, at just the point when you had been persuaded by his own self-deprecatory quietness that he had nothing to contribute, he would speak up, still quietly, but with such trenchancy that, whatever it was—perhaps no more than a proviso no one else had thought of—you immediately were obliged to alter your notion of the man. . . . I see that in some respects I'm describing Charley in terms very like those I used earlier for Alex; which is perhaps a revealing error. In this respect certainly—the pointed remark—they were somewhat alike; both could spring it on you; but there was a difference, a significant one: Charley's unexpected *aperçus* were delivered in a spirit of conciliation, if that were necessary, or helpfulness, without consideration of self, while Alex spoke most often from motives of a competitive or malicious nature, though she was skillful enough to hide this from most observers. . . . Charley was, in short, a complex person, like all of us. No hope of reducing him to a psychograph. His closest friends continually fell into the mistake that I have just made here—of presenting him entirely in terms of his sweetness, softness, tenderness, selflessness, his—so to speak—sibilant nature: but then there was that tic spasmodically screwing up his face, there was that upward-peering-through-the-forelock look—the attitude of a rat. Ratness was there, if you understand the full psychology of rat; in the center somewhere, deeply realized. The rat. Fear. Grief. Want. Pain. All good short words, hitting to the gut. The precise nature of Charley's permanent defeat can never be known to any of us, I suppose, who weren't there at Gespunsart, on the road to Reims, in the kitchen at Harfleur, wherever it was that the moment of downfall, final and irrevocable, occurred.

On the winter night when we were gathered at the captain's house in Palos Park, the blizzard blew down on us straight from the Wasatch Range—so it seemed—bringing old shrieks of pioneer families caught in the high passes. Middle-Westerners know this wind well, though it does not reach here to the east. . . . We all were subdued that night. Charley sat by the fireside on the bench,

112

his hands on his thighs, one up, the other down, and the firelight flickered on his hair and cheek. It was the only light in the room, just enough to illuminate our faces and leave the recesses behind us dark, the long recesses reaching away into the captain's partitionless house. Snow buffeted the glass wall, driving and swirling, drifting in a sloping line along the outer sill. Alex sat next to Charley but not beside him: I mean she left a foot or more of space between them. They were engaged to be married, but the wedding had not been scheduled, and I was not the only one who wondered whether it would ever come off at all, she seemed so remote. She wore a dark green dress, skin tight. I could see her navel. It was a depression in the smooth cloth, like the depression one makes in the ground with one's finger in order to plant a seed. That was the thought I seized on: planting a seed in Alex's navel, a zinnia seed; and I saw her walking later on, naked, an exaggerated waggle of her strong buttocks from side to side, and a huge, succulent, many-armed zinnia growing out of her belly, heavy with mauve blossoms. I snorted, and shifted my attention. Cienkiewycz, his close-cut white hair gleaming in the firelight, sat tilted back on a wooden chair, beaming, benign. He affected a desert style of dress: a painted leather shirt, a wrought-silver belt buckle inlaid with turquoise. He liked nothing better than to have guests at his fine house. His wife, a beautiful woman of forty, looked more serious: she was plotting the layout of beds in case the storm snowed us in, wondering whether Charley and Alex should be offered the double bed kept for married guests. This is the horrendous moment for American hostesses, I've discovered: do the boy and girl sleep together or don't they, and then, since they surely do, will they be embarrassed if they are offered the double bed, and will I (the hostess) be embarrassed if I offer it to them—questions asked every night in every university town and artists' quarter (I mean, obviously, the places where middle-class fears lingered still, a decade ago) in America. I have the impression these matters are more serenely adjusted in Europe and the Orient. . . . The other guests were myself and two young student-architects who were doing their internships, if that's the word, in the captain's office; crew-cut, buttoned-down lads from Princeton, uncertain whether to be witty, respectful, solicitous, or rebellious, and in consequence

113

veering continually and abruptly from one attitude to another. . . . As it turned out, the entire Middle West was snowbound that night. The two students shared the double bed, Charley and I slept on cots in the childrens' playroom, and Alex spent the night on a mattress which was placed on the floor in front of the fireplace. I was first up in the morning—having gone sleepless, as usual—and when I came into the living room, Alex was sprawled in a tumble of sheets and blankets, her head hanging backward off the mattress, her hair flung out across the brick hearth like strewn fire. She was dead asleep.

The storm had felled one of the captain's quivering aspen trees, and the tip of a branch had struck the glass wall, cracking the pane. Four long radial lines extended from the point of impact, three in one direction, the fourth in the opposite direction, like an ankh or a great bird-foot. It seemed to be a sign, hovering over the sleeping Alex, but the impression it gave was ambiguous—I couldn't say whether it was ominous or auspicious.

114

CHAPTER 25

Item. "He was a strong man, but pale as the Candle he studyed by. His pill (an opiate, possibly Matthews his pil) which he was wont to take in Turkey, which was wont to doe him good, but he took it preposterously at Mr. Wilson's, the Saddlers, neer Suffolk House, where he was wont to lye and where he dyed, and 'twas the cause of his death. As he laye unravelling in the agonie of death, the Standers-by could hear him say softly, *I have seen the Glories of the world.*"—John Aubrey recording the death of Isaac Barrow, who was my ancestor.

Item. "But contrary to our expectations, early in the morning having prepared their fire-works, they attempted to burn the house wherein we were, seconding their fire with the discharge of above four hundred shot against us, according to the soldiers' account, who afterwards told us how many shots they had made that morning, according to the emptying of their bandaliers; all which time, they told us, Captain Cooke stood behind such a great white oak tree, whom we heard encouraging his soldiers to come on with courage, thinking himself in safety; and so he was, for we discharged not a gun that morning, nor of all the time of their siege; but only two in the night-time at random, to scare them from working their trenches near unto us; for we had concluded to take the lives of none of our countrymen, unless they offered to enter violently upon us, which we only fitted ourselves to prevent such assaults, or else that we were forced out upon them by the firing of our house; only we perceived our words to be shot good enough to keep them aloof. For we called cheerfully upon the Captain to come on and bring up his men; for he should find us very cheerful spirits to deal with. . . .

"Shortly after this, there was a day appointed, wherein we were to receive our sentence from the Court, which was to be given in the afternoon; and in the forenoon, Master Cotton preached, having gathered up the minds of the people, in what they had observed, and perceiving the people took notice, that in what we dissented from them, was out of tenderness of conscience, and were ready to render a reason and ground for what we held and practiced, and divers such like things; to which he answered, that if we had done it out of ignorance, then there had been hopes of regaining us; but if out of tenderness of conscience, and able to render reason for what we did, (and other things of like nature) then were we ripened for death, urging them to agree together, and consent in one thing; that so it might be, else would not the Angels carry their souls to Heaven; for he was then speaking of the office of the Angels in that point. And when by all their examinations in Court, interrogatories put upon us in prison, and the public preaching, they could find nothing against us for the transgressing of any of their laws, they then proceeded to cast a lot for our lives, putting it to the major vote of the Court, whether we should live or die; which was so ordered by the Providence of God, that the number of two votes carried it on our side; and whereas both by law, equity, and act of Providence, they ought to have set us forthwith at liberty; yet notwithstanding, they proceeded further to censure, namely, confined us to several towns, and to wear bolts and irons, and to work for our livings, though it was in the extremity of winter, and not to speak of any of those things, which they had dealt with us about, and all this during the pleasure of the Court, and that upon pain of death.

"Here followeth a true copy of the Censure . . . as it was given unto us in writing by the Court; being extant and here set down, verbatim, as it was given to Samuel Gorton, the rest being the same, but only the change of the names.

"FOR SAMUEL GORTON.

"It is ordered that Samuel Gorton shall be confined to Charlestown, there to be set on work, and to wear such bolts or irons, as

116

may hinder his escape, and so to continue during the pleasure of the Court; provided, that if he shall break his said confinement, or shall in the meantime either by speech or writing, publish, declare, or maintain, any of the blasphemous or abominable heresies, wherewith he hath been charged by the General Court, contained in either of the two Books sent unto us by him or by Randall Holden; or shall reproach or reprove the Churches of our Lord Jesus Christ in these United Colonies, or the civil government, or the publick ordinances of God therein, (unless it be by answer to some question propounded to him, or conference with any elder, or with any other licensed to speak with him privately, under the hand of one of the Assistants) that immediately upon accusation of any such writing or speech, he shall by such Assistant, to whom such accusation shall be brought, be committed to prison, till the next Court of Assistants, then and there to be tried by a Jury, whether he hath so spoken or written; and upon his conviction thereof, shall be condemned to death, and executed.

"Per. Cur.

"INCREASE NOWELL, Secret.

"*Dated the 3d of the 9th mo. 1643.*

"In which condition we continued a whole winter season; in which time their Ministers stirred up the people, in their public sermons, to famish us to death, out of that place of the prophet Sephany, 11. 10. 11. This shall they have for their pride, because they have reproached and magnified themselves against the people of the Lord of Hosts; the Lord will be terrible unto them, for he will famish all the gods of the earth; and men shall worship him, every one from his place, even all the isles of the heathen. Samuel Gorton having intelligence from Boston to Charlestown, to which he was confined, that Master Cotton preached from that text in the prophecy Zephany, and how he applied the doctrine from it, to have all necessaries withheld from him, telling some eminent members of the Church, that if they either went unto us, to visit us, or sent unto us, to minister to our wants, the curse of God would abide both on them and their posterity, for so doing; the said Gorton hearing of these things, wrote a letter to the ruling Elder in Charlestown, a copy whereof (verbatim) here followeth, which

117

was consulted upon, by the Ministers immediately, together with the Governor Winthrop, as intelligence was brought unto him, but never answer given unto it, neither by word nor writing. . . ."— *Simplicities Defence Against Seven-Headed Policy*, by Samuel Gorton (1646). Gorton, also my ancestor, thus describes his difficulties with the Massachusetts Bay Colony.

Item. "At Provincetown, Nov. 18, 1771. I visited aged Mr. John Angell, ae. 80, born Oct. 18, 1691, a plain, blunt-spoken man: right old English frankness. He is not a Quaker, nor Baptist, nor Presbyterian, but a Gortonist, and the only one I have seen. Gorton lives now only in him: his only disciple left. He says, that he knows of no other, and that he is alone. He gave me an account of Gorton's disciples, first and last, and shewed me some of Gorton's printed books and some of his manuscripts. He said, Gorton wrote in Heaven, while on earth. He said Gorton had beat down all outward ordinances of Baptism and the Lord's Supper, with unanswerable demonstration; that Gorton preached in London, in Oliver's time, and had a Church and living of £500 a year, offered him, but he believed no sum would have tempted him to take a farthing for preaching. He told me, that his grandfather, Thomas Angell, came from Salem to Providence with Roger Williams, that Gorton did not agree with Roger Williams, who was for outward ordinances to be set up again by new apostles. I asked him if Gorton was a Quaker; as he seemed to agree with them, in rejecting outward ordinances. He said, no; and that when George Fox (I think) or one of the first Friends came over, he went to Warwick to see Gorton, but was a mere babe to Gorton. The Friends had come out of the world, in some ways, but still were in darkness or twilight, but that Gorton was far beyond them, he said, high way up to the dispensation of light. The Quakers were in no wise to be compared with him; nor any man else can, since the primitive times of the Church, especially since they came out of Popish darkness. He said, Gorton was a holy man; wept day and night for the sins and blindness of the world; his eyes were a fountain of tears, and always full of tears—a man full of thought and study—had a long walk out through the trees or woods by his house, where he constantly walked morning and evening, and even in the depth of the night, alone by himself, for contemplation and the enjoyment of

118

the dispensation of light. He was universally beloved by all his neighbors, and the Indians, who esteemed him, not only as a friend, but one high in communion with God in Heaven, and indeed he lived in Heaven."—Ezra Stiles, *Itinerary*.

Item. "Among the divers animals about this place were several ostriches, and one of our Hottentots found a nest full of eggs, and brought us a couple; he placed them in hot ashes, and by a small hole made in the end, stirred round the contents till they had acquired the consistence of an omelet, and certainly a better omelet never was eaten. Very often, in the course of my long journeys over the wilds of Africa, have I found an ostrich-egg thus prepared an excellent repast, and fully sufficient for two persons."—*An Autobiographical Memoir of Sir John Barrow, Bart., Late of the Admiralty* (1847). Describing an expedition to Graaff Reynet, 1797.

Item. "We reached Chadron in due time, and went into camp a little way beyond, on the banks of the White River, a stream which flows through Dakota and finally joins the Missouri. Our camp was on a little flat where the river bends around in the shape of a horseshoe. It seemed to be a popular stopping-place, and there were half a dozen other covered wagons in camp there. The number of empty tin cans scattered about on that piece of ground must have run up into the thousands. But there had not been a mile of the road since we left Valentine which had not had from a dozen to several hundred cans scattered along it, left by former 'movers.' We had contributed our share, including the gooseberry can. From the labels we noticed on the can windrow along the road it seemed that peaches and Boston baked beans were the favorite things consumed by the overland travellers, though there were a great many green-corn, tomato, and salmon cans."—*The Voyage of the Rattletrap*, by Fred Hayden Carruth (1897). Describing a journey made in 1882.

Item. Glories of this earth. Lake Michigan, for example, is 321 miles on its longitudinal axis, 118 on its other; 8,300 miles on its perimeter; and its surface is said to overlay 22,400 square miles. The water level is 1.6 feet higher in summer than in winter; and although its source, like that of all the Great Lakes, is only rainfall, Lake Michigan discharges 174,000 cubic feet of water per second. Its single natural outlet is the St. Lawrence River, 500 miles away, although engineers some years ago reversed the flow of the Chicago

River. Lake Michigan was formed by the recession of the glaciers, which in fact did not recede but melted; Lake Agassiz, named for a good man, was in glacial times bigger than all the modern Great Lakes combined, and extended into North Dakota, Manitoba, Saskatchewan, and Minnesota; it was formed by the famous Laurentide Ice Sheet, which reached south to Carbondale (well named, too) and was deeper than the White Mountains are high. The four glacial eras: Nebraskan, Kansan, Illinoian, and Wisconsin; and the three completed interglacial: Aftonian, Yarmouth, Sangamon. The Sangamon lasted 120,000 years, while so far our uncompleted interglacial era—following the Wisconsin phase—is 55,000 years old. The Wisconsin is divided into five substages: Farmdale, Iowan, Tazewell, Cary, Mankato—all good names, I think. Pleistocene! . . . In 1928 thirty passenger lines plied Lake Michigan on scheduled sailings, but now none is left, except one firm operating pleasure excursions.

CHAPTER 27

Linda is crying. So quickly do our joys decline. It is a hurt sound, scarcely a sound at all; unvoiced, almost unbreathed; deep in her throat. And yet it seems to resound in this cottage like a winter gale crying in the hemlocks: abject, grief-stricken. Nothing again, no word or gesture, will ever mean sadness to me after this crippled weeping. . . . What shall I do for her? What can I do? Don't mistake me, I am not abrogating my place, either as lover or as fellow creature, and I would do anything in my power to help her. But whatever it is that can help her is not within my means— nor anyone's, I imagine. Oh, I can stop her crying, for an hour or two. She will respond to me. But the grief is never assuaged, only suspended.

Somehow she has learned of the bomb, and now she believes, truly believes, in the end of the world. How she managed it I can't discover, since she is unable to read or hear; the newspapers and radio could not tell her, we have no television, we never go to the movies, her father had no television. Certainly I have done nothing to make her understand, nothing intentional, nothing I can think of. True, we developed a language between us, a rudimentary system of signs and grimaces, with which we can communicate our homely wants and equally homely gratifications; but this is a language of love, very profoundly, and I have never tried to use it as a means to tell her anything whatever about matters beyond our own circumference of hills and woods; nor would I ever do so in any circumstances. Nevertheless, somehow she has found out. It was New Year's Eve when she made it clear with one violent sweep of

121

her hand, razing the cottage, the woods, the hills, and everything; then she fell down and pulled me after her, and placed my hands palms together over my chest in the conventional attitude of death. She made the same sign with her own hands, first over her womb, then over her heart. And then she began to cry—silently. I could not doubt her meaning.

All this has been in my mind, too, and in all our minds, naturally. We got through 1961 by the skin of our teeth—you and I, all of us—but 1962? 1963? 1964? One year soon will be the last; we all know it. I myself—like most of you, I expect—am too tired to be scared, almost too tired to be sad: it has lasted too long, this terror. I am confident you know my feeling. Hence, although the end of the world has been in my mind, far down under all my thoughts, coloring every feeling and shadowing, I'm sure, these pages, the actual bodily sensations had been put away as too much to suffer in my daily life: I mean the pain of the fire-blast, the gut-burn of contaminated food, the tumescence and rot of carcinogenated flesh. Now they have come back to me. Linda, dumb Linda, has shown me the intuitive genius of the body. The peace I had built with her has been broken in its very heart, her heart. My self within her already flakes and chars.

Poor Linda. I never asked her if she believes in God or if she even knows what God is. I could try to teach her now? Perhaps. It would be a subject for a Daumier: an atheist (of fusty years) teaching a deaf-mute girl to know God while somewhere the immaculate hand inches toward the pushbutton. What an enormous explosion it will be, all wisdom going up in smoke and fire—wisdom that in its irremediable essence always reduces to folly. I guess that is the one genuine autochthonous human enigma which no one, philosopher or oaf, will ever explain.

Poor Linda.

CHAPTER 28

E: Watch it, for God's sake, will you?

C: Sure. What's the matter anyway?

E: What do you mean what's the matter?

C: You're so jumpy. You're in an awful mood, if you want to know the truth.

E: For God's sake, I'm in a perfectly good mood. You drive like my grandmother.

C: Come on now.

E: You should have downshifted for that grade and you know it.

C: Why? I'm in third now—

E: You're lugging the engine on that grade. I bet the r.p.m.'s were down to 1500.

C: I don't think so.

E: You were looking?

C: Kiss my sallow backside, will you? To hear you talk you'd think I'd never driven one of these things before. You think I can't *hear* the motor? What's the matter this morning? You were fine for the trials yesterday, but now you're as . . . as . . . what do you say—?

E: Irascible.

C: You're as crabby as an old maid.

E: I always feel lousy on Sunday. You know it.

C: Just like Alex. You Americans, you're all stuffed up like a Christmas turkey. Why don't you break down and go to church if you want to?

E: That's got nothing to do with it.

C: The hell it hasn't. You think I can't tell a *écrevisse* when I see one?

E: What in God's name is an *écrevist?*

C: Little thing lives in the water, always goes backwards.

E: You mean a crab?

C: Something like that.

E: What the hell's that got to do with. . . . Oh, I see, what you mean is a crawfish.

C: That's it.

E: Yeah—well, I'm no crawfish. All of us spend a certain amount of our lives backing out of situations, but—

C: Of course, of course. But the trouble with you is you never look over your shoulder. When you back out of one situation, you stick your ass right in another. No?

E: Who doesn't? *C'est la vie*—I believe that's the expression.

C: Okay.

E: Continual process of getting your ass in a sling. But that doesn't mean you have to go calling people crayfishes.

C: I thought you said crawfish.

E: Same thing.

C: Okay. Forget it.

E: What's the matter with Alex?

C: Who said anything was the matter with her? She just always feels lousy on Sundays.

E: What's the matter with her then?

C: Nothing. Same as you. Same as all Americans. Even if she is Jewish. But she hasn't got sense enough to know it.

E: Maybe she's got more sense than you give her credit for.

C: Maybe.

E: What's she do?

C: Nothing much. But I notice she always stays in bed on Sunday morning until church is over.

E: Old American tradition. Besides, the Jews have church on Saturday.

C: I know. But she's not Jewish like that. In fact, she's hardly Jewish at all—not like Jews in France anyway. For a long time— well, anyway, for the first few months after we got married I couldn't see anything Jewish about her at all, she seemed just like

124

any other American. You know?—ordinary American girl, which was just what I wanted her to be. But then sometimes—she's moody, as if she were getting through to someplace I can't see. Maybe that's her Jewishness?

E: More likely just female mystification.

C: What?

E: Never mind. Tell me, Charley, how did you come to marry her anyway?

C: Why not? What's the matter with Alex?

E: Nothing, nothing at all, I didn't mean it that way. I think she's fine. There's no reason in the world why—

C: Yes, I know. What you mean is why did Alex marry me?

E: Not precisely. Actually I think she got a better deal than she probably realized. But still—Alex does seem like the sort that might want something a bit . . . zippier? A husband with—

C: Plenty of money.

E: Yes, I guess so. But money plus something else. What they call glamour, the Sunday-supplement type, the sharpies. You yourself called her the American girl, and believe me that's what the American girl is looking for. That's what they're *trained* to look for —from infancy on—by their mothers, their teachers, their newspapers, radio, television, movies, everything—the whole damn shooting match.

C: Seems to me I've heard all that before.

E: I know. It's hard for me to lay off sometimes. All the time.

C: Well, I've been laying off for a long time . . .

E: What do you mean?

C: I mean I haven't ever told you how full of . . . of *nonsense* you are. Because I always felt you must know more than I do. Especially about things like this. But sometimes you are so damn blind and shortsighted it's enough to give anyone the gripes. No, wait a minute, listen to me a minute. You think because I can't talk as well as you do that I can't talk at all. You think I don't know *anything*. But I do. I know something about architecture, something about engineering, quite a lot about drafting and drawing. I've learned a lot since I came to America. And I can use these things. They give me a . . . a . . . I don't know what you call it. They let me understand things better than I could before. Not

125

only the things I see in America, but the things I remember from France too. Do you see?

E: Sure.

C: Okay. What I'm getting at is that I can give Alex as good a line as you can give your women. I did it. She thought I was pretty great—if I do say so. Hell, I knew some interesting people too, the captain, the students at the shop. That's why Alex thought I was okay. At first, anyway. And another reason is because I gave her a good time in bed. And another is because she thought I was going to amount to something, and I may yet, for all you know. Alex loved me—that's the main thing—and how do you explain that? It's like a sickness, or something you do in your sleep. And another thing—

E: Look, Charley—

C: No, wait a minute. There's more to it. I want to get this off my chest, I've been thinking about it for a long time. One reason Alex loved me is because I loved her. More than she'd ever been loved by anybody. But that's not the main thing. The main thing is that I loved her in a *way* she'd never been loved by anybody. None of this kidding and horsing around and ice-cream-sundae business you always see in American kids. I was *serious*. You know? Americans aren't ever serious. With them it's always horsing around, or else hearts and flowers.

E: Just what I've been saying.

C: Maybe. But I mean it differently. I wasn't just serious about loving Alex and wanting to marry her, I was serious about everything—about life. I don't know how to explain it. Maybe it has something to do with the way I lived during the war when I was a kid. But I know what life is worth. And when I told Alex I loved her I think she heard something in my voice she'd never heard before, and it *reached* her, it *got* to her, she really felt like somebody for the first time in her life, a real person.

E: That doesn't seem like enough to explain her marrying you.

C: No, not when you look at it afterwards, the way we're doing. But think how she felt then. You know what she'd always been before? A good kid, a cute chick. All anybody wanted from her was a good lay, and then a chance to walk down the street with her and show her off. That's all American men want—just a chance to

126

walk down the street with a cute chick so they can say look who's putting out for me. That's all they really get married for, most of them—so they'll have a perpetual excuse for showing off. And then when the cute chick turns out to be a real woman, that's when they start staying out with the boys and going bowling or drinking too much. I see guys like that every day at the shop.

E: Okay, Charley, but I still—

C: I know. She doesn't look like it so much now, but she really went for it then. The point is I gave Alex something different, and she appreciated it, she fell in love with me, she really did. I got her out of that cute-chick racket, and she went for me. Maybe too soon, or too much. But anyway she went for it. And there's another thing: here I am criticizing America and you agree with me. But there's a difference. You and Alex can talk about America as if it was the worst place in the world, but I know you don't know what you're talking about. The cute-chick racket is bad, but you can get over it, just like you can get over the rest of the "commercial civilization" you're always talking about. Sure, we don't have singing television commercials in France, not yet anyway. And I don't like them any better than you do. I've learned that much since I came over here. But that doesn't mean life in France is any bed of roses either. There's plenty of good things here and I say the commercials are a damn small price to pay. No, wait a minute—the point is that this is part of what I was giving to Alex too, and it's what made me so important to her. That's right, I wasn't just interesting or good for a laugh, I was important. Because I believed the things she wanted to believe but was afraid of, I mean the things about America. I showed her that underneath all the cute-chick business there are still real people in this country, the same kind of people you had in 1776. Go ahead and laugh. You've got to laugh, because if you don't it's too damn embarrassing: it means you're putting yourself in the same class with the television announcers and all the phonies. That's the way every American has to feel. The radio and television and movies are so full of crap you can't believe *anything* they tell you. You're the kind of guy that gets mad when you hear somebody on television say it's not nice to push your grandmother downstairs, or when you hear somebody say that Stalin was a son-of-a-bitch because he ordered the purge

127

trials, *even though you know perfectly well it's true*. . . . Well, on a different level Alex was the same way. And I showed her she really was a person—underneath, below all the crap. I showed her it was okay to believe what's true. Of course, that was only between us; to anyone else she still had to show she was just a cute chick right out of the Coca-Cola ad. But for a while with me she was a real person. You know, her mother and father came over from Europe, same as me. It's hard to realize it most of the time. But for a while I think Alex was like her mother—a little. She was tough, ready to live seriously. She really was like that. Anyway I thought she was.

E: What do you mean?

C: Lately she's been spending a lot of time away from home. Just like those guys at the office I was talking about. Lately she goes out even at night.

E: Normal. You're not honeymooners any more. What's she supposed to do while you're studying?

C: It's more than that. . . . Hell, I've been kidding myself anyway. All that stuff I was just saying—about France and America—that's what I used to believe. When I first came over. When I first met Alex. But it's all so complicated—I don't know what I think now. It *was* true then—for me anyway. I thought it was for Alex too, but now I'm not sure how far she went with me. All that stuff about being real people. We never had a baby, and I'll tell you the truth—the reason we never had a baby was because she never wanted one. So I guess she couldn't have gone very far with me even at the beginning.

E: Okay, Charley, I think you're right this time, I mean about all this being more complicated than you think. The cute-chick philosophy is everywhere, you know, in every country; and in every country there is probably an element opposed to it, like you and me. It isn't an American invention, at any rate, even if the Coca-Cola ad originated here. If we were living a thousand years ago we'd be blaming the Byzantines or the gypsies for the cute-chick philosophy, and later on it would have been the Albigensians, the Rousseauists, the . . . God knows what. The form it takes today happens to be American because almost all the forms of international vulgarity happen to be American. But you wait, in a couple of decades it may be Russian, and after that Chinese or Martian or

128

almost anything. And if we're being honest—well, the anti-American remarks of most intellectuals, including me, are a fake, a pose. Why not? You can't get by without poses, Charley. I know, you can't get by very long with them either. But to reduce everything continually to its elements, to be absolutely honest all the time, would be like continually acknowledging the complete chaos of reality, what you call the complications. Why, you'd blow your stack in no time at all. Life's too goddamn short. So you get by with poses—stock answers. Everybody's got one, or two, or a dozen. You try to get by without them and you'll wind up not being able to say a word, you'll be bugged by every object in the universe, each one of them putting forth its separate claims and appeals. Christ, what a nightmare.

C: It's not that bad.

E: You don't think so? I can't even think about it, it's so awful.

C: Because you're a goddamn natural-born pessimist—and—and—

E: Alarmist?

C: Yes.

E: Of course. But you can't reduce everything to a question of temperament either. Look at Alex. I don't know why the hell she married you and I think there's a lot more to it than your explanation. Anyway, now she's taken to absenting herself from the conjugal felicities, so to speak. Where's she go, by the way?

C: Wish I knew.

E: What you you mean—haven't you asked her?

C: Not right out. She says she's spending the time with Orville and Polly and that crowd.

E: You mean that guy lives down by Rainbow Park?

C: Orville Dinkoe, that's the one. And his wife Polly. And the Nickelsons and Henkels and some others, I forget their names. But I guess they don't stay home much. Hang out over at the Stadium—at least they did in the winter; Polly works in the ticket booth during hockey season. I guess they were in the taverns on Division Street most of the time. Now they go out to Hinsdale a lot.

E: Hinsdale? What the hell for?

C: Dinkoe belongs to some country club out there, or something

129

like that. . . . Alex asked me to buy her a set of golf clubs a couple of weeks ago.

E: What did you say?

C: What could I say? I'd like to give her some golf clubs, or anything else she wants. Why shouldn't she have them as much as anybody? But damn it, you got any idea how much golf clubs cost? She told me they had some secondhand ones out at this country club that they'd let go for ninety dollars. Let go!—and I guess from what she says they're not even really much good. My God, I'd let my left foot go for ninety dollars right now.

E: Hyperbole.

C: What?

E: Exaggeration.

C: Yes. Maybe so. You know what I mean, I haven't got that much money now for anything.

E: What did she say?

C: Nothing. She knows I haven't got the money.

E: Then why did she ask for the clubs?

C: She didn't really ask, she just mentioned she'd like to have them. And then I asked how much they cost and she told me. And then—well, of course I had to tell her it was too much.

E: Put your foot in it that time.

C: Yes.

E: So you can't complain.

C: No. I can't complain—ever, I guess. I'm lucky to have her at all. That's the way I feel if you want to know the truth. She's never unreasonable, just . . .

E: Remote.

C: I guess so. Something like that. Sometimes anyway.

E: Look, Charley, you got a perfect right to complain if you got something to complain about. Everybody has. That's not the point; the point is you got a beautiful, sexy, desirable, and bloody damned independent wife, and you're as hot for her as you ever were, and you think maybe she's beginning to take off on her own somewhat. Is that a fair statement?

C: You mean is it true? Yes, I guess so.

E: She's beginning to show possible signs of being bored at

home, and perhaps she isn't telling you quite the whole truth about what she is doing away from home . . .

C: I didn't say that.

E: I'm saying it.

C: Well, goddamn it, it's. . . . Okay, I was the one that brought it up, I suppose.

E: Let it pass. I haven't got anything to suggest anyway. Just trying to define the problem. Did it ever occur to you you might be better off without her?

C: No.

E: I thought not. Does she take any interest in your racing?

C: No. Why should she? She doesn't know anything about cars.

E: Nevertheless, if I had a wife I think I'd like her to share my—

C: Hell, you *had* a wife. What happened to her?

E: Very complicated story.

C: Sure, everything's a very complicated story.

E: Exactly. You needn't be sarcastic about it. . . . And I guess I needn't be so metaphysical, for that matter. None of it makes any difference.

C: Maybe it does. I mean I don't know anything about metaphysics. I'm not even sure what the word means. In fact, I wanted to ask you, because I read it the other night in Emerson's essays.

E: You're reading Emerson's essays?

C: Yes.

E: Great God, what for? Is that one of those book-club selections?

C: Yes. The American Treasury. What's the matter? They're good books, aren't they?

E: Yes, I guess so—most of them. But Charley, don't you . . . don't you find it a little hard going sometimes?

C: Emerson, yes. Sometimes I read three pages and I'm going around and around.

E: I should think so. You haven't got the background, Charley. What's the use?

C: Well, it's what I. . . . Oh, hell, how do I know if it's any use or not? Probably it's a waste of time. All I know is I'm an immigrant. That's how everyone thinks about me, including you. Including me, too. All I know is I'm ignorant as hell. I don't know

131

much about America or anything; and I want to find out. Maybe if I read books, a little of it will stick. Wouldn't you do the same if you went to live in a new country?

E: Maybe.

C: That's the trouble with you Americans, you're never immigrants, you're just—what-do-you-call-'em?—expatriates. I'm an immigrant. I don't ever forget it; nobody'd let me forget it if I wanted to. But I *don't* want to, not particularly. I don't mind being an immigrant. I think America is great, the best thing that ever happened to me, and I want to be the best American I can. . . . But it's not easy, you're right about that. If I'm going to be an architect I got to stick to the technical courses in night school, no time for history or literature. So I join the American Treasury. Is that bad? I get a lot of good books—$1.98 each, plus postage. They come once a month. Just about gives me time to read one book before the next one comes. Good books—Emerson, Mark Twain, Hawthorne, Booth Tarkington. I don't understand everything I read, but something sinks in—even if it's just a word here and there—

E: Like "sallow"?

C: What do you mean?

E: "Sallow"—it's a word you used a while back.

C: It's a good word, isn't it?

E: It's a fine word, just not the kind you expect to hear from a . . . a . . . well, from an immigrant—that's what you called yourself.

C: Okay, I said I don't mind. I like it. And if I'm using words you don't expect to hear from an immigrant, that means I'm making progress, doesn't it? Good. That's why I read these books— part of the reason anyway. You know something? I like some of these books. *Huckleberry Finn*—I read that book three times all through, even if I still don't know for sure what a huckleberry is. I know what it means to be sold down the river, I bet I know it better than a lot of Americans. . . .

E: I guess you do at that, Charley.

C: Why don't you say what you're thinking? You think I'm some kind of a nut or something, don't you?

E: Not at all. You're trying to needle me. I know damn well

132

you don't think I think you're any kind of a nut—or anything like it. If you did, this whole conversation would be impossible.

C: Okay, we're friends.

E: Of course. What else?

C: You been riding me pretty hard.

E: Sorry. I'm jumpy this morning. Don't know why. The race, maybe. Look, Charley, we *are* good friends, never doubt it. It means a lot to me, as a matter of fact. And if I take a tough line toward you sometimes, it's just that I'm a little worried: maybe I want to toughen you up a bit, maybe that's it. Because sometimes you seem to be awfully soft, Charley. A real sucker, I don't want to see you floored by something that anybody else would duck. And it *is* possible to be realistic about things without being cynical, even if I'm not a very good example of it myself. For instance, you've been over here—what? Three years now?

C: Going on three and a half.

E: All right, hasn't anything in all that time changed your attitude about America—even a little?

C: You mean the television commercials again—all that stuff?

E: No, there's a lot more to it. The whole ethos. Things like you see in the department stores at Christmas, everybody bulging with money and shoving each other around. Or maybe the way Cienkiewycz's clients are trying to nick him all the time.

C: That's just it, they *don't* try to nick him all the time. They're pretty damn decent, most of them. And the ones that aren't decent —well, at least they stand out so much from the others that everyone makes jokes about them. They're known all over town. As for the department stores, you're just looking at one side of it. I bet I can show you somebody being kind and helpful for everyone you show me that's being a bastard . . .

E: Okay, I just wanted to know. Actually I think you're right, Charley, part of the time anyhow. . . . But look at that guy up there in the Caddy; thinks he's driving the *Queen Mary*; I bet he pulls out in a minute. What about him?

C: Thinks he owns the road all right. But they got the same type in France, everywhere else too, I guess. Only ten times worse. You should drive in Paris sometime.

E: I suppose so. . . . Look at him, there he goes. Watch it.

133

C: I see him. Relax, will you?

E: Why didn't he look behind him? Guys like that would drive you wild, wouldn't they?

C: If you let them. Put them out of your mind, otherwise you go nuts. Anyway you can always blow it off in a poem, can't you?

E: Not now anyway. Besides, it never really works . . .

C: Listen to her. Sounds fine, doesn't she?

E: She really does. She ought to—after all we put into her.

C: It was worth it. She never sounded so—so sharp.

E: What's the water gauge?

C: Just under one-ninety.

E: A bit high . . .

C: It's all right, I think.

E: All right for cruising down Route 30 on a cool Sunday morning in May. How's it going to be on the track this afternoon with the sun beating down? Or later this summer?

C: She's running hot. We knew it. But she'll be all right, wait and see.

E: Maybe we should have put in that new thermostat.

C: Don't think it would make much difference. If she's running hot it wouldn't do much good to get the water into the block at five degrees sooner.

E: You're probably right. We'll have to do it later though. She'd blow up for sure on a really hot day.

C: She's built for England, not Illinois. But I wonder anyway. I bet so long as you kept her going she'd never blow up, even if the gauge got up to two-twenty or two-thirty—especially if you keep the water level low. . . . But you're right anyway. We'll have to do a lot more than change thermostats if my guess is right.

E: Carbon job?

C: At least. New valves too. She's beginning to get a hot spot. You know how it is when you shut off the ignition when she's hot, she jumps a bit on one cylinder?

E: Yes, that's right.

C: Probably carbon. Worn valves. We can do the job next month.

E: Us? Hell of a job, isn't it?

C: Not so bad. You can usually knock it off with an electric

134

drill and a steel brush. We could even probably burn it off without taking off the head, for that matter, if we had the right kind of gas. This rotten leaded gas, that's what does it in the first place; burns dirty and leaves carbon—specially in MG engines.

E: How's that?

C: Don't know exactly. But it's what you always hear. We'd have to ask an engineer. Maybe something to do with the low compression or the shape of the intake manifolds.

E: Maybe after we get some more people in the club, we can persuade someone to start selling it in this area—if we promised him all our trade.

C: Unleaded gas? Maybe: most people don't like it though. Anyway this club has a long way to go before it amounts to much.

E: They're dropping out already. I heard Burnshaw quit last week. And Jake told me half the members are behind in their dues.

C: It isn't that so much. Some people always lose interest, but we could get up the membership if we put on a drive. The main thing is that one club in Chicago isn't enough to keep up an interest in the whole area, and we need the whole area to keep up a decent track. Even if we got in with this new national club, we still couldn't run the track properly by ourselves. We need more clubs all through the state, and in Indiana. That's the only way we'll get a good racing program. And as long as people in this part of the country are more interested in the open wheel cars and stock cars, we'll have a hard time getting up a good program for road races. Look at this track. In the first place, you can't make an interesting track out of an old airfield, not unless you got a lot more money to spend than we have. In the second place, you have to do a lot more work on it than we've done. We still got tar ridges pushing up through the concrete on the aprons and off the pit area. Somebody'll get killed out here one of these days.

E: You take it easy this afternoon. Hear?

C: I will.

E: That's what you say.

C: I don't take chances, you know that.

E: You drive like a wild man. You're always gearing her down too late and revving too soon on the corners.

C: That's the only way to drive. Sure, if we had an Alpha we could drive easier. When you got a weak car on a small course you take every fraction of power you can get.

E: All right. But take it easy anyway.

C: I will.

E: You don't want to overrev and bust a rod.

C: Don't worry.

E: Okay, but I don't want to have a pile of junk at the end of the day. Racing is fine, but we haven't the money to be buying a new engine every month.

C: All right. Don't worry. . . . You want to drive?

E: No. It's your turn; that was the agreement. I'm just jumpy, that's all.

C: That's the way it always is, the guy who's not driving does all the worrying.

E: Almost there. We timed it right for once. You want to stop somewhere here and have some lunch first?

C: Let's get straight to the paddock, I want to have a look at the radiator and hose connections. She's up to two hundred now.

E: Okay, we can eat afterwards. Maybe the fan belt is slipping. Would that affect the water pump—if there was grease on the flywheel?

C: Might. We'll see when we get her opened up.

* * *

E: Don't look, old Pops Kowalski is coming this way—no, keep your head down. Maybe he'll pass us by.

C: Not much chance.

E: Keep your head under the hood anyway. If that old gasser starts in, we'll never make the grid with her.

C: Okay. Now hold her right there, that's it, and I'll tighten up. That ought to do it.

E: Yes.

C: Don't think it was the water pump anyway. But that ought to hold it. Nothing else we can do now, I guess. Watch it—here's Pops.

P: Whassa matter, boys? You got troubles maybe?

C: Hi, Pops. How are you?

P: I'm okay. Whassa matter? You got troubles maybe?

136

E: No, Pops. Everything's fine.

P: Whaterya foolin' with the gineraytor for? You don't never want to fool with the gineraytor before a race.

C: Why not, Pops?

P: Aw, yull foul up the belt for sure, git it too tight or somethin'.

E: We just adjusted it, Pops. Took up a little slack.

P: Yeah? Maybe you took her up too much, huh?

E: Hell, Pops—it's okay.

P: Aw, you squirts—you don't know nuthin'. Look at it, you got no moren hardly a sixteenth inch play in her. When she heats up good, she'll bust.

C: She's already hot, Pops.

P: Ain't nothin' like she's gonna be. Naw, you squirts—whadya know about racin' anyways? Lemme tell you, in the old days we did it right, see? *Measured* it! . . . Hey, that gineraytor don't look so good—start her up, why doncha—lemme listen to her?

C: She's okay, Pops.

P: Aw, start her up, lemme listen to her, I kin help you guys if yull let me.

E: What the hell, go ahead, Charley, start her up.

C: Okay. Keep her hot anyway.

E: Sounds very good to me.

C: Fine. What the hell's the old man doing?

E: Listening, I guess.

C: If he gets his head any closer to that fan he'll go home without his ear.

E: Ascultation.

C: What?

E: Nothing. Hey, look, here comes Push-Rod O'Shaughnessy heading this way.

C: Yes. We got a popular car, it looks like . . .

P-R: Hi.

C: Hello, Push-Rod.

P-R: What the hell's the old guy doing, looking for butts?

C: He's listening.

P-R: Yeah? I saw him looking for dinchers once under the back booth at Sharkey's, looked just like that.

C: He's all right.

P-R: Has-been, shot his wad . . .

137

C: Sure. That's all right.

P: Shut her off, *shut her off!*

P-R: He wants you should shut her off.

E: He heard him, for God's sake.

P-R: Okay, okay.

P: You got worn-out brushes in that gineraytor.

E: How in God's name do you know?

P: I kin hear 'em. Wonder you got enny juice at all.

P-R: You mean you can hear them brushes with the motor firing?

P: You think I'm dccf?

P-R: Pops, ain't nobody can hear them brushes with a engine going right under their ear.

P: Shows what you young squirts knows about anythin'! Anybody'd hear them brushes in the old days, hah!

P-R: Look, Pops, cut it out, will you?—we had enough of that old-timey crap.

P: Old-timey crap! Hah! We had cars in them days like you kids never seen in your lives, you know that?

P-R: Cut it out, Pops, cut it out. You old Indy windbags are done. Why in hell don't you admit it?

P: Yeah? I'd like to see enny of your cars nowadays run against some of them babies we had. Lemme tell you somethin', we'd take anythin' you put on the track.

P-R: How come they ain't still running them, Pops?

P: Cause they changed the goddamn formulas, that's way! Yeah, you know it as well as me, you're just stickin' it in me again, ain't ya?

C: That's right, Pops. Go easy, Push-Rod.

P-R: Well, I get tired of these old windbags all the time talking about them sixteen-cylinder supercharged monsters they had in the old days. You call them cars? Goddamn locomotives, that's all. Too bad they didn't all blow up, like most of them did. And take these old windbags with them!

C: Easy, Push-Rod.

P-R: It's the truth, ain't it? Look at the Indy races now—ruined, that's what, ruined. All them cars exactly the same, going around

138

and around. What kind of racing is that, huh? I tell you them Offy's ruined it.

P: That Offenhauser's a mighty fine engine.

C: Sure, Pops.

P: And Indianapolis 500 is a mighty fine race.

P-R: Supercharged monsters, that's what they are.

P: What the hell's that Alpha Romeyo you kids are allays talkin' about. Blown, ain't it? You betchur sweet life it is!

P-R: Aw, they're done! They got that one-five liter bug blown so high it's burning up its own plugs for fuel. They're done, I tell you. Watch them new four-five liter Farraris coming on. Unblown, see?

E: They're not winning many races.

P-R: You just wait. Them Alphas are running at 9,000 r.p.m.'s with two blowers, see?—as big as grapefruits. Maseratis the same. They can't carry the gas for all that blowing and they can't lighten the engine or it'll bust its slats. So what's going to happen? So the unblown jobs are taking over. With the compression they get now they can stand the extra weight. And they got less pit stops too.

P: Maybe.

P-R: You bet. You know what? I bet they change the Formula One specifications next year, year after. Get rid of them blowers altogether.

P: Maybe. Allays room for changes—

P-R: Now you're talking sense, Pops. Say, you ever drive on a road circuit.

P: Sure. Plenty of times. I remember once out at Silver Lakes somebody set up a course. Before you was born probly.

P-R: What was you driving, Pops?

P: Me and Jolly Chandler had one of them new Duesenbergs —what did they call it?—Model J? That was it, Model J—a real hummer, blieve me.

C: Was it a good car, Pops?

P: One of the sweetest I ever seen, made beautiful—you couldn't ast for nothin' better from a regalur production model. Oh, them engine parts was machined beautiful, and all shiny casings. And power?—you could drive a ship with one of them engines. Think it had somethin' like 270 tops at maybe 4,000 revs. Course it weren't

139

so good on handlin'. Weighed something like two tons—too heavy for a tight course.

C: What did it look like?

P: You know, like a sports car, like this here one of yours, 'cept it was a lot bigger and we didn't call 'em sports cars in them days. Mostly we called 'em roadsters or two-seaters. Course the one Jolly and me had was cut down some.

P-R: You mean you and this other guy took shifts at it?

P: Nope. This was a old-time auto race; least that's what it was sposed to be—like the ones I seen when I was a kid, back round nineteen ten, eleven. You know? A regular road race, dirt roads, 'cept the course was shut off. Jolly and me rode together. Him drivin' and me mechanic. He was bettern me for driving, and anyways he was too jumpy to ride passenger.

P-R: Yeah? How'd you make out, Pops?

P: Threw the right rear wheel on lap thirty-eight; the tail was draggin' and the tank bust and she burned up.

P-R: Yeah?

P: Yeah.

P-R: Ain't that something?

P: Yeah.

P-R: Anybody killed?

P: Naw. Jolly, he died later—the same year maybe—1929. Drownded in Lake Michigan.

P-R: What do you know?

C: Look, Pops, are you really serious about that generator?

P: Course I am, what you think?

C: But there's no time to do anything about it now.

P: Aw, sure—what time you got, Push-Rod?

P-R: Quarter past one. We got a full half hour, plenty of time. Huh, Pops? We can do it easy. Say, Pops, seems to me I heard them rockers banging, maybe we should do something about that?

P: Aw, this heap's got a million things wrong with it.

P-R: Yeah, but they ain't going nowhere at all with them tappets loose like that.

P: Yeah, that's right. Tell you what, you slip out that gineraytor cover and turn the brushes, see, and I'll set the valve clearances— if I kin borry a sprocket wrench somewheres.

140

E: You leave that engine alone.

P: Take it easy, kid. What you got them clearances set at?

E: About seventeen.

P: When she's hot?

E: Yes.

P-R: Tighten them up, huh, Pops?

P: Yeah. Sure. Course with them weak brushes maybe we should cut the spark some. Whatcha got the gap at?

E: About twenty-two.

P-R: What you think, Pops?

P: If only we had a good magneto to throw in there. Hell, they ain't got nothin' in this bucket of bolts but this here old air-cooled coil. Weak?—why it couldn't burn the fuzz off your old lady's ass.

P-R: So what we going to do, Pops?

P: It's like this. If only we had a good magneto to throw in there. We could maybe even up the gap to twenty-three, twenty-four, you know? And if ony we had a hot coil we could maybe leave it where it is. But like this? We got to cut that gap to twenty, maybe nineteen.

P-R: Think she's worth it, Pops?

P: She's a pile of junk, kid, if you wanna know—but what the hell, we gotta do the best we kin with what we got as the Greek said when he stuffed the cat in the meat-grinder.

P-R: Yeah? Say, Pops, that's pretty good.

P: Yeah. Hell, I figgur they even gotta have distributor trouble with this heap. Timing all off. So then with the punk gineraytor she misfires or fouls, and who knows what happens, she blows a gasket, busts the mannyfold, throws a rod—and you might as well take her to the river and push her in.

P-R: That's right, Pops. Say, you got it all figured out, ain't you, Pops?

P: Sure, kid. Now I'll tell you what to do, git that valve cover offa there quick, see, and go to work on them rockers, but yull hafta use a screwdriver and a ordnary wrench cause we ain't got no time to go borryin' now, and I'll be gettin' them plugs outa there and settin' the gap down, if I kin get them out when they're hot, and then maybe we kin advance the distributor a fraction, see, so the stroke is longer and maybe that way she'll get by.

141

P-R: Yeah, yeah. Say, Pops, you sure know what you're doing, don't you?

P: Wull, I ain't been round these heaps for forty years for nothin'.

P-R: That's right, Pops.

P: Now git goin'—there's some tools laid out over there where the guys was gettin' ready to pack 'em up.

P-R: Okay, Pops.

E: *Listen, you two flea-brained bastards, neither one of you is going to lay so much as a greasy finger on*—oh, for Christ's sake! —you tell them, Charley.

C: That's right, Pops. See, the steward's just blowing his whistle. Time to line up.

P: Huh?

C: Yes, Pops, the time's up.

P: Wull, what do you know 'bout that—we never even got to open her up.

E: *You're bloody damn right you never got to open her up, you old*—

C: Yes, he means you took too long discussing it, Pops. Now we have to fall in on the grid.

P: Wull . . . wull . . . wull, keep the revs up anyways, that'll help some. Don't let her idle on the line no moren you hafta.

C: I won't, Pops.

P: Say, who's your pit crew?

E: I am, and nobody else is going to—

C: That's it, Pops, we can handle it ourselves.

P: Aw, you gotta have moren one. Spose you git hung up with a tire change and somethin' else too, huh?

C: We'll manage it, don't worry. This is only a sprint, Pops.

P: You kids is crazy, that's what!

P-R: You said it, Pops.

C: We can handle it.

P: But you gotta have somebody with some 'sperience in there, don't you?

E: For Christ's sake, come on, come on, if you want to see the race so bad. Bring your buddy. Bring your old lady!

P: My old lady's dead.

P-R: Yeah, Pops? How did she die?

P: Sa funny thing, she was walkin' out the front gate in Davenport, that's where we was livin'—you know, Davenport?—well, it's like this, she was walkin' out the front gate, see, and this kid comes along on a bicycle, see, and he clips her, just like that, right in the ass . . .

P-R: Yeah? Say, that's a laugh, ain't it, Pops?

P: What's so goddamn funny?

P-R: You mean it really happened?

P: Sure, whadya think I yam—she fell down and bust her head and she died. Whadya think I yam, a goddamn comedian or somethin'?

* * *

P: What did you clock him at?

E: Forty-seven point one.

P: Pretty good.

E: Pretty good!—it's sensational. Hell, that thing's not rated more than seventy-five, eighty flat out. You can't get her much over sixty-five on this course. Charley's brought his time down from fifty-five point three in nineteen laps. That's damn good driving.

P: Six laps to go. Forty-seven point one, huh? How long's the track?

E: The way they laid it out this time it's nine-tenths of a mile. Too damn short.

P: Yeah. Say, he's clockin' close to seventy at that. Maybe too much for the track. With that heap of yours, anyways.

E: If he can hang on, third is cinched, and a chance for second. Best we've ever done.

P-R: If that Alpha'd conk out you could even win, ain't that right, Pops?

P: No chance. She's hittin' forty-six, forty-five regalur and ain't even tryin', far as I kin see. She'll coast in. What is she?

E: That's a 1900 Sport. Damn fine car. Almost new.

P: Well, you might take the Bristol.

E: Might. Damn good car too. Showing its age though. I tell you, I think he can take that Bristol. Look at him, he's pushing the Bristol on the corners and he's cornering fine.

P: You think so. Maybe. From here it looks like he's gonna spin

143

her into them markers next time round. She's nosin' down, he's goin' in too hard.

E: Don't you worry. Charley knows what he's doing.

P: Okay. I didn't say nothin'.

P-R: Hey, look, there goes that yellow Crosley. Jeez, look at her smoke.

P: Oughta take alla them Crosleys off the track. Look at him. Blew out a oil seal, differential burnin' up—hell, that's the last thing oughta happen to a racin' car. Look at him throwin' smoke in the Alpha's face. That'll slow him up.

E: They're giving him the black flag.

P: You sure got some lulus runnin' today.

E: What else can you expect? Not many around here got cars, not amateurs anyway. If you're going to get up a race more or less in the same class, you have to let in some punks. The Crosleys haven't a chance, but that doesn't mean their owners don't like to drive.

P: What's the limits on this race?

E: Twelve hundred to two thousand cc's. Sure, it's phony. But it's the best the club could do with what we've got. That's why those old cars are in there. Beauties too, some of them, but not fit to race today. Like that Aston-Martin Le Mans; it's twenty years old. And that AC 16/80.

P-R: What's that white one?

E: Called an Alvis. British car. Never saw one before.

P-R: Here's Charley.

P: What's the time?

E: Forty-seven point four.

P: He's holding her steady. Guess he's probly got her doin' as much as she'll do.

E: Ten to one he breaks forty-six point five?

P-R: Take him up, Pops, take him up!

P: I'll tell you kids somethin': never bet on a race.

P-R: That's right, Pops.

E: Did you notice anything wrong, Pops?

P: Naw, looks okay, sounds okay. But look at him on that corner —like he's diggin' pavement.

E: He always does that, Pops. Don't worry.

144

P: I'll tell you kids somethin' else: never touch your brakes in a turn unless you're better drivers than I think you are.

P-R: Something going on in back, past the esses. Look at the crowd over there.

P: No smoke, can't be afire.

E: Probably one of the Crosleys threw a wheel or something.

P-R: Hope it ain't Charley in no trouble.

E: No, not Charley. Couldn't be.

P: Naw. Never git to worryin' till they come around anyways.

E: Charley always gets through the esses with no trouble at all.

P: Can you see him on the south turn?

E: Not yet.

P: What's the clock?

E: He's due.

P-R: There, there—that's him, ain't it?

P: Hard to tell from here. There's so many of them red TD's on the road.

E: Yes. . . . That's Charley. You can tell by the slant in the left fender. See? It's a bit off. That's where I rammed the marker last summer.

P-R: Yeah?

P: Here he comes.

E: Look at that, look at that! Flat out. Hear it?

P: What's the time? Did you forget to press the button?

E: No. Forty-six point eight. Didn't I tell you? He's working it down, lap by lap.

P-R: Look at him! He's nosing inside the Bristol on the turn!

P: Too fast, too goddamn fast! Don't he know when to shut off, for God's sake?

E: He's all ri——

P-R: Lookitim, lookitim!

P: He's gonna spin!

E: Charley. . . .

P: Jeezus, look at him!

P-R: He's flipping, Pops, he's flipping!

P: Left front caught one of them tar ridges. Caught it at a angle.

P-R: Up and over! Lookitim, lookitim!

145

E: Charley, Charley—

P-R: Oh, man—again!

P: Flipped three times—

P-R: Lookit, she's blowing up, she's blowing up!

E: Look out.

P: Hey, grab him!

P-R: I got him, I got him—

P: Hold him!

P-R: I can't, he's getting away!

P: Slug him, for Christ's sake! Sit on his head! Now hold him. . . .

P-R: Jesus.

P: Take it easy, boy, take it easy now.

E: I'm okay.

P: Sure. Whadya tryin' to do, git yourself kilt or somethin'? You can't just run outen onto that track any time you want to.

E: I know, Pops.

P: What did you think you was doin' anyways?

E: I don't know, Pops. Just wanted to be there, I guess.

P: Wanted to be there—I reckon you did! Now, look. See? No reason for it. Charley's out, he's okay, see? He's walkin' around. See him wavin'? He's okay. Look at him walkin' around lookin' at the car?

E: Thank God.

P: Yeah.

P-R: Boy, you sure got a mess out there now, ain't you? Scrap metal, that's all.

P: Aw, maybe, it ain't so bad as it looks. Sometimes you take and straighten them out, they goes as good as ever. You know? Little paint here, a new hunka tubing there—hell, you kin do a lot.

E: We'll see. It'll take a lot of money.

P: That's a fact—sometimes it ain't worth it. If you take her home like she is and put her in the barn, maybe she'll be a classic someday, you kin sell her for a coupla thousand bucks, who knows?

P-R: Ha-ha. That's a good one, Pops, ain't it?

P: Well, you never know. Many a little lady's turned out to be better'n anybody'd figgured in the long run.

P-R: Hey, there's the Alpha getting the flag. Race is over, Pops.

146

P: Yeah.

P-R: Let's hit the road, Pops.

P: Yeah. Okay.

P-R: So long. Better luck next time.

E: Thanks.

P: Yeah. So long, kid. Don't take it too hard; it don't never pay. Hope we see you sometime—somewheres when our tracks cross. So long, kid.

E: So long.

PART III

CHAPTER 29

"Rot," Alex said. "Perfect utter birdlime."

She stretched, running the backs of her fingers along the head-board, so that the nipple of one breast peered—inquisitively, it seemed—over the edge of the sheet. For an instant I could have sworn it blinked. Of an absolute circularity, not a millimeter off, if I may be permitted a pedanticism, it was a color between mallow and coral, like a mulberry nearly ripe.

"What do you know about birdlime?" I asked.

"Nothing whatever." She subsided, folding her hands on her stomach and twiddling her toes under the sheet. Her tone of voice became flat. "Nothing whatever. But you'll admit the word has an appropriate ring."

"Why?"

"Because-you-are-talking-drivel-and-you-know-it."

"The fact remains that Charley keeps a gun, which I must say shocks me considerably, aside from the perso—"

"Why should it shock you?" She looked at me under weighted eyelids, without turning her head. "Lots of men keep guns."

"Of course, of course," I said, with only half simulated impatience. "But I didn't think Charley was the type, I still don't think he's the type. Something is out of line. Which is to say, keeping a gun suggests an element of Charley's character that is either wholly illusory or has been hidden until now. In either case, I'm having a hard time fitting it into my conception of the whole man."

"Why don't you talk like a human being?"

"Oh, for Christ's sake—"

She thumped her pillow loudly and lay down on her side. "Go on," she said.

One breast sagged a trifle in the direction of the other, creating a soft inverse curve that furled downward from the tendon of her throat. Instantly four poems came to my mind, four celebrations of that tender arrangement of loved flesh, four poems that should have been written by Skelton, Wyatt, Ben Jonson, and perhaps Sackville or Waller; but they didn't write them, and neither did I. People who complain—with some justice—about the number of poems that are published, should think of the number, including some superb examples, that are never written.

"Well," I said, "it occurs to me that—by the way, what kind of a gun is it?"

"Colt .38 automatic."

"I see you are knowledgable in such matters. Is it loaded?"

"No."

"How do you know?"

"I looked."

"All right. Assuming you know how to tell. Where does Charley keep it?"

"Bottom drawer, right side, desk in living room."

"Did you see any cartridges?"

"When?"

"When you looked, naturally."

"No. But that was some time ago."

"You haven't looked recently?"

"No. Why should I?"

"If I were living in the same house with a gun, I'd prefer to keep tabs on it."

"That's the kind of a person you are."

"What do you mean by that?"

"I mean if we're talking about character and elements of character, you never open your mouth without giving some of yours away gratis."

"I see. And what do you infer from what I just said?"

"Never mind. I keep my own counsel."

"Don't you, though?" I leaned over and kissed the end of her nose. "Bitch," I said. I took a cigarette from the pack on the night

152

table, lit it, blew a long gust of smoke at the ceiling, and briefly, silently cursed the little stitch of pain that tightened in my right lung.

"Recapitulation," I said, trying to collect my thoughts, which for the moment seemed to have scattered as far as the dispersed parts of Charley's (or my) character. "Charley, in a moment of unknowing self-revelation, says he is going to kill me. Don't interrupt: I know he didn't realize he was talking about me and also that he didn't realize there was any real occasion to be talking about anybody; and beyond that I know that after the first shock wore off I myself discounted Charley's statement, thinking it too much at variance with the man's real character to be credible. But there is still this business of the gun. I'll tell you, the more I think about the gun the more I find myself in doubt. I remember the tone of voice in which Charley said he would kill anyone he found messing around with you. It may have been a bit hesitant; but not boastful or affected. He was feeling his way toward a true knowledge of himself, toward that hidden element of his character we've been talking about. Which he, perhaps, was too innocent or good-natured to recognize previously. At any rate, I was."

"You? Innocent and good-natured? Don't make me laugh," Alex murmured, examining her fingernail to find a rough place. "You look like a pirate and you are."

"Not, by God!" We had been through this before, and Alex knew we had reached the point at which I was beginning to decide to refuse to accept her aspersions as simple kidding: she was interested in seeing precisely when the preliminary flickers of lightning would be superseded by the main bolt. However, I wasn't ready to launch it yet, and she gauged this immediately.

"Okay, you're a sweet, good, kind—poet," she said.

"Contradiction in terms, and you don't have to rub it in." Alex was biting her nail with great care; she didn't answer.

"Anyway," I continued, after a pause, "I can't help beginning to suspect there is more to Charley than meets the eye, and that's really a damn stupid way of putting it; he and I have been close friends for a long time, I thought I knew him, I still think I know him a lot better than I could through any meeting of eyes. But I'm puzzled, no doubt of that. This new element is upsetting. Pri-

153

marily, of course, because I'm the guy he's going to take a shot at when he finds out what's going on, but secondarily because—hell, I just don't like people to go overturning my concepts of them. And don't tell me that's because I'm a poet. I know what you think of poets, but in this case, at least, I'm behaving perfectly normally. Nobody likes to discover concealed motives in their friends."

"Look," Alex said. She took the cigarette from between my fingers, sucked on it greedily with her head tilted upward, and stumped it out in the ashtray without asking me if I wanted it back. "You and Charley may be good friends. But he's my husband—"

"Thanks."

"It's a fact of life, for Pete's sake—don't be so unrealistic. All I'm saying is I know Charley better than you do. I probably know him better than anyone in Chicago, anyone in America—if what he says about his life in France is true, I must know him better than anyone in the world. I'm his wife. I've lived with him for two and a half years. All right, we're not an old married couple; he hasn't got gray hair and I haven't got varicose veins; but two and a half years is something—in fact, it's a pretty long time. And I say you're cockeyed. Charley wouldn't hurt a fly."

"How long has he had that gun?"

"I don't know. He's had it since before we got married."

"Where did he get it? Has he got a license for it?"

"I don't know, I don't know—what difference does it make?" Alex was turning snippy.

"Dearest—be patient. It's important, after all. What I'm driving at is this: what the hell does he have the gun *for*? I mean if he isn't going to shoot anybody. Do you know him well enough to answer that? Certainly you must have wondered about it. Did you ever ask him?"

"Yes, I did." Alex shifted onto her back again, and turned her head to look out the window into the hazy, hot morning sky of September. Street noises came to us, the whine of a trolley-bus on 47th Street, kids banging on the iron fence out front. "You know what he said?"

"What?"

"Nothing. Or rather, he found some way to change the topic to something else." She smiled a small smile that scarcely moved

154

the corners of her mouth. "When Charley thinks I'm asking questions which aren't any of my business, that's the way he lets me know."

I raised myself on my elbow. "Then doesn't that support my view? If he won't tell you what he has the gun for, isn't that another indicator of this element in his character we've been talking about? Something concealed? He's got a hard side to him, too firm, too determined—it's the sort of thing that betrays a suppressed rage."

"Birdlime. *Birdlime!*" She sat up and clutched her knees. "You make me sick."

"Oh, I do—"

"You're just not thinking." She turned her head in order to look into my eyes, very earnestly. "Charley is a European; that's the first thing to remember. But he's also an American, a kind of obsolete American, two hundred years behind the times. You know how he is about that. All right, as a European he holds certain ideas about the family and marriage; I don't have to tell you what they are because you probably know more about them than I do; but I'll tell you this: Charley just takes them for granted, that's all. He doesn't press them, not ever, do you see? If I questioned them, if I said a wife's role in America isn't exactly what he thinks, why he'd probably abandon his ideas immediately. But I don't question them—" she was speaking now with measured emphasis "—and I never will question them, whatever else happens between us. That's the way I love Charley, and if you don't understand that you don't understand the first thing about me. No, don't say anything yet. There's another point: did you stop to think that the American Constitution says every man has a right to bear arms? Probably not; you probably haven't read the Constitution for years. Neither have I. But Charley has; he's read it and studied it, he's been reading it and studying it, off and on, ever since he came to this country—remember that. And another thing: you probably don't know that Cienkiewycz carries a pistol with him all the time, don't ask me why. Okay, put these things together. I think Charley keeps that gun for several reasons, reasons that overlap. One—" she began counting on her fingers "—he believes it is a husband's duty to defend his home. Two, he feels, perhaps dimly, that the gun is a

155

symbol of his freedom as an emigrant to America. Three, he is imitating Cienkiewycz. Four—" she began talking faster, excited by her ability to think of more reasons than she had expected "—he unconsciously wants to put himself on a level with the soldiers who lorded it over him for so long during his childhood and who all bore arms, at least on parades. Five, it cost a lost of money and consequently is a symbol of financial success. Six, remember the reason he gave himself; it *is* a beautifully made machine and Charley loves machinery. Seven . . ." She paused. "Hell, that's enough, isn't it? The point is there are lots of reasons for him to buy a gun, but not one of them is sufficient to make him use it. Not on you; not on any human being, for my money. Charley isn't firm or determined or anything like that, and you know damn well you're just building fantasies about all that stuff. All he is ever trying to do is be clear—clear in his own head, his thoughts and feelings. That's all; it's his whole purpose in life, if you ask me. And it isn't firmness. Just the opposite."

"Possibly, possibly, but don't you—"

"Don't I think Charley can change, don't I realize matters are complicated, don't I this, don't I that? I know, this is what you always say. But now listen to me. Yes, of course matters are complicated, but it's not such a damned original remark as you think it is. And here's another thing, if matters are as complicated as you say, knowing this, recognizing it, is no help whatever to most people. Just the opposite. Most people have simply got to find a straight way of looking at things if they are to keep themselves from going insane. And who's to say their view isn't as good as yours, and as true? You don't know so much, you said that yourself plenty of times. Then why can't you listen to somebody who does know something, *me*? If you want to go around pulling a long face all your life, that may be all right for you. But not for me, I'm not going to tell everybody I don't know anything when I know damned well I do know something. I'm not smart, I pulled out of college, I've never read many books; and furthermore I'm not ever going to read many books, I don't give a damn for books. But I'm not stupid, and I know that however much I don't know I still know something. I believe what you know is a lot more important than what you don't. And that's what most people think—they

156

agree with me. If you think anybody can live a decent life on the basis of any other theory, you're crazy—plain crazy." Alex brushed the hair back from her forehead. "Lord, I'm talking too much. Haven't been this wound up for years. It's no good for a lady, all this serious conversation, changes the color of the circles under her eyes." She swung back the sheet and stepped to the mirror to peer at herself. "What's the difference, Poppy? Let's not talk about it any more, okay? . . . But I'll say this for Charley. His attitude, I mean about America and marriage and all that—well, you know, it's stupid, isn't it? Just doesn't have much to do with the facts of life; everybody knows it. It's Charley's dream, as cockeyed as they come. Yet I don't care. I think it's sweet, goddamned sweet."

"So do I. I wish I didn't."

With her forefinger she felicitously nudged a speck on the point of her chin, and leaned forward to examine it more closely. "Do I dare ask what you mean by that?" she said.

"You dare ask anything you want," I answered in a soft tone. "You know that. My anger—if that's what it is—will never last long with you: I'm too scared of you."

"Now it's my turn to say thanks."

"You needn't be sarcastic," I said. I felt suddenly weak and worn out, soft, unaccountably close to tears. "It's exactly what you want."

Alex said nothing. I reached for another cigarette and lit it; this helped—the pain crouching in my windpipe. And so did looking at the volute carved in Georgian frumpery at the end of my living-room mantel; the soapy whorl of wood caught the light in a peculiar way when seen from the bedroom, and always made me think of a brain—out there, detached—object of a thousand former nightmares and daymares. My mind ratcheted back through these remembered images, like my own head tumbling through the mirrors of a barbershop. I felt better; replaced again firmly on top of the poker chips of my days.

"After all," I said, spouting a long jet of smoke toward the ceiling, "I have a little reason to be angry, or at least hurt—which comes to the same thing. Charley the innocent, Charley the sweet, Charley the prince charming, and so on and so *on*. I've had a pretty stiff dose of it in the last twenty minutes."

157

She turned around and leaned back against the edge of the dresser, bracing herself on her straightened arms. "You asked for it," she said to the Saito lithograph which hung on the wall above my head.

"I suppose so," I muttered. "But do you think I'm made of steel?" I drew on the cigarette. "Isn't a man entitled to a little jealousy? For God's sake, every night you climb into bed with that guy right behind this wall—" I reached up above my head and rapped the wall with my knuckles "—and you know damn well it kills me. Do you realize how much sound comes through? I suppose you're having a first-rate time these nights—you, you insatiate . . ."

"Hush. Isn't anything out of bounds for you?"

"Out of bounds!" I sat up straight, but then subsided again. "I'll say this much: I have the distinct impression that although you are unwilling to talk about your bedtime activities over there to me, you would be more than willing to discuss your bedtime activities over here with Charley—critically and with relish, dwelling on every detail."

"Don't be silly," she said. She came to the bed and stood beside it, looking down. She ruffled my hair. "Anyway—as I've said before this morning—what difference does it all make? Poppy, let's enjoy life, can't we?" She took the cigarette from my fingers, turned, and walked through the door to the living room, trailing a blue scarf of smoke behind her nakedness.

CHAPTER 30

Have I pointed out that Alex was lame? Probably not: it is easy to forget. For that matter, most people never knew it, never observed it; for it detracted not one syllable from the syntax of her flowing movement, her expressiveness, her being. Yet Alex had been born with a left leg three-eighths of an inch shorter than her right. A defect; so she herself proclaimed it—in private. But a defect easily disguised if not remedied; and Alex had her shoes made by a cobbler on South Michigan Avenue, a pocked and pagan Anatolian, from the prolix recesses of whose shop issued footware in the *haute mode* for Chicago's bunioned and spavined gentility. His price was as low as $175 a pair for simple suede, and his clients paid up without a murmur, being careful only to demand a smudgy receipt for their husband's tax files.

On the street, thanks to the Anatolian, Alex walked altogether levelly, drilling passersby with her arrogant and smoldering stare; and only those who saw her in undress could tell she was a gimp. These could; but not many did. I am not speaking here only of the men who attended her—joyous, jealous fraternity. Alex occasionally went to swim and sun at the 57th Street beach, wearing a bathing costume which, however little it left to the imagination, nevertheless incited more fantasies than one cares to contemplate —many a young man in her presence wished his own costume more inscrutable—yet I wonder how many of the spectators who retained sufficient composure to examine her critically (spleenish wives and injured sweethearts) detected the limp. Alex possessed other arts than those conferred on her by the Anatolian. Like all gimps, she had learned them in childhood. She never approached the water with a walking gait, for instance, but always at a run, no matter how icy the prospect; nor do I mean one of those giggling, hippity-hoppity, tooth-gleaming caprioles which decorate the travel posters from Nassau: Alex's immersion was accomplished in a smooth, athletic run, executed on the balls of her feet, ending in a skimming splurge and fifty yards of Australian crawl. Not a trace of a limp. Coming out was more difficult, and she had various tactics. One, less successful than others, was simply a reversal of her entry; but it is hard to run *out* of water. A commoner expedient was a slow, intermittent progress from water's edge to blanket, interrupted by much hopping on one foot to shake out her hair, turning to wave to someone still in the lake, stopping to take a pebble from between her toes, etc.; by this means she could traverse as much as a hundred feet of sand without once taking a normal step. Alex wasn't ashamed of her short leg. If anyone there, the savagest rival, had come up and asked in a loud voice whether or not one of her legs was short, Alex would have replied, "Of course"—equally loudly and without a blush. But she regarded her limp as . . . I was about to say an esthetic blemish, but I think her feeling was more moral than esthetic, though she would not have recognized this with any clarity; only in retrospect can I surmise it myself. She was Jewish, remember that—half-Jewish, to be precise. Her lameness may have been a mark of God's overbearance, a sign of interminable heaven's war against human dignity and sanity. Like Job, she preferred to bear the insult alone.

As for myself, I held a different attitude toward her limp: far from being a defect, it was a saving deviation from an otherwise too-perfect symmetry, and a special correlative of my affection. Too-perfect symmetry?—something like that, I suppose, for in every other aspect Alex possessed total balance: eyes equally large and well placed, breasts ditto, nose as straight as twelve o'clock, hands, wrists, arms, shoulders all perfectly equilateral; and she was ambidextrous. Hence the limp was everything, in a sense; the humanizing factor, giving, it seemed, an attainability and intelligibility to her poised hauteur as well as her poised pelvis. Believe me, she might very well have lacked these qualities if she hadn't possessed the limp. Without the limp Alex could take form in my

160

projecting mind—or yours, I dare say—as a woman who, by the age of fifty, will necessarily have discarded all gestures but those of pride; with the limp this is impossible.

And so I lay stretched out on my comfortable sack with my head inclined at the comfortable angle against my headboard, and I watched Alex walk away from me: through the bedroom door, into the living room beyond, past the Georgian mantel, up to the three tall windows which looked out over the roofs of 47th Street. Thank God for suntan lotion. From the whiteness of her buttocks her color verged to honey-brown, then to the dark gold of her hair; and the thin, dissipating, blue veil of cigarette smoke was the perfect garment for this richness. Her shoulder blades moved gently and supplely beneath their cover, and an alternating luminescence shone in the backs of her knees as they twinkled slowly away. . . . Sorry to be so lush. I recognize that my words may produce grotesque images for you, and of course the temptation to render an exact description in such subjective matters is just what the professional writer ought to reject. The job can't be done with words. How much less adequate then my language would be for conveying the brain turbulence produced by that little lurch as she stepped down on her left foot. Talk about sinuosity, lissomeness, silken undulatency, etc., etc.—my God!

As she approached the windows, the light from the sky took precedence over that indoors, and she receded into silhouette—posed in dynamic stasis against the hazy brightness of a sky whose cowl of cloud scarcely withheld the flood of hot September sunlight above it. She looked out the window for several minutes, and flicked her ashes into my malnourished azelea, which had kept itself alive since the previous Christmas by mere good luck. Its brown and parched appeals were generally unnoticed. Not now, however. Alex called out: "For Pete's sake, Poppy, why don't you give this poor plant some water?"

I got up and gave the poor plant some water.

161

CHAPTER 31

Alex sat down on the sofa, tucking her feet sideways. "God," she said, looking at them, "they're filthy. You might have your floors swept once in a while."

"Nothing but complaints. As a matter of fact, the cleaning lady can only come in the mornings," I answered. "So I told her to stay away until further notice."

"Oh." Alex sat for a while without speaking; she continued to study her feet, and with her slender forefinger traced a blue vein down her instep. I sat in the leather chair. Abruptly Alex said: "Guess I'll take a shower. Okay?"

"Okay," I said.

She walked away and I heard the water spurt on, the first crash and then the steady downpour. I moved over to the sofa and sat where she had been sitting. . . .

It was a good arrangement we had—good, that is, in the mornings, pretty rotten other times. I mean the convenient accident of living not only in the same apartment house but on the same floor, virtually in the same apartment. (Accident? But perhaps we would never have fallen into adultery if the accident hadn't occurred first. Can an accident be its own convenience?) I see I must say a word about the house itself, however. It was the standard pre-World War I urban dwelling house of Chicago and most Middle-Western cities: a unit three stories tall, with one apartment to each story—"Pullman" apartments, they are called, from their resemblance to the old sleeping cars. Each apartment had an inner corridor running from front to back, with eight rooms opening off

162

it, though there were also direct connections between most of the rooms. The front room had a bay in one corner, with three tall windows, so that from the outside each three-story unit appeared to have a single tower at one corner, leading it off on a slanting course like a ship with a lopsided prow. Often this asymmetry was rectified by building two units side by side or with a single shared partition; sometimes there were four, six, or eight such jointures, or a whole blockful—the units were uniform and interchangeable, all culled from the same architectural source; but often, too, a single unit would be left standing by itself, as you can see it in a painting by one of the realists—Sheeler perhaps?—with the hard Middle-Western sky above and behind it, and the vacant rubble-strewn lots, called prairies in Chicago, extending on either side. In a neighborhood of decaying gentility such as ours, these apartments were often divided into smaller accommodations, sometimes even into single rooms, but more usually into two four-room apartments, four rooms in the front and four in the back; a practice considerably accelerated during the housing shortage after World War II. And even though these cut-down apartments were furnished with individual locks, there was still a good deal of intimacy between the tenants of the front apartment and those of the back: they shared that inner ("Pullman") corridor; which meant that a person could go from the front apartment to the back one without being seen at all on the outside—in the main hall or on the stairs. A convenient accident, as I said; for I occupied the front half of such a divided apartment, and Charley and Alex occupied the back. The house stood on the corner of Woodlawn Avenue and 45th Street.

The manner in which these accidents came about—if they were accidents—was simple enough. After that first stormy night when I had met Charley and Alex at the home of Cienkiewycz, I continued to see them from time to time, and then with increasing regularity. They were not members of the primary circle of acquaintances among whom I had to spend a good deal of time by virtue of my job: people from the university, artists and writers, a few of the wealthy who solaced their hours away from meat-packing and railroading with the company of the local intelligentsia. But Charley and Alex soon became close members of the smaller circle in which I spent my better hours, so far as my enjoyment was concerned: a mixed group, but having in common a certain honesty, openness, *genuineness*, which made them the natural society for Charley. Alex, of course, was welcome anywhere, everywhere; all she needed to do was arch her bosom a quarter of an inch and the Dalai Lama (bless him) would have invited her to lunch. Cienkiewycz was on the fringe of this smaller group, too much interested in his home to spend much time away from Palos Park; usually we saw him only when he invited us to come out, for he found means to evade our invitations to come in. Others were a young antiacademic bookstore owner from the university neighborhood, an instructor at the municipal junior college, a semantically minded piano player who worked in a modernist trio at Christy's Mill on 55th Street and read Korzybski between sets, a graduate physicist at the university who was engaged in a mysterious experiment on the "creep" of plastics and had to return to the laboratory every two hours day and night to take measurements, no less than three female painters, the director of publicity at the union stockyards—well, a complete list isn't necessary. Wives, husbands, sweethearts, of course, were included or at least tolerated. It was a drinking crowd; everyone was fouled up one way or another—that goes without saying in those years after the war. I was convalescing from divorce, ridden one day by bitter misogyny and two days later by devouring lust—as battered, between these extremes, as a defeathered shuttlecock. We met mostly in each other's rooms, or in the saloons of the South Side.

My association with Charley and Alex was closer than with any of the others, or at least soon became so, if only because we lived in such intimate proximity. Not at first, of course. After that first meeting at the home of Cienkiewycz, I continued for some time —perhaps two or three months—to think the two would not marry; their dissimilarities were too great, close to antipathies. So I thought, so everyone who knew them thought. But as I learned to know them better I saw, not that the dissimilarities were illusory —in fact they weren't, but were, then and later, as plain as day— but that Charley and Alex could not see them, were totally blind to them; and this too continued, inexplicably, to the very end of their relationship. But they weren't in a hurry to be married. Then sud-

164

denly they were. What hit them, God knows; something, something hot and hard. Not lust; they were sleeping together. But some celestial bolt of sentiment that knocked them on the tops of their bedazzled heads, with the result that they must be married immediately—with the further result that Charley must find a place for them to live in immediately. Not an easy thing to do in those times; but by accident (again!) the rear half of my floor fell vacant at that moment, and what was more natural than my offering to introduce Charley to the landlord? It was done. With the now known consequences.

For more than two and a half years I was the front tenant, they were the rear tenants, and we made splendid neighbors, supping at one another's tables, sharing one another's wine and salt, giving one another little presents on birthdays and Christmas, bringing to one another our problems (though not the really intimate, troublesome ones), taking care of one another's flats when vacations came around, etc., etc., etc. Charley consulted me about the problems he encountered in his reading, about the proper conduct of a young man on the way up, about his night studies to become a draftsman and ultimately (he hoped) an architect. I can't remember that I ever took to him any problems of my own. Except for the trials of writing, which I discussed endlessly, of course, with writer friends, I kept my private despairs to myself, nursing them alone—they were too messy to expose to others. But certainly I shared many interests with Charley; I taught him, for instance, all I knew about jazz, which was a lot, and we shared our record collections; then in 1950 we bought the MG, a model TD in bright red with an Abarth muffler, Weber carburetors, the standard equipment. The following spring (1951) was the time of Charley's accident, or perhaps I should say the MG's, since Charley survived it without injury (thanks to the roll bar and safety belt), while the car was sold for parts to Kurt Bergomann for $300. In all this Alex played no active role, of course, and so far as the racing went not even a passive one; but she was there, we were friends, we had respect for one another's capacities. . . .

That summer—our momentous summer, 1951—Charley decided at last that he was a sufficiently "well oriented American"—his term, picked up no doubt from Cienkiewycz—to apply for natural-

165

ization. Often in the evening he came to my flat with a few records, and after we had listened to them and discussed them, we primed for the examination: names and dates of presidents, Declaration of Independence, Constitution, wars, battles, voting procedures, names of contemporary federal and local incumbents, the whole rigmarole. Charley was tough, on himself and on me—he asked the goddamnedest questions I've heard from anyone, and sent me to a good many steamy hours in the pages of the *World Almanac* and the *Encyclopaedia Britannica*. He was determined to have it all cold—the whole business—from Peter Minuit to Harry Truman. It was absurd, the judge wouldn't be interested, the examination was a simple matter of one or two questions; but when I remonstrated with Charley, I got the impression that nothing mattered in the world but his own self-knowledge, when he stood before the court and took the oath, that he was a thorough American, which for him meant primarily a "well informed" American. There were no drafting school classes in summer, and through June, July, and August Charley beat the books, memorizing everything—at night in the hot flat, during weekends on the porch of the cottage at Lake Jones. He was a demon. And he was scared stiff by the time the day of his examination arrived.

Which was today. So I remembered, with a start, as I leaned forward on the sofa to scratch a particular spot on the small of my back. And then—the party for Clambert Fillermine. Lord, Lord —a hot day and too much to do. Why not climb in the car and go away to the green fields of Wisconsin and sleep in the shade of a. . . . I got up and went into the bathroom, where Alex was still moving around in the shower, making athletic noises. I looked at myself in the mirror.

Same old mug. A mug's mug. "Mug, mug, mug. . . ." "What?" Alex said. "Nothing." Black hair growing on a bulbous skull like old cobwebs on a battle helm in the cellar of a museum; a beard like iron filings; hooked beak; evil eyes, hemirimmed in white, with bruised flesh gangrening underneath. The face no one could love. She didn't love it, I was confident of that; but it held her, she was, for the time being, addicted to it, and she would never, never forget it, I was equally confident of that. . . . Obviously I had a hangover. I'd forgotten it, and was glad to be reminded—it's the

166

sort of thing a man shouldn't put too easily out of his mind. I went to the icebox and got a cold can of beer, with the moisture beaded on its rouged and polished face like sweat on the face of a corpse. I opened it and took it back to the bathroom and sat on the john and drank it. The coldness and bitterness were delicious; they sat in my stomach like money in a bank. Alex was humming the theme from the slow movement of the fourth Brandenberg Concerto, but interrupted herself.

"What are you doing?" she asked, raising her voice above the noise of the shower. Steam was billowing from the curtain, fogging the mirror.

"I'm having a beer."

"Give me a swig." A dripping hand and arm wound through the opening in the curtain, a thick stem of orchid winding through the humid rain forest. I gave it the beer can; it receded and after a minute reappeared. "You haven't forgotten Charley's naturalization?"

"No," I said.

"What's the schedule? Do we still have to go to that party for what's-his-name—the English poet?"

"Yes. No way to escape it, at least for me. You going to the courtroom with Charley?"

"Of course."

"What time?"

"Ceremony's at three."

"Then you and Charley can come to the party afterwards. You'll probably get there about four. We can duck the party at five or five-thirty, I think. . . ."

"What about dinner?"

"You two are eating alone, aren't you?" I assumed Charley would insist on that at least.

"He wants you to help celebrate. Says it's your doing as much as his."

"That's ridiculous. But I don't mind helping—naturally. Where shall we go?"

"Charley wants to go to De Jongh's for the snails. Then afterwards we're supposed to pick up the rest of the crowd at Christy's."

"I see. What about lunch?"

167

"Can't."

"Why the hell not?" I'd been counting on it.

"Date."

"Date! Who the hell with?"

"Don't be so huffy, you're supposed to be calmed down now. Why don't you take a shower?"

"I will if you ever get out of there. Who's your date with?"

The shower stopped running. The orchid reappeared. "Give me a towel," Alex commanded.

I did so, and in the silence which followed I set the empty beer can on the tiled floor with a little clink. In a moment Alex, bright red and with the towel draped like a wimple over her head and shoulders, groped her way through the shower curtain. A cuculate lobster.

"Who's your date with?" I asked again.

"Go on, take your shower, for God's sake."

She began rubbing herself some more. I climbed in and turned on the water, and soon I heard the bathroom door open, then the icebox door. I stood under the hot water, face turned up, thinking about my bones. Not a jealous bone in my body, not a jealous bone in my—just old bones, bones for the bone picker, fossils, pickled bones, alcoholized, limp rubbery bones, smelly bones, but . . . coming alive in the warmth, diluvial warmth, equatorial, Jurassic; coelacanth lifting bleared eyes through the warm slime. Dissolution and resolution. *Ecce homo!* Not a jealous bone in my body. . . .

"Who the bloody ignominious hell is your date with?" Alex was sitting on the bed, eating herring from a jar, when I came out of the bathroom.

She smiled and chomped a morsel, and patted the bed beside her to indicate I should sit down; which I did. She swallowed, and put the jar on the night table and stuck the fork in it, and kissed me—cheekbone, nose, lips, throat, lips again. I put my hand along her chin and kissed her well.

"You stink of fish," I said.

"You forgot to shave."

She put her arms very closely around my neck and shoulders, and we fell back, her thigh slipping between mine.

168

"Insatiable," I said.

"Yes."

As luck would have it, I was moderately insatiable myself that morning. . . .

Afterward she went back to her flat to dress; and I shaved quickly and dressed myself quickly, thinking I might finish before she did. But when I entered Charley's living room—once in it I always knew it was Charley's, not hers—she was sorting things into her purse while she sat, dressed and ready to leave, on the arm of the sofa. She snapped the handbag shut, looked at herself quickly in the long mirror that hung on one wall, twitched her hips and smoothed her skirt. She made a kissing motion with her mouth toward me and opened the door.

"Who's your date with?"

"Friend of Dinkoe's."

"What's his name?"

She shut the door, and her footsteps hurried down the corridor, shump-shomp-shump on the carpet, through the outer door, clup-clup on the bare wood, down the stairs, tunchy-tunchy-tunchy on the stair carpet, one flight, turn the corner, second flight, ten steps on the bare wood of the second story, third flight, turn the corner, fourth flight more faintly, clickety-clickety on the vestibule's distant marble. . . . The house door squealed and the latch burped . . . clackety-clack on the brick steps . . . was it she?—or another noise in the house. . . . She was gone.

I looked around Charley's living room, so familiar. The big threadbare secondhand sofa, gift of a friend. The new armchair upholstered in broad shiny stripes, crimson and beige—Charley had chosen that, unaware of the vulgarity. Dear Charley. There were his books, the shelf of uniform bindings in sedate blue—the American Treasury—Charley's treasury, so well beloved. . . . Damn Charley!

Damn me, damn my rotten jealous greedy insatiable soul!

Damn Alex. . . .

CHAPTER 32

February now. We had our midwinter thaw last month. The snow is old: yellow and tabid. In the meadow the southern slope bares its moss, russet and gray, shifting like sea colors as the clouds pass over; and in the forest by the brook the willows are as yellow as parsnip flower, by the pond the alder stems are reddening. People here say we shall have more snow before long, blizzards and fierce Canadian winds perhaps, and it's true the winter has not ended—yesterday I broke a hemlock branch but no sap flowed. The sun is warm though, the brook is full. The forest has a faint musical sound—unidentifiable. The seasons interfuse; in winter the thin ice on the brook blossoms like ferns, in summer the bluejays cry of a barren land. And only a week or two ago I saw a milkweed pod that had filled last August on the roadbank split and loose its feathered seeds; the wind whirled them across the snow and into the dark frozen woods, life dancing in the domain of death. It is all mixed together.

I have been working hard. Very hard, in fact. I must finish this. But if three pages a day are done, I fall into exhausted stupor, so obdurately do these old memories resist my shepherding: I must whip them, lash them, herd them with dog and stone—until I am lame, bleeding. I thought physical labor would refresh me, and went into the woods to cut fuel for the fire; and I found many aged pines carrying a weight of dead branches, which I have been trimming away, carefully, neatly, so that the trees are handsome again and grateful. I carry the sticks and logs on my back, a heavy load. It drives my knees through my shins. I walk the last hundred

170

yards to the cottage on bruised stumps through the snow. I fling down the logs and my legs vanish, and when Linda comes to sit on my lap she sinks through to the chair. Madness—such sensations of the unwilled, unwilling flesh. My body is insane. . . .

Linda's is rational, I should say. At any rate it vomits every morning after breakfast, which is the only sane response to our diet of bread fried in salt pork, morning sickness or no. My money has gone, nearly all of it; and still so much remains to be done. But I get plenty of milk for her to drink from Harley Marion, the dairyman, who is one of the few people here that were kind to Linda in former days. I told him I couldn't pay him. "Forget it," he said. "It ain't no hardship on the cow, what *she* drinks," and he nodded his head toward Linda. All he asks is to be permitted to see what I've written. Each Tuesday, Thursday, and Saturday he stops with four quarts of milk, and then sits at the table in the kitchen to read the new installment. "That Alex," he says, "she's a topper now, ain't she?" And he gets up and winks at Linda and pats her belly—no offense, none whatever—and goes out the door shaking his head. Linda won't drink the milk, though. It's a good day when I've persuaded her to take two glasses; one is usually all she can manage. I've tried everything—cajolery, lovemaking, even anger—but that, of course, didn't help, she only cried harder than ever. I make soup, potatoes and cabbage boiled in frankfurter juice, and she likes that the best, though I suspect it isn't so much a question of liking as a desire to show she is happy to have me make soup for her. She takes the vitamin pills I bought for her, eight dollars a bottle.

Next Wednesday is Saint Valentine's Day, and I've been wondering what to give Linda for a Valentine; but I don't know whether or not she understands. How can I explain? We can say love and sex and hunger and hot and cold and I-have-to-go-to-the-toilet and look-at-the-pretty-bird and—many things. But saint? Saint's day? Celebration? It's hard to tell if she understands such things. Perhaps it is better not to give her anything, though I am deeply in need of giving. . . . Perhaps, on the other hand, she does know about Valentine's Day, and will be disappointed if she receives nothing; perhaps she learned of it in childhood. I don't know. I don't know what I could give her anyway, what could

171

possibly arouse her interest at this point. Even her bells are neglected. I have tried hard. One of the reasons the money is gone is that I bought art books for her, expensive books that cost twenty dollars at the bookstore in Salisbury; and for a while she looked at them, turning the pages slowly, backward and forward, her long thin hair falling over the pictures. But I wasn't careful enough. One of the books contained a dozen or so reproductions of Goya's cartoons. You can imagine the result.

She is the only woman I have known whose weeping does not exasperate me.

If some of the people I have been writing about could see what I am writing here they would say I am driven by guilt for having made Linda pregnant. Oh, I remember well that hard tone of voice, the smart voice, the city voice. But it is not true, I swear it. Linda's child will be my child—my sanity! She is creating it. I am doing my best to create her, I swear it.

When I write she stays in the kitchen, looking out the window at the chickadees and tree sparrows. When I am in the woods . . . I don't know what she does then, of course. Often when I come home she is pouring the coffee. She must watch for me all the time I am away, because she cannot hear me coming.

Guilt? That is absurd. There is no guilt in the world now, or else so much that it can no longer be felt. Only pity is real. Pity and this infinitely tender love.

CHAPTER 33

In the woods I sometimes encounter Alfred, who comes there to chop sticks for his fireplace also. Alfred keeps a workshop; he makes colonial weather vanes—copper roosters, horses, and fishes, which he sells in summer to the tourists who come to visit the Berkshires, a profitable trade. But it is more than a business with Alfred, who is an artist; he is dedicated to the perfection of his weather vanes, aware of his role in society. No two weather vanes are exactly alike, he says, and he takes great care in weathering them, aging them; indeed, he has sixty-five weathering now in the field behind his house, under the snow. "You'd be surprised," he says, "how quickly the patina grows." Yes, Alfred is an artist, and like all artists he makes a creative use of fakery. He does not precisely tell his clients that the weather vanes are genuine colonial antiques, but neither does he tell them that they are not. He is silent on the matter, as an artist should be. One cannot give away one's secrets.

Alfred worries a good deal about his relationship to the world. "The television," he says, "all those news reports—terrible, terrible. Makes a man feel kind of lost, doesn't it?—out of everything. What good are weather vanes now, with so much suffering and fear everywhere?" We rest from our labors, sitting side by side on a fallen birch with our axes, like hieroglyphic birds, perched where the blades have been driven into the log. But Alfred says he would go nuts working in a factory or an office—"crazy as a coot," he says. Hence he doesn't know what to do.

Momentous, indeterminate speculations. "It's a problem, all

right," I say to Alfred. But mostly I keep my thoughts to myself, like a proper middle-aged man. I think: the nation, by which our ancestors meant the cumulative historical ethos, has given way to mass civilization, and the characteristic features of the tradition have ceased to be decisive forces. They survive—in the library, the classroom, the studio, safely hermeticized. What good is that? And I am not thinking now of Athens or Florence or the scalds, or of anything particularly grand; I have given that up. I am thinking instead of the homelier, nearer earth: of Ethan Allen and Lyman Beecher and Trumbull, Winthrop, Brewster, Alcock, Brainerd, Bulkeley, Stiles, Allyn—of all the voices unheard, unwanted, unremembered. The dead are a mixed lot. Some had the vision of humanity, though. . . . Library, classroom, studio: necropolis. Today poets live there, but of their own accord, and so that's all right—perhaps. But what about Charley, the plain man caught up in the vision of humanity, the irregular survivor? How ground down he is between the mass of unguided desire and the mass of inalterable history! I do not wish anyone to think that there is an implied morality in what I am writing. Remember, I am hopeless, because I know enough of history to rejoice in my incompetence. All I am suggesting is that after a long time—half a century? a century? two? two and a half?—of falsely arrogated sensibility, the artist must now surrender his title as *homme d'esprit* if he is to save his self-respect at all. It belongs to Charley. . . .

I dream about Alfred often, always the same dream, though in various disguises. Once he was cutting a slender beech sapling with a huge ornate axe, a battle-axe, but he made a bad job of it and the sap gushed from the wound and spilled over the rocks like a cataract of champagne. Another time he was sitting in his field, surrounded by his copper roosters and horses and fishes, all milling around peacefully like good domestic animals; and he was flinging some sort of feed to them from a bucket he held between his knees—it looked as if he were throwing out scraps of bloody flesh, but the animals gobbled it up before I could see properly. Alfred winked at me and said: "It's all right, I've made *sure* the meat is poisoned this time."

CHAPTER 34

A few minutes later, when I myself was clonking down the brick steps disgruntedly, it occurred to me I might have taken the opportunity in Charley's living room to look for his gun and see if there were any shells lying around. I still could have gone back, pretending, for the sake of any onlookers, that I had forgotten a book in my own flat; but I didn't. The hell with it, I said to myself.

I found the car a block down Woodlawn, where I'd left it the night before, climbed in, methodically rammed the car in front and the one behind to make room—a technique all good Chicagoans must learn sooner or later—and pulled out and headed down Woodlawn toward the 39th Street entrance to the Drive. Filth everywhere. Newspapers flopping in the street like decapitated chickens. Graystone and yellow brick housefronts decaying, peeling, scaling: the caries of urban blight. Shopwindows grimed with soot, cobwebs, grit; signs broken and hanging askew from their brackets; old placards drooping; scatologia and brutality crayoned densely on every wall. At 37th and Lake Park Avenue the intersection formed a triangular island, which held a statue of some meat-packer—he ought to have been astride a rampant pig and waving a cleaver, but he wasn't, he stood there with his hand on his belly like Yeats visiting the schoolchildren. Newspapers embraced his ankles—the dirty present pleading with the gross and nefarious past. A wrought-iron fence enclosed the tableau, leaking rust. Do not think I exaggerate; Chicago is a city in which the corruption is exceeded only by the misery, corruption so deeply embedded in the whole organism that the occasional infusions of rationality at the top never purge the

175

rottenness from the bowels, the heart, the million limbs. Over it all, that day, hung the whitish sky like a winding sheet; but the city had been imperfectly mummified: it was still alive, stirring greasily in its cerecloth.

I shifted down satisfactorily, double-clutching, and ground the old Chevvy in first around the big turn of the ramp; silly perhaps, in such a car, but I always liked to get the most out of her. The lake heaved restlessly and oilily at the stone barrier, lipping over occasionally like an enormous vulva. The color was citrine; on the horizon the water department's red brick pumping station smeared the haze like a swatted mosquito. I pushed the Chevvy into a slot in the traffic and headed downtown. Damn fool, damn fool, damn fool, I said to myself. I wished I had gone back to look for that gun.

I was hungry. Hunger, I've discovered, is the worst thing in the world for nerves. I looked at my watch: twelve-fifteen—with luck I'd reach the office before Paula and Rollo went to lunch, in which case I could go with them. Of course, everyone would be in a dither over Fillermine today, Lord knows how the schedule might be upset. I goosed the Chevvy a bit anyway, and bent toward the inner lane, easing forward cleanly between the white stripes. Damn fool, damn fool. I couldn't convince myself of the soundness of Alex's complacency, not in my bones, where it counts, nor in my fidgety heart; but at the same time I knew my fear was more a function of my shame than of the objective circumstances. A fool doubly damned. In my mirror I saw a cop crossing lanes about seven cars back, a black and white car like a skunk—you couldn't miss him. I let the accelerator ease off, glanced at the speedometer, then pushed on past a matronly Oldsmobile that was riding the white line. Moreover, it wasn't the thought of an unexpected shot in the back that disturbed me . . . at least I didn't think it was, though to tell the plain truth I couldn't decide from one minute to the next whether I was afraid of Charley's gun or not; a question of wavering, coming up close to the fear and then being so fearful of the fear itself that I backed off again into courage. Doubly, triply damned. . . . But there couldn't be the slightest doubt that I was afraid of Charley's wrath, of his discovery—without knowing precisely what form it would take. Simply being *known* by Charley as

176

the man who was sleeping with his wife, that was the sword which hung over my head. Involuntarily I looked at the ceiling of the Chevvy. Nothing there but the stained plush. I lit a cigarette; the smoke plummeted through my guts like a bubble of vitriol, and I gagged slightly, sucking my navel in close to my spine. I looked at the cigarette—god-awful tack! But I swallowed my repugnance and took another deep drag, and my hunger abated somewhat. Clearly my attitude toward Charley was still love of the boy . . . man, I should say. No other explanation could lie at the base of my fear and self-loathing than the extreme reluctance to give pain to Charley. This was what shook my voice like a housewife shaking a dust mop whenever I spoke to Charley now, this was what made my hand tremble when he came into my presence. And yet . . . and yet every morning I awoke in knots of anxiety and expectation, thinking of the minute when I should hear Charley's footsteps scuffle down the corridor, down the stairs—eight-seventeen or eight-eighteen usually—because then the way would be clear for Alex to come to me. And on Saturday and Sunday mornings, when Charley didn't work, she couldn't come, I was ill with hatred. On the mornings when she chose to go back to sleep instead of coming to me, I burst in on her, raging like a wounded boar. I took her in her own bed. Charley's bed! And every moment of it, kissing her, touching her, climbing between her feet, I knew that what she gave me was not worth the sacrifice of even a scrap of Charley's love. What she gave me—nothing! Except the possession for an hour of that hot, pulsing, magnificent flesh. Oh, Alex, were we given sex for the sake of bondage to the likes of you?

Do not misconstrue me, I wouldn't have been in such a fix at all, probably, if I hadn't cherished sex, or some idealized view of it. Look at my poetry. It's all there. But adultery? Rationalize it any way you like, you can't make it natural: not in our society, not in our time. And by "our society" I mean roughly the whole historical complex issuing from the marriage of Abraham and Sarah. Was there ever an adulterous love in this swatch of human history that was—merely comfortable? Could the adulterous man and woman ever look at each other with untroubled eyes? What happened to Abraham and the Egyptian bondwoman? But of course no one knows what happened to the bondwoman; probably nothing,

177

probably she looked straight into Sarah's eyes the next morning. Because the women are unperturbed, only the men suffer agony. How could I not know it, with Alex always in my mind, her slow gaze burning me without a trace of remorse? *And she loved Charley!* Make no mistake about that, she was the one who may have loved him the most of all. . . . It wasn't that Alex organized all life to suit her own bodily and temperamental desires. She was one of the world's few human beings who can say to themselves that they cannot organize life at all, not one little patch of it, not even the atom of it lodged in their own skulls. She acknowledged this freely, willingly; and then took—no, permitted—whatever came along. God, what a creature!

Not a man in the world could do it.

The Chevvy's tires sang on the metal openwork of the bridge, then hummed down the hill. I took the left lane for the left turn at Grand Avenue, but as usual I had to wait for the green arrow. Then the Inner Drive to Huron Street, and one block west to the parking lot. When I reached the office, the time was twelve-thirty-five and I had to use my key to get in. From habit, I looked at the wire basket of unread manuscripts, and saw that it was stuffed; it was always stuffed; this time, in fact, the stacked envelopes had spilled over onto the wrapping table, where a couple of dozen of them were soaking up the water from the upset sponge dish. Great, I thought, just fine—nobody's taken a manuscript out of that basket for a week. And immediately was plunged into one of my perennial moral dilemmas. Paula and I were the only paid members of the staff, and she was secretary-office manager-receptionist-filing clerk-subscription clerk-check writer-inventory clerk, while I was editor-production manager-advertising manager-circulation manager-publicity director. Reading unsolicited manuscripts wasn't her job, and I didn't have time for it; the volunteers were supposed to do it. And how can you admonish volunteers if they don't keep up to scratch? Instead you must thank them for volunteering in the first place and hope like the devil they don't poop out on you altogether. But if they volunteer for a job they damn well ought to *do* the job, shouldn't they? At the same time, they are human beings, and it just isn't human nature to. . . . You see what I mean. I grabbed thirty or forty envelopes in my fist and started toward

178

the back room, where my desk was. On the way, the middle dozen squirted out—like pumpkin seeds—and then the whole stack sprayed onto the floor. Sweet Jesus, blast these manuscripts! Blast the idiots who wrote them! On my hands and knees in the dust of thirty years, I collected the manuscripts. Vile, vile! At my desk I opened my briefcase and rammed the manuscripts inside. "I'll take them home tonight," I said aloud.

In the bottom drawer of the second filing cabinet next to Paula's big desk in the front room, I found the bottle of Imperial and put about two ounces in a water glass. I lit a cigarette, and then walked around the office as I drank and smoked. It wasn't often I had a chance to be there alone. I loved that office. I loved the job, the only job I've ever loved, and gave myself to it heart and soul; and in turn the job gave me as much as a man can hope to get from work. Not in money, Lord knows, since the salary was very small. But I was the youngest editor ever to have charge of *Pegasus*, perhaps one of the youngest men ever to edit any literary magazine as important as *Pegasus*. I don't mean to be conceited; I got the job through a fluke, at about the time of my divorce—it saved me from the wildness that was close beside me then. I was proud of my job, but at heart very humble too. Now I walked back and forth in the three rooms, savoring the dust and dirt—literary dirt that was so much more palatable than the city dirt outside— warming myself in the heat that seemed to be generated in the files of back copies stacked high along the walls. Many famous poems and essays were in those old magazines, much heat had gone into them, and a little of it remained there still—so it seemed to me.

You can tell by the old-fashioned name—if you don't know already—that *Pegasus* was an old magazine, and by all the laws of literary evolution it should have either folded or gone moribund years ago. It was founded in 1897, back in the days of Moody and the Vagabond. But it hadn't gone dead. On the contrary, when the "new poetry" came along before the First World War, *Pegasus* had the sense to side with Pound and Eliot and Fletcher and the rest, and it had been a chief organ of the *avant-garde* ever since. There had been some depressed periods, all right; damned depressed; and damned depressing when you go through the old files—the spark

179

had burned low for quite a while. But then things picked up again, and under my editorship *Pegasus* seemed to be flourishing. Not that I can take much credit. It was simply a matter of knowing whom to write to for contributions, and I was not bashful about asking. In 1948 there was still more good material lying around than magazines in which it could be published, and I had been snooping long enough to know who had the good stuff. It came to me, I published it, I fired up a few controversies with my own editorials—shameful, stupid trash, I now know, but at least opinionated enough to catch people's attention. That was enough, that got the mechanism started; and by 1951 things were running smoothly; all I had to do was keep on top of the incoming manuscripts, deal with the printers, advertisers, distributors, etc., and worry about money. Not that that wasn't work enough.

The office comprised three rooms on the ground floor of a small stone building on Huron Street east of Michigan Avenue, a neighborhood of somewhat arty shops, somewhat arty people, somewhat arty saloons—all far too somewhatty to be taken seriously. Indeed, one of the saloons was owned and managed by a retired officer of the Syndicate, as respectable a fellow as you'd care to meet. Chicago lacked a genuine Bohemia; there was the slumland of junkies and grifters on North State around Division Street and Bughouse Square, the domain of Nelson Algren, and there was a little dilapidated island of painters and jazz novelists on the South Side near the east end of 57th Street, sustained by memories of Lorado Taft and Frank Teschemacher; but neither of these could claim the depth of internecine intellectualism that makes a true Bohemia useful to the artist or the community at large. As for the university, it was a fake Gothic enclave where in battlemented towers old and young graybeards, sealed away from the grime of the city, puzzled out the hard fate of Gil Morrice or the precise executive relationships between the chairman of the Atomic Energy Commission and the Cabinet. Nothing the matter with that, I suppose. And of course there was that infamous squash court under the university stadium where the first controlled nuclear chain reaction was set off. . . . A queer-looking place though, the university. Somebody once told me that Thorstein Veblen, when he was teaching there, was observed one afternoon ducking curiously this way

180

and that as he walked across one of the quadrangles, and at the same time squinting timorously upward. When asked what he was doing, he replied: "It's those goddamn crossbowmen up there. Man, look out!"—and he pointed toward the crenelations on the surrounding roofs. Another time he spent a delighted hour walking around behind a party of workmen who were, under orders from higher up, sowing grass seed in the cracks of the flagged walks. Passersby noticed that he was smiling broadly—a rarity—and rubbing his hands.

What Professor Veblen said, or would have said, about *Pegasus*, I can't be sure, of course, but he might have held that it was another case of growing grass on sidewalks. At any rate, a lot of money had been pumped into the magazine over the decades, and nothing equally negotiable had ever been known to come out. It was a continual chore to raise funds, a disagreeable chore. Part of my editorial duty was writing hundreds of requests for help: letters to rich men or, more commonly, their wives; to foundations; to institutions of any kind that might conceivably put up a few thousand dollars; and regularly I traveled east and west in search of money. Almost all this activity was futile, and *Pegasus* continued to be fed, as he had been from the start, chiefly by handouts from local patronesses, the society matrons of Chicago who could be bullied or cajoled into subscribing five hundred or a thousand dollars a year to the cause of the city's cultural prestige. This was accomplished by means of an indirect suggestion that their own prestige—social prestige—would ultimately be served, something far beyond my capacities; it was Rollo's province.

We couldn't have been luckier. Rollo presented the exterior of a perfect con man, the type whom everyone can recognize but whom rich middle-aged ladies can never deny. Handsome, perennially forty-nine years old, with a trim rufous mustache; no observable wife; a trifle less than middling tall; in other words, sexy, gallant, polished, a suggestion of the military, yet still compliant, submissive, subjugable. Irresistible. Remember, I said this was the appearance. Rollo could turn it on and off like a neon sign. Actually, he had a wife to whom he was devoted, an unfortunate slip of a girl who was more or less permanently confined to a sanitarium, and he was an unhappy, good-humored, hard-drinking man

181

like the rest of us—except that he was well off. Not rich; but he had made enough in the grain elevator business in Iowa to set himself up comfortably for the rest of his life. He could have been rich, we were all convinced, if he had wanted to be. He was a characteristic figure of our time—the superb businessman who hates business. He had quit when he had enough, and had become the magazine's staunchest volunteer. He managed our finances and our ladies; without him—especially as printing and paper costs began to rise sharply after the war—we would have folded quickly, there can be no doubt whatever of that, and I wish he could have a paragraph or at least a footnote in some literary history of the future; he deserves it a lot more than the punk poets and prissy short-story writers who will be there in his place. In his fund-raising capacity, Rollo's trick was simply to see that the ladies had three or four good parties a year, and to make sure that the *Tribune's* society photographers were in attendance. The blowout for Fillermine was one of them; and the astonishing part of it was that *Pegasus* didn't put up a cent—the Blackstone's ballroom, the liquor, the decorations, the engraved invitations, the whole damn shebang came . . . I'm damned if I know where they came from, out of thin air maybe, or more likely out of the ladies' own pockets: they had their party and paid for it too. It was Rollo's doing. The middle room of our office had been assigned to him, and there at his desk, which was set in the darkest corner of the room, facing the wall, Rollo brooded and hatched and brooded, reading unsolicited manuscripts betweentimes by the light of a desk lamp with a blue fluorescent bulb. His taste was good and I trusted him to help me get through the burden of mail, though he tended to go overboard for poems in the manner of Elinor Wylie. By accident I discovered one night the reason for this; I was at his house, having a few drinks, and when I went to look for the john I opened the wrong door and found myself in his bedroom, where I saw a photograph of his wife on a large bedside table that was loaded with books. The resemblance to Mrs. Wylie was extraordinary, filmy veil and all.

I sat down at Rollo's desk and pressed the button on the fluorescent lamp: the curious cold blue light flooded down on the blotter. I looked up, but my eyes were forced down again by the dark walls, the dark filing cabinets, the dark shelves of letter boxes

182

which surrounded the desk; I felt as if I were in a cockpit—or a womb. At that desk attention could not stray from the ovum; here Rollo bent over his conceptions in concentrated oblivion—the lonely lovemaking of work. For the first time I felt the whole force of his misery. It smoldered like a deep, dying ash in that pit.

More than ten years have passed since that time, yet I remember Rollo well; more clearly, in fact, than others who were closer friends. And I remember him particularly in a scene which was wholly a vision of my imagination, though for that reason perhaps truer than the rest: Rollo as a man of twenty-five, in his vest and shirtsleeves, his white collar and cuffs well starched, his gold watch chain hanging loose from his vest, sitting by a country stream in Iowa on an afternoon in spring, reading the poems of Elinor Wylie to his beautiful, frail young wife.

With a certain reluctance, I switched off the lamp then, got up and walked into the inner room, which was my own workplace. I stood with my whiskey in one hand, the cigarette in the other, and surveyed my domain. It was less tidy than Rollo's, less intense. The view was broader, the desk more cluttered, the table where I "made up" each issue of the magazine was littered with strips of paper left over from cutting and pasting the proofs. A portable-typewriter case hung lopsidedly from the hatrack, letters and envelopes lay heaped on top of the filing cabinets where they had been waiting, perhaps for years, to be filed, the photographs on the walls hung askew and were thickly filmed with dust: one was a picture of the Revered Founder sitting on a wicker settee with Rabindranath Tagore, who was wearing a white robe; another showed Yeats seated at the big desk in the front room, his white hair tousled, his expression uncharacteristically joyful—I used to wonder if he hadn't been hoisting a few before the photograph was taken. My desk was littered with papers; the address file was open, and stamps were spilling from the Chinese box that I kept them in. I had no inclination to sit down, not with my nerves jumping and too many complexities on my mind. Yet the scene—certainly there was enough detail, even in the little space, to qualify as a scene, and much of it seemed to be growing naturally, as in a landscape—the scene was a soothing one for me, and I imagine it would be for most writers. I remember a photograph of "Thomas Mann at Work," which showed the author in a starched collar and tie, smoking a huge cigar, sitting at a carved mahogany desk as big as the President's, staring at a pile of manuscript; perhaps he actually worked in such quarters, I don't know, and very likely there are writers, the Hollywood sort, who work in offices with bleached modern furniture, cocktail tables of inlaid tile, glass walls, etc. But most writers form an image of the writer's workroom early in life, a place of clutter and dust and comfortable broken furniture, conveying at the same time an impression of hard work and an aura of sanctity. Few writers ever find such a place; but I had found mine, and it shed an additional numinosity for having been occupied by several famous poets before me. It isn't simply fantasy-making to say that I felt their presence, because I did; not in any cheaply psychical sense, but as if the good work they had done here had imbued the objects of the room with the power of inducing further good work. A lucky feeling—and no doubt all nonsense. Still, I don't think any young artist should be denied, or should deny himself, the far from insubstantial reassurance which comes from communion with his predecessors in the special places that evoke their characteristic power and goodness.

I wandered back to the front room, a bigger room than the others. Paula kept it reasonably presentable, but it was a place of work and looked it. There were wrappings on the floor, the sponge dish for moistening stamps had, as I said, spilled over, the magazine rack which held exchanges needed rearranging. Paula's desk was huge, about six feet long, with a slatted top that rolled up and down between little tracks at either end. There were dozens of pigeonholes, all stuffed. Her typewriter was a big new Remington, the best in the office, and she had two telephones and a buzzer on a small table at one end of the desk. Her chair was a tall-backed swivel chair; and both the chair and the desk had originally been the divan (in the older sense) of the Revered Founder. . . . There's no point in sentimentalizing Paula. She knew where everything was, she knew how to make reapplications for second-class mailing privileges, she understood the copyright law, she kept the books, mailed out proof, and remembered the names of all the poets in the world and their addresses and the names of their current mistresses and *their* addresses. Not a single small business office

184

anywhere could function for a quarter of an hour without such a person to supervise it, and since there are hundreds of thousands of such offices, there must be hundreds of thousands of such persons —devoted, intelligent, hardworking. Paula had been a drama student and actress, but had abandoned her hopes when she discovered she was far too nervous ever to succeed as a performer. She was saddened by this, no doubt; but at the same time so relieved to have escaped her stage fright that she was quite happy in her role as head stable hand for *Pegasus*. In addition, she was a joy to the rest of us: cheerful, quick-witted, shy, pretty—she would have been quite lovely if she hadn't always had lipstick on her teeth and cigarette ashes on her blouse.

I sat down in Paula's chair and tried to imagine what it would be like to be her. This is an exercise which I suspect most men attempt from time to time. I never get far with it myself: just to the point of thinking what a ghastly discomfort it must be to have breasts that bump up against the edges of everything. I didn't try to force matters that day; but gave up quickly, finished my drink, took the glass back to the seaweedy washbasin in the middle room, and departed, glancing with my usual pang of pride at the out-to-lunch sign on the door which hadn't been moved, so far as I knew, once in the past six years. Paula and Rollo had probably gone to the Domino Club for lunch, and I walked south on a street whose name I've forgotten (parallel to Michigan, one block east) two blocks, and entered the dark barroom. Paula and Rollo were sitting in a booth at the back, and I sat down next to Paula. There was nothing on the table except an ashtray.

"Hello. We wondered where you were," Paula said. "We've been over at Schreiber's getting some last-minute things."

"Last-minute things? I thought you'd gotten everything days ago."

"Forgot the special napkins," Rollo said. "You always forget something."

"Napkins? Doesn't the Blackstone supply . . ."

"It does." Paula adopted a patient, explaining tone. "These are special napkins for Fillermine to sign. You know, autograph. Made out of some kind of paper that will take ink, but they still look like napkins."

185

"For the ladies," Rollo added. "To take home with them."

"What will they think of next?" I said. "Have you ordered?"

"Yes," Rollo said, waving to one of the waitresses. "What'll you have?"

"Martini."

"Do you think you should?" Paula asked. "We decided we wouldn't—today." Her cigarette waggled in her lips as she spoke.

"You mean because of the party? But I feel like hell."

"You look all right," Paula said, squinting at me through her cigarette smoke.

"I look like hell and you know it," I said.

"You always look like hell," she said. "But you look all right."

"I'll still have a Martini." I said it a trifle aggressively and immediately wished I hadn't.

Rollo looked thoughtful. "Maybe we all need one," he suggested, sighing. "We can go easy this afternoon, and God knows there's a lot to get through before things get started. What do you say—it'll give us a new dimension in life?"

"Hell is paved with new dimensions," Paula remarked absently.

The waitress came up and pushed her pneumatoid abdomen against the end of the table. "Hold the steaks," Rollo told her, "and bring us three Martinis."

"Okay," she said. "I figured you'd change your mind." Then to me: "What do you want to eat—same as them?"

"Yes," I said.

Rollo and I lighted cigarettes; Paula squashed hers in the ashtray, and then immediately lighted another. I decided not to say anything about the beer and whiskey I'd already had, especially since they hadn't done any good, but I wondered, as always in such circumstances, whether or not my breath smelled: I sucked hard on my cigarette and blew a fat cloud of smoke into the aisle.

"Where's Fillermine?" I asked.

"Down at the university," Rollo answered. "The English faculty is giving him a lunch."

"Will he show up?"

"Damn well better," Paula said indignantly. Like most people who work on literary magazines, she didn't care much for writers.

"He'll show up," Rollo said judiciously. "Pocksman's got him in tow. Pocksman's reliable."

186

Ralph Pocksman was the university's eighteenth century man, specialist in the pre-Romantics. His book on Blake had been reviewed in *The New York Times* Sunday book section—more or less favorably.

"Yes," I said, "Pocksman will show up all right, you can bet on that. I got a batch of poems from him a couple of weeks ago. He'll come nosing around to find out what I think of them."

"Good," Rollo replied. He eased himself down a notch, sliding his fanny across the polished wooden bench. "You know, I wasn't as confident as I sounded—about Fillermine getting here, I mean. But if Pocksman has got an axe to grind, we're safe. He'll get the guest of honor to the appointed place on time come hell or high water, if I know Pocksman."

"The poems any good?" Paula asked.

I wrinkled my nose.

"Well, for God's sake, don't tell *him* that!" Rollo puffed smoke out of his lips vigorously. "Let him rest easy for today—as a reward for good deeds."

"Okay," I said.

The waitress came back with the Martinis and put one in front of each of us on paper doilies. The glasses were beaded with moisture and little sparkling fragments of ice clung to the rims. We said cheers and each had a sip.

"I must say," Paula said, "the first sip is a blessing. Nectar for the gods."

"Yes, well, I just hope they're not pouring too much of this nectar into old Fillermine right now," Rollo said. "Be a hell of a note if he shows up crocked. He's got to be presentable for the photographers."

"Don't worry," I reassured him. "Fillermine's not much of a boozer now."

"No?" Paula asked. She spilled ashes on the table and swept them onto her skirt with a deft stroke of her palm.

I explained: "The English tradition—or whatever it is. You know, they booze like hell to age forty-three and then suddenly they become public figures with public responsibilities and they quit. I don't mean they quit drinking, they still put it away by the jugful, but they stop showing it."

"Like Churchill," Rollo put in.

"Exactly. His booze must run to hundreds of dollars a year, maybe thousands, but nobody calls him a lush."

"What's he like?" Paula asked.

"Churchill?"

"No, silly. Fillermine."

"Well, you—"

"Never met him," Paula interrupted. "But I've heard he's very handsome."

I pulled on my cigarette and looked across the dimness toward three businessmen in faintly striped suits who had their heads close together. "Yes, he's good-looking," I said. "Fantastically good-looking. Probably the best-looking poet alive."

"He'd have to be to catch five wives," Rollo said.

"Six, isn't it?" I replied.

"The *Tribune* says five."

"Maybe they don't count the one that died," I said.

"Is he married now?" Paula asked.

"No. At least I don't think so. You can't be sure. . . . Anyway, he's good-looking—"

"How?" Paula interrupted.

"Oh, he's tall. Very tall for an Englishman. And he's got a good strong face. And a hell of a lot of hair—wavy hair. Mostly white now, I guess—but that only adds to the effect."

"You know," Rollo said, "what he really looks like is an American, maybe a Texan. Not an Englishman at all."

"That's it," I said. "A real broad-shouldered type. And he dresses like an American too. None of those little dickey-coats, or whatever you call them. Good suits, nice shirts, ties tied with a Windsor knot—the whole business. I tell you, Paula, he'll knock you off your feet."

"Not me," Paula said. She stamped her ballet slippers clumpily under the table. "I only go out with sailors."

"Thought I detected a rolling gait," Rollo muttered.

Paula blushed. "Now look," she said. "You've made me blush. You know I hate it."

"It's very becoming," Rollo said.

"Shows your modest upbringing," I added.

"Modest upbringing my foot! It's a simple neurotic response.

188

If I wanted to get laid by a sailor, why in heaven's name shouldn't I say so?" She blushed again, violently. "Oh . . . oh . . . you see? Just like a sunset, a bloody technicolor *sunset!* Damn." She hid her face in her hands. "Go on saying what you were saying, will you?"

"What I was saying was that Fillermine will probably knock you off your feet."

"Well, that won't do any good, will it? What you want him to do is knock the old *whores* off theirs."

"Exactly," Rollo said. He folded his hands on the table and leaned forward. "Exactly. I'll tell you something. I hadn't intended to say so before, but—well, if this party goes off and if old Fillermine performs as expected, we stand to do better on this than we've ever done on anything."

"Why?" I asked.

But before Rollo could answer, the waitress brought the steaks— our usual one-dollar pieces of flank, surprisingly edible. That's one point in Chicago's favor: the meat is good. Rollo unfolded his hands and leaned back, and we swallowed the remains of our Martinis while the waitress slammed our meal onto the table. We dug in. I remembered, gratefully, how hungry I was.

After only one bite, however, Rollo resumed his subject. "Look. I'm pretty sure, almost dead sure, we've got Mrs. Rheinklugel this time, the old fruit. She's coming, she promised Mrs. Carlow and Mrs. Prunier she'd come with them. I tell you, if we can once get her into a picture with Fillermine, the *Trib* will give it full play— you can count on that. The Rheinklugels are too damned important to neglect. And if that happens, I think I can go around to their place next week and get a fat check. I mean really fat."

"Watch it, Rollo," I said. "You're letting this thing run away with you."

Rollo's voice slumped, along with his shoulders. "Maybe I am. Just because her husband owns three stockyards and two railroads, or something, doesn't mean that—"

"Don't pay any attention to him, Rollo," Paula said. "He got up on the wrong side of somebody's bed this morning. You can do it, I know you can."

Involuntarily I caught my breath and a mouthful of salad entered the wrong pipe: I coughed and gasped. In my choking, pure bio-

189

logical panic seized me, the body fighting for life; but it subsided quickly. "I'm all right," I said.

Paula was pounding my back, and Rollo had half-risen from his bench.

"I'm all right," I said again. I took a sip of water.

Rollo sat down. "You should be more careful," he said. "People choke to death that way."

"It's that rotten salad—"

"Say," Paula interrupted, "there's nothing wrong with the salad, except it tastes awful." She turned to Rollo. "You know when he started choking? When I said something about him sleeping in somebody else's bed."

"Yes," Rollo said unenthusiastically. He wasn't interested in the byplay Paula and I habitually carried on. He was sorry the conversation about the party had been broken off.

Paula said: "Tell us whose bed it was, Mister Editor. Who's the lucky husband whose wife is putting out for the greater glory of Middle-Western literature."

I wasn't enthusiastic about this line of discourse myself. "Nothing like that, Paula," I said. "Just this rotten salad—"

"Salad my kneecap," she said.

"I still think I can get a good contribution out of Mrs. Rhein-klugel. If she shows up," Rollo said.

"Good," I answered quickly. "I didn't mean to be a wet blanket, Rollo. If you think it can be done I'm sure there's a good chance. God knows, we need it."

"Exactly," Rollo said. "It all depends on Fillermine. Whatever you think of his poetry, he's—"

"I think his poetry is damned good," I put in.

"Well, whether it's good or bad, at least he's famous—about the most famous poet we've had passing through here in five or six years. It's a break for us. And he *is* handsome. And charming—at least I guess he is."

"Most people think so," I replied.

"Okay. But is he cooperative? That's the point. Mrs. Rhein-klugel is a fool. Worse than that, she's a damned tedious fool. Not to be confused with our real supporters. Why should Fillermine put up with her? She's nothing to him."

190

"But poetry is. I know, that sounds hopelessly corny. But when you get down to it, this whole business is shot full of corn, even if we do spend half our lives trying to disguise it. And perhaps the corn isn't a bad thing. The point is, Fillermine knows our troubles, if only because he's been connected with half a dozen literary magazines himself, and he knows what we're trying to do to overcome them, because it's the same thing that every little magazine does. And he believes, damn it! He believes in what we're doing, same as we do—otherwise we wouldn't be here and neither would he. He's a good poet. I'm a good poet. Both of us have ways of covering it up, and neither of us especially likes the other, but we both know we're good poets and we both know what we have to do to keep poetry going—it's an obligation we were born with, or at any rate one we accepted a very long time ago. Don't worry, he'll help—all you have to do is say the word to him."

"Will you say it?" Rollo asked. "I've never spoken two words to him. I mean I just talked to him a couple of times on the phone."

"Okay, I'll ask him."

"Good."

"What don't you like about him?" Paula asked.

"His accent."

"Just British, isn't it? What's the matter with it?"

"I don't know. It just doesn't go with him, for one thing. In fact his whole personality doesn't go with him. He looks big and handsome and intelligent and . . . well, American. Strong and likable. Then he opens his mouth and this little crappy accent comes out—"

"What do you mean little crappy accent?" Paula interrupted.

"He talks the way they do at the London School of Economics."

"Horsepiddle! What do you know about the London School of Economics?"

"Nothing."

"You've never even been in London, have you?"

"You know I haven't," I said.

"Well."

The steaks were finished. The waitress brought our coffee, and we put in sugar and cream and stirred, without saying anything.

191

"Tell me what I should do, Rollo," I said, when we had lighted our cigarettes.

"Nothing. Just be there. Be a good host."

"Yes, I know that. But what time? Do you want me to do anything beforehand?"

"No. The invitations said three-thirty. If you're there by four that'll be soon enough."

"All the dirty work has been done by your loyal henchmen," Paula said.

I was quiet a moment. Then I said: "I know. Don't think I don't." I have learned that an unexpectedly heartfelt word from time to time is worth any amount of flattery. "Shall we go?" I said, after another pause—breaking the tension of my candor.

We walked out of the air-conditioned dimness into the heat and glare of the street. By the time we reached the office, all of us were half sick from Martini, cheap steak, and sunstroke.

CHAPTER 35

At my desk, tilted back in the creaky chair, my feet crossed on top of the typewriter, I watched my cigarette smoke rising like a blue vein toward the ceiling: at a certain point the vein writhed and broke, for no apparent reason—not an air current stirred in the little room. Perhaps it broke of its own accord, from the tension of its own slender beauty. Paula was talking on the phone in the front room, but I couldn't distinguish her words. The White Sox-Browns game on the radio in the basement, where a cabinetmaker kept his shop, was perfectly clear, however. The Browns were at bat in the third inning; no score. Rollo was occupied with his silent thoughts in the middle room. I jogged my cigarette a sixteenth of an inch, and watched the tiny spasm climb up the vein of smoke. Why write poems when nature produces these symbols so effort-lessly?—but that was all settled two hundred years ago. Make yourself useful, for God's sake.

I reached for the briefcase, dropping my feet noisily from the typewriter, with the intention of getting out the stack of new manuscripts; but then decided I should have another look at the Pocksman poems first—just in case. I liked Pocksman. He was thirty years old, long-legged and short-waisted, pasty-faced, not very bright, inclined to get somewhat overjoyed at parties; but he was friendly and good-humored and . . . interested. He asked questions, that was his amiability, he listened, he wanted to know—at least more than most of the university people. How did you happen to think of this? he would say, hauling out a copy of the *Nation* and pointing to a line in your latest poem; which (no matter what anyone says) is a damn pleasant thing to happen when you've just published a poem. Yes, yes, he would say, I see, I see, and then, of course, you, etc., etc. Very good for a rainy Saturday afternoon over a few beers at Christy's Mill.

Pocksman's manuscripts were in the Second-Look File. Frankly, this was a hell of a place for any poems to be. Limbo, nothing more or less. The poems which for one reason or another the editor couldn't or shouldn't or wouldn't dispose of immediately went into the Second-Look File, where as likely as not they remained for months. Some poems in there had been filed away by the predecessor of my predecessor—old, creased, smeared sheets that I looked at from time to time with spiritless guilt and then replaced. Lord knows what the poets thought. Maybe they were dead. . . . I reached for the folder in the bottom drawer of my desk. The Pocksman manuscripts were on top where I had put them a week or two before, a dozen gleaming pages of stiff, expensive bond, neatly and blackly typed, pinched together by a bright copper paperclip. The first poem was called "Office Hours":

> *Hoping so much that she is all pencils and*
> *eyeglasses, clinging meekly to my desk:*
> *"I think I understand, sir, I think I . . ."*
> *Hoping so much that she is all incunabula.*
> *And the four corners of my wordy skull burst*
> *like the four winds, professors of compasses.*
> *"Oh, thanks, sir . . . just love your classes . . ."*
> *Hoping that she is all inkstains and that*
> *points-of-breasts won't jut against her blouse.*

And so on, another ten lines; Lord, Lord, if only he wouldn't hit that dead level, that *exact* dead level. Five thousand manuscripts a month come in to us, and four thousand are this poem, the dead sea scrolls—in many shapes, many sizes, various tones and colors perhaps, but this level, damn it!—over and over again. You come to love the people who copy verses off greeting cards and send them in under their own names, they are so blessedly, idiotically fraudulent. What's the matter with Pocksman, couldn't his gray heart *feel* the encounter with this coed? Surely if he had felt it, his feel-

194

ing would have forced some clarity of organization on the poem, some quantum of originality out of his imagination. . . . No, that's wrong. That's the temptation—to say Pocksman didn't respond— but you've got to resist it . . . to the death even. He did, he undoubtedly did, poor old Pocksman, feel it, his timid lust was genuine, and his fear for his wife too. He probably hadn't slept half the night, thinking about that girl's bosom—and the winds, the professorial winds. He had his fingernails on a good thing there, perhaps. But it got away from him, it will always get away from him, forever and forever. Damn Pocksman. Hasn't he ever read anything good, can't he tell? Presumably he's read Blake at least, if he wrote that book about him—but all for nothing, except a scrap of a new theory about the influence of the Epimetheus legend on certain parts of the *Book of Thel*. A question of comparative sensibilities. Pocksman is moved by some of the good things in Blake and he is moved by his own poem, and he cannot tell that one is not of the same quality—no, he wouldn't say quality, he's too modest—but the same order as the other. . . . Professorial winds; a good incongruity. Something might be worked out of that. Fillermine—how would he do it? Something in shocking understatement, you can be sure, with an abstraction or two thrown in, a prosy rhythm and some ironic rhymes. . . .

> The philological patina of her blouse—
> Forgive me, the morning by implication only
> Said in her conic breasts carouse, carouse,
> But the room was damp, and I . . .

Drop it, drop it—even fake Fillermine, even parody, wouldn't be as absurd as that. . . .

> But the room was damp, and I inopportunely
> Coughed—

Drop it! Idiot, that way madness lies—understand? Madness, mind running wild. Yet Fillermine might have done it, might have pulled it off, you never can tell. A word changed here, a cadence there, and you pull a good poem out of a burlesque like a foot pulled out of a

195

sock. Fillermine would know the trick, a word in the first line or two that burgeons reflexively with moral energy when you look back on it, a leer toward the end to show that sex really stands for politics. . . . Oh, well.

I threw the manuscripts down on the desk. Pocksman, at any rate, was no one for such antics: but you couldn't help feeling that at age thirty he ought to have learned to keep his verses at home. Would he become one of the mad inexorable ones? Would my successors be returning unacceptable poems to him ten years from now? Twenty? There were such stalwarts, insane, monomaniacal— I knew their handwriting well, and the individualities of their typewriters. Nothing could daunt them. But Pocksman was a man close to literature, an academic man, perfectly sane, as rational as a textbook. Yes; at forty. But at forty-five, or fifty-five? Insanity begins in a disguise; only at the end of the party, when everyone is drunk and wild, is the mask ripped off and the hideous face revealed. . . . Pocksman had enclosed a large, five-cent Manila envelope, addressed and stamped, with his manuscript, and Paula had slipped it under the copper paper clip at the back of the sheaf. I unclipped it and put the manuscript inside, and licked the flap— an ashy taste on my dry tongue. I got up and took it into the front room and dropped it in the basket for outgoing mail. Pocksman would get it in the morning.

Paula had on a party dress and fresh lipstick; she had been to the ladies' room to change. For the first time I noticed her overnight bag under the wrapping table. She and Rollo were ready to leave. Rollo was irreproachably dressed, as always: a soft shirt, neutral-colored Palm Beach suit, yellow shoes—no, I don't mean yellow, that would leave the wrong impression, but shoes of that curiously elegant color of . . . all I can think of is laundry soap, and why that should be elegant I can't say. A translucent beeswaxy color. Is that any better? Fifty-dollar shoes anyway, you can bet on that, and in perfectly good taste, given Rollo's general appearance and social tone. He said: "We'll go down early—to make certain everything is in order. See you later?"

"Yes," I said.

"No later than four?"

"All right," I said.

"Pocksman?" Paula asked, and nodded toward the out basket.

196

"Yes," I answered, keeping my sigh barely audible.

Paula shrugged elaborately and went out. With his hand on the door, Rollo said: "At least he won't get them till tomorrow." He went out too, closing the door softly behind him.

I went to look at myself in the scurfy mirror over the washstand. How did Rollo contrive it?—to look so unworn. I saw a wrinkled collar, seams of grime and sweat on my face. Eyes like decapitated mice. The mirror with its scaling silver took little patches out of me, as if a wind were blowing through me. A professorial wind. Absurd! . . .

Ethical wind; wind of principia; the bounden wind, calling across the world. Absurd!

As I drove home to change, a new weather plunged across Chicago from the plains, as so often happens in that flat country; a sharp wall of cold. The air flowing in my car window changed abruptly. I looked out over the lake. Different strata of clouds intersected overhead, moving at different speeds, revealing different colors. The wind was long and steady, the waters of the lake wallowed in irregular upheavals, a tethered cormorant struggling to rise into the air. The trees along the Drive bent before the wind.

> The world bird floundering in his wounds
> Writhed on sodden wings, and a low cry
> Rode on the four and fatherly winds
> Across the rising immanence of the world.

More absurdity. Unintelligible pain; injury. At home I let the lukewarm shower drain away my sweat and grime, thinking the water might restore my sense of orientation. The water beat against the shower curtain like wind on a beech forest rattling the leaves. The professorial wind. . . . What I had really been hoping was that Alex would be at home, returned from her luncheon. That was why I had decided to go ten miles for a shower and a clean shirt. But when I had knocked at her door there was no answer. I went in and found no one. I looked in the bottom drawer of Charley's desk. The gun was there all right, black and precise and evil against the papers that lay under it and partly over it. It rested there like a cat on an unmade bed.

But what was I to do? Steal the gun? More absurdity. You can

197

do something to the firing pin so it won't work, I remembered. But I hadn't the least idea what. I closed the drawer and went to my own flat.

In the shower I trembled uncontrollably, and the water crashed against the curtain like a huge wind breaking the windows of a hospital.

When I left the house and climbed in my car, the air was still cool. My skin tightened over my ribs, an icy drop of sweat rolled down from my armpit. Death of cold, death of cold, death of cold, I thought. The trees along the Drive stared at me, crying their identities. My hands on the steering wheel vanished—all feeling gone. Where was I, for God's sake, what had become of me? Person was gone. The lake rose in grotesque shapes, struggling sadly. I was in the lake, gone to a new home. I saw the lampreys, millions and millions of gray-white worms twined in a great squirming mass, a horrible ganglia at the bottom of the world. Mindless, thoughtless. They said the lampreys were destroying all the fish in Lake Michigan, a great disequilibrium in nature, out of control. And now the fish were gone, and the lampreys in their evil were sucking each other, mouths tearing their own flesh, the mass of soundless agony at the bottom of the world. And the lake rose and fell, rose and fell.

> *The spent lovers, pinioned in their evil,*
> *Woke in their mess and the eating chill,*
> *Wallowing, foundering breast to breast,*
> *And North and South and East and West*
> *Up trod the four and fartherly winds,*
> *Their long, uncertain, unsyllabled yell,*
> *A cold birthcry for a new cold world.*

CHAPTER 36

Late February now. We had our blizzard. Snow like heavy cream flows deep everywhere, drifted up to the windowsills, heaped in frothy waves beside the road. And still it snows, the wet and warming aftermath of the storm. The gray, unfriendly sky slavers on us continually, gouts and spittle in a damp wind. Even when the wind is from the northwest, it is damp. A Baltic sort of wind. Geography all bugged up, who knows where anything is? All the same, I go to the forest for my woodcutting, sloshing through the snow in my boots. Do you know the quality of a late snowstorm—? Essence of malevolent nature. Walking now is like marching through a valley of tripe in a country inhabited only by blind, starving canaries. The apple tree is out of sight.

Once in a while I have to get away from Linda's noiseless weeping for an hour.

I bash the dead pines and snow-crippled birches, cursing with every stroke.

From one day to the next my axe grows rust, an orange fur. I could oil the blade, I suppose, but as a matter of fact I have a theory that rust is the axe's self-sharpening mechanism, each night removing the little clefts and nicks that the day's encounters with frozen knots have imposed. Probably nothing in it.

A gentleman by the name of Glenn has circumnavigated the globe three times in five hours by means of some sort of rocket, and is in consequence receiving the congratulations of almost everyone. Why not? I congratulate him too. He has done well. I am the last to suggest that what he set out to do was not worth doing. It would be pointless anyway. The flight was an action precipitated by previous actions, the "course of events," and so there was never any serious question of not doing it. It occurred; it evolved; it—so to speak—grew. The serious question is, on the contrary, is it interesting? Superficially, yes—in the sense that you or I would probably be glad to step into the next room to look at a perpetual motion machine if someone took the trouble to build one there. But beyond that? Hardly, I should think. Can we who are fighting here for our lives in the world of reality take much serious interest in fiction, science fiction at that?

The sky bleats, shedding its dirty wool. . . .

By the way, if any of you were aware of the hiatus between Chapter 25 and Chapter 27, do not be disconcerted. I have cut out Chapter 26. In reading it over a day or two ago, I saw that if I left it in it would give the whole show away.

CHAPTER 37

The Blackstone Hotel on Michigan Avenue, Chicago, is an honorable old stack, presuming honor is an adjunct of any explicitly public aspect of civilization. There are other hotels in town; a good many, in fact, since Chicago has always enjoyed a good business from travelers who had to stop there whether they wanted to or not: a question of the more or less fortuitous itineraries of the transcontinental railroads. Some of these other hotels are prettier than the Blackstone, more modern, more elegant, more expensive. On the other hand, a great many are uglier, older, less expensive, and decidedly less elegant. The Blackstone comes somewhere near the top of the list in these respects, but not at the top itself. Nevertheless, if it is possible to extract an "essence" from the great American hotel myth, then the Blackstone is "essentially" Chicago's most honorable, most venerable hotel. Because for years it has been the gathering place of powerful men. Some of the juiciest deals in the manipulation of American industry—mergers of railroads, for instance—have been cooked up in the Blackstone, I have no doubt; and as for politics, the smoke-filled room, an indispensable element of American folklore, is virtually by definition a Blackstone room— this, I am sure, all politicos (if they have any sentiment for the traditions of their calling) will concede. Chicago is par excellence the city of political conventions. The jet airliner may rob Chicago of its status as the nation's foremost stopping-off place, but nothing will diminish its attraction to the politicos—nothing. The blandishments of Los Angeles, so sordid, so crass, may prevail upon one or the other party from time to time, but you can bet they will always come back to Chicago. Los Angeles is mistaken in its belief that simply because a V-8 bosom over a twin-cam ass, hotly idling, will invariably pack the theater with paying spectators, sex must also be what the politicos are looking for. Far from it. Politicos are the least sexy of mankind; ask their wives; even their mistresses. After all, when you are hunched contentedly in conclave, totting up lists of delegates, rolling your tongue around a succulent fifty-cent Havana *claro*, soothing your ulcers with the larruping twelve-year-old sour-mash Jack Daniels that always appears at convention time, this is just when you do not want the irrelevance of some rutting broad draped on your shoulder. Fact. It is an axiom of all political theory that the center of a woman's brain is her pudendum; no idea ever occurs to her which does not concern passage one way or the other through that portal. Nothing implicitly wrong with this, of course, but. . . . It's a matter of power concepts, comparative study thereof. Chicago knows this. Take it as a general rule that all women fare badly in Chicago—you won't go far wrong. It is a man's city. Perhaps this is true of all prairie towns: Lewis Mumford would say they have no containing principle, essential to the femininity of a place. Be that as it may, Chicago offers no sex to the politicos at convention time, except to minor female delegates who must be shunted off to the fleshpots of North State Street to get them out of the way. Instead, Chicago offers the far more illuminating and encouraging spectacle of the stockyards. Just what the politicos require—a vision of God's creatures marching docilely into one end of a machine, from the other end of which issues a steady stream of money. Can anyone doubt that this is the inspiration which calls the politicos eternally back to Chicago? It is demonstrable that the important political orbit at convention time lies between the Blackstone Hotel at one end and the Union Stockyards at the other.

If, in any presidential year, neither of the major parties selects Chicago for its convention site, a minor party is almost sure to do so: Prohibition Party (1869); Greenback-Labor Party (1880); Anti-Monopoly Party (1884); Labor Party (1884); Anti-Saloon Party (1886); Irish Nationals (1895); Prohibitionists (1900); Socialists (1904); Independence Party (1908); Progressive Republicans (1911); Communist Labor (1919); Farmer Labor (1920); Workers (1924); etc. In 1932 the Republicans, Democrats, Com-

202

munists, and Farmer-Laborers all convened in Chicago to watch the steers march in. Lord, there were some notable nuts in Chicago that summer, I believe. The first important political convention in Chicago—remember, the city was founded in 1832—was the Republican gathering in 1860 which nominated Lincoln. A pretty lucky shot in the dark, you will agree. Since then, the Republicans have journeyed with great frequency to Chicago, hoping for a repeat, I suppose. So far without much success. On the theory that Lincoln was a Democrat at heart, the Democrats go there too, almost as often and with about the same results. Don't blame the Blackstone, though. If good bourbon, good tobacco, thick carpets, dark paneling, and well sealed chambers could produce good presidents, the Blackstone would be our true mother of statesmen. . . .

I left my car in the parking lot by the Art Museum and walked to the hotel, debating whether or not to slip downstairs to the public bar for a fortifier ahead of time. No chance. In the dark lobby I saw Pocksman dancing toward me obliquely (pronounce as in the Army) among the ocher marble columns. Our hands met damply and fluttered together like tangled underwear on a clothesline.

"Hello, old man. Nice to see you," Pocksman tittered.

"How are you?" I asked without enthusiasm. "Am I late?"

"A bit late, old man. A bit. Most of the crowd's already here."

"Ummm," I murmured. "Mrs. Rheinklugel?"

"Not yet, old man."

"Ummmm."

I wondered about inviting Pocksman down to the bar, but decided against it when I remembered I had to avoid discussing his poems with him. I pulled out a pack of cigarettes and proffered it.

"Thanks, old man—I'm a pipe-smoker, you know." He hauled a great knobby pipe out of his pocket and poked it into his dancing face. It clung there like a gourd on a vine.

"Well, let's go." I made a grimace signifying mock-bravery.

"It's not so bad, you know. Fillermine's a quite decent chap, once you get to know him." Pocksman gamboled a step or two, trying to fall into my stride.

"I wasn't thinking of Fillermine."

"No? Oh, I suppose you mean Mrs. Rheinklugel."

203

"Exactly."

"Not a bad sort either, as a matter of fact. We made her a trustee of the New Augustans last spring, she really takes an interest, you know."

By way of reply I stopped to drop cigarette ashes into an urned gum tree with elaborate circumspection.

Pocksman was dancing on, trying to light the dottle in his pipe and talk at the same time. "I wonder, old [puff] man, if you [puff, puff] have had an opportunity [puff] to glance at those [puff, puff, puff] *poems* I sent you a week or two [puff] ago [puff, puff, puff, puff, puff]?" He coughed and struck another match.

"Well, I haven't had much—"

"Oh, I know how it [puff, puff] is. You editorial fellows— always deep in [puff, puff, puff] *literary machinations* . . . eh?"

"Well, I wouldn't say—"

"Still, I think perhaps [puff, puff] you might possibly find . . . something of interest?—yes, in the [puff] poems, you know. You see, I'm entering a new [puff, puff, puff] *phase of my work* . . . so to speak?"

"Very interesting. We must have a talk about it sometime."

"Yes, I [puff] knew you'd be [puff, puff] sympathetic, old man." He was on his fifth or sixth match by now, and most of them had burned nothing but his fingers. "You see, I have this little—ah— theory, you might say, [puff, puff] about—ah—the function of the [puff, puff, puff] *symbology of consciousness* . . . in the poem, you know?"

"I see."

"Yes, and—well, it's a question [puff] of . . . what you might call dialectics—the moral and libidinous centers of [puff, puff, puff] *imagery?*"

"Sounds like a very useful con—"

"Oh, yes—first-rate, you know. Really. I'm surprised myself— but, you know, all sorts of possibilities open [puff, puff, puff] *up?*"

"I daresay."

"Of course, there's a lot more [puff, puff] to it. I've got it pretty well worked out, you know, all the [puff, puff, puff] *details?*"

"Of course," I said.

204

By this time Pocksman was striking matches and talking and dancing and puffing at such a rate that he looked and sounded more or less like a toy steam engine the moment before it blows up; and I began to wonder if I shouldn't do something to subdue him before we entered the ballroom. Again he forestalled me— danced precariously ahead, peered into the room, raced back, jamming his pipe—still unlit—in his pocket. "Ah," he said, "Fillermine's talking with a bunch of those . . . *Notre Dame instructors?* You must allow me to introduce you to him."

"As a matter of fact, we've already met several times," I said. Whether I realized that Pocksman's aim in intercepting me in the lobby had been chiefly the pleasure of officiating at this introduction—whether I realized this before or after I made my reply, I can't at this moment recall.

"Oh," Pocksman said.

I motioned to indicate that he should go in before me.

"After you, old man," he said, smiling and showing his carved mahogany teeth.

* * *

Clambert Fillermine projected, like the Acropolis, above a huddle of overcrowded tenements, the shabby skulls of Notre Dame instructors. Tan and fit, meticulously brushed, he gazed serenely, classically, impartially down upon his admirers. He was clad in smooth Palm Beach cloth and thin Italianate shoes. The instructors, except for one, were clad in crumpled seersucker; the one was a very young, very round priest, whose black, sweat-soaked serge was mildewing before our eyes.

"Of course, if one is committed, as I presume all of us are, to a— num, num—representational form of government, with its attendant benefits, then one must indubitably, I suppose, accept its attendant ills; among them being, as we see with increased clarity virtually every day, the segregation and, I may say, denigration of the arts as a matter of—num, num—public policy; and, indeed, one can scarcely expect more, can one?" Here the Acropolis describes a quarter-turn, so as to distribute its radiance on a new sector. An immaculate fingernail touches imperceptibly an unruffled eyebrow. "In an age of universal education, after all, the . . . ah . . . what we

205

may call effective electorate?—as distinguished, you see, from the enfranchised but apolitical masses of a previous era—the effective electorate, which has increased manifold, may easily impose not only its will but its—num, num—taste upon the procedures of government; but while, in an age of universal education, it may be feasible to raise the effective electorate to a status of technical literacy, very little can be done, one fears, to increase its intelligence or its keenness of sensibility. Just so. The dilemma of democratic man, as you see, but cast in peculiarly and, I suggest, painfully contemporary terms." Here the hands touch, with no more than a faint intimation of wringing. "And yet, may there not be found in the old theory of representational authority an indicator of the solution?" Another quarter-turn here, a shade more energetic than the other. "I invite you, if you will, to consider the known but often forgotten fact that representational theory in itself nowhere requires a government whose authority derives—solely, at any rate—from the citizenry considered as a—num, num—indiscriminate conglomeration. On the contrary, the notion of *proportional* representation is, if you will forgive me [a cold smile here], a product of nineteenth century American political practice which, however suitable it may have been to cultural and social conditions in the United States a hundred years ago, appears radically unsuitable today. In fact, is it not true that the more or less forced imposition of the *proportional* system upon newly emergent cultures throughout the world, and even, for that matter, upon the traditional cultures of Europe, is accountable for much of the political . . . ah . . . neurosis which is now evident on every hand? But representational government has in the past often enough been organized upon other grounds, and indeed vestiges of former systems survive in the British House of Lords and your Senate, do they not?" Another judicious quarter-turn, a slightly deprecatory dropping of the hand. "Suppose, for example, that our parliamentary bodies were readapted to a multiplex society, suppose that our representatives were chosen as the delegates, not simply of miscellaneous units of population, but of purposeful groups—trades, businesses, professions. Then artists, though insufficiently numerous to effect a controlling influence, would at all events be heard, and would no longer be submerged in the mass . . . ah . . . insensibility, so to speak. You will protest, perhaps, that the organization of such a

206

parliament upon lines of justice would be intolerably difficult and always subject to disagreement; but, in the first place, the system of what we may call *purposeful* representation need not be grounded merely upon concepts of privilege, as it so often has been in the past, and, in the second place, surely our instruments of sociological analysis have now reached a degree of—num, num—refinement which will permit the accurate collocation of social groups. On the other hand, bear in mind that the element of free choice might be retained by providing for the individual elector an unrestricted opportunity to denominate the representational group to which he prefers to belong. But these are technical matters. I feel assured that a revival of the notion of *purposeful* representation will be the . . . ," etc., etc.

London School of Economics. To a T.

After half a dozen further resonating sentences—they spilled from his mouth like water over the lip of a sluice—Fillermine caught sight of me, parted the circle of admirers with a delicate slicing motion of his hand, and floated toward me like a torpedo boat with its power cut. He shook hands perfectly: not one pump, like a German; not a dozen, like an American; but three, firm and vigorous and dry. No Gallic hand-on-my-elbow; no Viennese hand-on-my-biceps; no Roman hand-on-my-shoulder. Thank God for the English; they may be funny looking, but at least they know how to behave.

"How pleasant to see you again," he said.

"How are you, Clambert?"

"Truth is, I feel awful."

I was taken aback. "Do you?" I said. "You look fine."

"Matter of climate, I daresay. Terrible tropical city, Chicago— as you know." He tapped his forehead. "All clogged up inside."

"Well, I grant you—"

"No, no, no—I mean *my* head. Not the city's. Actually, I rather like it. I mean the city."

"Try a drink," I suggested. "Try some gin. Everybody in the tropics drinks gin."

"I'm holding off. For the time being, you know. Necessary to keep on one's feet." He smiled.

"Say, Clambert, were you ever a student at the London School of Economics?"

207

"Heavens, no. How curious of you to ask."

"You talk like it—sometimes."

"I talk like it! What a hell of a bloody American sort of a thing to say. I don't believe it."

"Fact."

He scratched his eyebrow. "How can you tell, if I may ask?"

"You may. Absolutely pure essence of London-School-of-Economicism. Can't miss it. But tell me, Clambert, do you believe that guff you were handing out over there?"

"Yes."

"Well, damn it, are you *interested* in it?"

"As a matter of fact, yes."

"All right. Sorry I asked. Forget it. I guess I just don't understand the English."

"We do try to speak more or less like civilized men."

* * *

Cienkiewycz was there, also looking tan and fit. For that matter, Cienkiewycz and Fillermine superficially resembled each other; both were tall, beforehandedly gray-haired, handsome. The resemblance went no further, though. Fillermine gave Cienkiewycz a good span in breadth of shoulder, and something also, I think, in depth of humor. Cienkiewycz, solely by adoption, was nevertheless a frontiersman—laconic, wry-tongued, independent to the point of near-crackpotism. A great Martini man too: nothing would keep him from the bar. And that was where I found him, his back to the rest of the assemblage, tilting an icy Martini to his lips.

"Hello, Captain," I said. All of us followed Charley's mode of address in speaking to Cienkiewycz.

"Mr. Editor," he said.

We shook hands, and I took a Martini from the tray on the improvised bar. We both drank.

"Good," I said.

"You bet your life," Cienkiewycz said.

"I suppose we really ought to hold off till Charley gets here."

"You mean to celebrate?"

I put down my drink and lit a cigarette. "Well, I expect he'll be pretty elated. Being a citizen means a good deal to him."

208

"Maybe he won't make it."

"Oh, he'll make it all right. Couldn't possibly miss. Right now he can answer the judge's questions better than either you or I could, and don't think I exaggerate. He's been studying like a demon."

Cienkiewycz pulled at his Martini, then turned around, facing the room, and leaned his back against the bar. "Then what the hell's been on his mind so much lately?"

"Charley's?" I went on my guard. "Well, he's the worrying kind. Even with all his studying he tends to be afraid of the questions. But what do you mean?"

"He looks like a mighty worried man to me. I wouldn't say it has anything to do with this citizenship business, not directly anyhow. He's full of anxieties. Lost all his equanimity."

"All?" I sounded surprised. "I hadn't thought it was anything as bad as that. A little let-down maybe, but. . . ." I gestured with my cigarette and raised my Martini with the other hand.

"No, something more than that. More serious."

"You mean he's slacking off on the job?"

Cienkiewycz tapped his fingers against his huge belt buckle. "No. Charley will always give you fair measure—fair measure and more. As an employer, I've got no complaints. But I can't help seeing that now he's working more from a sense of duty than for the love of it. His enthusiasm is gone." He looked at me squarely. "You know, Charley had more zeal for his job—in a quiet way— than anyone else I've ever seen, when he first came to work in the office."

I glanced away, over the heads of the crowd. "Well, a certain loss of drive is normal, isn't it? And he *has* had this naturalization business pretty much on his mind. But I don't know what else." I was running scared now, without doubt. I hadn't the faintest idea what Cienkiewycz might suspect; I only knew he was shrewd enough to suspect something. The strain of the conversation was rising, and I felt the resonating implications of what was being said twanging, as it seemed, on every nerve in my body. Which meant I had to put an end to Cienkiewycz's line of inquiry immediately, either by forcing him to tell the real extent of his suspicions (which might turn out to be nothing) or by making him lie (out of

209

embarrassment) about having any suspicions at all. I turned to him again and gave him a point-blank question: "What's your theory?"

"General disillusion."

Not very helpful. "Yes," I said, "but that's scarcely enough to account for this extreme anxiety you speak of. And it's not at all evident in his pursuit of the citizenship business. He hasn't slacked off any there."

"No. I mean on the job."

"But you said he was doing all right?"

"In a sense. He does his work, does it well; he's beginning to be a good draftsman. But he knows now that's as far as he'll go."

"Oh." Immediate draining of tension, flooding in of old stable emotions—affection for Charley, respect for the captain, confidence in juniper hooch. I inched a trifle closer to Cienkiewycz. "No hope, is that it?"

Cienkiewycz turned on the ball of his foot, quickly, brusquely. He set down his empty glass and picked up a fresh Martini. "Great glabrous godlings!" he muttered—at least I think that's what he muttered. "Look, what have you got to be so happy about?"

"Me happy? I don't—"

"Come off it, for Christ's sake. You detest Charley and you know. . . . No, that's not right either." He lit a cigarette. "No one detests Charley, I guess. But I know you—better than you think. You're a poor fouled-up son-of-a-bitch, a second-rate artist, wrecked sensibility, neurotic misfortunate, outsider, alien, and so on and so on—the whole rigmarole. Well, all that means nothing to me, not a goddamn thing. See? For me the adjectives are so much offal, I shovel them out. A plain ordinary unadorned son-of-a-bitch, that's what you are, nothing more—and I should have told you so a long time ago."

"I must say I had no idea you—"

"I know. Hospitality of my house, pleasant conversation, all the old jolly bung-ho—so how come now I'm jumping on you? Well, lots of reasons. But the way your face lit up when I put my finger on Charley's rotten luck—frankly, I've never seen anything like it."

I felt the conversation was turning wild, dreamlike, fantastic. But strangely interesting. I wasn't in the least disturbed. "I should

210

think you might consider the possibility," I said, "that my feelings were caused by something quite different from what you imagine, something not related to Charley at all."

"Impossible." Cienkiewycz swallowed a third of his drink and looked intently at the remainder, turning his glass slowly between his thumb and finger. "I don't say your immediate feelings and motives are known to me, though they may be. I simply say that in the rather concentrated tissue of meanings which had emerged in our talk it was impossible for your response to be unrelated to Charley. Maybe not Charley as an individual person, for all I know. Maybe just Charley in the abstract, what he stands for. But don't think that makes you any less of a son-of-a-bitch."

I looked across the room. Pocksman was dancing from one foot to the other in front of the little fat priest. It was the courtship ceremony of an extinct species.

Cienkiewycz went on: "I'll tell you what ought to be clear to you. There never was any hope for Charley. Do you understand? For Pete's jug-handled sake, I know enough about poetry to see that Charley is no poet, can't you try to know enough about architecture to see he isn't an architect? No, not you. You think words are the only passkey to existence. Listen. If I'd known Charley was so dead set on being an architect, I'd never have agreed to his coming over here in the first place. But I didn't, I only found it out when he arrived. Not that it would have made any difference. I think the point is this: Charley's ambition to become an architect, fantastic as it was, was deeply connected with his whole vision of life in America. Now God knows what will happen. Something. As I say, it all probably doesn't make any difference in the long run, not even your being a rotten son-of-a-bitch. Charley decided to be unlucky long ago."

Which was, I suppose, a rather penetrating remark. How true was it? I don't know. Charley certainly strove, he was a first-rate striver: he came to this country, after all, he made an effort to alter his destiny. And he studied at night school, he worked at the shop, he pushed back when circumstances bore in upon him. The ordinary observer would have said that Charley's temperament was far from that of a fatalist. Yet I feel that Cienkiewycz was essentially right; Charley did make his own decision to be unlucky, and prob-

211

ably had made it long ago. As for Cienkiewycz, he said a few more words and then walked away to another part of the ballroom, and I never spoke with him again. I liked him, I still like him, and I've always thought we should have been good friends. I remember his words clearly and I've set them down here accurately. Odd that I shouldn't have altered them perhaps, but I wasn't tempted. The truth is I didn't know then and don't know now what to think of much that he said, there are so many imponderables. But I think perhaps I'd rather be a son-of-a-bitch according to his lights than a fine fellow according to most people's. Cienkiewycz was a pretty good son-of-a-bitch himself. How else could he have existed in the charmed and charming circle of Charley's creators?

* * *

Cienkiewycz walked away among the other guests, treading deeply, it seemed to me, like a man entering the ocean. I watched him until he disappeared. I looked up at the ceiling, a high ceiling of molded plaster, supported by intaglio pillars and arches traced on the walls. At the far end, saffron sunlight entered through tall French windows; above the heads of the guests a heavy winding of tobacco smoke squirmed like a baldachin. I stood at the bar and gazed outward with proprietarial decorum, wrapped in warmth and well-being like a quilted sultan. Solely the effect of alcohol, as I was quick to recognize; I was safe now, safe for hours, if I used a little good judgment; safe in my alcoholic objectivity; I could afford to be charming, witty, the equal of any occasion.

Without doubt, the entrance of Mrs. Rheinklugel was an occasion, though the exact modifying adjective to go with it escapes me at the moment. Let it be enough to say that Mrs. Rheinklugel came in. . . . No, damn it, wrong from the start. Mrs. Rheinklugel probably never came in in her life, she always came on . . . less like an actress coming onstage, I may say, than like a general coming onto a parade ground, accompanied by color guard, drums and bugles, and assorted aides-de-camp. Farfetched? Not at all. In this case, Mesdames Carlow & Prunier fluttered and simpered on either side of the General in a manner spectacularly aide-de-campish, two bellboys from the Blackstone staff carried the General's handbag and tartar sable stole with evident awareness that they were flourishing the insignia of rank, and as for the drums and bugles,

212

I imagine the press corps can do service here, for the General's entrance was signaled by a splendid fanfare of snapping shutters and blaring flashbulbs. The General herself was short, broad-shouldered, and chesty; she walked like a pit terrier and wore her campaign medals—excuse me, her diamond-and-sapphire brooch—proudly. I have no doubt she had earned it on many an arduous campaign. Once on the parade ground, she halted and surveyed the assembled company. Carlow whispered decorously in her ear, Prunier motioned the bellboys to stand back. The photographers knelt, petitioned, and were granted a frosty smile. Mrs. Rhein-klugel had arrived—for the umptieth time. I caught sight of Rollo hurrying through the throng to perform the official greeting, and with a pleased sense of my own benignity and serenity, I went forward, without being sought out, to lend a hand.

"Mrs. Rheinklugel, permit me to introduce our editor."

Rollo was at his courtliest, and I duly loaned my hand.

"So-o-o glad to meet you. I've heard so-o-o-o-o much about you. I think it's just wonderful what you are doing with our *Pegasus*, just wonderful. Why, I was . . . ah . . . just saying to—"

"Yes," the Carlow struck in. "She was just saying on the way up how marvelous it is for the city, you know, having such a . . . a . . . gallant cultural . . . enterprise . . . yes . . . ah . . ." Obviously, the Carlow's job was to bail out the General when the General seemed about to founder. I wondered who bailed out the Carlow.

Naturally, the Prunier. "You see, we all are so appreciative of your good work on behalf of . . . ah . . . on behalf of . . ."

"Yes. But of course. That's it exactly. Isn't it?" The Carlow resumed the burden.

"Exactly," the General beamed.

"It's very good of you to come," I said. "We are always grateful for the support of the—" here I bore down hard "—*aware* members of the community." As well as I could, I smiled.

"Well, you know, I've always just loved poetry. . . ."

"Yes, indeed," interposed the Carlow. "You ought to see the books and book of poetry on her . . . ah . . . bookshelves. . . ."

"Books and *books*," said the Prunier.

The General beamed.

At this point, fortunately, Fillermine appeared. As I've already remarked, praise the Lord for the English, they always know what's expected of them. Fillermine knew, and dutifully performed. "Mrs. Rheinklugel, it is a great pleasure for me to," etc., etc.

Flashbulbs blared.

"Mr. Eliot, how marvelous! It's a marvelous thing, really—I'm so-o-o-o-o-o glad to—" The General broke down, beaming.

The Carlow: "It's really such a great honor, you know, for us and for. . . ."

The Prunier: "Terribly flattering, just terribly—why, I'll remember this as long as . . ."

Fillermine: "Very kind of you, I'm sure. But there seems to be a case of misidentity. My name is really," etc., etc.

More flashbulbs.

"Dear me, Mr. Prufrock, to think you've come all this way—you really must come tomorrow for . . ." The General beamed.

Carlow: "Yes, indeed, for tea, Mr. Prufrock, the day *after* tomorrow . . . for tea . . . in the afternoon. . . ?"

Prunier: "Oh, yes, Mr. Prufrock. Do-o-o-o come. Day *after* tomorrow? Tomorrow is the governor's wife, you see, and we couldn't really . . . could we?"

Fillermine: "No, indeed, but I'm afraid I shall be in San Francisco on," etc., etc.

Flashbulbs right and left.

"Dear Mr. Sweeney, tell us, have you written another play since the . . . ah . . ."

Carlow: "*The Peacock Tail?* Oh, we enjoyed it so-o-o-o-o much. So-o-o-o-o amusing. . . ."

Prunier: "So-o-o-o-o profound. . . ."

Fillermine: "Well, as a matter of fact, you see," etc., etc.

Minor regrouping here, supervised by Rollo. Then more flashbulbs. But I had reached my limit. "Mrs. Rheinklugel," I said, in what I judged were painfully suave tones, "perhaps a little refreshment?"

Rollo took it up. "The photographers must be finished now."

"Well," the General enunciated laboriously, "perhaps . . . just . . . a . . . little . . . you . . . ah . . ."

"I'm sure the bar has some excellent sherry," Rollo said maliciously.

"Oh, but I . . . well . . . I think . . . perhaps . . . I . . ."

214

Carlow: "Yes, it is . . . isn't it? Getting on toward . . ."

Prunier: "Time for . . . ah . . ."

Rollo braced his shoulders. "Most of us are having cocktails. Perhaps a cool drink for a warm day? Something with a touch of rum perhaps?"

General: "Ah, yes, well . . . sometimes I . . . that is . . . I . . ."

Carlow: "When it comes to cocktails, you know . . . well, one mustn't be . . . must one?"

Prunier: "Indeed, not . . . ha, ha? We . . . you see, we . . . prefer . . ."

"Martinis," the General beamed.

"Of course," Rollo said. "Shall we go this way?"

"Delighted," said the General. "So-o-o-o-o-o nice to have seen you, Mr. Possum, so-o-o-o-o-o nice. Till tomorrow afternoon then?"

Carlow: "Wonderful, wonderful, Mr. Possum—I wouldn't have missed this for worlds, not for worlds! Till day *after* tomorrow. . . ?"

Prunier: "I . . . ah . . . oh, yes, Mr. Possum—day after tomorrow? At four?"

When they were out of earshot, I said: "Look here, Clambert, I knew it was going to be pretty rough, but I had no idea—"

He silenced me with a half-raised palm. "No apologies, really. There's no need—I'm used to it, God help me. Besides, I've seen worse."

"Worse?"

"Far worse. There was a South African woman in Florence once who told me for a half hour how much she adored my sonnet beginning, 'Leave me not in the marriage of two minds.' . . . Really, this is nothing, nothing at all. Anyway, it's in the good cause. One mustn't complain." He smoothed his eyebrow with a delicately arched finger.

"You're an astonishing fellow, Clambert," I said.

"Nonsense. Nothing of the kind."

Nevertheless, I detected a tremor in his eyelid as he turned away, and I thought to myself that it was the most eloquent gesture I had ever seen from a deathly weary man.

* * *

Resumption of atomic testing in the atmosphere. To think— to *think* with minds that by every objective criterion are accounted

215

rational—that adding to the forces of destruction will accomplish anything but destruction! And now shelters, "fallout shelters," shelters for everyone—to protect us in case of a thermonuclear war. *In case of a thermonuclear war!!!* My God, what has happened? What is going on out there? Has everyone gone mad? Am I the only sane one left in the world, hidden away in these snowy woods and hills? "You can save yourself," the radio says. Exactly what the pimply boy said who came to my door a week ago and pressed a copy of the *Watchtower* into my hands. Illusions. Saved in a world whose very rudiments—earth, air, water—are being turned into the food of death? Saved in a black burrow while topside every needful and beautiful thing is thrown down, burnt, contaminated, mutilated, destroyed? I ask you.

The beginning of this book was difficult, as I made a great show of announcing to you, but what a hollow show it was. Now, now the words come hard. I was brave enough then—faced with my little anxieties about style and form—but now the words come hard. Hard, I tell you—"you," whoever you are, whatever you are, *if* you are. The man who said one can write for art's sake, or for the purpose of pleasing oneself or shaping the truth of oneself or any of that jazz . . . he lived in no such times as these. Now, now when you out there are being snatched away from me by this insane fury, now when you are virtually gone and I sit here totally alone, now the words come hard.

I hammer them onto the page. One by one. Like spikes. Hammering up these little words against my sense of nullity.

Linda does nothing, lost in a dream of nothing.

I had thought I could keep these notes on the present segregated from the rest.

Is my method better than Linda's? I have absolutely no idea. I only know I must pursue my reason as she pursues hers. We are the two sane ones, that much is clear, but which sanity will prove the more effective? I guess the effectiveness of either will be so little that it doesn't matter. I simply go on. Putting down these sad and funny words. It ought to be easy, really; that September afternoon ten years ago was sad enough and funny enough, you might think, to call up its own language from the force of its own being. But it doesn't. The words come hard.

* * *

216

"Have you any idea how rotten and lousy a life Rollo leads?"

I looked across Paula's head toward the gaggle-at-large. In my present condition of carefully nurtured interior placidity, I wasn't sure I liked the direction the conversation was taking: these fierce questions about the private lives of one's friends always lead to disturbing commitments.

"He hasn't got anything," Paula continued. "Just dreariness."

"Come now—he enjoys his work, he's got us."

"You think so? Maneuvering these old biddies all the time?" Paula sucked vehemently on her cigarette. "Listen, if he's getting anything out of the work it's not what he does, you can be sure of that—it's just knowing that possibly it all means something in the end. That, plus the chance of associating with you every day."

I looked doubtful. What else could I do?

"I agree," she said. "It's nonsense. But you may as well know that's the way he feels." She looked away. "He thinks you're a genius."

I shrugged. "So do I." Paula made a gesture of impatience, but I went on. "All right, I like Rollo too, I think he's a splendid fellow, and so on and so on. But isn't that just what I said to begin with? He's got us. If we've got to be maudlin about this, I'm serious, I mean what I'm saying." This wasn't what I wanted to tell her: too dangerous; but I couldn't think of another gambit quickly enough. I went on: "One of my chief pleasures in life is working in the office and being with you two. You're good company, everything considered, and it's a pleasant way to work; I'm fond of both of you. The point is, if Rollo gets the same pleasure out of it, so much the better. I know how it is."

"But it's so little."

"You expect too much, Paula. Practically everyone has to settle for too little out of life. And Rollo's reached the age when he knows it, and if he doesn't accept it, he at least doesn't rebel against it foolishly. You know, you can't burn with a fine gemlike flame all the time."

"I never burned in my life and you know it," Paula said. "I wouldn't mind burning once in a while, if that's what you mean."

No, it's too much, I said to myself; time to break away. But I couldn't think of a ploy. I smiled, tentatively. She remained

217

unsmiling, however, and began speaking before I could attempt an excuse to leave. Her thoughts hadn't been moving in the direction I feared; her mind was still on Rollo.

"Whatever he gets out of the work," she said, "it isn't enough. Life means more than that—I *know* it. What does he do at *night*, for God's sake? And he's so old."

"Rollo? He's not fifty yet."

"But that's old. Practically ancient."

"Good Lord, Paula—Rollo's got years ahead of him."

"What kind of years?"

"Why, what's the matter with him? He's healthy, isn't he? Full of vigor, I'd say."

"Yes, that's all you think about—work. Of course he's good for a lot more years maneuvering the biddies, adding up the accounts. But what else?"

I turned it back to her. "What do you mean?" I said.

"Well. . . ." She blushed.

This time I smiled genuinely. "If it makes you so uncomfortable, I asked, "why do you keep talking about it? You've got an obsession."

She looked down. "I guess that's what an obsession is, isn't it?" Her tone was rough-edged. "Something that makes you uncomfortable."

I let that pass, and reverted to Rollo. "Don't you think Rollo's sex life is his own affair?"

"What I think is, you ought to be concerned about your friends' lives, and help if you can."

"Meddlers get into trouble—"

"I'm not going to *meddle*," she interrupted. "But sometimes you can sort of . . . *arrange* things so a person can take advantage of them if he wants to."

"There's a word for that," I said. "It's called seduction."

She blushed again. But she didn't say anything.

"I see," I said, "I see." I confess I was shocked. But the pathos of what she was doing, or trying to do, overcame my surprise. "How do you know Rollo isn't perfectly well satisfied already?" I asked. "You said you don't know what he does with his nights. How do you know he isn't popping out to Cicero or someplace

218

like that three or four nights a week and whooping it up with the girls? And what the hell do you want me to do anyway?" I pumped these questions at her rapidly, almost angrily.

Paula sighed. "I don't believe it. And neither do you. Does he seem like that kind of a person to you?"

I agreed he didn't. "Still," I said, "I wouldn't be surprised if he had something going, something more modest perhaps."

"I would," Paula replied. "Can't you tell? By the tone of his voice, that dryness and misery? By his clothes, so correct and color-less? It's gone out of his life, that's what I think—out of his whole being. He's forgotten *how*." She paused. "Not literally, of course," she added.

I jiggled the coins in my pocket. I wondered how much she'd had to drink.

"I know what you're thinking," she went on. "But why do you think I brought this up to you? Because you're the one person I know who I thought might understand. You're thinking of his wife—or rather, you're wondering what I'm thinking about his wife. Well, I think that's just not enough. Not any more, anyway. Do you know how long she's been gone?"

"A few years," I said.

"Seven," she said. "Seven years. Maybe a person can keep it up for a while, maybe two or three years, but seven?—it's too long. Do you know she hasn't even been able to recognize him for over two years?"

"As bad at that."

"Yes," she said. "And I think he's just sort of slipped into this way of being sort of half-dead—damn it, I know I'm floundering. Why don't you help? It's a sort of un-being, isn't it?"

"A common case. Perhaps I've tried not to see it in Rollo."

"Well. . . ."

"You want me to be your pimp." I hit her very hard with this. The alternative was a complete deterioration.

Paula bit her lip.

"What the hell do I know about pimping?" I said.

"A great deal: you do it every day."

"What—"

"Oh, yes. Don't get starchy about it. An editor and a pimp are

219

practically the same thing." Paula blushed—the third time. "What do you think makes anyone a pimp? The money? I doubt it—not often anyway. Pleasure, can't you see?—the pleasure of bringing together people who need each other—in your case, the writer and the reader."

"I fail to recognize the cogency of the analogy."

"Never mind, it's not the point anyway."

I let my placidity return. "Still," I said, "Rollo's wife is someone. Someone very deeply embedded in his life, I imagine. He's a lot older than you, remember. You can't truly understand the quality of his existence. Neither can I. Neither can anyone. But people— some people—can live on memories, you know, on illusions, on fictive identifications."

"I know," she said. "Rollo's just the sort who might do it—in his quiet way. I've been thinking, though. There's a kind of . . . of relationship, isn't there?—where you are just friends." The fourth blush. "No, I mean more than friends, but—well, something between being a friend and a . . . a wife? At least that's what I read in the novels and poems you people are always writing."

"I suppose so—in certain circumstances."

"Something like that might work with Rollo," she said simply.

"All right," I said. I looked at her, at her eyes suddenly very soft. She was in love, and again I was surprised. Her hair was rumpled, a thin strand fell over her eyes. She had ashes on the front of her dress, a smear of lipstick on her teeth. "Go fix yourself up a bit," I said. I smiled, and picked the lock of hair off her forehead and placed it among the rest. She smiled too, shyly. I leaned down and whispered in her ear: "Tell me now, whom am I really pimping for, you or Rollo?"

* * *

The fat young priest was expounding earnestly to a schoolgirl, who looked as if she might be a student at a junior college. Probably the daughter of one of the older guests. He said: "No, but you've got to go beyond that period, the period of the 'Jellyroll' record. Russell was great then, no doubt of it, but still working in the older vein. He scarcely deviated from the tonic. But so much as a year or eighteen months later he has made marked progress, very marked progress. And my contention is that he antedated

220

many of the harmonic and especially rhythmic innovations of Parker and the other habitués of Minton's."

"Such a hypothesis seems difficult to sustain," the girl replied thoughtfully. "When you consider the extent to which Parker, Gillespie, Edwards, and the others acted as a group, abetting one another's experiments. This climate of experimentalism, it seems to me, was the essential ingredient. Pee Wee Russell, after all, was working in virtually complete isolation, not even associated with the main earlier developments of Lester Young and Roy Eldridge."

The priest's forehead was runneled with sweat. "In the first place," he said, "you neglect the importance of the intuitive leap as an element in creative development. Russell was capable of it. He was—and is—one of the three or four white geniuses. He could do in isolation what a lesser artist could do only as a member of a coterie. But in the second place, do you imagine that Russell was unaware of developments in the Basie-Ellington orbit? True, he was working primarily at the other end of town; but I think there is good evidence that, first, he didn't care for his location and wouldn't have chosen it if he had been permitted a free hand, and, second, he was extremely interested in the harmonic devices used by the others and adapted some of them, particularly Eldridge's, to his own style."

"I don't deny the truth of what you say," the girl responded, frowning in concentration. "But I still believe you would be straining a point if you refused to acknowledge the genuinely revolutionary nature of the events which occurred *after* Parker came to New York. The extraordinary efflorescence in the middle of the decade must have sprung from a more immediate source than these scattered impulses from the early years. At best Russell was a precursor, not himself the innovator."

"He could scarcely be an innovator in the sense you mean when no one was willing to pay attention to what he was doing," the priest said, and then turned to me, speaking with a note of appeal in his voice. "Don't you agree?"

"Oh, I'm with you all the way," I said. "Definitely. But I didn't catch your reference to that record you mentioned earlier, the 'Jellyroll' record? Can you give me the full title?"

* * *

221

Trays of assorted good things—miniature sandwiches, sausages spiked on toothpicks, *pâté* and melba toast—were being carried among the guests by Negro waitresses, all of whom seemed too small to be entrusted with such burdens. One, particularly slight, a beige girl with maroon hair and freckles on her nose, lifted her tray for my inspection.

"A tempting array," I said. "What do you recommend?"

"Oh, they're all very good, sir."

"You think the customer should make his own choice?"

"Yes, sir. We put the *carte blanche* before the *hors d'œuvres.*"

"What?" I said.

* * *

Charley stood, looking downcast, at one side of the main door. He seemed poised in a peculiarly dryadic stance, as if he were about to vanish among the folds of drapery which, in design and color, were a somber foliomort.

"Have you been here long?" I asked, as I came up.

"No," he said. "Five minutes, I guess."

"Where's Alex?"

"I don't know," he answered, shifting his pose. "What a jam! Do you have to have so many people?"

"Afraid so," I replied. "Good for the cause. See here, Charley, don't be evasive—do you mean Alex didn't show up for the naturalization proceedings?"

"No."

"Then what—"

"I mean yes, she didn't show up."

"Oh," I said. "Charley, that's terrible. What happened? Have you heard from her?"

"No. She was having lunch with a friend; she told me she might be late." He straightened his cuff. "It's all right, she didn't really take much interest in this citizenship thing anyway." He straightened his other cuff. "Like you," he added.

"Oh, well, after all—you can't get very worked up about something you're born with. At any rate, most of us can't. Come on, let's have a drink."

We walked across to the bar, edging Indian fashion among the knots of guests. By this time, the party was in full swing. "Excuse

222

me," Charley said to a blowzy socialite who had stepped backward just in time to transfix his instep with her stiletto-shaped heel. "Think nothing of it, honey," she said. And she kissed him. At the bar Charley wiped off the lipstick with a balled handkerchief dredged from his pocket, and ordered a Dubonnet. The bartender was pouring a shakerful of Martinis into iced cocktail glasses set out on an aluminum tray. "Yes, sir," he said, and began searching among the bottles swimming in a tub of half-melted ice behind him on the floor. He came up with the Dubonnet, poured out a glassful of the lovely solferino with evident satisfaction, and asked, "Lemon?" Charley said, "Please." As the bartender twisted the peel and handed the glass to Charley, he said, "Congratulations, sir." "What for?" Charley asked. The bartender picked up his pitcher of Martinis and resumed pouring. "You're the only sensible man in the house," he said.

I chose one of the newly filled Martinis and turned to Charley. "You know perfectly well, Charley, even if we don't take citizenship seriously ourselves, we're interested in your naturalization." I sipped the Martini, warming the cold gin on my tongue. "If only because you're interested," I continued. "I'm astonished Alex didn't show up. Do you suppose anything has happened to her?"

"What could happen to her?"

"I don't know."

"If you mean an accident," Charley said, "I'm not worried. I had to learn that long ago. She's often late; and sometimes it seems as if she chooses the worst times to be the latest."

"Characteristic of the species."

Charley swirled his glass and watched the lemon peel turn slowly in the wine.

"How did it go?" I asked.

"Simple."

"What did the judge ask you?"

"He asked me what was the procedure for ratifying an amendment to the Constitution."

"That's all?"

"Yes."

"Bit of a letdown. . . ."

Charley smiled crookedly. I thought of the months of study, the questions he had asked me, the anxieties he had endured.

223

"Well," I said, "three cheers anyway. And congratulations. You know, I think you really are the most sensible man in the house, after all." I raised my glass.

"Thanks," Charley said. "I'm glad it's over." He sighed. "It doesn't seem to mean so much right now. But I guess that's just the letdown, isn't it? Later on, tomorrow, it'll be more like what I thought. . . ."

"Sure," I said. "That's the way it is."

Charley looked around the room. "There's the captain," he said. "I'll go tell him."

"Yes, of course. He should have been the first to know."

When he had taken two steps, Charley turned. "Don't worry about Alex," he said. "She'll turn up."

* * *

The General: "My dears, isn't it too marvelous—all this . . . all this for the sake of *culture?*"

The Carlow: "But really, you know . . . well, you know . . . without you—"

The Prunier: "Yes, indeed, my dear. Yes, indeed. Without you . . . well, after all, without you it wouldn't be . . ."

The General (beaming): "Come now, my dears, we mustn't be too . . . must we? It's all for the . . . ah . . . the *poets*, you know!"

* * *

"How's it going?" I asked.

"All right, I think," Rollo said. "Everyone seems pleased. No fights so far. Of course, you never can tell about Rheinklugel, you never can tell what's going on in her brain—if she's got a brain."

"Yes, I must say she's a tough case. I hadn't expected much. But that—that's about the bottom of the barrel, isn't it?"

"Depends. In some respects it's the nearest to the top we've ever been. She's got the money, don't forget—stacks of it. She could bail out *Pegasus* for the next decade out of the money she spends for . . . for storing her furs, *par example*."

"I'm sure." I proffered a cigarette and was tendered a light. "Let's hope it works then. At least old Clambert came through in good style."

224

"Like a trouper," Rollo said.

"He's really a considerable asset, old Clambert."

"No one else could have got the Rheinklugel to attend—I mean for the sake of the photographs. You can thank him for that."

"Really, Rollo, in that case I don't see what we have to worry about. Obviously she was pleased. Tickled pink, I'd say—even if she actually doesn't know who he is. The party's a rousing success."

"Let's hope so. We'll see later. Everything's gone smoothly so far, at any rate. Thanks to Paula—she's done a good deal more than her share, you realize."

"And I've done less than mine."

"I didn't say that."

"True, nevertheless."

"You're being self-pitying," Rollo said. "Your job is to hold up the editorial end—a damn difficult job. No one's ever done it better, that's what I think. And the only reason the rest of us are here at all is to keep things going so you can—"

"Okay, Rollo, lay off—I'll shut up." I blew cigarette smoke in the direction of the other end of the room. "There's Paula now, making up to the fat priest. Doing her bit, all right. I must say she looks okay, don't you agree?"

"I guess so. What do you mean?"

"I mean when she fixes herself up a little she's actually rather inviting looking. Bedworthy, in a wholesome way."

"You think so?" Rollo watched Paula smile at something the fat priest had said. "Wholesome, yes—I've always thought that. I expect she might be receptive, though, if you approached her with . . ." He waved his hand vaguely.

"No thanks," I said. "I'm otherwise occupied. I was thinking of you."

"Me?"

"Why not?" I dropped my cigarette ash into an empty Martini glass that was standing on a marble table, on a copy of Fillermine's *Prologues and Passpennies*. "You two spend a lot of time together. Most people probably already think you're—"

"Preposterous!"

"No, I'm not exaggerating. Besides, nobody would be anything but pleased, especially Paula. I repeat: why not?"

225

"I'm old and tired and disgusted and empty and forlorn and puritanical and spiritually impoverished and—"

"Yes, and Paula is young and tired and disgusted and empty and forlorn and so on and so on. Rollo, there isn't anyone alive in this city right now, anyone with an ounce of sense, who doesn't feel the same way for one reason or another. Or probably in any other city, for that matter. It's the times, Rollo—and for God's sake, don't let me get off on that. But seriously, you know as well as I do the malaise isn't essentially personal; it's epidemic. The point is there's a certain periodicity to one's susceptibility. And the further point is we still have to live—"

"Why?"

"You mean that."

"Of course."

"No one can answer that question for another person, Rollo. You fight it out alone, don't ask me how. Obviously, I was wrong; you don't have to live. Somebody said the question of suicide is the only topic left for serious inquiry. I agree; we should face it unashamedly. However, one point remains where we have no freedom of choice, if that's any comfort. *If* we live, then we have to be human beings, we can't escape it; and that's what I meant to say in the first place, I guess. We have to be what we are, the *sum* of what we are. Which means the sum of what everyone else is or ever has been. You may say this is meaningless, too big a statement to be useful; but I disagree. What do you think Paula does at night?" I smiled inwardly at myself for adopting Paula's tactic. "You can tell me she sits at home and reads and mends her stockings, but you damn well know what the truth is—she sits at home and suffers. No less than that. The most ordinary thing in the world. But another ordinary thing is the termination of suffering, or at least its interruption, its temporary suspension. That happens every day too. The cyclical movement is a human mechanism—inescapable. All you have to do is let it happen."

Rollo dropped his cigarette butt into the Martini glass, where it hissed gloomily. "You should never try to talk rationally," he said, "especially when you've been drinking. It doesn't suit you. However, there's a speck of meaning in your flummery." He turned to look again toward Paula, who was still listening to the fat priest.

226

"I couldn't go it alone, not for a whole evening—I've pretty well lost my hand for this sort of thing. What's the program tonight?"

"We'll be at Christy's on 55th Street after dinner," I said.

He lit another cigarette. "I guess the first thing to do is rescue her from the Church.

*   *   *

Alex, Alex!

Did you live? Were you real?

I didn't know. Never before had I been so touched, shaken, by the emotional cogency of the old philosophies. Good Dr. Berkeley, I palpitate in the apprehension of your living heart: what *are* the structures of reality? Out of sight, out of mind—so people say. We few, the unnerved, say more: out of mind, out of the world. It seemed to me, as I wandered from group to group that September afternoon, that the alive warmth of Alex still clung to my body, but then it seemed to me that this was illusory, it seemed to me—a spasm of possibility—that there had never been such a woman, but that I had invented her. Seemed, seemed, seemed—my skull echoed. But what *is*? Do I love? Hate? Feel anything at all? But of course, Charley had been speaking of her only a moment ago.... *Was Charley real?* I spun and stumbled. There, at the far end of the room, still talking to Cienkiewycz. Thank God. But the three tall French windows wavered in the intense saffron light like three crones hobbling together. Hé, hé, hé, they snickered, winking at me.

A moment's sensation, no more. Then the alcohol took precedence again. With nonchalance, I observed the stability of the room; the din of the party in my ears; the world resuming its customary implacable objectivity. I noted, calmly, that reality was in no danger: it was I, driven by fear and longing, I, the indispensable nub of consciousness, that had momentarily disintegrated.

That such a thing should happen to a man! Ah, Alex.

*   *   *

Pocksman dancing around Fillermine like a child around a Christmas tree. When I came up, he began dancing around me too. Two Christmas trees: the thought occurred to me that it was

227

well past Christmas Eve, more like Twelfth-night—we were dry, our lights were burnt out, and we'd soon be taken down.

"Ah," Pocksman said, "glad to [puff, puff] see you. I was just telling Fillermine here about this article I read by Robbe-Grillet —you know his work, of course?—in . . . ah . . . the *Nouvelle Revue Française*, in which [puff] he holds that the chief romantic . . . ah . . . fallacy is the humanization or . . . ah . . . anthropomorphosis of external [puff, puff, puff] *things?* Ah, you will say, the old pathetic [puff] fallacy, Ruskin *à la gauloise*. Yes, but . . . ah . . . with this [puff, puff] *difference?* Robbe-Grillet is interested primarily in . . . ah . . . isolating the explicitly or should I say implicitly —ha, ha!—human element . . . ah . . . as opposed to the alien unknowableness of [puff, puff, puff] *things?* And you see, of course, how interesting it all . . . ah . . . is—and how it fits in with my own concepts of the dramatic symbology of consciousness, what I was telling you [puff, puff, puff] *about?* Because, you see, if the symbolic force is dissipated into objects unintegrated in the precise drama of withinness . . . ah . . . well, you see what I mean. . . . Fillermine says it's very [puff, puff, puff, puff, puff] *interesting?*"

"Yes, indeed," Fillermine said. "Although I've always tended to think that the—num, num—*procedural* theories of *writers*, as distinguished, you see, from the *analytical* theories of *critics*, are significant chiefly as rationales for the creative act and have little objectivity validity in themselves, if indeed anything does."

"Oh." Pocksman slumped visibly. But then brightened up again. "Of course, I see what you mean, the [puff] poem is the . . . ah . . . main thing, after all, isn't [puff, puff, puff] *it?* Now at the moment I happen to be working on a longish . . . ah . . . dramatic monologue tentatively entitled 'The Defense of Sheba,' which embodies," etc., etc., etc.

* * *

I engaged the Prunier, incautiously, in conversation. She was pretty well crocked.

"Tell me, Mrs. Prunier," I suggested, "have you enjoyed a pleasant summer?"

"Oh, yes . . . yes, indeed. Marvelous, just marvelous."

"Really? Rare these days to hear anyone confess an honest enjoyment."

"Yes, isn't it? Ah. . . ."

I risked another question. "Were you in the country?"

"Ah, well, you see, ah, not really, that is, only a few weeks."
She gulped at her Martini. "Yes, only a few weeks, you see. Mostly
we were in Madrid. Yes, and Barcelona."

"I see. You spent the summer in Spain?"

"Oh, yes. Of course. That is, we always do, you know . . .
invarial—inveeri—in-VARE-ably."

"Indeed? You must be deeply attached to the—"

"We go for the fights."

"The fights?" I inhaled deeply.

"Oh, yes . . . in Barcelona and Madrid, you know. We always
go. Ah, are you an—ah—*afficionado?*"

"I'm afraid not, Mrs. Prunier. I've never yielded to the spell.
Perhaps you can tell me the source of the enchantment?"

"The source of the . . . ah? . . . yes, I see. Well, you know—have
you read a writer named Hemingway?"

"Some time ago."

"Yes, he has rather gone out of style, hasn't he? Yes. Well, he
says—by the way, have you ever . . . ah . . . met him?"

"No. No, I haven't."

"I see. Well, you know what he says about the fights, they're
so . . ."

"Graceful?"

"Yes. Yes, that's it exactly—graceful. And . . ."

"Exciting?"

"Yes. Oh my, yes, indeed, very exciting—why when they put
the . . ." She staggered, and braced herself briefly with her hand
against my chest. "When they put the—the *estoque* in . . ."

"Yes."

"So exciting, so-o-o-o-o-o . . . . exciting."

"I have no doubt."

"My heart just goes . . . my heart just goes . . . ah, you know?"
She lowered her voice. "I like it best when they bleed a lot."

"Who?"

"Well, the—no, no, you're joking, I can tell, I can *tell*—you're
pulling my . . . ah . . . Yes, the bulls. Of course, the bulls. Never
the matador—oh no, they never bleed. Cover 'em up quickly, get
'em out, yes, sir—no blood. But the bulls . . . oh my. Black blood,

229

you know?—like . . . ah, er . . . *mud!*" She touched my forearm confidentially. "You know? No? Like mud, like earth, that's what it is, all running down, but so strong and thick. And the smell, you know? No? . . . Oh my."

She was rubbing my arm softly. I noticed that the skin which folded inside her collarbone somewhat resembled the pleats of an old leather valise.

"Oh, the brave bulls. Oh, the brave bulls. Bleeding, bleeding, you have no idea . . . so-o-o-o-o-o exciting. You have no idea. . . . Have you any idea, Mr. . . . er . . . Mr. . . . er . . . no, you have no idea. And the smell—like . . . ah . . . like a warm baked potato . . . YES, BY GOD, A WARM BAKED POTATO . . . oh my. . . ."

"Mrs. Prunier, I say, Mrs. Prunier, I wonder if you'd mind— Mrs. Prunier, I wonder if you'd mind—you're spilling your Martini down my shirt, oh, damn and blast and a bloody shaft in the— excuse me, Mrs. Prunier, I see a gentleman at the bar with whom I must have a word."

She nodded slowly. "And then, of course, and then . . . in Madrid . . . we shook hands with the Generalissimo, yes . . . such a dear man. We shook hands with the Generalissimo after the fights . . . oh my. . . ."

* * *

Alex came in at about five-thirty, in company with a tall, dark, slender, scholarly-looking apparition.

Cool this time, I decided. No frenzies. I pretended not to notice. Alex and her friend sought out Charley first—near the windows—and then all three joined me at the bar. Introductions were performed; the apparition's name, it turned out, was Rignum Bruno—Rig, for short. Alex and Charley were holding hands.

"Isn't it wonderful about Charley's citizenship?" Alex said. "I'm so upset, not making it on time. Rig and I lost all track of the clock."

Charley smiled shyly.

"Calls for a drink anyway," I said. "If you're not loaded already."

"He's trying to be funny," Alex said to Bruno. "If anyone's loaded around here, we know who." She shrugged and smiled.

"We certainly should toast our new compatriot," Bruno said. His voice was astonishingly deep and rich.

"Champagne," Alex said. "Mumm's, '36, at least."

"None available," I said.

Bruno looked grave. "Why not let me call down to the public bar for a bottle?" he asked.

"No, no," Charley said quickly. "Let's not do that—it wouldn't be polite, would it? Having champagne, I mean, all by ourselves in the middle of the party."

"I don't think anybody would mind, would they?" Bruno asked.

I didn't like Bruno. "It might be frowned on," I said.

"Hell, Rig, give it up," Alex said, "before I die of thirst." She took a Martini from a tray on the bar. "Who likes champagne anyway?" she said, smiling.

Bruno took a Martini, too. Charley asked for another Dubonnet and the bartender, saying, "Yes, sir," with a tone all of us recognized as conveying friendliness beyond the call of duty, poured it out. I hesitated, thinking perhaps I ought to change my drink as an inward gesture of anti-Brunoism, but then took another Martini anyway.

"Who'll make the toast?" Alex said.

"I think you should," Bruno said.

"Oh, no," Alex demurred. "I wouldn't know how."

I said: "Why not? Perhaps the female should speak for us all."

"I think so too," Charley said. His voice seemed to float gently on the hubbub from the rest of the party.

This is the only time I can recall Alex disconcerted. She turned and placed her handbag on the bar, and took longer than necessary to stub out her cigarette in an overloaded ashtray. When she turned back to face us, she held her glass stiffly before her, and spoke with uncertain solemnity: "To a new American, who has been long in our hearts and is now in our country, may he always be prosperous and happy and . . . and . . . true!"

We raised our glasses. But before we could drink, the bartender said, "May I join in?" Charley nodded and smiled. Quickly the bartender poured some Dubonnet into a shot glass, and we all—all except Charley—put our glasses to our lips and drank.

"Thank you very much," Charley said.

* * *

231

The bathetic qualities of this scene, including the awkward toast spoken by Alex, may seem to you egregious and worthy of concealment; I dare say they do. But I have reported the interchange faithfully, without expurgation, because in my remembrance a vestige of the occasion's warmth and feeling still lingers. The words uttered by Alex, Bruno, and me cannot convey this to you, of course. Neither could any words that I might make up now, artfully tinted and parceled out to the speakers retrospectively. All I can do is assert—as I do—on the simple authority of a participant, that the feeling was there; in all of us, I think, even Bruno. A complex emotion, since each of the three of us—Alex, Bruno, and I—was hiding something, a guilt in our breasts as real as a tumor; yet the warmth of our feeling for Charley and the simple, childlike evocations of the event overrode, for the moment, our tensions. Put it down to the booze if you like. But consider also the possibility that in this complex machine of spinning hates and loves, this four-personed mechanism, the directive force was Charley. Was it likely that he could dominate and subdue our loves and hates by the unanswerable appeal of his simplicity and goodness? I remember him standing there—a little stooped, his blond hair ruffled—and it seems to me that this was precisely the case.

* * *

Mrs. Rheinklugel, I saw, was turning aside from a group near the doorway to say something to the young girl who had been discussing jazz with the fat priest. She (Mrs. Rheinklugel) smiled vacantly. In the center of the room Paula was whispering to one of the waitresses. To the left and at the end, under one of the high windows, Alex and Bruno were now standing with their shoulders touching as they looked at something in a magazine Alex had just taken from the window seat. I felt a stomach twinge, and for a moment the noise of the crowd seemed unbearable, like a sudden burst of pigeons through a narrow street.

* * *

Later I found myself caught up with Bruno in one of the party's circulating eddies. For a hideous moment we turned round and round tête-à-tête. His black hair was thin, gone altogether in front.

232

My eyes fixed on the alarmingly deep depression between the frontal bones—called, I believe, the metopion.

"Very pleasant to meet you, Mr. Bruno," I snarled. "Do you live in town?"

He licked his lips. "No. Oh, no. Out in the Hinsdale section."

"Ah, the real country," I growled.

"We like to think we avoid some of the city's . . . entanglements," he sobbed juicily.

"Your business is in Hinsdale too?" I snapped out.

"Oh, yes," he bawled.

"What . . . er . . . is your line of—"

"I breed horses," he gasped. "Racehorses."

"Fascinating occupation," I thundered.

"Really more of a hobby, you know," he muttered.

I blasted at him, "I see—a gentleman farmer?"

"You might say," he coughed balefully.

"Fascinating, fascinating," I howled, and leaned into the scorching wind.

"You must come out sometime and let me take you on . . ."

But his words were swept away in a blast of hellfire, and we lurched apart.

*   *   *

It was some time before I could capture Alex, bind her, so to speak, and lead her—trailing smiles like bread crumbs—to the dark end of the bar.

"That's your date?" I eructed. "Humbuggary!"

"None of that," she said.

"For God's sake," I implored, "why do you *do* it?"

"Why not? I like him—"

"And he's rich."

"Moderately. You think that's the key to—"

"To you, yes."

"Sweet boy. Such a dear." She smiled, then frowned. "Give me a cigarette, will you?" We lighted cigarettes, and she continued, her tone dry and earnest. "You've got to be angry, I suppose. I despise it, but—you can't say I'm not a realist. Not in these matters; not at this stage. All right then, go ahead and be angry, be insane,

233

be a proprietary male. But don't expect me to pay much attention."

"To whom should you pay attention if not to me?"

"You see?—that's just the tone I was talking about. If it satisfies you, go ahead—perhaps you need it. But does it serve any purpose?"

"My purpose," I said coldly, "is simply to elicit one plain fact. Why—why the double—triple—cross?"

"That's exactly the term you'd use, isn't it? How do you know it isn't a quadruple cross, or a quintuple?"

"My God, I don't."

"And I don't accept your imputation!"

"Imputation, hell—it's a fact. It's as plain as the—"

"No. Not at all. Only if you apply your terms, your rotten criteria. I don't apply them." She puffed seriously on her cigarette. "Look, you know I'm no—what do you call them?—moralist? I don't give a damn for that. You want to know why? Because life is too short, *life is too goddamned short*. That's all I know, or care about. Maybe it seems simpleminded to you—"

"It does."

"All right, write a book about it. But while you're at it, tell me this: we've had a good time, haven't we?"

"God, yes—glorious. What do you think upsets me so much?"

"You mean you're upset because you had a good time? That's silly. You're silly. Love is a good time, fundamentally, and if it isn't a good time, it's not worth bothering about. And you're making a mess of it."

I caught myself shrugging my shoulders, as if to ask some unknown kibitzer what you could do with such a woman. "And I suppose you think we should go on as if nothing were changed, I suppose you think we should go on having a good time when we know perfectly well you're . . . you're . . . cultivating that horse breeder."

"Anybody wants variety in his garden—no, I don't mean that. At least not the way is sounds."

"Variety! My God—"

"No. Wait a minute. Do you believe in different kinds of love? Just like different kinds of life? The way you live part of your life at the office, part at home, part somewhere else?"

"Possibly, but—"

"Then why can't there be many kinds? An almost infinite number of kinds?"

"But it's customary to limit one's investigations of them to one partner. One at a time anyway."

"Customary to whom? Where? Why? You're being sentimental. And very old-fashioned."

"I'm being—"

"One person can write several kinds of poetry, isn't that so? But how much variety would you have if you never read any books except those by a single poet?"

"This is absurd. What has poetry got to do with it?"

"I don't know. What I'm saying is that life is so goddamned short. Can't you understand? You'll be sorry someday—you're getting older every hour."

I almost shrugged again. "At least I'll have the satisfaction of knowing I haven't stuck a knife in anyone."

"What have I done to you—aside from giving you an opportunity to love and make love and be a better person for it?"

It was useless. I saw with sudden insight that the whole course of my feeling was futile—completely without hope. The universe at large, reality itself, was in opposition to my smallest needs, and nothing I could do would make any difference at all. My anger subsided into sorrow; I was nearly crying. "Alex," I said, "you've spoiled it all—don't ask me to analyze it, I can't. It's over; all done; that's as much as I know."

She put her hand on my arm. "No. Don't you see? It needn't be."

"Christ, Alex, have you any idea what you're saying, how monstrous it is?"

"Was it monstrous with Charley, too? What about him? What about when you were worrying about his gun?"

"I know. That was foolishness. I should have known better—at least I should have known Charley better."

"I wouldn't be sure . . ."

"What do you mean?"

"He knows."

"Knows what? About us?" The banality of my question struck me; then the banality of the whole episode, from that hot day in August at Lake Jones until this moment in September at the Black-

235

stone Hotel. But my sense of melancholy could not yet give in to my sense of the absurd.

"Yes, about us."

"Who told him? Cienkiewycz?"

"The captain? No, how could he know? Some of the kids in the building told him."

"The little bastards." I staggered a bit. "Alex, what's going to happen?"

"Nothing, Poppy. Don't you see?—we're not the sort of people who do things, we're really not people who ever take action at all if we can avoid it." Her hand was still on my arm, and she pressed gently with her fingers. "Don't worry. Not now. We can't decide anything until later anyway." She opened her handbag and looked at herself in a mirror that was set in the back of the cover. "We can meet tonight if you like."

"Good Lord, no. I couldn't."

She looked at me, moving her eyes but not her head.

"How could you get away from Charley—tonight of all nights?" I said.

"It could be managed."

"No," I said.

She closed her handbag and walked away, brushing the back of my hand with her own as she went.

* * *

Ten minutes later I learned that Bruno was a eunuch. My first thought was that my brain had been put out of commission; it couldn't absorb so much in such a short time; it had gone dead. Someone at the far end of the room laughed, and the laughter tinkled in a high corner of the ceiling. My second thought was: why in hell couldn't Alex have said so? Actually, the one who told me was Rollo. A case of disability incurred in the war, he said.

"I find it hard to believe"—this was all I could manage by way of response.

Rollo sipped an obviously warm Martini that he had been nursing. "Why?" he asked. "It must have been a common enough type of casualty. Probably there are more of them around than we realize." I remembered that Rollo didn't know what I knew—or thought I knew—about Alex and Bruno, and hence couldn't share

236

my bewilderment. I let him continue talking. "Think of the danger from land mines and booby-traps," he said. "Very widely used in Europe. No doubt thousands were injured in the same way. . . ."

I mustered a semblance of aplomb. "I suppose so," I said. "Hideous business."

"Makes you shiver," Rollo said.

"But how do you know?" I asked. "He a friend of yours?"

"I've met him once or twice. But he makes no bones of it . . . er . . . I mean he doesn't hide it—he even wrote a little book about it, published it himself and sent it around to friends. There's a copy in the office somewhere. Sort of little paragraphs; prose-poems I guess is what you call them—the sort of thing done by Fiona MacLeod, if you remember her . . . er . . . him. . . ."

"Yes, yes, I know what you mean," I said. "Curious, though. . . ."

"Why? What do you mean?"

My aplomb was slipping, I saw. I faked an answer. "Well, he doesn't look it, does he? Appears virile enough, in a slimy sort of way. You might think he'd be fat or have a squeaky voice or something like that."

Almost as in a dream I knew what Rollo was going to say. "No, that's not how it works apparently. Provided you've already acquired the secondary sexual characteristics at the time emasculation occurs, I guess your appearance doesn't change much."

"Apparently not," I agreed.

"Makes you uncomfortable though, doesn't it? Wouldn't care to spend much time in his company."

"Neither would I. A case of autosuggestion in reverse, perhaps."

"*In extremis*, I'd say."

"Wonder why Alex bothers with him. . . ."

Rollo said he had no idea, and we were each carried away in separate vortices—the party's indeterrable momentum.

* * *

I was eager to get to Alex again, of course, and throw this new perplexity at her—the incongruities between my conversation with her and my conversation with Rollo, the disparity between Bruno's now known disqualifications (for Rollo's information was trustworthy, I felt) and her evident involvement with the man; an involvement which, moreover, as anyone could see who took the

237

trouble to look at them, was expressible in the lover's ordinary sensuous terms of gesture, glance, and touch. It was damned disquieting, as you can imagine. As I anticipated my talk with Alex, my spirits rose and my enthusiasm returned: I couldn't take the rivalry of a eunuch as a serious threat. Her motives were obscure, of course, but whatever they were, I felt now that Alex was simply putting me through some kind of trial by torture. An old trick, really. Well known female perversity. I was certain that when I confronted her with what I knew, she would laugh, confess, and take credit for having exposed my gullibility; and in my certainty I put out of my mind the knowledge, which at another time would have been my first thought, that this sort of thing simply wasn't Alex's way. . . . Owing to the party's demands and limits, however, I didn't find another chance to speak to her alone that afternoon.

*　*　*

"Tell me, who is the blonde, the—what-do-you-call-them—sexpot?" Fillermine had drawn me aside to ask his question. "Over there." He indicated direction with an eyebrow.

I looked across the room. Of course it was Alex: a lambent head and a gray-blue cocktail dress of raw silk glimmering through the haze. "Name of Alex Dupont," I said. "Friend of mine."

"I say, you're not offended, I hope?"

"Not at all. Sexpot is the precisely accurate term."

"Indeed," he murmured. "Appearances are sometimes deceiving."

"Those who dress the part won't play it when the chips are down?"

"Exactly. Maskers, I find, are seldom doers—when, as you say, the chips are down."

"In this case, however," I said, "the appearance is a declaration of . . . well, she's safely married at all events."

"A pity."

"Many regard it so."

"I have no doubt." Fillermine smoothed his eyebrow. "Still, I'd be glad to make her acquaintance."

I examined the alternatives: to perform the introduction in the hope that Alex would snub him and then give me a chance to talk to her alone, or to forestall the introduction on the grounds that there were enough cooks stirring this pot already; in my momentary exuberance, I judged for the former.

"Come on," I said. "I'll introduce you."

When we arrived, Alex was sitting next to an elder and minor female poet—Leyden Starr—on the wicker settee; they were discussing a recipe for *pâté de foie canard au Canadien,* and Miss Starr was embroidering a design of colored threads on what looked like a piece of old burlap. She was elaborately lipsticked and kohled, stained with granular pigments on her cheekbones, and smelled as if she had sprinkled herself with ground cloves. Her split Chinese dress exposed a sinewy thigh. Charley was standing at the other end of the settee, his back turned to Alex and Miss Starr, listening to Pocksman and the fat priest. As Fillermine and I approached, I heard the words "but Robbe-Grillet definitely says that the denatured universe is a cosmological necessity in his program of," etc., etc.

Mr. Fillermine, Mrs. Dupont; Mr. Fillermine, Miss Starr; how-do-you-do; very-pleased; charmed; etc., etc., etc.

"There is a belief among central European dressmakers," Fillermine essayed, looking at Miss Starr's needlework with a keen eye, "that when a seamstress pricks her finger with a needle it foretells great pleasure for the person who will eventually wear the garment upon which she is working at the moment."

"How interesting!" Miss Starr said. "How ever do you suppose such a superstition got started?"

Alex said nothing.

"A curious belief, as you say," Fillermine agreed. "You might think the association would be, in the normal course of things, just the reverse."

"Of course!" Miss Starr exclaimed. "The drawing of blood should be an evil omen."

Alex said nothing.

"It may be," Fillermine went on, "that this is a case of mythological inversion owing to Christian influence."

"How exciting!" Miss Starr applauded. "But what do you mean?"

Alex said nothing.

"One can see a glimmer," Fillermine ventured, "of some such origin as the Arachne legend. . . ."

239

"How clever!" Miss Starr interrupted.

Alex said nothing.

"And then, you see, as the momentum of Christianity forced pagan elements underground, and then permitted them to re-emerge in the form of folk culture—"

"Yes, yes!" Miss Starr interjected.

Alex said nothing.

"Why, we know that in such cases meanings were often inverted," Fillermine continued doggedly.

"I'd never have thought of it!" Miss Starr declared.

Alex said nothing.

"But really, it's terribly unimportant, isn't it? So tedious and pedantic. You must think poets are dull fellows, Mrs. Dupont."

"Not pedantic at all, Mr. Fillermine!" Miss Starr said angrily. "Why, you could make a poem out of it!"

Alex said nothing.

"I'm afraid I write very little nowadays," Fillermine said modestly. "Are you connected with *Pegasus*, Mrs. Dupont?"

"I too!" Miss Starr sighed. "One does lose one's creative force, doesn't one?"

Alex said nothing.

"I wouldn't say that precisely," Fillermine objected.

"Oh, no, of course not!" Miss Starr trilled. "But there are so many other things to do these days, aren't there?"

Alex said nothing.

"Indeed," Fillermine said ruefully. "So many other things to do."

"Still, a poet of your extraordinary gifts never gives up!" Miss Starr responded. "You'll produce something soon, never fear. I know what deep designs must be occupying your thoughts!"

Alex said nothing.

"You do?" Fillermine said with surprise. "I mean yes, I'm sure— all in good time."

"One must keep one's hand in!" Miss Starr laughed. "I write every morning for two hours, whether I feel like it or not."

Alex said nothing.

"I'm sure that's the best way," Fillermine said. "But as you say, there are so many demands. . . . I see a friend beckoning me now, as a matter of fact. You'll excuse me, Mrs. Dupont?"

240

"Of course!" Miss Starr replied. "So nice chatting with you, Mr. Fillermine. Cheerio!"

Alex said nothing.

"My God," Fillermine said, when we had broken away, "talk about cold fish. I thought you said she was . . ." He smoothed his eyebrow with a finger which trembled almost imperceptibly.

"She has moods," I explained.

"Clearly."

"I'm sorry, Clambert. Not much anyone can do when she decides to be bitchy."

"No, I daresay not," Fillermine said.

Only then I remembered my original intention to maneuver the conversation toward a private talk with Alex. Her performance had taken away, if not my breath, at least my volition.

* * *

The departure of Mrs. Rheinklugel and entourage was accomplished with difficulty. The scene was played in two simultaneous actions. The General herself, occupying center stage, took the leading role, blustery and domineering, showing she could hold her drink like a trooper. Her chief attendant was Fillermine, while Rollo hovered at the opposite elbow, these supporting roles having been defaulted by Carlow and Prunier. The two aides-de-camp, in fact, had been painfully stricken by Demon Gin, and in bedragglement and hauteur were assisting each other offstage as best they could, their bubbly sopranos piping an obbligato to the main discourse. This is a point in the narrative which would benefit from the cinematographer's synoptic view; but I'll do the best I can.

The General (nodding toward Rollo and speaking in a low voice): "Confidentially, Mr. Sandburg, this gentleman here is going to ask me for money—for his magazine, of course. You know, I can *always* tell. They have such an *interested* look. I may not be very bright, Mr. Sandburg, but I am not so dumb either, and I know if anyone's interested in *me*, it's not because I'm . . . well . . . you know, Mr. Sandburg?"

Rollo (in a cautiously sophisticated tone): "Perhaps you underrate yourself, Mrs. Rheinklugel. And in any case I should warn you I can hear everything you are saying."

241

The General: "Well, then there's no point in whispering, is there? Ha, ha, ha. But it's true, Mr. Sandburg, I *know* it; he's going to ask me for money, you just see if he doesn't. And confidentially, what I want you to tell me is, should I give it to him?"

Fillermine: "Actually, you know, in the first place, my name is really—"

The Carlow: "Oh, my dear, I'm—oops!—frightfully shorry, I didn't mean . . ."

The Prunier: "Thass quite all right, my dear, thass purfeckly all right, you juss lean on me, my dear, and don't worry, we'll . . ."

The General: "You don't say? Funny, I thought all along you were Mr. Sandburg."

Fillermine: "A natural mistake, I'm sure, in the circumstances."

Rollo: "Mr. Fillermine is from England, Mrs. Rheinklugel, a British poet and a very distinguished one."

The General: "Of course. I knew *that*. But you see, Mr. Silvermine, I still don't know what to do about this request for a donation? There are so many demands these days."

The Carlow: "I say, my dear, you haven't got a shafety-pin, have you? My hat's coming apart."

The Prunier: "Let me see—oh, dear, iss not your hat, iss your hair-piesch—seems to be coming apart. . . ."

The Carlow: "Wait'll I get my hands on that Antoine. I said to him, I said, Antoine, will it shtay? And he sez sure, sure, he sez, it'll shtay, he sez, you can dee-pend on it. . . ."

The Prunier: "The rat. He ought to be shtrung up, thass what. Shtring him up, I shay!"

The Carlow: "Eggzackly. . . ."

The Prunier: "Whatchue want to do with it?"

The Carlow: "Whass that?"

The Prunier: "This hair-piesch—whatchue you want to . . ."

The Carlow: "Gimme the goddamn thing, I'll shtick it in me pursh. . . ."

The General: "Now Mr. Silverling, if you could just tell me, speaking as a expert—ha, ha, ha—what do you think of this magazine?"

242

Fillermine: "Really, Mrs. Rheinklugel, I think there's no doubt that—"

The General: "Because, Mr. Seiberling, you see—as a matter of fact, I was told by one of my good friends at the D.A.R. last week that—you must never say I said so, of course—that, well, frankly some of these people are—*Communists!*"

Rollo: "Mrs. Rheinklugel, that's absurd. We aren't—"

The General: "But Mr. Seidlitzer, everyone knows poetry is so— *radical.* Isn't it?"

The Carlow: "My dear, they muss have put something *awful* in . . ."

The Prunier: "Purfeckly *awful.* I've never had a shimple little Martini affeck me so. . . ."

The Carlow: "My dear, iss what comes from soshiating with these whaddeyacallum—*poets!*"

Fillermine: "All told, Mrs. Rheinklugel, I'm certain it is safe to reassure you on that score."

Rollo: "And besides, Mrs. Rheinklugel, one should support a balanced program of—"

The General: "Are you *sure,* Mr. Singleton? Because my husband —Mr. Rheinklugel?—he always says how it's the—how they're ruining the country, you know. He'd never forgive me if I donated money to the Democra—I mean the *Communists!*"

Fillermine: "I think you can set Mr. Rheinklugel's mind at rest, Mrs. Rheinklugel."

The General: "Well, it *is* hard to know, isn't it? I mean to know what to *do.*"

Fillermine: "Often it becomes a problem—"

The General: "Yes, I'm so glad you agree, Mr. Singlevine, so glad to find a—kindred soul. Ha, ha, ha. Why, do you know last year after I had given to the Catholic Committee for Overcrowded Families, the people from the Methodist Orphanage Fund told me that the Pope is against birth control? So-o-o-o-o perplexing."

Fillermine: "Yes, indeed. I quite agree."

The General: "And my husband—Mr. Rheinklugel?—you know he can only give me two hundred thousand for the annual charities budget, which does sound rather a lot, doesn't it? But when you

243

come to try to fit everything in . . . Think of it—three schools, two churches, two museums, a clinic, an orphanage, and then there's that Mr. McCarthy from Wisconsin who came to dinner and my husband says we have to give him . . . well, you know, it's awfully difficult, really."

The Carlow: "Iss what I all-ways say, my dear, eggzackly—you givvum a ninch and they'll take a *mile*. . . ."

The Prunier: "Ain't it the truth—*isn't* it? My dear, you juss *know* these people'll be all over ush now. Now we've come to this pa-a-arty. . . ."

The Carlow: "Eggzackly, juss what I was saying, my dear. Them and their filthy poison gin. . . ."

The Prunier: "My dear, all the po-e-tree anybody needs's in the Book of Common Prayer. . . ."

The Carlow: "Eggzackly, my dear, egg-zackly."

Fillermine: "I sympathize with your predicament entirely, Mrs. Rheinklugel. But at the same time, I think our friend here will give you good advice."

Rollo: "You may rely on that, Mrs. Rheinklugel. If perhaps it would be convenient for you to—"

The General: "I don't know, I just don't know, Mr. Filtermane, I'm sure I don't know what I'll do. It's so-o-o-o difficult. But here we are, aren't wc?—the end of a lovely party, and now it's time to go. Thank you so much for inviting me, Mr. Fillimore."

Fillermine: "But I didn't give the party, Mrs. Rheinklugel. You must thank this gentleman for that."

Rollo: "It has been our pleasure, Mrs. Rheinklugel. I do hope that—"

The General: "Never mind, Mr. Filmername, it's been a lovely party anyway. I've just *loved* meeting you. And I do so-o-o-o appreciate your listening to my troubles."

Fillermine (a bit briskly): "Not at all, Mrs. Rheinklugel. I sympathize with your difficulties. After all, we're all more or less in the same boat, aren't we?—though of course some of us go tourist class. Ha, ha. Good-by. I'm sure you'll solve your problems. Keep your pecker up."

The General: "My WHAT?"

Rollo: "Very gracious of you to come to our party, Mrs. Rheinklugel. Please allow me to—"

The General: "Well! . . . Come along, my dears, time to go home. . . ."

The Carlow: "Yes, juss what I was saying myshelf, my dear. . . ."

The Prunier: "Eggzackly, she was juss shaying. . . ."

The General: "You're fried! Both of you—*fried!* . . . Oh, well, lean on me, my dears—we'll manage, never fear. . . ."

So they paddled away, the old goose and her two goslings, one bald and the other speckled, bobbing and babbling as they went.

* * *

The departure of Mrs. Rheinklugel was accomplished, as I say, with difficulty. But it was worth it.

In her wake a cool wave of sanity flowed into the room.

"My God," Rollo said, and stood leaning against the drapery at the side of the door.

I went to the bar and got a strong highball and brought it to him.

A general departure of the ladies set in—the society ladies, most of whom, fortunately, were more rational than the General—and with them went the hangers-on: fops and fairies, mealymouths and assorted Magyars. The press had left earlier. The fat priest, dripping like a fountain, shook hands all around before he scurried to catch the South Shore express. "Damn good show," he said. "Be sure to let me know when you're in South Bend." Miss Starr, too, went home, leaving a parting shot—"Do come and meet my father, he's making his death mask in case no one remembers later on"— which remains among my uncherished memories.

Only the stalwarts were left, a small, brittle group in the echoing ballroom. We clustered at the bar, having a last one. Fillermine was restless. Paula stood on tiptoe to whisper something indistinguishable in my ear, and she and Rollo departed together, her heels ticking on the parquetry. "Drink up," I said, "time to go." The bartender looked grateful.

"Yes," Alex said. "Are we still bound for De Jongh's?"

"No reason to change our minds, is there?" I asked.

"No," she said. Then to Charley: "You don't mind if Rig comes too, do you, sweetheart? I told him he could."

245

Charley smiled and said no.

"I say, please tell me frankly if I'm butting in, but the fact is I'm at loose ends," Fillermine said. "Would you permit me to join you?"

Alex looked blank.

I said: "We were planning a little celebration for Charley. You see, it's his—"

But Charley broke in. "No, no—of course, you're welcome. Please come with us."

Fillermine started to speak, but Pocksman got in ahead of him. "I'll come too," he said, "and then we can all go over to my place afterwards for drinks and things."

"We wouldn't think of imposing," Alex said.

"No imposition at all. I'll go call my wife and tell her to fix up a few goodies." He danced away in search of a phone.

"How do you suppose she stands it?" Alex said.

"His wife? No one knows."

Fillermine smoothed an eyebrow. "I had no idea you were—"

"Never mind," I said. "It's only a little dinner to celebrate Charley's naturalization—as an American, that is. We'll all have a fine time."

"But I do rather resent finding myself in the same category with . . ." Fillermine nodded in the direction Pocksman had taken. "Gate-crashers—is that what you call us?"

We all smiled, being sympathetic and friendly. Bruno passed around his faïence cigarette case.

"I guess sometimes everyone finds himself in a category he doesn't like," Charley said.

PART IV

CHAPTER 38

I hope I have made clear the importance, the cardinal importance, of the day of Fillermine's party, which was so filled with conflicting events. There isn't anything particularly unusual in this: troubles never occur singly, we habitually say, and everything happens at once. During the course of the day (and night), my responses to this plethora of experience shifted as my emotional stamina flowed and ebbed. The dinner at De Jongh's, for instance, was a low point; so low, in fact, that I remember now only a few things which were said around the table; and for this reason I propose to adopt the artifice of *monologue-intérieur* in reporting it to you.

An outmoded artifice, I grant you—much frowned upon at present by those who set the fashion in literature. It was invented in the dear dim days beyond recall by writers who hoped it would lend greater "realism" to their work. How quaint—as if there could be grades of reality. . . . People always adduce the example of the one-legged man who still experiences the sensation of his lost foot. How much more pertinent to consider the degree of unreality which has become attached to our own two feet, we who are thought to be "whole." . . . But it is all the same.

Still, as a technique of journalism, the artifice may be serviceable. I hope so. What few words I can recall from the talk at the dinner table, I shall put into double quotes in the ordinary way, and the rest you must imagine as my own psychic flow at the time. One utterance which I do distinctly remember was the waiter's answer to my question about the quality of the *escargots*. He was Italian:

249

clean-shaven but with such a heavy dark beard his face looked like a half-tone. He said:

"You like 'em, they're good. You don't like 'em, they're bad. Me, I don't like 'em and they stink." Brothers under the skin, *mon semblable*—don't know why I asked in the first place. Conformity; bugaboo of being thought unequal; but why must I eat snails and stinky mussels-and-truffles merely because I am dining with a Frenchman? Red meat, my dish, American fat of the land: five-dollar steak, seared and juicy—eh?—and if one must be French, *béarnaise* on the side please, to vary the bites with. To begin?— hell, waste of time—all right, the broiled grapefruit, full of Vitamin C. . . . That's it. Thank God I snagged a chair next to Fillermine instead of that Bruno guy, the—the what? Going to call him queer. That's not right. Can he be queer when he's a eunuch? A eunuch, an eunuch—funny word. Alien word, yes; never said it before, that's sure, and where have I read it?—the Bible no doubt (Philip), but can't think of a single poem. So no queer; but behaving damn peculiarly for all that—hankering after a woman of the flesh. A sexpot. Don't know, can't tell, a queer fellow all the same; horse breeder. Compensatory device? Wonder if he goes out in the corral or wherever they do it and watches the stallions at work. Wouldn't be surprised, standing there supervising the work he can't perform himself. Merely vicarious lubricity?—faint vestigial tingle of prurient itch aroused in his own flesh from watching animals in heat? Laughable? Pitiable? Both—it's always both, the world's re- sistance to simplicity. . . . My God, a peeper, guy hooked on a goddamn peep show, and if stallions and mares then maybe. . . . No! Wouldn't, couldn't. Could she? Could, damn her. Alex and some lusty gent, some servant, some stablehand—the stableboy!— the goddamn groom. Groom? Know the type precisely, damn his eyes, whamming hell out of her; and she loving it; and that de- bauched Bruno gazing. . . . Christ, no! The filth, filth of it; the filth —and me trembling, shaking, ready to bust, the anger growing, growing inside me—don't let it out! . . . Eh? What? "You should have tried the snails, they're really superb." Ah, Pocksman, you ass, for once you spoke up in time, nick of time—only absurdity could have intercepted *that* detonation, it was coming on fast. But look at him, look at that Pocksman, eating snails as if he were eating Lord

250

knows what, dog turds or something, and his face like a rotten lemon, and then saying they're *superb!* Fool. Who cares? It's that Bruno—what does she call him?—that *Rig* that worries me now. And I know nothing, nothing whatever . . . except my own rottenness. The filth. . . . Guy may be perfectly okay, a great joe—how the hell do I know? Don't care for his looks, that's a fact, don't like the way Alex looks right now either, that's another fact, don't like the way they look together, that's a third bloody fact and pretty damn cogent too . . . if you ask me. . . . Philip, Philip, sweet guy, sweetest of them all, but I could not do it. . . . Exorcised unclean spirits crying with loud voice in their victims—ah! Philip. . . . Bruno such another? Incredible. But what is credible to me is . . . almost nothing now. Dear Philip. . . . Look at that Pocksman, hates snails worse than I do, but look at him!—flourishing *pincettes* like he used them every day and talking about the *Revue des Deux Mondes* like he could read it without a dictionary. Probably can, the bastard. Ass stuck on his own folly, professor swallowing his own learning. Not worth scorning—but Christ! so easy, pouring my self-loathing into a caricature of Pocksman. Poor Pocksman. Fool. No more than most. You ass! Filthy, frightened, envious—*envious?* Of Pocksman? Yes. Security, confidence—how else could he commit his follies? Fools always enviable. I am no fool. Too bad. Conscious wrongdoer, culprit, thief, betrayer, raked with guilt. Repentant? Christ, yes. What good; wonder how the church argued it?—probably never was an unrepentant human being in the world—for a minute, an hour. Drive to screw-all resumes. . . . "I don't like them either, as a matter of fact, but I order them once a year or so to see if my taste has improved." British point of view. Fillermine despicable in a way, low and grubby, you can't help setting it against the American self-reliance, specially in Chicago. Reliance an aspect of pragmatism—Emerson, all that. Then you got to admit British grubbiness works—somehow. Beautifully, in comparison with the rest. Here's old Clambert plugging away on the snails, driven by God knows what motives of conscience and duty, and eventually he probably *will* end up liking the damn things. . . . What's the difference? Fond of him though—in a way. Surprising. Better poet than I am. *Little children, which bud of April sows your eyes with apathy?* Good line, good sentiment, good

251

honest feeling. That's important. Let the critics rant. . . . Never have it, never. Fillermine, at any rate, is enviable, whatever Pocksman is. Yet I don't hate him, not like a year or two ago. Age? Getting older? No doubt. Too many competing hatreds? More like it. Not *true*, not *true*—*not* hatred, I swear. Never! Not what's in me. Love—can't you see that, you idiot? . . . Round and round, round and round. . . . Wait, Pocksman working up to something. Look at him; here it comes. "I say, Mr. Dupont, now that you are . . . ah . . . one of us, so to speak, have you decided to forego your origin entirely, or will you teach your children to speak French and . . . ah . . ." *Now why did Charley throw me that quick glance?* Should have looked at Alex, shouldn't he? Not having children is *their* quandary. Then he does know, by God, he does—Alex wasn't being funny, for once. And Charley looked at me in his shame, shame of horns. How could it come to this—so hurtful? I didn't know. Must mean more, though, more than shame. Alex pregnant now? Maybe. God, wouldn't that be . . . And Charley doesn't know who planted the seed. *And neither do I.* Neither of us will know until the child is born. Horrible. But possible. My God, is it? Why not? Alex would have told me if she were—but no, point is she might not, just might not, the bitch! Love, she calls it. Lies, jokes, fears, a man could bear them; but mockery?—too much, too god-damn much. Alex herself wouldn't know whose child she was carrying until it was born, maybe not ever, and she wouldn't care. Though for that matter Charley and I don't look much alike. . . . If it came to that, a child there between us—among us. . . . Horrible. Have to leave, of course—the simplest part, the best—cutting out, cleanly, completely; erase my memory from their minds. But Charley would remember—not Alex, but Charley, forever. Christ! . . . Now look, a simple fantasy, contrived worry, false product of anxiety. No? Yes. Alex not pregnant, bet your life on that—no one more careful, knows she's the fertile type, prob-ably even realizes she'd be a sucker for a child, true dumb maternal animal. Who knows?—maybe she even recognizes this is the only love she'll ever be capable of in the fullest sense, because the only kind that will return her complete satisfaction, exactly the satisfac-tion that brings an end to need, desire, purpose—existence. Who knows? Only just now beginning to recognize this about her my-

252

self. In any case she's hardened her heart against it—against all of us. Can't face anguish of being fulfilled. Blame her? Probably not; blame no one. Woman can't be expected to work her way out of that one, jammed into a false category by a false society. Even so, there's an answer. . . . Like eating steak, probably. Good red meat. Natural enough thing to do, yet capable of assimilation to highly refined concepts of value. Poets dining, all that sort of thing. . . . And the child was born of Pocksman's inanity. It's too much. . . .

—Yes, it is too much, here and now, nineteen hundred and sixty-two, early spring. I can't keep out; don't ask me; all those old thoughts and feelings, they pluck up my heart by the roots now—by the roots! If only Alex had had a baby. . . . It would have been something, anyway. So much. The last remnants of snow lie rumpled like soiled sheets in the valley. The skunk cabbage has appeared in the low places, the red alder and the red-winged black-birds in the swamp. The crows have come back to the woods from wherever they spent the winter, and the day is logical with their vociferations. (I think they spent the winter on the town dump.) The air is good, a cleansing wind; the sun is good. Even Linda is more rational—by her criteria. Her purpose is sharper, clearer. A hunger strike: don't ask me how she decided, where she heard of it, *if* she heard of it, how she, a poor, lost, bitterly ignorant, deaf-and-dumb girl in America, could have this communion with India's great good man and martyr. It's happening, that's all I know. Her protest, her eloquence. Above all, her dignity. But the child . . . yes, the child. It is my rationality that dies this spring, I think. Starving in Linda's withered womb. Even if the child had been Charley's—if Alex had been pregnant—that would have been something. In a way, a bit of me. . . .

—Charley knows, without a doubt he knows: inclemencies and unheavals befall us now, the moral weather shrieks in turbulence, hang up the hurricane lamps lest we have no light at all. Poetry, hyperbole. Bombast even for yourself? Imbecile! Always the show, mask, pretense; no decent substance left. If Charley shoots you, you'll collapse like a tent, all your trappings will flop on the ground. Poetry again—a curse, a defect—bestowed on you as blindly, uselessly, painfully as terror in a rabbit's eyes. Can't think without it. "I can't quite follow Mr. Pocksman on this point. It

253

seems to me that the artist's subjugation to his art, as he calls it, is primarily esthetic, not moral. Don't you agree?" Look alive now, Fillermine's throwing it at you. Got to be intelligent. But what the hell is it about? What are they up to? Say yes, for God's sake, quickly. "Well, actually isn't this the old dilemma posed so often in our schooldays in terms of form and content? I've always thought there may be an alternative consideration, the aspect of pure utility. You may say this is begging the question; yet in practice it is always possible, I believe, to resolve a conflict in terms of its elemental necessity, and from this it may be feasible to erect an esthetic of relative values which would be both functional and self-consistent within the . . ." What the hell are you saying? What kind of jargonistic mess have you got yourself into now, idiot? Everyone staring. Couldn't just say yes, could you?—fathead, turnip! Ah, well, Pocksman's caught it up, off and running again; thank God for that. At least there's a spark of sense in what you said, even if you did smother it. Could write it out for them, which is more than Pocksman'll ever do. But why does Pocksman insist on being so goddamn highbrow? Poor old Charley, look at him, tic going like a machine, tzip, tzip, tzip, I wonder if he knows it. Of course he does. Eyelid jumping like that, how could he not know, even if he weren't so sensitive about it? No complacency against the oafish nerve. All you can do is eat steak and rub your gut, like a pawnbroker in his back room, and when the anger beckons, when the nerve leers and belches, look the other way and think of your profits. But at least they could talk about something else for Charley's sake—at his party. . . . Charley now, is it anger with him—that tic—corrupted desire, madness of jealousy, threatened selfhood? God, we're told every day how the saint's placid exterior and his good work hide only an extra portion of guilt in the heart, we're told how the world runs on energies converted from lust and wrath. Sublimation. Loathsome idea. All very well to say a positivistic analysis of motives cannot destroy the value of good actions—à la Pocksman—look at him sucking on a lobster claw, a spider miscegenating with a wasp—but if the whole world agrees that sublimity is perversion—? Jaysus. It'll be an amateur psychoanalyst who pushes the button, I bet. . . . Charley's no psychoanalyst, nor rationalist, unless you can catch it from reading

254

Huckleberry Finn: that's his phase, doesn't seem likely he'll reach much beyond. The boy, wise in nature. . . . Charley, Charley, name of innocence. Gunning for me? Is that what the tic means, violence suppressed—for the moment? Is that what the glance means, thrown at me when it should have been thrown to Alex? Complicity and guilt: complicity of two who sow their seed in the same golden furrow, complicity of two who assist each other through the labyrinth of a crime—murderer and victim. Easy for me to imagine—in my rottenness. Filth and scum, stew of ego. But look. Rottenness is going, receding, draining away like life's blood. Look, look. Purification, I am risen, nothing, an eye. A knot in the beam. Sure and passionless. An eye never winking. Steady and clear. Looking down. Look. These strangers, the fecund woman eating lobster, butter on her chin; the white-haired handsome man poking into his pompano *en papillote;* the spidery man; the monkish man; the steak-eater, glowering; the boy with the tic: all laid clear, the natural ones, the community of insects, far down, performing its ordained function before the season ends. And good, good. All goodness. Yes, see the tic of pure love that can never be anything else: embarrassment for the other, fear for the other—the deepest instinct. Tic of goodness, nothing else. Look. The perfect truth. *
* *
* *
* *
* *
* *
* *
* .

CHAPTER 39

A place to end? Perhaps. It might be pleasant to conclude with an affirmative gesture; if that's what it was, that closing cry, and not merely a sign of my own crookedness, warp, eccentricity—what do you call it? Unreason? . . . But in any event there can be no hope of ending now. I go forward inexorably, machinelike. The typewriter seems an extension of my fingers; I hold it in front of me as a kangaroo holds her young. Writing, writing; and now I cannot even say why. I would be inclined to think that I am swept by a current, but—I *am* the current. With no more consciousness than transparent water. Flowing; flowing resistlessly. Among gullies, sandbars, deltas, shapes of my own making.

Art, it has been said, is the largess of life.

The doctor has been with Linda, and now she is weeping—a long sigh falling and rising in the house. Before he left the doctor said she must be sent to a hospital, where she may be properly fed —forcibly if necessary, against her will. If necessary, he said, I must "commit" her. He cannot feel the shock of it, the shock turning into laughter. I commit Linda? He cannot feel much of anything, if the truth were known—Linda's purpose, Linda's being. He is blind. He sees only the body breaking. *Doctor, look around:* I nearly shouted it at him; but it would have done no good.

Linda knows perfectly well what she is doing. I am certain of that. And I am also certain that she knows the alternatives, has studied them, has rejected them with quiet (ha!) recognition of the consequence. Can I tell her she is wrong? Can I say some other course would be better? Can you? Linda is hurting me terribly, kill-

256

ing me; but her entire value as a human being, I mean her value to the world, to me and to you—what "value" does she have to herself?—lies in her keeping faith with herself, and with her need and reason. If her need and reason destroy her, that is a quality of her existence. If they destroy me, that is her curse. And mine. And yours. But let us not on that account turn one another into non-beings, for then we will have lost everything, everything. As it is, we have little enough to get by on. Linda must be herself. She must *be*. I, too. I must go on writing, every day, while this terrible spring-time unfolds.

Art, you see, is the largess of love.

CHAPTER 40

Dinner ended in the usual strong coffee, cigarettes, cheese, armagnac. Alex ate some tortoni; Fillermine declined coffee. The table was littered with cups and glasses and soiled plates, over-spilled ashtrays, empty wine bottles. The heavy white cloth was rumpled where I had caught it in crossing my knees, and a blotchy taupe stain stretched from an upset wineglass. Pocksman's pipe fumed, emitting a sour reek. There were six people at table—six gnashing bellies. "The trouble with dining out," Bruno said, "is that afterwards one has no place to lie down." I was embarrassed for him, momentarily. I studied the twin eminences of his frontal skull, glittering in the hard light: they reminded me of a scene in the Apennines, the shallow fracture falling away southward from Ariano, between two high knolls. I remembered that Ariano was where I had seen a priest beating a small girl through the street with an olive rod. Alex was pursuing the last droplet of tortoni in its paper cup with a little silver spoon, frowning intently. She licked the spoon, more or less delicately, and placed it on the dish; then she straightened, yawned more or less delicately, moved her shoulders in a more or less delicate stretch, pointing her breasts toward Fillermine. Fillermine was impressed. Charley smiled.

"Shall we go?" Pocksman announced. "Margaret will be ready for us now."

"Margaret?" Alex said.

"Mrs. Pocksman," he mumbled.

"We had planned to drop in at Christy's for a while," I said.

"The jazz place?" Pocksman's voice quavered with disappointment.

258

"Yes," I said. I held to my point, on the grounds that I had told Paula and Rollo we would be there, though chiefly I was interested in finding other friends who would be more to Charley's liking.

"We don't need to stay long," Charley said.

"All right, all right," Pocksman interposed briskly, heading off any further abortion. "And then we'll go on to my place." He got up, and the waiter cursed—"*Geeee*-zus, mac, watch it!"—as he caught the rungs of Pocksman's chair across his shins.

Paying the bill, tipping the waiter (Pocksman gave him nothing, I noticed, so I left double), searching for purses and hats, filing out—the sheepish procession of the overfed, oo the dinner ended. M. De Jongh, goatee bobbing, false teeth clacking, intercepted us on the threshold and told us again the story (new to Fillermine, of course) of his fortuitous escape from Antwerp in 1940. How awful, we said, and let's hope nothing like that ever happens again, etc., etc. M. De Jongh hauled out a dropsical wallet and displayed a snapshot of Mme. De Jongh, who unfortunately hadn't made it at the last minute. Poor woman, even in the photograph her destiny clung shadowlike to her eyes. A ferlie tear glistered behind M. De Jongh's spectacles.

We were at Christy's soon after nine. Not much doing. The trio —piano, cello, bass—was tinkering on the stand behind the bar; Ernesto at the piano fingered the chords to "Gee, Baby, Ain't I Good to You," very slowly and hypothetically, the cellist was bowing dissonant arpeggios, while the bassist was writing on a small piece of paper which he held against the shoulder of his instrument. Three students sat together at the bar, drinking beer. Two couples occupied one of the forward booths; they were arguing and had open books spread on the table between them. Two bartenders were setting up for the night. Christy sat, as always, on the rearmost barstool, facing forward, one fat elbow propped on the bar. She was smoking a cork-tipped cigarette. She wore a purple sweater—blotchily died—and raspberry-colored paisley slacks. Christy seldom spoke and seldom moved; no one knew what manner of life she led. Her characteristic gesture was the slight and solemn lifting of one ham whenever she broke wind.

We pushed through the dimness toward the back, where there were a few round tables for larger parties, nodding to Christy as we passed. She shook her head, smiling grimly. When we were seated,

259

a waitress—hefty and gray-headed—came to take our order. Cigarettes were lit, the drinks arrived, everyone said cheers and *salud*; we didn't worry about taking on more booze because obviously Christy's shot glasses were phony. More customers filtered through the haze, and the trio, having struck on an amiable sequence of changes, moved into serious work. By the end of half an hour the atmosphere had deepened to blue tenebrosity, most available spaces had been filled, and our table had broken up into separate, more or less peripatetic groups. As I edged back to the men's, I reflected that half an hour was about the average time required.

My piratical image loomed in the freckled mirror like Neptune rising through the foam. I poised my left eyebrow at the sexy slant and glared at myself. Not bad. Considering the stress of recent hours, that is. I always looked better at night. Of course, to be completely honest, I needed to shave twice a day; but the murk of Christy's disguised my emerging stubble. Really, not bad at all, I decided. I gave myself a parting scowl, and returned to the bar with an easy, self-confident tread.

Fillermine and Alex were seated at the bar, and I could see he was, as he would say, having another go at it: lust glazed his eyes, which were turned toward me. I paused a moment in admiration, surprised at being required to admit to myself that they made a supremely handsome pair. As I've had occasion to remark already, Alex from the back—as I saw her now—can be just as dramatic as from the front. In her smoky blue dress she balanced on the barstool, one foot drawn up and tucked behind the calf of the other leg, which extended with a pointed toe along the flare of the stool. Her spine beneath the taut fabric curved upward from its root like a wisteria stem, her dark-gold hair burned and smouldered. Fillermine faced her, hovering on tense haunches, white-haired and broad-shouldered—he looked lean, hard, tall. Two animals, I reflected, caught in an old deadly game; I could almost hear the tiger's scream of sexual torture splitting Christy's subtropical gloom. It was, in fact, an awesome but tantalizing spectacle for civilized man to behold. Yet how complex these animals were. And how complex their game had become. I decided to intervene.

"Do you imagine," Fillermine was saying in a sneering tone, as

260

I came to stand beside them, "that you can throw your sex about in that manner without arousing interest?"

"I do not throw my sex about, Mr. Fillermine," Alex replied. Her voice was full and hard, and at the same moment the cello throbbed on a strong, vibrant note. "You talk as if I waggled my hips like a common whore."

"Nothing of the kind," Fillermine said. "Your style is superb."

Alex uttered a mock laugh. "Thank you. And what do you suggest I do to save visiting firemen from my snares? Dress in long black robes and walk like a nun?"

"You should damn well not display it unless you intend to . . . use it."

"Nonsense. I'm not displaying it, except to some." She was looking steadily at the tip of his ear. "What do you mean?"

"Your dress, movements . . . your *smell*, for God's sake!"

It was as if I weren't there. They paid no attention to me, though I was standing at their elbows, and I could see that one of the bartenders was listening too. Clearly, Fillermine was in a bad way.

"You exaggerate," Alex said.

"Not a bit." A muscle flickered in Fillermine's jaw.

"Well, you've got a peculiar way of trying to persuade me to sleep with you. You Englishmen, you think you're so clever. All this line of being so rational and open-minded and objective—"

"Do you think for a minute I'd attempt to use a 'line' on someone like you?" Fillermine turned away for a moment, and some of the tension went out of his bearing. "Look here," he said, turning back to Alex, "at this point I've given up—as you know perfectly well. It's clear you're not going to sleep with me, though I'm damned if I know why. Certainly you're not the sort to be impeded by affectations of fidelity—"

"Don't be so sure."

"Why not?"

"Just don't."

"Very well. Fidelity or no, I'm certain pleasure comes first with you. And let me tell you I'd give you more pleasure than you ever had with—"

"Be careful."

261

"No. I'm perfectly sincere. And I'm not boasting—at my age I don't need to." Fillermine smoothed his eyebrow. "Have you ever been in England?"

"No."

"Then what do you know about Englishmen?" He leaned his elbow on the bar. "I can tell you something about the English, if you'd care to hear it."

Alex nodded.

"There's not a woman in the British Isles who could give the appearance of being aware of what her natural body's for, the appearance that you give in every movement—you and a dozen other American women I've seen on the streets of Chicago alone, in the last two days. You can do it beautifully. You're superbly healthy, for one thing, and you can afford good clothes, for another. And you're taught from childhood the techniques of allurement. But you're bogus, you're all so many brummagem dolls. You can't play the game through—"

"*You're* being silly—you know that? It's just not true."

"Wait a minute." Fillermine made a slight expostulatory movement. "I don't mean American women haven't succumbed to me, if you'll permit the word. In fact, most of them do, the ones I have a go at. But what's it like?" His voice hardened. "I have no illusions about it, believe me. These women accept me because I'm a poet, they're the kind of women who can't resist a poet, and America is full of them. But when it comes to the thing itself— why, your hip-waggling whores have more respect for it than you do. You've got the show, the appearance, the display, but that's all—like your magnificent frigid movie stars. Any English girl. . . ." His voice trailed off.

"You're not so clever, after all. How can you oversimplify like that? People are different, not countries."

"Oh, no—don't make that mistake. People are different, yes. But so are countries; so are cultures and civilizations. Perhaps I exaggerate the differences for the sake of my point, but they're still real differences."

"Birdlime! A woman is a woman, English or American."

"Nevertheless, I've had both. You can't deny I'm—"

"You know what I think you are?"

262

"What?"

"Filth."

Fillermine smiled, as if to himself, and got down from the bar-stool and walked away. I took his place.

"Hello, Poppy," she said.

I warmed instantly, of course. "An admirable performance," I said, crinkling my eyes. "But did you have to be so rough with him?"

"He asked for it, didn't he?"

"Perhaps. But I think he was honestly trying to seduce you. He was being complimentary—at first, anyway."

"I didn't think so."

I fished up my pack of cigarettes and lighted two, handing one to her. "Have another?" I asked, pointing to her glass. She nodded. I signaled the bartender, and when he came she said bourbon and water and I said the same. "What about your theory that you can't have too much?" I asked, putting a wary sarcasm into my voice.

She looked thoughtful. "It might have been fun to knock down his pride a bit. The fool!" She drew a circle on the bar with the point of her finger. "But it really wouldn't have been worth the trouble, not with a guy like that. Anyway not tonight. When things get too complicated there isn't time to . . ."

"Savor it?"

"Something like that."

"You're a wonder, Alex. My God!"

We drank our drinks.

I asked: "Is there time for me?"

"I hope so, Poppy. Naturally." She smiled sweetly.

I touched her knee with mine, under cover of the bar. "When?"

"Oh, I can't tell yet. You leave the arrangements to me."

"Of course," I said. I increased my pressure slightly, and moved my knee so that I could feel the resilient flesh just above her kneecap; and a hand fell on my shoulder. I jumped back, quaking.

It was Rollo. "Glad to find you still here," he said.

"Hello," I said. I swiveled round, regaining some of my composure. "How's it going?"

"Splendidly," he said.

"Where's Paula?"

"Over there." He removed his hand from his pocket, and waved it vaguely toward the front. I looked, and saw Paula near the entrance, standing beyond the front curve of the bar, looking especially vernal in that blighted atmosphere. She was talking with Fillermine.

"Where you been?" I asked.

"We had dinner at the Pump."

"Foreclose somebody's mortgage?"

Rollo smiled. "I thought she deserved a little high life," he said, "after her labors in the cause."

"It was a lovely party," Alex said. "I'd say you both deserved it."

"Thank you," Rollo said. He looked well pleased.

Alex slid down from her stool. "Excuse me," she said, "I think my husband needs rescuing from the professor." I saw that Pocksman had Charley pinned against the wall at the back of the room. Alex nodded, almost imperceptibly, toward Paula and Fillermine. "Watch out for that guy," she said, and walked away.

Rollo raised his eyebrows.

"True," I said. "He's stalking any game. Fair or otherwise."

"Oh," Rollo said.

"Raiding poets always think they can bear off any prize. Come on," I said, "Paula needs rescuing too."

I started toward the front, but Rollo put his hand on my arm. I saw from his sober expression that his confidence had weakened. "Maybe we'd better not . . . I mean maybe she'd rather we didn't. . . ."

"Rollo." I said his name sharply. "For Pete's sake, don't give up now."

He said nothing, but made no move to accompany me. He was looking at Fillermine—indecisively, I thought.

I determined for strong measures. "Look, Rollo," I said, "I happen to know Paula will be exceedingly disappointed if we don't rescue her. Exceedingly."

"You know?"

"Yes." I gave him a straight look.

Rollo set out then, and I followed, down the aisle along the bar. When we reached the front, Rollo stepped close to Paula and took her hand. "Hello," he said. "I've brought the boss."

264

Paula smiled gratefully. I kissed her temple. "Blessings," I said.

"We were wondering what the program for the rest of the evening is," Fillermine said.

I'll bet you were, I said to myself. Aloud: "I don't see why we shouldn't push on to the Pocksmans'. The liquor'll be better, at any rate. And since we have only ourselves, the company can't be any worse."

"Good," Rollo said.

"I'll announce the sortie," I said.

As I walked back along the aisle to collect the others, I waved to Ernesto, who was deep in a long solo on "Wrap Your Troubles in Dreams." He made a tremolo on a diminished thirteenth, and winked.

CHAPTER 41

The end of the weather disturbance brought cool, placid stillness to Chicago. A trailing wind moved across the face of the water, and moaned, far off, until it was no more than a resonance in the mind, like Linda's weeping. The clouds wore thin; they frayed and parted. One by one, then more quickly, the stars came out, diminutive beacons riding on all the horizons of the universe, conveying friendliness and hope from the immense distances; and the three-quarter moon set sail, high and bright. The long roll of the waters slackened, settled, and slowly fell to rest. That night autumn came to the lake.

Let our angers, too, be stilled, I thought. And then: all in good time.

CHAPTER 42

Pocksman lived on the other side of the Midway. For the sake of non-Chicagoans, I should explain that the Midway is a broad green strip cutting across the South Side, near the university. It is all that remains of the Columbian Exposition of 1893, which is a considerable point of aggravation to students of architecture: I remember Cienkiewycz more than once lamenting to me the disappearance of the exposition buildings which had been designed by Louis Sullivan. On certain foggy nights Little Sheba still dances on the Midway, to the faint winding notes of the syrinx and for the delectation of befuddled young students on their way home. Pocksman lived in a house of intricate and long-faded elegance, a three-story wooden structure cowering in a cul-de-sac off Woodlawn Avenue; it was a house which baffled the eye with its complexity of porches, bays, turrets, colored fanlights, gingerbread, and fish-scale shingling, and there was a tangle of soot-blackened rosebushes in the front yard.

Our three cars—Pocksman's, Bruno's, and mine—hove to at the curb, and the company disembarked; we had been joined, I saw, by two female artists and one male philosophy student. A streetlight shed its moldy glimmer on the scene; the moon, beyond the housetops, seemed remote and cold. Our small noises resounded in the night: car doors slamming, high heels clattering, a few words in different voices dropped like coins on the pavement. Someone flipped a cigarette into the street, where it burst like a tiny rocket.

Led by Pocksman, the company assaulted the flight of wooden steps which led to the porch, rumbling like a cannonade. I thought

267

of Mrs. Pocksman waiting inside, alone. How did these thundering footsteps sound to her? Frightening, amusing, or only tedious?

Impossible to tell. She was waiting behind the door, and met us with old-fashioned courtesy: so good of you to come, very happy to meet you at last, please come in, let me take your hat, etc., etc. Her dress, too, was a trifle old-fashioned, and like her manner was more formal than anything to which we had been accustomed by the events of the afternoon and evening so far; it was a light print of some expensive fabric—silk?—which fell nearly to her ankles and was clasped at the breast with jade. She wore a jade ring. She had been a beauty once, unmistakably. But the luster had been corroded by—well, I thought I saw the shadow of fear, the shadow of the expectation of fear, darkening in her eyes. Her features were still fine; but her mouth turned down and she was too thin, her brownish throat was sunken. Her movements intimated weariness. I did not know quite what to think of Mrs. Pocksman. A mousy type, obviously, I said to myself at first; but then almost immediately I was caught by something in her expression which uncovered the wells of sympathy in me—forgive, please, my stupid way of saying it, but in fact I did experience a slight overflow. I liked her, I decided; all the more when I looked around. Within that hideous dwelling she had created a pleasing, interesting world. It was her doing, I was sure, not Pocksman's. Nothing costly or ostentatious, but much that expressed the woman's good taste: there was a large shallow bowl of beaten pewter I'd have liked to own myself, and on the escritoire other fine objects of pewterware; the only picture was a sixteenth century Genoese map of Hierosolyma. There was one bold note, excruciating in its intentionally corny assertiveness; how I knew, on such short acquaintance, that it was not only intentional but intentionally corny, I don't know; but I was certain of it. The shallow pewter bowl contained a wooden hand, female and delicate, exquisitely made and jointed with dovetails—I took it for either an artist's or a glover's manikin, and I have the distinct feeling that such a hand occurs somewhere in a painting by De Chirico—which lay palm upward with loosely curved fingers, and held a porcelain egg, softly tinted with rose.

It is creatures like Mrs. Pocksman who make young persons of thirty, as I was then, so deathly afraid of being forty.

In the next room the dining table supported a layout such as

268

I've never seen elsewhere except in a professional eating house, and seldom enough there. Memorable: the term is not excessive, since obviously I remember it. Tiny spareribs with a spiced honey-and-pineapple sauce; Italian sausages; baked prunes wrapped in bacon; corn crackers covered with an impasto of shredded ham and grated provolone; mushrooms stuffed with minced smoked turkey; a whipped paste of avacado and mint, served on saltines; a huge bowl of cold boiled shrimp; another of raw cauliflower, to go with a roquefort-and-cream-cheese dressing; a third of fresh apricots; and, of course, sardines, herrings, gefüllte fish, smoked oysters, anchovies, and Lord knows what all. Plus olives, celery, carrots, radishes, pickles, nuts, chutney, coconut, cucumbers, pretzels, mints, candied fruit, English biscuits, and (so help me) a cheesecake as big as a . . . a . . . well, say a medium sized suitcase. . . . Paula, Alex, and I stood at one end, transfixed.

"My God," Paula gasped. "When could she have done it? She must have been working every second since she got that phone call."

"I should think so," I said.

Alex said: "Can you imagine anyone taking the time? Or having the ambition? I thought this sort of thing was repealed by the nineteenth amendment."

"It was," Paula said.

"Speaking from the masculine point of view," I remarked, "it's a sight to gladden the heart."

"Mine, too," Alex said. "Strangely."

"But we'll have to *eat* it," Paula said. "I can't say it gladdens my stomach."

"Not much choice, is there?" Alex replied. "We can't ignore it—not after she's put so much into it."

"But we just ate!" Paula said in protest. "I don't see how I can." She picked up a stuffed mushroom and experimentally popped it into her mouth.

"Oh, well," Alex said thoughtfully, "not right away. There's a little time to wait, isn't there? What time is it, anyway?"

I looked at my watch. "About ten-thirty," I said.

"I shouldn't think we'd be expected to take all this very seriously till after midnight," Paula murmured. "Would you?"

"No," I said.

269

"Definitely not," Alex said.

"Just think," Paula added, "we might not have shown up at all."

Pocksman appeared, lighting his pipe.

"When I was a young graduate student," he said, "the chairman of my [puff, puff] doctoral committee once took me aside and told me: 'Pocksman [puff, puff, puff], the mark of a true scholar is that he always [puff, puff] gets out the hooch as soon as the guests arrive.'"

We said ha, ha.

"Shall we have a drink?" Pocksman added.

We went back into the living room. A card table had been set up in the middle of the floor, and covered with about fifteen layers of newspaper; on it stood an assortment of bottles, an ice bucket, glasses, a pitcher of water.

"Not very genteel," Pocksman apologized. "My wife frowns on it. But I say to her: 'Dear, the eatables are your department, let the booze be [puff, puff, puff] mine.' Ha, ha."

We all smiled.

"What'll you have?" Pocksman asked, sweeping the room with a ghastly smile.

We all said bourbon, except the philosophy student, who said rye.

"Rye?" Pocksman sneered. "I didn't know anyone around here drank rye whiskey any more."

"I'm from Weehawken," the philosophy student said.

"New Jersey?" Pocksman asked.

Paula hiccuped. "Excuse me," she said.

"Well, I haven't got any rye," Pocksman declared. "What else'll you [puff, puff] have?"

The philosophy student said bourbon.

Pocksman fixed the drinks, making them all very dark except one, which was about the color of rheum. He handed the drinks around, giving the colorless one to Mrs. Pocksman with a little bow. "Here's to the future of drinking," he said. "Ha, ha." He held up his glass.

We all gulped.

"Let's sit down," he said.

We all sat down.

"Had an interesting thing happen in my novel class the other day," Pocksman said. "One of the students [puff, puff] said, 'If Zola wanted to be a genuine naturalist, why didn't he write about what he knew best, the natural life of his own class?' Set me back a bit, I can tell you. After all, what do you suppose is responsible for the perennial affinity of the artist with . . . ah . . . shall we say, low [puff, puff] *life*? Fundamentally, I mean."

Silence. Someone was tapping his foot. I looked, and it was Fillermine.

Finally Bruno said: "Maybe it has something to do with the artist's rebellion against his early surroundings. Isn't that considered practically mandatory for anyone who wants to write?"

"A [puff, puff] surface explanation only, I believe," Pocksman said, hopping up and down on his chair. "It may suffice to account for the artist's *initial* overture to the . . . ah . . . muse, but will it sustain a lifelong [puff, puff] *endeavor*? You see what I mean."

Silence. One of the female painters blew her nose vigorously on a Kleenex. She had a bad cold.

Mrs. Pocksman said: "But it isn't true of *all* novelists, certainly. Take Jane Austen, for—"

"Ah, my dear," Pocksman snarled, spinning on his chair like a machine gun, "you don't stop to think that Jane Austen's characters drawn from her own class—Mr. Bennet, say—are caricatures, while she lavishes her fondest attentions on the villains, Wickham and Darcy."

Silence. Alex jiggled the ice in her glass; Rollo ran his forefinger under his collar.

Mrs. Pocksman said: "But surely, dear, you don't say that Darcy was a representative of the low li—"

"Inversion, that's all. A simple inversion—the same rule applies," Pocksman snapped. He jammed his pipe in his mouth.

Silence. You could have cut it into strips and sold it for insulation.

At last there was a whirring sound from the next room, and a clock undertook to announce the hour. We all counted the strokes. Eleven. We all looked at our watches—to make sure.

"Mrs. Pocksman," Charley said, diffidently. "I wonder if I could turn on the radio for a few minutes. I'd like very much to hear the weather report. We're planning a trip in the morning."

271

"Why, of course," Mrs. Pocksman said, rising immediately. "It's here, in the dining room."

Good old Charley—not one of the rest of us could have found the tact to do it so well. He got up too, and so did a number of the rest. There was a general stirring about, talking, lighting of cigarettes, and so on—the ice was broken at last. Lord knows how it had got frozen so solid in the first place. The party was under way.

CHAPTER 43

Before long, the course of natural events led me in search of the john. Do not fear, I won't try your patience with an exercise in the description of my ritual exertions, though this has, I know, now become the *experimentum crucis* of every proper prose-writer. I decline to commit myself to the trial. Which is not, sadly, so much a question of principle as of simple humane feeling. When you are living in the same house with a person who has not gone to the bathroom, one way or the other, for more than forty-eight hours, such a game loses its appeal. To say the least. I mean Linda, of course, beautiful Linda, serene Linda. This may seem to you a peculiar way of recognizing her falling away into grace. All I can say is that it does not seem peculiar to me. What her thoughts may be I can no longer even guess; but she smiles now, and will smile for hours as I sit holding her hand, looking at me from time to time from beneath her attenuated lids. Her eyes are lustrous and deep, though she has no fever. It's I who have fever, the pain now is all mine, I think, although the cure can only be worked in her. But no cure exists for this illness. If I somehow, anyhow, could revive the force of that young lucid body, if I could. . . . But the mechanism is broken, like a flower the wind has cracked.

You see—don't you?—the urgency which besets my task.

In the course of searching—I resume; have patience—I found the john. A good enough john, though old. It was on the second floor, the last room but one in a hallway extending the length of the house. When I reached it, however, the door was closed; and

I wandered on a few steps to the end of the hall. The final room, beyond the john, was open, but dark. I looked in, I struck a match and held it up—the room was small and bare, except for a small bed. My match burned my finger and I blew it out, but went on in, feeling my way to the bed: it was covered with a plain white counterpane, made of some ribbed fabric, and had only the mattress underneath—stripped for action, so to speak. The speculations that you can imagine as well as I crossed my mind as I came out again into the hallway and resumed my vigil. Fortunately, I had learned some years before not to wait till the last moment when I was at parties, and so I wasn't suffering. When the bathroom door finally opened, Alex was the one who came out.

"Hey, come here," I said, unerringly. "Hurry."

"Where?"

"In here." I showed her the room, almost pushing her in. I struck another match, turned on the light, shut the door and slid to the small bolt that locked it. Only then I noticed that the window shades were already drawn. I sat down on the bed. "Cozy, eh?"

"Very," Alex said, coldly. She walked a few steps, but then came and sat beside me.

"What do you suppose it's for?"

She looked at me. Her expression wasn't in the least promising: she seemed undecided whether to laugh or jeer. "What the unutterable hell do you think it's for, you old letch?" She turned away. "An alcoholic letch, at that."

"I was just asking," I said. "No need to get spleenish about it."

"Just asking!" Alex expelled a breath gustily. "You think I don't know when I'm being propositioned? It's an empty room," she said, speaking with exaggerated precision, "just an empty room. If you lived alone with your middle-aged wife in a three-story house, don't you think you'd have an empty room?"

"The point is," I said, my voice wobbling, I fear, between unction and acrimony, "it's not empty—it's got a bed in it."

"All right then, have it your way. Mrs. Pocksman is taking tricks on the side—to earn Christmas money."

"Okay, okay." Alex is the only woman I've known who could be genuinely shocking. "I just meant it's . . . hell, it's convenient,

274

I don't know why it's here but it *is* convenient, and I thought . . . But let it pass. What's come over you anyway—you're more changeable today than I've ever seen you?"

"Not true. But I do have some sense of propriety."

"And I don't, I suppose?"

"No, Poppy, you don't—especially when you're tight."

"I'm not ti—"

"Yes, you are. Pretty much anyway." She smiled. "There's a time and place, you know. For everything." She put her hand over mine. "Not now. And not here."

"Okay."

"That's for the university kids, that back-room business at parties. University kids and poets."

"Well, I *am* a poet."

"Not when I love you," she said.

"I see," I said. "Well, at least you laid that on the line."

We were both silent, looking at the uncovered floor.

Then Alex spoke. "Do you realize it's only been a few weeks—not even two months—since . . ."

"Lake Jones?"

She nodded.

"Yes. It does seem longer, doesn't it?"

She nodded again, and got up from the bed. She bent, raised her skirt, pulled down her slip by the hem.

"Have you made the . . . arrangements yet?" I asked.

"I'll be on the Promontory at one o'clock," she answered.

This time I nodded. I got up too, staggering momentarily. Pocksman's bourbon was better than Christy's, without a doubt.

"You'll be a dead fish by one o'clock," Alex said.

"Not a bit," I said. "I'll go easy after this."

I unlocked the door and turned out the light, and we stepped into the hallway; but we were caught—by Fillermine. He had just turned into the hallway from the stairs as we went through the door.

"Hello," he said. "I thought it was the next-to-the-last room." He raised his eyebrows and smiled.

"It is," I said pleasantly. "Help yourself."

Alex slipped past Fillermine and hurried down the stairs.

275

"Then what's in here—as if it weren't obvious?" He peered into the last room. "A bit functional," he observed. "But adequate, adequate." He withdrew his head and turned toward me. "But I see my chief hope has been thwarted."

"It wasn't much of a hope, Clambert."

"Obviously," he said. "Congratulations. But tell me—I wasn't properly introduced to the two young ones—would you mind?"

"The painters? Not at all. Their names are Ruth Travicic and Mary Donaldson."

"So many Biblical names in America, aren't there? Heritage of separatism, I daresay."

"Perhaps. There's a lot of it around," I said. "Frankly, Clambert, I don't think your hopes are particularly rosy in this case either."

"No? I suppose they're both head over heels in love, eh? The young and brave?"

"That's the ticket."

"Spirit of pietism." He spoke with quiet exasperation. "What kind of men do you have in this country, that can lock up a young female's . . . ah . . . constituent parts and then stay home and sleep while the dear thing goes galloping around and showing off? It's . . . it's Ptolemaic." He frowned. "See here, just for curiosity's sake, whom are they in love with?"

"With each other, I imagine."

I patted his arm sympathetically, and slipped into the bathroom ahead of him.

When I got downstairs, I was drawn, inevitably, to the card table. Pocksman came forward and began making drinks for both of us.

"Easy, man, easy," I protested. "The night is young, relatively."

He blinked. Then: "Quite so, old man. I'm beginning to feel a bit loopy myself." I couldn't see that he diminished his own portion any, however.

"Cheers," I said.

"By all means," he said, and swallowed a large gulp. "I say, old man, I was wondering about those . . . ah . . . poems, you know?" He filled his pipe from a greasy pouch. "I mean, I'd rather like to know when I might expect to hear?" He struck a match. "Your

276

decision, that is. I'm [puff, puff] rather eager, you know, to [puff, puff, puff] place them definitely because [puff, puff, puff, puff] well, frankly, I've been asked to give something to the . . . ah . . . university literary quarterly?"

I gasped involuntarily as Pocksman's acerbic tobacco smoke enveloped me.

"Sorry, old man," he said. "Bit strong for you?"

"A little gamy," I said.

"Ah," he said, putting the pipe down on the card table. He pulled again at his glass. "As I was saying," he went on, "about those little verses of mine, I rather wonder if you could let me have some sort of . . . ah . . . timetable, perhaps?"

"Oh, it'll be soon now, very soon," I said offhandedly. "Been busy as hell with this party for Fillermine," I lied. "Had to wait till this was wound up before I could tackle the new manuscripts."

"Ah, yes. Of course. Well, I just thought I'd mention it. Happens to be a rather ticklish business for me, you know? Meeting the quarterly's deadline and waiting for your decision at the same time —all that sort of thing." He picked up his pipe again and struck a match. "I mean, I'd much rather have the [puff, puff] verses in *Pegasus*, of course—you know how it is—but at the same time, you [puff, puff] see, I've been definitely *asked* [puff] by the quarterly?"

I gasped again.

"Sorry," he said. He rammed the pipe into his side pocket. "Habit, you know."

"Don't apologize," I assured him. "And don't worry about your poems—you'll be hearing in a day or two, a week at the most." I lied again; quite expertly, I thought. "I say, old man—" I cursed inwardly for my weakness in imitating him "—excuse me, will you? I want to have a word with Paula." I turned away before he could answer.

I couldn't find Paula, but Rollo, who was standing with Mrs. Pocksman, beckoned to me. They were near the foot of the stairs.

"Splendid party," I said to Mrs. Pocksman.

"Thank you so much," she replied, her voice lowered. "But I'm afraid there's some unpleasantness." She gestured hesitantly toward the upper floor.

"What's up?" I said cheerily to Rollo.

277

"I'm not quite sure. Seems Fillermine's up to something."

"Ummm," I said. "Little room at the end of the hall?"

"Yes, I'm afraid so," Mrs. Pocksman said.

"Who's with him?"

"Mrs. Pocksman thinks it's Paula."

"Well, get up there, get up there!"

"But what the hell—excuse me—can I do?"

"Listen," I said, "if you care anything about that girl, anything at all, you understand?—you'd better do something. . . ."

"All right." Rollo looked worried, but turned toward the stairs.

Mrs. Pocksman smiled. "Wait," she said. "I didn't realize . . . I mean, I didn't know you. . . . Well, anyway, I think I have a plan. Let's all go up."

We mounted the stairs—a rather odd trio, I thought, to be going to the bathroom, but no one appeared to notice.

When we came to the last door, Mrs. Pocksman said, "Let me. . . ." She rapped on the door gently. The murmured voices inside stopped. "Mr. Fillermine," she called. "Mr. Fillermine, telephone for you." She paused. Then: "It's from London."

It worked. Fillermine knew, obviously, when he was licked. The door opened almost immediately, and he came out, looking unruffled, brushing a speck from his sleeve. "I say," he smiled, "from London? How appalling!" He stepped around Rollo deftly and headed toward the stairs.

"Hurry!" Mrs. Pocksman whispered with a surprising hiss, and she pushed Rollo, with her hand squarely in the small of his back, through the door. Before he knew it, he was inside and she had closed the door with a soft click.

She turned and scurried after Fillermine.

I was left standing alone in a state of discomposure which was equaled, I'm afraid, by Rollo's. I went into the bathroom and looked at myself; raised my eyebrows; clucked my tongue; straightened my tie and nodded knowingly to myself. Feeling reassured— less like someone who has just arrived at a bus stop in time to see the bus pulling away—I came out again. Since Rollo was still out of sight and since I had heard no cries for help, I shrugged my shoulders and walked to the stairs.

The view from the top of the stairs afforded a tableau of the company at large. Fillermine and Mrs. Pocksman, standing under the archaic map, were bathed in laughter and complaisance, getting on famously. The poet had taken the hoaxed telephone call with good grace, and I silently commended Mrs. Pocksman's finesse. The two painters had Pocksman half smothered between them on the sofa, babbling in both his ears simultaneously, showing him something on a sketch pad; for once the professor looked out of his element. Charley and the philosophy student were seated on straight chairs by the escritoire, leaning their elbows backward on the opened lid; they were talking, smiling, enjoying themselves, Charley was sitting in a slouch with his ankles crossed, there was no trace of a tic. I wondered what they could possibly be talking about. Alex and Bruno were not in sight, I noticed with some trepidation, but I thought they might be in the kitchen or dining room. I descended the stairs slowly, lighting a cigarette, and wandered through the other rooms, but found no one but a large English bulldog asleep under the kitchen table. From among the folds of his obesity, he pronounced my doom with one flaming eye, and went back to sleep.

I approached the card table, and spooned up a fresh piece of ice from the puddle in the ice bucket, plopping it into my glass. Charley was saying, behind me: "Oh, no. We don't swaddle the infants any more—only in the most backward areas. But maybe French kids get the same result from their sleeping—uh—arrangements. We're always overcrowded, especially in the cities."

Smiling, I turned around, picked up a ladder-back chair, and went to join them. "Don't let me interrupt," I said.

"We're just talking—not seriously, you know. We tried a bit of philosophy, at least I asked a few questions, but—" Charley shrugged. "I wasn't up to it," he said simply.

"It's too bad, in a sense," the philosophy student said. He was a redheaded boy, thin, pale, good-looking. "But when you study the damn stuff so much, you necessarily get kidnaped by the techniques and you can't talk without them. Same problem everywhere, of course. Dangers of specialization. Still, I'm naïve enough to think philosophy ought to be for everybody."

"Depends on what kind of philosophy it is, I expect," I ventured.

"Yes," the student answered. "Yes. That and a man's readiness to admit that life is problematical. Most people won't, you know."

"There, you see?" Charley said. "Just when I think I know what

279

problematical means, or some other word like that, I hear it in a new sentence, and then it seems to me I don't understand it any more."

"The so-called language barrier, Charley," I said. "We've all got it, more or less. And ultimately it's not important."

"Well, it's damned inconvenient," Charley said.

"You do remarkably well, it seems to me," the student put in.

"He does indeed," I said, "and he really knows more words than he thinks, only he's afraid to use them. Perfectly understandable."

Charley studied his hands. His tic began working, like a hairspring in his eye.

"I'm hungry as a bear," the student said. "When do we get a chance at the eats?"

"Any time you like, I guess. We've all been holding off because we had enormous dinners."

"Well, I didn't." As a matter of fact, he looked as if he hadn't eaten a full dinner in years. "I think I'll . . . give it a whirl," he said, rising with a certain embarrassment.

"We'll go with you," Charley said.

Soon we were standing beside the table, guzzling spareribs and sausages.

"Good," Charley said.

"Damn right," the student seconded.

"Formidable," I agreed. "Hadn't realized I was so hungry."

"Thank God for the lowly pig," the student said, stoking himself with sausage.

"Ummm," Charley muttered. "Try some of these cauliflowers and cheese."

"Uh-uh," the student replied. "Right now I'm carniverous."

I was moving on to the ham-and-cheese canapés. "Try these, then. Lots of protein—and they're a dinner in themselves."

We stood around, chomping.

Paula and Rollo came in, looking well pleased. I concluded the episode abovestairs had been comparatively successful, though I was more interested, naturally, in the long-range prospects. "Hi," I said. "Come and pitch in." I reflected that Alex was wrong—partly wrong, at all events. In condemning the "backroom business" out of hand, in saying one must always choose one's time and place.

280

Occasionally the time and place do the choosing, and then it is right as rain.

"I recommend these spareribs," the student said. "You shouldn't miss them."

"It all looks so good," Paula sighed. "It's hard to choose."

She took a couple of spareribs though, and some celery and olives. Rollo stocked his plate. We all stood around, chomping.

"Good," Rollo said.

"A gas," the student said.

Rollo looked startled. He chomped a while, then said: "Say, did you notice that hand out there with the egg in it?"

"Couldn't help noticing, could you?" the student said.

"Curious," Rollo muttered, and returned to his chomping.

"What I'm wondering," I said, "is whether or not one dares cut into that cheesecake."

"Why not?" Paula asserted. "She wouldn't have put it there if it weren't to be eaten."

She found a serving knife on the sideboard, and cut chunks of the cake for each of us. More chomping.

"Man, this is living," the student said. In the marveling quality of his voice I thought I recognized the possible tones of Lazarus.

"It's very good," Charley said. "Wish I could eat more."

Mrs. Pocksman poked her head through the doorway. "So glad to see you in here," she said. "I was afraid no one was going to touch it."

"It's delicious, Mrs. Pocksman," Paula said.

"Magnificent," Rollo added.

"Emphatically," the student said, with his mouth full. "Have you ever tried rhubarb sautéed with veal?"

"I'm so sorry," Mrs. Pocksman called, as she ducked out again. "It's upstairs in the medicine cabinet."

"What did she say?" the student asked.

"I think she thought you were asking for bicarb of soda," I said.

"Oh."

"Time for us to be leaving," Rollo said.

Paula concealed a yawn. "It's been a long day." Actually she looked as fresh as ever.

"It's getting on—we'll all leave soon," I said. But this is fine, I

281

thought. If the beginning has been made in the security, so to speak, of numbers, he ought to be able to carry on in private.

"Good night."

"So long."

"Drive carefully."

"Oh, we will."

"See you tomorrow."

"Yes—not too early."

"Thanks for everything, you two. The magazine owes you a lot for this afternoon—whatever comes of it."

"Don't be silly. It had to be done—that's all."

"Well, good night."

"So long."

And they were gone.

"Me, too," Charley said.

"Yes, it's time to cut out," the student said.

I looked at my watch. Quarter past twelve. Not late by any means; but I had an appointment to keep. "Yes," I said. "I'll be leaving too."

"Can I catch a lift with you?" Charley asked. "I left my car at home this morning—didn't want to risk getting hung up without a parking space at the courthouse."

"Of course," I said. "Can I drop you off too?" This to the philosophy student.

"No, thanks. I always go for a walk at night anyway."

"Okay," I said. I took Charley aside to a corner of the dining room. "What about Alex?" I asked. "Has she gone home?"

"No," Charley said, looking down at his hands. "She went with Bruno. He's sick, something the matter with his heart, I think—she drove him home in his car, then she'll get a taxi back."

"I see," I said. "Okay, we can leave in a minute. I need to make a visit upstairs first, though."

"I'll wait in the front room," Charley said.

I climbed the stairs again. In the john I saw I'd declined somewhat from my best hour. Coffee, I thought—that's what I need. Get some when I get home. Funny there wasn't any here: Mrs. Pocksman lying down on the job. I smoothed my hair, wet my fingers, wiped them on a pale green towel. I heard footsteps in the

282

hall outside. A last glance; then I opened the door, stepped out, and saw at once who was there: Mrs. Pocksman, followed by Fillermine, was just entering the little room at the end of the hall.

Bravo!

No point in attempting to thank mine hostess, I thought, but better seek out mine host; I tramped, a little heavily, down the stairs.

I hadn't far to seek. Pocksman was waiting for me, weaving soddenly, at the foot of the stairs. From his pinched face sprang two red eyes and a gnash of mahogany teeth. He was jumping up and down on both feet, with his arms outstretched. "You!" he howled. "Miserable editor! Thief! Cheating poor poets of their just due! You black bastard, I'll have the law, you understand!—you, you poem-snatcher, I'll have the law! Hah! Drinking my liquor, eating my food—and what do I get for it?" Tears of rage gleamed on his papery jowls. "My poems stolen, fruit of my anguished hours! *Stolen,* do you hear? Stolen away from me." He clutched my lapels and shook me. "Give them back to me," he wailed. "Give me back my poems."

"Easy, Pocksy, keep your shirt on," I said placatively. "You'll have them back in no time, I promise."

"Ah-h-h-h-h," he shrieked. "You won't read them! I knew it, knew it! God in Heaven, he doesn't even open the manuscripts! Justice! Justice!"

"But of course I read them, Pocksy," I said. "Very interesting too. But there are so many—"

He leapt. "Out!" he bawled, whipping his finger toward the door. "Out of my house! You'll not trespass on my hospitality another instant! Do you hear? Out! Out! . . . Oh, merciful heaven, justice! Pour down retribution on this . . . this . . . this ba-a-a-astard!" He broke into inconsolable weeping.

I feinted around him, and broke for the front door at a run, pushing Charley ahead of me.

CHAPTER 44

I drove in silence, Charley also did not speak, we moved north on Woodlawn, past 55th, 53rd, 47th, across the quiet night. A few people were about, a few cars and buses. The bars were lighted. This fellow Charley, I thought, how shall I take him now—the one who was to kill me, the one whom I was to kill? Absurd: Alex was right to laugh at me. Yet I can't say there isn't a terrible enmity between us. A mortal enmity. He says nothing, does not move. Is it benevolence or malignity that he radiates? Or neither? Perhaps his placidity is only a disguise for the universal human bewilderment, fermenting in him now with particular unintelligibility. Perhaps he simply doesn't know what to do or think. God knows, I don't either. Defeated, both of us, brought to rest before the inconceivable—a human being. As I say, it was a mortal enmity.

I parked at some distance from the apartment house, taking the first space I saw. We climbed the stairs. "Coffee?" Charley asked, and I nodded. We both went into his flat. I paced nervously in the living room while he boiled water and measured coffee in the kitchen. The house, so well known to me, increased my nervousness, enclosing me in its walls; the identifying environment of my life, Charley's life, Alex's life. I was the adulterer, the odd man, and I was here. My danger seemed acute.

Charley came in with two steaming cups, and handed one of them to me. He sat in the crimson-striped chair, and I took my cup to the end of the sofa. The cup rattled. My tension—still unanalysable and still perhaps unnecessary—reached the point at which a break was imperative.

284

"It's been a red-letter day for you, Charley," I said, and quickly sipped my coffee.

"Yes, red," he said. "Red stands for hell."

I put my cup on the low table and pressed my hands under my knees. "That sounds ominous."

"Onimous? I'm not sure what that means. It's been the worst day of my life."

"Charley, I'm astonished. What is it?"

"You know. You must."

"I? How can I know?" My breath strained in my throat. "What's eating you, Charley?"

"Everything's gone to pieces, that's all."

I got up and began pacing, slowing, regularly, along the carpet. "You better tell me," I said. "I suppose it's Alex—her behavior tonight. At least I don't know what else could make you so upset."

"It's Alex, all right. But I don't know, I don't know what to say about her, what to call her. Do you understand? Maybe she's just a bitch, a common bitch. You must know. . . . I think she must be just a bitch, and yet she's done so many fine things."

"I don't think Alex is a bitch, whatever she's done. And I don't think I know what a bitch is anyway. I don't trust classifications."

"No, I suppose not."

"What *has* she done, Charley? What's it all about?"

"I don't know. I can't say now. I think you're the one who could tell me, if you wanted to."

"Me? I haven't the least idea what you're talking about, Charley. Honestly."

"Maybe."

"Look, Charley, if you have suspicions, perhaps it'd be best to spill them out. Talking helps sometimes. Maybe what you think is untrue."

"I don't know. I can't talk about it now. It'll all be out in the open, one way or the other, soon enough."

"When is Alex coming home?"

"I don't know." He scowled at his hands.

"Charley, it's late, I'm sure this whole business seems a lot worse now than it really is—you've been building it up in your mind. Tomorrow it will assume its right proportions."

285

"I don't know. We'll see."

I picked up my cup and gulped the coffee. It was now half cold. "Can I do anything, Charley? You want to come over to my place for a nightcap?"

"No. No, thanks. I'll just stay here."

—And Linda is sleeping now, I've just gone to see, her breath passes in and out as lightly as a summer breeze in the forest, and her breast quivers like the leaves on a beech sapling.—Charley would not sleep; I didn't know what he would do that night, but I knew he would not sleep.

"I'll be getting home, Charley. I'm done in."

"You know something? You say you don't know what a bitch is, and maybe I don't know what a son-of-a-bitch is—but sometimes I think you're one. Do you know you always talk down to me? I don't think you even know it. It's true though—you always do."

"I do know it, Charley. Maybe I'm a son-of-a-bitch. I guess I am. You're not the first one to tell me so, at any rate. But I do know when I'm talking down to you, I'm probably just as aware of it as you are. Maybe more, even. I can't help it. I do my best—most of the time—but I can't help it. Maybe that's my curse, Charley, as much as yours."

"Yes, yes. I knew it wasn't worth mentioning."

"I've got to go now, Charley."

"Okay. Good night."

"Good night, Charley."

I went out, closing the door carefully and quietly behind me.

Did Charley know?

He must.

CHAPTER 45

I took off my coat, tie, and shirt, and washed myself. When I wash Linda her arms are like paper, they stay where I put them, and the skin of her belly is translucent, as if the light inside were shining through. I shaved, gently because my face was still raw from the shave I had had in the morning. I put on a fresh shirt, and a different tie and coat, transferring my wallet and cigarettes. I went out. I walked as quietly as I could down the stairs, down the front steps, along the sidewalk to my car. But before I reached my car I heard other footsteps on the walk behind me, and before I started my car I heard another car start up. Charley. . . .

I drove south on Lake Park Avenue to 55th and put the car in a vertical slot in front of a hotel. Another car was behind me, too far back to be distinguished in the night. I looked at my watch: one minute to one. When I got out of the car, the cold air hurt me, chilling the perspiration on my forehead.

The walk to the Promontory leads down from the street, across a small park, through a tunnel under Lakeshore Drive, and out onto the Promontory itself, which is a rocky spur jutting a hundred yards into the lake. A path leads to the farthest point and there are benches beside it. As I walked across the park, I heard footsteps on the street; when I entered the tunnel, I heard heel-taps quicken behind me. In the dark tunnel, I thought I saw a shape crouching ahead of me, but I did not flinch and it was nothing. Before I reached the end of the tunnel, the steps behind me had entered, echoing cavernously. I hurried. I was panting now, and sweating in the cold. My perspiration clung to my ribs like rime.

287

Charley has a gun, I thought. Charley has a gun. He actually has it, owns it, possesses it—a real gun. No dream, no metaphor. Deadly metal, cold and tight. He is walking behind me now, here.

In the cold of late night my back was scorched with fear. It burned with the fire of the gun.

But when I saw Alex I was more afraid, because she was sitting on a wooden bench with Bruno, at one side of the Promontory. And I thought: Charley will kill all of us, it will be a cataclysm of blood and death, a newspaper scandal, here by this park bench in the darkness.

I came up to the bench, and in a few second Charley was beside me. Alex looked at us. "I have something to tell you both," she said. "That's why I asked you to come."

Now, Charley. Now. Now.

But nothing happened. I was faint, but heard then, remotely through my vertigo, the words which Alex had said, as if for the first time. She had asked us both to come. Charley had been *asked* to come. He wasn't following me, he had come of his own accord. He didn't know, he still didn't know.

CHAPTER 46

"Rig and I are going away together," Alex said.

Charley said: "I know. I mean I thought it must be that. Why, Alex?"

"I have to leave, Charley—sooner or later you would ask me to. I'm not good now, not for the part you want me to play. It isn't what you think, not altogether. It's just that I'm—not strong enough for it now. You don't understand."

"No, Alex. That doesn't matter. I do understand how people can get strong in time. I'd be glad to wait for it, Alex."

"No, Charley. It might never happen, it would take too long. Lives are to be lived, Charley—yours too."

Charley made no answer.

Alex said to me: "I asked you to come too because I want to leave Charley in your hands. You and I love Charley more than anyone else does."

Bruno sat half in a shadow.

I hesitated. Then: "I'm not very good at that sort of thing, Alex. I can't even take care of myself. But all this is fantastic anyway. Fantastic. Have you lost your reason?—all this calm sweeping away of people and events, you can't do it, it's not sane."

"Don't worry about sanity and insanity so much."

I didn't know what to say to that.

After a few seconds I put my hand on Charley's shoulder and said to him: "Do you mind, Charley—Alex and I had better have a word or two alone?"

"No, of course not," he said.

"Let's walk a bit, Alex," I said.

We left Charley and Bruno on the bench, sitting at opposite ends. We walked toward the water's edge. The waves were running in lightly, stumbling against the stones. We stood by the point, looking out.

"Alex," I said, "I've eaten too much, drunk too much, and God knows heard too much. I'm not thinking well, I know. But what in the sweet hell is it all about? You say I love Charley, but I love you too—very simply and completely, in spite of all our muddlement. You know you're killing me?"

She raised her head. "Yes, Poppy."

I went on, hurriedly. "All right, forget about me. I think I must be really half-dead; I don't know what I think or feel. Perhaps I do love Charley enough to think of him first. I think tonight I do. Let's say you *can* ditch me—just like that. No regrets, no reproaches. But Charley? You're not only breaking his heart, you know. It's not as simple as that. You're breaking him completely."

"I know."

"Then why? Why?"

"I've told you—I'm broken too, I can't be Charley's wife any longer. That's a duty, an . . . obligation. Too much, far too much. I can't perform it any more."

"But—" I stopped. "Oh, hell, I think this is crazy, whatever you say. For instance, is it possibly, conceivably true, what they say about Bruno being a—"

"Yes, it's true."

"Then for God's sake, it's madness—madness compounded. Why? Why? What are you up to?"

"Rig needs me," she began. "But that's not it, others would do as well. I need him—terribly. In the first place, I need someone to pity, you must have seen that long ago, and I don't think I can pity Charley any longer—it's the other way around now. He doesn't want it or need it, and my pity's worn out. For you too."

"Alex, that's rationalization, and a poor job of it at that. You don't leave your husband on any such flimsy grounds. Or your lover."

"I know. Wait, can't you? I'm coming to the point. The most important thing is that not only my pity's worn out, *I'm* worn out,

290

totally, the whole thing. I'm gone now, vanished—the part of me I always used to mean when I said 'I.' Am I making sense? All I can do is love now, crazy, mad love—yes, I'm using your terms. Crazy, mad love without a single constructive element, just taking, taking, grabbing everything, even things for which I have no use. I'm one total, simple, famous sex machine, that's all. And when you reach that stage you really haven't any sex left at all, sex means nothing. I'm sexless, just like Rig. The two of us make a perfect couple."

"You're not being clear, Alex. What is it really?"

"That's it really. I'm defiled, you muddlehead—can't you see it? Smell it, feel it? I can. I'm totally defiled. Only instead of being loathsome, I'm beautiful—too beautiful, a total beauty. Like some great flower, some hungry orchid, a perfectly natural thing. But I don't want to be a flower, I don't want to be a natural thing, I want to be a human being—at last. Above all, that's what I want. Why do you think I was so rough, as you said, with Fillemine this evening? Just to make him squirm? Of course not; he isn't worth it. I was trying to get back a bit of my own humanity. And it worked, I haven't felt as well as I do tonight for weeks."

"I hadn't noticed."

"No. A sex-driven man never notices. A woman is different, if you want to know the truth."

"Alex, it all sounds like metaphysics to me. . . ."

"I don't care what it sounds like. To me it's just a need, like air, like water. . . . Probably I haven't said it very well."

"You tell me you're defiled, beautifully defiled. I must say that's a curious defilement. But by whom?—or what? I don't understand."

"All right, you force me. By you. And it isn't the defilement that's beautiful at all, believe me."

"By me? I don't understand."

"Of course, by you. You've been responsible for the break between Charley and me just as surely as if he had known about us and had taken matters into his own hands."

"But he didn't know about us. Apparently he still doesn't—though Lord knows what I can believe from you now."

"No, he doesn't. That's the truth."

"But then—" I stopped, then went on. "You say you're defiled,

291

you say I've done it, you say that's why you must leave Charley. But Alex, you're talking like someone in an old melodrama. You make me sound like the wicked landlord. This is today, tonight. You can't tell me a woman with your capacity for experience is defiled, as you say, simply from taking a lover."

"Oh, no. You don't escape that easily. It wasn't just sleeping with you, or loving you. And probably any other man in the world could have taken me and then left me intact. It's you, you yourself. Only your touch could have made me dirty."

"What a hell of a thing to say, Alex."

"No. My words are what you yourself have said many and many a time. You are saying them now."

Yes, I was.

But not now, not with Linda, I swear it—it's not true at all. I swear by the bell—what else can I swear by in a defiled world?— the bell she loves no longer that I keep here on my desk.

292

CHAPTER 47

Spring. Rain. April rain. Steady and cold in the dark. For three days now; and the snow melts, the last of it. Yellow foam crumbling in the woods. Water everywhere, puddles, streams, lagoons. I lean on the windowsill, looking out, and the water surrounds us, wavelets running in the starlight. Across the water, the apple tree shimmers indistinctly. It's as if the cottage were an ark, toiling and turning away on the flood, bearing us off to refuge, Linda, I, and the other.

Alex went to her refuge. She had discarded the blue dress now, and wore a white, simple, almost classical garment, white as alabaster in the starlight; and her hair was ruffled by the night wind. Bruno led her away, down the walk from the Promontory, into the tunnel. For an instant the two were framed in the tunnel's entrance, poised frailly arm in arm against the interior blackness.

CHAPTER 48

In Charley's flat again, we drank—first the remains of the booze we found in his cupboard, then the bottle I brought from my kitchen—and we scarcely noticed that one was bourbon, the other gin. Again Charley sat in the crimson-striped chair, I sat on the sofa. Charley's books, the uniform blue-bound volumes of American treasures, were ranged in a cabinet beside him. For a long time he brooded, studying the titles. A few tears were in his eyes, like strands of cobweb that have escaped the broom; the tic alternately dozed and wakened. He got up and stalked from room to room, pursuing his image of despair, mocking it. His footsteps groaned on the carpet like frogs in a dry pond. At last he came and sat again in his chair.

We were both drunk. But our minds seemed active and sober. No drink could intoxicate them now, short of unconsciousness.

"I don't understand," Charley repeated over and over. "It is an evil thing, isn't it? Why does it happen? Who makes it happen? How can the world go on, how can anything work, if an evil thing happens—it will all come falling down. Thump."

"Some good may come of it," I said.

"How? What good?"

"Your bearing it, or not bearing it—that might be a good. In the long run. In you."

"Oh, I don't understand you!"

We were both silent, drinking.

Then Charley: "I tell you if a bad thing happens to a man out of a clear blue sky, then it is death, nothing but death, it is death for everything, the world goes to pieces, there isn't anything left to be trusted, not the sun if it shines or the wind if it blows."

"But you will still live, Charley. And eventually—"

"No, it's death. Death. You can't put the world together again. Never."

Silence. We drank and smoked.

Charley asked: "Did you know?"

"Perhaps. Something was wrong."

"Yes. Yes. She's a bitch, isn't she?" But he held up his hand. "No, not a bitch. If only she were a bitch, things would be better. If she were a bitch then there would be not-bitches. But she is not a bitch, and so there are only—what? Alexes, Alexes everywhere."

He brooded on the titles of the books. Finally he reached out and took one from the shelf. He read the title from the stamping on the cover. *Huckleberry Finn.* Slowly he opened the book, turning pages at random, and then he tore a handful of pages from the center and flung them into the air over his head, letting the mutilated book drop to the floor by his side. The pages slithered and sprawled. He reached for another book—*The Red Badge of Courage*—and tore its pages and flung them in the air, letting the mutilated book fall to the floor by his side. A third book—*Great Battles of the Civil War*—was torn in the same way; and a fourth, a fifth, a sixth—*The Essays of Bronson Alcott, Martin Eden, The Federalist.* In a fury now he swept a dozen books to the floor, kicked them, spat on them, ground the pages under his heel. He took his glass and poured his drink over the debris. Tears shone on his face; his white shirt was drenched.

I reached out and touched his hand. "Enough, Charley," I said. "You've made your point."

"Je suis appellé Gaston," he said. "Actuellement."

He rose from his chair again, went to the desk, opened the bottom drawer, took out the gun.

"Actuellement," he said.

I watched, very tense.

"What do you think?" he said. "Bruno—that guy Bruno?"

Relief, triumph flooding my veins. I was quiet.

"Bruno?" Charley repeated. "You have to do something, don't

295

you—do something at a time like this. Isn't that so? They always do something, don't they?"

I held my drink tightly in my fingers, squeezing the knuckles white.

"Bruno," he said.

He put the pistol in his pocket and went out the door, lurching.

CHAPTER 49

But it was madness. What the devil was driving me? Of course Charley would never shoot anyone but himself—never in any circumstances.

But it is Linda now; Linda, so ill, sleep broken and scattered; there will be none this night. This clear night, the stars shining on the waters beyond the window. I must gather the strands together. Linda, convulsed, writhing, trembling like a candle flame.

What the devil is driving me? I cannot recognize myself. There or here.

And I hurried, I did my best—down the stairs, clattering; banging the door open. Time then only to see Charley's car swerving across 47th. Where was he going? Surely the Promontory again, I knew that. I stumbled into my car and drove again, trembling again, down Lake Park to 55th to the hotel parking space.

But the cottage whirls, spinning away in the blackness, turning round and round, turning upon its center—Linda. Things are miscarrying. Lord, I write, I run, I clutch the window, watching the stars in the waters, turning.

Across the park, through the tunnel, waiting for the loud explosion. It must come. Now. *Now!* But this thing is dead, Linda. Oh, my dear. And the tunnel snarls at me with echoes, bites me; and I run, cold and wet. Onto the Promontory where the blazing stars of the sky blaze too in the waters, all turning around above and below the pit of the universe—dead, dead—but Charley stood there—stood!—between stars and stars, whirling. *"Where is the gun, Charley?"* And he points into the starry waters, down, far down, and I look, and I can almost see—dead, dead. And I fall, I am lurching down to the stones, laughing, laugh, my God, Linda—where are we?—throwing laughter everywhere clattering among the stars—the cottage turning away—through the stars—laughing tears blinding the stars—laughing—

CHAPTER 50

Later now. And elsewhere. I am calm, pain subsides, the days have moved. Safe now. Again. Locked up again. Here the first daffodils are blossoming on the grounds, the lawns are turning green, bees and wasps investigate the window. I lean on the deep sill, pressing my forehead against the grid, so that two indentations remain in my flesh when I turn away. This is not foolishness, though doubtless the others think so; they don't laugh, no one laughs here, but they look at me and then away again; this is not foolishness, my pressing the bars, but simply a ritual means—rituals are important!—of communing with the solidarity of the place. Even more, the stolidity, the changelessness. Though, as a matter of fact, one or two changes have occurred since the last time. Additional beds, a new intern. The old-timers greet me as if I had come home from a journey to a foreign country.

I lean on the windowsill and look out because—it took me several days to understand this—because it is spring. You see how strong is the old necessity? I'd like to lie in the sun and listen to someone reading from Hesiod. Though I know practically no Greek.

Well, five days from now the T-and-O (tests and observation) will be over. I'll be able to go out in the yard with the others.

Meanwhile, I have been given pencil and paper.

I had intended to present you with a workmanlike book, not one of those lapidarian ornaments of literature that are so much admired in these years—I haven't the skill for it and frankly don't think I care much for the type—but something at least sturdy and

299

straightforward; I know I have gone extremely wide of that mark; I had planned to go back, of course, amending, amplifying, improving wherever possible, cutting away false impressions I may have created in my haste, reordering some of the misplaced remembrances which I originally set down as they occurred to me; but now there is no opportunity for even these minor repairs. Probably there will never be an opportunity. This place is not a workroom, needless to say, and the job of amending my book would be difficult anyway, perhaps impossible. Because, you see, you are receding from me, you who have been with me so long, receding farther and farther away, now that the real meeting I had envisioned between us will almost certainly never occur. I mean, of course, the time when you would sit with my book, finding me on the white pages and in the clean print. Now there will be no pages, no print, and the loss, I imagine, in the circumstances, is only— well, let it pass.

I use my regained equilibrium only to say this hopeless afterword to myself. (Though I still speak to you. Is habit inextinguishable?) Usually people who write books try at the end to dispose of their narrative in a tidy way, but I can't do that: I don't know what has become of my old friends and enemies. Paula, Fillermine, Pocksman, Cienkiewycz, Alex herself—they are elsewhere, no longer in my book, or in me. On the contrary, it is I who am in them, I don't know how—I can *feel* myself in them, scattered, remote, but living still. Rollo is the only one who has been "loyal," in the vulgar sense; he came to see me here from time to time in the previous sojourn, perhaps a dozen visits over the years. Through him I learned that Charley went back to France, was conscripted to serve in the French army, and was killed in a street skirmish at Dienbienphu. Rollo found out, when I asked him to, by writing to Charley's sister Angélique, whose address he obtained from Cienkiewycz—I felt I couldn't write to Cienkiewycz myself. Rollo is a member of an Owenite community near here. Well, I call it Owenite, which annoys Rollo somewhat. He says the group's principles are much more sophisticated than that. He has a beard and wears tennis shoes tied with black string.

Rollo believes that my sense of living in the others is an abrogation of responsibility to myself, an acquiescence in my forced

300

"withdrawal." On the other hand, the doctors say it is a guilt-projection. I don't really care which, if either, is correct, since I'm sure no one who ever lived has been wise enough to tell. It's all the same anyway, all one. I read a good deal of history from the library here.

Charley is dead, then. I would know it even if Rollo had not written to Angélique, for long ago I ceased to feel Charley's existence, though I remember him perfectly. Can I trust this sense? That's the important question now, today; not whether it is explainable, but whether it is reliable. If it is, then Linda is alive; but I have no corroboration. They have done something with her, but they don't tell me what. They told me that when I was sleeping, after they had given me the injection, I said, "Let her die, let Linda die," and they asked me what I meant. I told them it doesn't matter, but perhaps it really does. You see, I believe in one thing, my mind understands one truth, that reality is fortuitous. Don't mistake me, I don't deny cause and effect, I am practical and a realist; I simply say that causality is will-less and also infused with a radical and cosmic multiplexity. Hence it is neither predictable nor governable in any terms comprehensible to intellect as we know it; reality is fortuitous. Which means that the notion of justice is a fiction—worse, a self-contradiction. But a lovely notion, nevertheless. The most beautiful of all. If anything has meaning, anything, then there ought to be justice, someone, some human being, ought to succeed. My body—blood, bone, nerve—is a pain of yearning: let there be one success, only one. If in my sleep I asked it for Linda's sake, perhaps that was a personal vanity—wanting the thing to happen within the ambience of my personal knowledge. Perhaps it might better happen elsewhere. I can only say that Linda is worthy, a pure heart and a clear intelligence. I love her. I love her more than anyone, past or present. But that is another aspect of yearning, perhaps not germane. In reality, no one succeeds. Not one of us. Ever.

The baby didn't. It is dead. But it *was* alive—briefly. They told me it probably came out living, and that in a sense it brought on the miscarriage itself through its own blind living desire to escape from the dying world in which it found itself . . . so luminous, so

301

purposive that small existence was. And now a vacancy, nothing more.

Have they dropped the bomb yet? Has it begun? Is it coming nearer? We have little news here.

These are unconnected notes, you understand. No attempt to bring matters to a smooth ending. You must forgive me—there isn't any way to work intensively or deliberately here. I wonder, would I have been better off if the opportunity to work in concentration had been denied me all along? I aimed very high—you understand that also, I'm sure; all my fine writing, word-searching, pressing for ultimate meanings, it was perhaps bound to collapse simply from its own weight. At any event, I couldn't support it. And the real folly was that I should ever have thought for an instant that I could, as if I hadn't been through defeat after defeat. But I hoped for a moment—a few months—I might ask this little for myself: those lovely hills and woods, that cottage, Linda; a chance to discuss with you who might be my friends the things we know and care about. Was it so much to ask? A meaningless question.

Remember Charley, though. I thought for a while I would ask you to remember Linda and me; but that was foolish. I thought of asking you to love us and to pity us in our adversity; but it is enough that we love you, and that we shall never be the ones who start a war. We are the principles of love, Linda and I, and so you need not remember us; indeed, you cannot—you can discover us only within yourselves, in which event we shall have different names and faces. Linda and I do not exist, as we ourselves are the first to recognize. But Charley exists—outside you, beyond you; he is one of the rare persons in history who can tell you something about yourself that you do not know and cannot discover by yourself. He is a teacher. He teaches you the impersonal validity of existence: the protest which was his life was lived not for his sake nor for ours, but so that the protest alone might have the dignity, however ephemeral, of a name. It was an act of pure transcendence. This is why I think you should—must—always remember him.

April 19, 1962

302